What Others Are Saying about Sharlene MacLaren and *Summer on Sunset Ridge*...

In *Summer on Sunset Ridge*, Sharlene MacLaren has constructed a heart-stopping story wrapped around one of the most tragic periods in American history. MacLaren is sure to please her ardent fans, and to develop new ones, as well, with this full-bodied tale featuring brave, Christ-loving characters who will stay with readers long after the book has been closed.

—*Debby Mayne*
Author, *High Cotton*

MacLaren has created a touching and sweet love story in *Summer on Sunset Ridge*. Giving readers an intimate look at Quaker life and beliefs, MacLaren brings the Underground Railroad and the abolitionist movement to life. From the memorable characters to the intriguing plot, readers will be sure to savor every page.

—*Jody Hedlund*
Christy Award-winning author, *Luther and Katharina*

I've long been a Sharlene MacLaren fan, and *Summer on Sunset Ridge* may well be her best novel yet, populated by characters so realistic that they seem to leap from the pages as their mettle and their faith are tested. This story features the perfect blend of adventure, plot twists, romantic tension, and historical accuracy. You'll want to make room for this one on your "keepers shelf"!

—*Loree Lough*
Award-winning author of 100-plus titles

Summer on SUNSET RIDGE

Summer on SUNSET RIDGE

A NOVEL BY SHARLENE MACLAREN

WHITAKER
HOUSE

Publisher's Note:
This novel is a work of fiction. References to real events, organizations, or places are used in a fic-
tional context. Any resemblances to actual persons, living or dead, are entirely coincidental.

All Scripture quotations are taken from the King James Version of the Holy Bible.

Summer on Sunset Ridge

Sharlene MacLaren
www.sharlenemaclaren.com
sharlenemaclaren@yahoo.com

ISBN: 978-1-62911-796-6
eBook ISBN: 978-1-62911-797-3
Printed in the United States of America
© 2017 by Sharlene MacLaren

Whitaker House
1030 Hunt Valley Circle
New Kensington, PA 15068
www.whitakerhouse.com

Library of Congress Cataloging-in-Publication Data (Pending)

1 2 3 4 5 6 7 8 9 10 11 ᴡ 24 23 22 21 20 19 18 17

Dedication

To my wonderful, loving parents, Richard and Dorothy Baker,
who taught me about Jesus and are, even now, basking in His presence in
their eternal home. I will see you both again.

1

Fifth Month, 1855 · Philadelphia County, Pennsylvania

Rebecca Albright lifted the brim of her bonnet to swipe at her sweat-slicked brow, then pulled back her shoulders to help release the tension. Tossing her braid of dark brown hair behind her, she readjusted her tired, sore knees on the hard earth, and blew out a loud breath that caused her hot cheeks to puff out like two pink balloons.

"How much longer must we work at this, Becca? My aching back can't take much more."

Rebecca glanced up and down the long rows of vegetable plants yet untouched, then cast a weary glance at her petulant younger sister Lydia. "We're not even halfway done."

"But I'm perishing in this heat," Lydia whined.

"Thee cannot perish on me yet. Wait till we finish. Then thee can perish."

"That was rude."

Rebecca hid a grin as she yanked up another weed. Of her seven siblings, fifteen-year-old Lydia tended to be the most candid.

"Take a drink of water." Rebecca nodded at the nearby jar.

"It's not even refreshing," Lydia droned. "The sun has made it as hot as a boiling kettle."

"That's a bit of an exaggeration."

"Is not." Lydia reached for the jar, unscrewed the lid, and took a couple of swallows, then wrinkled her nose and wiped her mouth with her sleeve. "Awful, that's what it is."

Rebecca could hardly blame her sister for complaining. It was dreadfully hot, especially for being so early in the spring. Even now, the sun scorched the back of Rebecca's dress so that she feared it might burst into flames at any minute. Silently she cursed the stubborn weeds that refused to come forth, requiring hours of labor that left her palms red and blistered. If Lydia were to overhear her utter even so mild an expletive, she would fly faster than an arrow to Mother to snitch. Staunch Quakers that the Albrights were, they kept their language—nay, their entire manner of existence—clean and free from clutter. Members of the Religious Society of Friends led simple lives; "plainness" was their code, manifest in their mode of fashion, their furnishings, their speech, and their architecture.

Rebecca glanced at her red-faced sister. "Go sit in the shade for a bit."

Lydia raised her eyebrows hopefully. "May I?"

"Thee does look tuckered out."

"I don't know how thee can keep such a cheery attitude."

"Only by God's grace."

"Thee is a good Quaker, Sister."

"Not always." Rebecca shrugged. "Today, I would just as soon be pulling weeds in my undergarments."

Lydia giggled. "And wouldn't that be a sight? Imagine if Elder Thurston Byer came calling on Papa. Thee would be shamed almost to death."

Laughter bubbled up from both of them, and Rebecca noticed that Lydia did not follow her suggestion to rest. "And Thurston would fall off his horse in horror," Rebecca added. She tried to push up one of her sleeves, but the wrist cuff was too tight. It wasn't that she wished to wear fancy hats or frilly dresses such as those she observed on other women during her trips to the city; but the plain bonnets and shawls did bore her from time to time, not to mention overheat her on days such as this. On the rare occasion that Mother permitted her daughters to pick out a lightweight fabric with a simple floral pattern for skirts, Rebecca and her sisters jumped with glee.

The two sisters returned to their tasks, and for five minutes, at least, Lydia allowed Rebecca some blissful contemplation. In such times, Rebecca strove to listen for God's Inner Voice. But, of course, the silence didn't last.

"Will thee be seeing Gerald Tuke again this week?"

Rebecca gave a tiny groan. Lately, Gerald Tuke had been joining the Albrights for supper every Fourth Day, and paying special attention to Rebecca. "I suppose, but seeing him at First-Day Meeting would be soon enough for me."

Fleetingly, she wondered if she would ever find a suitable mate. She couldn't think of a single man in the Society of Friends she would consider marrying. Her parents believed Gerald Tuke made the perfect match, but she would rather drown in a pool of mud than be his bride. Nothing about him appealed to her, and she couldn't understand what it might be, except for his Quaker beliefs, that made her parents so fond of him.

"I suppose he is somewhat ungainly, with that overlarge nose and those ears that poke out from under his hat," Lydia acknowledged. "Poor fellow probably won't find a wife if thee doesn't marry him."

Rebecca groaned. "Am I thinking too highly of myself to hope I'll find someone more comely-looking to marry?"

"Indeed."

Rebecca jerked her head up and scowled, then tugged at her sleeve with irritation. "Thee didn't weigh thy response for very long."

Lydia laughed. "Didn't have to."

"Scoundrel!"

"Those thick spectacles make his eyes look as big as boulders. Sadly, he might well be thy only choice. Thank goodness Papa and Mother don't consider me to be of marriageable age. I can only hope that, when they do, someone more fascinating than Gerald Tuke comes along."

Rebecca yanked a long, stubborn weed out of the ground and flung it across two rows of plants, hitting her sister square in the chest.

Lydia gave a yelp and brushed the dirt off before narrowing her eyes at Rebecca. "Thee will pay for that," she growled.

"Don't do it, Lydia May," Rebecca warned her.

Lydia tugged a weed from the tomato patch. "Thee asked for it."

"Did not."

"Did!" Lydia aimed and threw, but Rebecca ducked just in time.

A mischievous strain welled up in Rebecca as she gathered another fistful of earth—more dirt than weed—and pitched it across the garden. Lydia fired back, and soon the air between them was a cloud of dirt.

"Getting your work done, daughters?"

They halted their foolish play as Papa approached from the barn. Gracie, the family's collie, trotted along at his heel, her black-and-white body moving back and forth with every wag of her tail. Dust billowed around Papa's boots as he moved toward them on his way to the house, his tool belt rattling with all manner of carpentry tools, which he used to build furniture that was sold to folks from miles around. His reputation for fine craftsmanship, along with the produce of the family's hundred-acre farm, kept the Albrights well-fed.

"Hello, Papa," Lydia chirped with feigned jubilation while hurriedly brushing herself off. "Our gardening is coming along fine, as thee can see, mostly because I work circles around my sister. If thee will notice, I've weeded three rows to her two."

Rebecca shook her head as she pulled another weed. She was tempted to heave it at her sister but added it to the pile behind her, instead.

"Is that so?" Papa paused beside the garden and surveyed the rows. "I could've sworn I saw a dirt battle going on."

"Becca started it, Papa. Just look at my shirt."

"I don't suppose thee had it coming," Papa said.

Lydia sputtered. "All I said was—"

"Never mind, Lydia May," Rebecca put in. "Papa is not interested in our foolish talk." She didn't want Papa to know they'd been discussing Gerald Tuke, lest he might presume she favored him.

Papa tipped his face to one side, and the sunlight revealed the glimmer of a smile beneath the shadow of his hat brim. "She is thy oldest sister, Lydia. It is thy duty to show her respect."

Rebecca lifted her chin at Lydia and gave a light sniff.

Lydia glared at her, unspeaking.

Papa turned and resumed his walk toward the house, his left leg dragging just slightly, still stiff from a break he suffered in a fall from the hayloft many years prior. "Tomato plants are looking a bit wilted," he called over his shoulder. "When Levi returns from the field, he'll give them a good soaking."

Upon reaching the porch steps of the rambling stone farmhouse, as substantial as the day Grandfather Albright built it five decades earlier, Papa paused, removed his tattered hat, and ran a work-worn hand through his thick, silvery hair. "See you shortly for the noon meal."

"Yes, Papa!" Rebecca answered.

When the screen door closed behind him, Rebecca went back to weeding.

With a sigh, Lydia followed suit.

2

Sheriff, come quick. There's been a murder at Magnolia Hill Plantation!"

Clay Dalton's stomach gave a jolt. He shot out of his chair, Julia foremost on his mind. "What? Who?" His eyes alit on the young man who'd just bolted though his office door, his face dripping with perspiration. Years of training had taught Clay to react calmly in most situations, but it wasn't every day that one responded to a reported shooting at the residence of his betrothed.

Clay glanced at his deputies, Harmon Clark and Walter Gibbs, whose faces reflected the alarm he felt.

"It ain't yer fiancée, so you can let out yer breath," the young man assured him. "It's her ol' man. I hear tell one o' his slaves shot and kilt 'im. Some's sayin' he acted in self-defense. 'Course, anybody with smarts knows that ain't true. No, siree."

Clay gulped and cleared his throat. Poor Julia would be beside herself. "Was anyone else harmed?"

"Everyone else's fine, far as I know, 'cept Mrs. Wellesley. She's shriekin' like there ain't no tomorrow. Yer Miss Julia is doin' her best to comfort 'er mother. I hear tell them brothers o' hers are madder 'n hornets. As fer the slave what done it, his name's Horace Spencer. Him an' his li'l brother took off before anyone hardly knew what happened. Cain't nobody figure out where they went off to, but they're gone. Ain't no Negroes talkin', neither. Somebody sent for the doc, but it won't do no good. All he'll do is pronounce 'im departed for glory."

Clay leaned down, pulled open the lowest desk drawer, and snatched his holster belt and gun. After fastening it hastily around his waist, he grabbed his hat and slapped it on his head. Then he turned to his deputies. "Harmon, you come with me. Walt, you stay here and field any calls that come in."

"Yes, sir," the men replied in unison.

Clay and Harmon traveled on horseback to Magnolia Hill Plantation. They entered the property by way of the big arched gate, then rode down the pebbled lane to the circular drive in front of the three-story house with its massive pillars and covered porch. Behind that was the massive barn, and beyond it were rows of long, ramshackle buildings that housed the Wellesleys' slaves. From all sides, extending as far as the eye could see, were fields and fields of tobacco plants. Here and there were large groups of Negroes picking tobacco leaves.

A group of men and women, probably friends or neighbors of the Wellesleys, had assembled and were talking in loud voices, but Corinne Wellesley's wails rose above the din. Clay sought out Julia amid the small crowd of frenzied folks and found her talking to a woman he didn't recognize. His fiancée appeared collected; perhaps it was due to the contrast with her mother's hysteria.

Clay hadn't seen Julia for a few days. He'd decided to distance himself from her following a disagreement over their wedding and future plans. Clay wondered how she would receive him now, in such tragic circumstances.

He glanced toward the barn and saw a few men standing near an oblong figure draped in a blanket—presumably the body of Joseph Wellesley. There was no sign of either of the doctors from Ellicott City. Perhaps whoever had summoned the doctor had told him not to bother hurrying, since the victim was already deceased. Still, the sooner someone removed the body from the premises, the better.

Soon a number of folks stormed Clay and his deputy, their voices exploding as they clamored to report one thing or another about what had transpired. Clay and Harmon dismounted their horses and handed the reins to a Negro boy who immediately led the animals to a watering trough. Clay instructed Harmon to see to the mortally wounded Mr. Wellesley and wait with the body until a doctor arrived. As Harmon set off in the direction of the barn, Clay turned toward the gathering throng.

"Clay! Oh, Clay, it's just plain awful."

He turned and saw the ample Corinne Wellesley coming toward him, leaning heavily on the arm of her son Joseph Jr.

"He shot him, Clay—shot him dead. That wretched Horace Spencer. What are you going to do about it, Clay? Hang him—that's a given. What else?"

"Well, I'll have to find him first, Mrs. Wellesley. It's my understanding that he's fled."

"He's fled, all right. But you will find him, Clay, won't you?" This from Julia, who rushed to her mother's side, her blue-green eyes bloodshot and moist.

Clay wanted to reach out and touch her arm, but they hadn't talked since their argument, and he felt strangely distant from her. She would need him now more than ever, but his priority had to be tracking down the man who had killed her father.

He scanned her pretty face, then met her teary eyes. "I will do everything in my power to find him." Then he gave his attention to her brother. "What can you tell me about all this, Joseph?"

The bearded fellow's eyes burned with rage. "Not a lot, Clay—er, Sheriff Dalton. I just returned from town a few minutes ago. You'd best ask somebody who was here when it happened."

"I was here!" shouted Floyd Piper, who ran the local general store. "I was making a delivery at the time of the incident." He gestured with a thumb at a wagon laden with merchandise. One of the two horses that were hitched to the rig snorted and pounded his front hooves in the dirt, as if to show his impatience.

"And I was just arrivin' to deliver a package to Mrs. Wellesley," said a fellow Clay recognized from the post office. He still held a parcel under his arm. "I take it upon myself to make personal deliveries whenever a parcel arrives for Mrs. Wellesley."

"I see," Clay said, looking from one man to the other. "Well, I'd like to talk to each of you in private, if I may."

"I'd like to hear what they have to say," Joseph Jr. piped up.

Clay thought a moment before responding. "I understand your wish, Joseph, but surely you understand the nature of investigating a crime. I wouldn't want your presence to influence or taint the witnesses' testimonies."

Joseph Jr.'s eyes narrowed to red-hot slits. "We already know that wretched slave shot my father dead. Don't see how a couple of witnesses are going to make a hair of difference. I want that brute found and hanged, no matter what anybody has to say about it."

"You don't need to ask how it happened. We all know Horace Spencer kilt him," said Harv Maynard, whose property bordered the Wellesleys'. "You gotta keep slaves under control at all times, or they'll take advantage o' you. That's what happened here. He prob'ly didn't want t' carry out some order, an' so he just pulled a gun on Joseph. Yessir, you can bet that's what happened."

Mentally setting aside the remarks, Clay surveyed the crowd once more. "Anybody else here who was present at the time of the shooting?" He waited a few moments.

"My brother is right." Julia spoke up. "That man needs to hang, the sooner, the better." The strength of her voice almost startled Clay. She stood taller, sucking in her tiny, corseted waistline. "Horace Spencer has always been a rebellious sort. I've heard Daddy complain about him on more than one occasion. Why, just last week, Daddy had him whipped for insubordination. That despicable man must pay for what he did. I trust you'll not waste any time in finding him."

The sharpness of her tone sent a convulsive shudder up Clay's spine, reminding him of one of the reasons they'd argued the other day. He loved her—truly, he did—but he didn't appreciate her dictatorial ways, and he'd told her so. Lately, she'd been issuing all manner of instructions regarding the tasks she expected him to complete before their wedding day—painting the interior walls of his house a pale green, hanging floral wallpaper in the dining room, updating the kitchen, and so forth. On top of that, she'd ordered new living room furniture from a company in New York—without his knowledge, and evidently unaware of the state of his bank account. He knew her family could well afford to pay for all their needs, but he'd been trying to explain to her that he didn't wish to rely solely upon the family's wealth for their survival. Convincing her to scale back on her lifestyle could prove to be a hardship, however, and that worried him. He'd dismissed her behavior as typical conduct of brides-to-be, but then he'd started to notice the forceful, domineering comportment of Corinne Wellesley, not only with her household staff but also with her husband and children, and he feared Julia would turn into the same woman. Of course, he hadn't expressed his fears to Julia in quite those words, but he'd hinted at his concerns. He'd also reminded her that she wasn't marrying a money-bag, just a county sheriff who'd never needed "things" to make him happy. "The love of a good woman was riches enough" had seemed a sentimental yet compelling argument at the time. But Julia hadn't particularly taken it the way he'd hoped she would. "And what gets you the love of a good woman but to please her, to see to her every wish and whim?" she'd asked. Then she'd poked out her lower lip in a pout, fluttered her dark eyelashes seductively, and purred, "You *do* want to make me happy, don't you, darling?"

It had been their first real argument, and now he wondered why it hadn't happened earlier. Had Julia's rare beauty so entranced him that he'd lost the ability to speak his mind? Was he so completely wrapped around her finger? He'd courted her exactly six months when her father had approached him and asked, point-blank, when he planned to propose. Joseph Wellesley said he considered Clay a good match, that he liked the idea of his daughter marrying a man folks held in such high esteem, not to mention one who enforced the law. "Besides," he'd said with a wink, "my daughter needs a man with a strong hand. She's too much like her mother, and I never could keep her in line." He'd meant his remark as a joke, but the more Clay observed of that overindulged, unyielding side in Julia, the more he wondered if there was any man capable of managing her, least of all himself.

Clay reined in his thoughts and addressed his fiancée. "I understand your anger, Julia, but you need to let me do my job. Why don't you take your mother inside, and I'll come check on you later?"

Julia pursed her full lips until they formed a tight, thin line between her tear-stained cheeks. Clay realized it was outrage upon grief, for in her mind—and in the minds of most people—there was no need for an investigation. A slave had murdered his master, an unthinkable act. Motive was a moot point, even if Spencer had been provoked.

Clay pulled his gaze away from Julia, noting that she had no intention of guiding her mother toward the house, and focused on Floyd Piper and the fellow from the post office. "Let's take a walk, shall we?"

The three of them ambled off toward a tobacco field. Once they were out of earshot of everyone else, Clay said, "I'd like to know what you men saw and heard, so I'll take your stories one at a time, if you don't mind. Mr. Piper, would you kindly wait over by that tree while I talk to mister...."

"Mitchell, Sheriff. Ronald Mitchell." The man still clutched the undelivered parcel under his arm.

The rather gangly Mr. Piper gave a stiff shrug, and as he walked off, Clay turned his attention back to Corinne Wellesley's personal mail carrier.

"Pleased to meet you, Mr. Mitchell. Now then, what exactly did you see?"

The middle-aged man scrunched his brow, chewed his cracked lower lip, and gave a nervous glance back at the plantation house. Through the open windows of the residence, the wails of Clay's future mother-in-law carried on the hot breeze.

"Try not to let the commotion distract you, Mr. Mitchell. I just need an honest account of what you saw."

Mitchell's grimace grew as he shifted his weight and scratched his balding head. "Well, sir, there's no doubt that slave had a good scoldin' comin' to 'im. He probably said or did somethin' Mr. Wellesley didn't like, so the spat between 'em had to have come from a good cause. But...." He paused, taking another worried glance over his shoulder. "Folks can get into trouble for defendin' slaves in these parts," he muttered.

"All I'm wanting is the truth, Mr. Mitchell."

"Some folks don't like knowin' the God's truth." Mitchell was almost whispering now.

Clay sighed. "We have a serious crime on our hands, and I need to get to the bottom of it. I promise to keep private whatever you might tell me. Now, did you actually see that Spencer fellow kill Joseph Wellesley in cold blood?"

"It wasn't what I'd call 'in cold blood,' Sheriff."

"Is that so?"

The fellow gulped. "Well, sir, it's like this. I see Mr. Wellesley take his gun out of its holster and point it at that slave man's temple. He starts cursin' 'im, tellin' 'im he's gonna kill 'im. That slave man just stands there a-shakin' in his boots. It's not that I felt sorry for 'im. The way Mr. Wellesley was screamin' an' rantin' at 'im, I figured he done somethin' really bad. Then another Negro runs out of the barn—looks to be a young kid—and falls on his knees with his hands folded, like he's prayin', an' starts beggin' Mr. Wellesley not to shoot his brother. Mr. Wellesley turns and shoots at the boy but misses, and that's when the slave tries to wrestle the gun outta his hand. In the scuffle, the gun goes off, and Mr. Wellesley falls down." Mitchell took another deep gulp. "I was so busy lookin' at the crumpled body, I didn't see where that slave and the young boy took off to. They just vanished like dew on a leaf. About that same time, some folks, includin' Mrs. Wellesley and her daughter, come boundin' outta the house. A couple o' slaves run out of the barn, too, but then they skedaddled back inside, so's not to get yelled at, I s'pect. Mrs. Wellesley falls across her husband's body and starts shriekin' real loud, 'He's dead, he's dead!'" Mitchell shifted his stance nervously as his gaze darted about. "That's what I saw, Sheriff, and nothin' more. Can I go now?"

Clay pursed his lips. "You sure you got nothing else for me?"

The man gave a fast shake of his head. "No, sir. Just want to get on home to my wife an' kids. I'm scared these folks are gonna turn on me if they find out what I told you."

"You don't have to worry about me saying anything, Mr. Mitchell. I appreciate your telling me what you saw. You've been very helpful."

Floyd Piper's account wasn't much different from that of Ronald Mitchell, except that he corroborated the identity of the young boy as Horace Spencer's brother, Amos. According to Piper, who identified his source as a slave handler he'd spoken with while making a delivery at the plantation, Horace had a bad knee that often buckled and impeded his work in the tobacco fields. Amos would try to cover for him, which irked Joseph Wellesley to no end. The handler had been about to deliver a thrashing to the older man for failing to meet his daily quota.

Clay glanced back at the barn and saw the white-bearded, wire-bespectacled Doc Pickering standing over the body of Joseph Wellesley. His funeral wagon was parked nearby. The doctor peeled back the blood-ied blanket covering the deceased, then reached inside his black bag, produced a stethoscope, and held it against the man's chest—a formal-ity and nothing more. With a slow shake of his head, the elderly doctor draped the blanket over the dead man's face again. He then nodded to several bystanders, who proceeded to lift the body into the back of his wagon. As they did, Corinne Wellesley's howls rose several degrees in volume. Joseph Jr. steadied her with his hand, then turned around and gave Clay a hard stare. Clay could almost read his mind: *Find that lousy so-and-so and string him up. Tomorrow isn't soon enough.*

With little time to spare, Clay would say his good-byes to Julia, then head back to his office and prepare to ride out of town before sunset in search of Horace Spencer. He would trail an extra horse on a lead, for use in transporting his prisoner back to Ellicott City. His deputies would stay behind to keep the peace as best they could, with Harmon in charge for the direst of emergencies.

Plenty of people would probably insist Clay form a posse, and would even volunteer their services. Others would tell him to hire a slave catcher or a federal marshal. Clay snubbed both ideas. A slave catcher might very well find Spencer, but he would have no compunction about hanging him from the closest tree. No, this was something Clay had to do alone. He had a good nose for sniffing out escapees, and he intended to find Horace Spencer and haul him back to Ellicott City to face a judge and jury. It was the only way to handle the matter. Everyone, slave or free, deserved his day in court. And Clay would make sure Spencer told his side of the story, if it was the last thing he did.

Didn't matter the color of his skin or his lot in life, he deserved a fair trial.

3

The delightful smells of vegetable stew and fresh-baked bread greeted Rebecca and Lydia when they entered the farmhouse. Mother issued the girls a hurried glance from the cast-iron cookstove. As usual, her graying hair was pinned back in a bun beneath her white prayer cap, a simple accessory without which she looked only partially dressed. The only times Rebecca had observed her mother bareheaded were just before retiring for the night and first thing in the morning, on the rare occasion she discovered her still in her sleeping attire. Of course, Rebecca and her sisters wore the traditional bonnet outside and in public, but the headpiece was the first thing they tossed off once inside the house.

Two-year-old Chrystal popped up her head at her older sisters' entry. When she spotted Rebecca, she dropped her handspun rag-doll, leaped to her bare feet, and waddled over with outstretched arms. Rebecca bent down and scooped her up.

"Becca be in garden?"

Rebecca kissed the tip of her baby sister's petite nose. "Yes, Becca's been weeding in the garden, and it's hotter than a duck in a closet out there."

The child's face contorted into a frown, and she glanced at the pantry. "Duck?"

Rebecca laughed and tweaked the girl's chin. "It's just an expression, silly." She set the child down and went to wash her hands at the sink, while Chrystal protested with tears and lifted arms. Rebecca hurriedly dried herself with a towel then scooped up her baby sister again. "How can Becca help Mother if thee insists on being held?"

Obviously sleepy, the child nuzzled Rebecca's neck with her chubby face.

Mother made a half turn to glance at Rebecca. "Thy holding her is help enough for me."

The eight-foot pine table, with simple wood benches on either side, stretched across the dining room like an oversized boat in a small inlet. It was set with the white ironstone dinnerware passed down from their maternal grandmother. Frances, seventeen, seemed likelier even than Rebecca to take up Mother's housekeeping mantle. Besides her domestic skills, she was the beauty of the family, with blue eyes and long blonde tresses framing her flawless face. With art and efficiency, she sliced a loaf of bread, arranging the pieces on a serving platter and dropping the crumbs into the slop bucket on the floor at her feet. After the meal, one of the boys would take the slop outside and feed it to the hogs Papa intended to sell come fall. The family didn't eat meat, since Quakers believed in the sanctity of every living, breathing being, yet Papa thought nothing of making a profit from others who did.

"I'm hungry," piped up four-year-old Henry, the youngest boy. With all the commotion, Rebecca hadn't even spotted him, kneeling by the stone hearth over a puzzle Papa had fashioned in his woodshop.

"Well, get ye to the table, Son," Mother said as she hefted a hot kettle from the stove, using two thick towels to protect her hands from the scorching handles. She set the vessel down on a board on the table, then began ladling vegetable soup into the bowls Frances handed to her. The rest of the family—Papa, eleven-year-old Samuel, and seven-year-old Milton—seemed to emerge from every direction to gather at the table. The only absentee was eighteen-year-old Levi, still out in the field.

After Papa offered a blessing, the meal began as any other—in utter silence, save for the clatter of spoons against bowls, and the discreet sounds of chewing and swallowing. Mealtime tradition dictated that no one was to speak until Papa initiated conversation. Rebecca supposed the rule stemmed from Papa's need for rest and respite after a tiring morning. No one knew for sure, but everyone accepted it. Even Chrystal and Henry managed to follow the rule, for the most part.

"Laura, did thee pack a lunch for Levi?" Papa asked, breaking the silence.

Every set of shoulders relaxed. As if on cue, baby Chrystal let out a little wail for more soup. Lydia quickly brought another spoonful to the child's mouth.

"Yes," Mother replied. "I just brought it up from the root cellar." Her gaze trailed to Frances. "I'll ask thee to deliver it to him, Frannie."

Frances stopped chewing, her spoon midway to her mouth, and widened her oval eyes at Mother. Then her gaze shifted to Papa. "What if someone should come to call on me?"

Papa's eyebrows flickered a little. "Was thee expecting someone?"

"No, but I like to be prepared."

"One trip out to the field and back shan't take long, Daughter."

"But I'll soil my dress."

"Not if thee stays upright on thy horse this time."

Giggles and guffaws sputtered around the table from those who understood what Papa was getting at. The previous week, at Mother's request, Frances had delivered a fresh loaf of bread to the new neighbors; on the journey home, her horse had spooked and bucked Frances right off. On the ground, up-close with the snake that had presumably startled the horse, Frances leaped up and took off, screaming and squalling, toward the house, her bonnet strings flying, her skirts flaring, and her arms flailing. Papa had gone out to investigate and found the curled-up reptile, which he identified as a harmless eastern milk snake, a critter that helped control the farm's rodent population.

"I am never going to live on a farm. There are too many snakes, and I just don't care for all the...the dirt," Frances said while delicately dipping her spoon into her steaming soup. "I wish to marry a merchant or a banker, or perhaps a lawyer."

"Is that right?" said Papa. "I don't know many Quakers who aren't farmers."

"Sometimes, thee must take what is available," said Mother while dabbing her chin with her napkin. "Farming is an admirable profession, and thee would make a fine farmer's wife." She sipped of her water, eyeing Frances over the rim of her glass.

Everyone knew better than to argue with Mother, so Frances quieted and concentrated on her meal. Mother always had the last word. Even Papa was careful not to contradict her.

"Why, consider Gerald Tuke," Mother continued after setting her glass down. "He's made a fine career out of farming with that large collection of livestock and those flourishing fields of wheat, barley, and corn. Before long, he'll be one of the most prosperous farmers in the area. It is a boon that he has taken such an interest in Rebecca."

Lydia stifled a laugh with a loud cough, and Rebecca rolled her eyes but kept them focused on her soup bowl. If she had to fight to her death, she would not marry Gerald Tuke. But the dinner table was not the place for starting a war. In an attempt to change the topic, she raised her head at Papa. "Does thee have a special delivery to make tonight, Papa?"

He picked up his napkin and pressed it to his beard. "Indeed, I do."

"I wish I could come along. I know I could be of assistance." Ever since she'd joined the Philadelphia Female Anti-Slavery Society, her father's work with the Underground Railroad had become a source of fascination to her, and she felt a yearning to help.

"The distribution of supplies to these poor souls is a job more suitable for men," Mother said.

As usual, Mother had to have her say. Rebecca searched Papa's eyes for some sense of understanding and approval, but he shook his head. "Thy mother is correct. It is a dangerous mission, not to mention an illegal one. Aiding runaway slaves is a federal crime, and the Fugitive Slave Law prescribes punishments that are quite severe. I cannot risk having thee fined or put in prison."

"But there are many brave women deeply involved in the endeavor, Papa. Harriet Tubman, for one. It's reported that she's been making twice-yearly trips from New York to Maryland to lead slaves to freedom in Canada. It's rumored that Louisa May Alcott is a strong supporter, as is Susan B. Anthony, a Quaker."

"Those are rumors, and thee should know that Harriett Tubman has a price on her head," Papa stated.

"What's that mean?" Milton asked.

"It means that if anyone catches her, she's not long for this earth," Samuel supplied.

"I shouldn't want to be in her shoes," said Frances.

"Nor I," said Lydia. "But Becca has an adventurous personality. She doesn't mind a bit of danger now and then."

Rebecca sent Lydia an appreciative grin, then looked to her mother again. "I am passionate about abolition, Mother."

A tiny muscle flicked in Mother's jaw. "Sometimes, one's passions do not serve one's best interests. Thee should be looking toward marriage, not running around after dark assisting runaway slaves. As Papa has said, the Railroad is not a safe endeavor. 'Twould be best to leave matters in his hands."

"I'm aware of the dangers involved in the Railroad, and I'm ready to face them," Rebecca insisted. "Harriet Tubman has demonstrated amazing bravery, and has even faced death, on more than one occasion. But God has kept her safe and allowed her to continue her work. I believe God will protect me, as well. If I wish to do my part, shouldn't I be allowed? At twenty-one, I'm certainly old enough to make my own life choices."

"Thee has more important matters at hand," Mother maintained. "Namely, considering thy future with Gerald Tuke."

"Mother, thee knows I don't wish to marry him."

"Nonsense. The two of you will make a fine pair. Now, let us cease with talk of that for the time being and focus on something else, shall we?"

But Rebecca could only focus on her fear that Mother really meant what she'd said.

After the meal, Samuel and Milton headed out to the barn to help Papa, Frances went to deliver Levi's lunch, and Mother escorted Henry and Chrystal upstairs for their afternoon naps. That left Rebecca and Lydia to clear the table and do the dishes—a chore Rebecca didn't mind, and one she almost would have preferred completing alone, if only to spare herself from having to listen to Lydia's loud complaints. When they had finally finished, Lydia announced her leave-taking for a trip to the necessary, and Rebecca happily waved her sister out the back door.

Mother came back downstairs after putting Henry and Chrystal down. She mopped her glistening brow with the hem of her apron, then sat down at the table. "Would thee mind getting me a glass of cold tea, Becca?"

"Of course."

"Get one for thyself, as well."

Rebecca knew what that meant. Mother wished for her to sit a spell and have a chat, no doubt about Gerald Tuke. Rebecca took a deep breath as she went to retrieve the pitcher of tea from the icebox. She reached for a couple of tall thumbprint goblets from the shelf above the sink, filled both glasses, and carried them to the table. Then she pulled out a chair and sat down across from Mother.

For a few minutes, the two of them sipped their tea in silence. It was neither awkward nor uncomfortable, though, as Friends were expected to weigh their words with care before uttering them, and speak only that which was good and necessary and true.

Finally, Rebecca could bear it no more. She decided to initiate the conversation she knew was coming. "I've already told thee I don't wish to marry Gerald Tuke," she said quietly. "I don't love him, Mother. In fact, I don't even much like him."

Her mother's head shot up. "Rebecca! He is a good man."

"He may be a good man, but he isn't my type."

"Of course he is," Mother insisted. "And if thee doesn't marry Gerald, thy chances of finding a mate within our Society will diminish almost entirely. Thy sister Frances is approaching the appropriate age for marriage, and it would be a pure disgrace for her to marry before thee."

"Perhaps that is true, but the fact remains I don't love him."

A tensing in Mother's jaw betrayed her frustration. "Thee has made that more than clear, Rebecca. I can only assure thee that love will come in time."

"But I want to love my future husband *before* I marry him."

Mother pinned her with a calm stare. "Let us not dispute this any further. Gerald Tuke has spoken with thy father, and they've arranged a proper date of the eighth month, sixteenth day."

Rebecca's stomach tensed. "For what?"

"For thy wedding."

She jolted. "My—wedding? Thee and Papa have decided this without my consent?"

Mother fingered the edge of the tablecloth, not meeting Rebecca's eyes. "Gerald Tuke wants to hold the ceremony before harvest's busiest time."

Rebecca opened her mouth to protest further, but Mother held up her hand and rose to her feet. "If thee has anything more to say on the matter, thee can take it up with Papa. Just know this, Rebecca: we want only what is best for thee. We have brought the matter before the Lord, and we believe the two of you, with the Lord's help, can make a good life together. Thee must simply open thy heart to the possibility."

Rebecca tried to argue further but came up short. Was it true that she had not opened her heart to the possibility of a life with Gerald Tuke? Could she indeed grow to love him? Was she being stubborn, refusing to look for the good in him and seeing only that which was undesirable? Had she placed too much importance on outward appearance? Panic surged through her veins and made her stomach clench.

O Father, please come to my rescue. Thee knows better than I—and even better than Mother and Papa—what is best for me. Please, Lord, help me to seek Thee above all else and to find the path Thee has already carved out for me. If it means my marrying Gerald Tuke, then help me to surrender. If it means going another direction altogether, then help me to obey Thee without dishonoring my parents' wishes and desires.

4

Seated beside her father in the Albrights' wagon as it rocked and pitched along the potholed road where untold thousands of wheels had carved a two-track path in the hard earth, Rebecca grinned to herself. It was a grand day for a journey, with a sapphire sky above and a perfect sun warming her shoulders without scorching them. A gentle breeze cooled the air just enough to keep her comfortable in her long-sleeved shirtwaist. She'd dared to unbutton the top two fasteners, and if Papa had noticed, he'd said not a word. Rebecca's long, thick hair hung loosely around her shoulders. She so enjoyed letting it fly in the wind, and was glad Mother was not there to insist that she braid and pin it up beneath her prayer cap. Rebecca desired to please God, but she somehow doubted that the style of her hair mattered even one iota to Him.

Rebecca knew good and well why Mother had insisted she accompany Papa to Philadelphia, and it wasn't to ensure that he purchased all the grocery items and supplies on her shopping list. No, Mother wanted her to speak with Papa about marrying Gerald Tuke. Oddly, Papa hadn't brought it up yet, and Rebecca certainly wasn't about to broach the subject. What would she do if Papa gave her no choice in the matter? Could she disobey him outright? The closest she'd ever come to defying his wishes was refusing, as a young child, to eat her cooked spinach. He'd made her sit at the long farm table until she'd finished each and every wilted leaf. To this day, she detested the vegetable.

So, for now, Rebecca relished the opportunity to have Papa all to herself, and to discuss anything and everything other than Gerald Tuke.

"When is thy next preaching trip, Papa?"

"Hm?" He glanced over at her. "The overseers have been discussing sending me off Sixth Month. I shall discuss the schedule further with Mother before committing."

"And where will the overseers send thee this time?"

"They are suggesting we travel to Dover, Delaware. I believe Elias Fox is to accompany me. He has a great heart for our Dover Friends."

"How does thee decide what to preach on, Papa?"

"I make it a practice to sit in silence and wait upon the Holy Spirit to guide me."

"Thy keen discernment for the voice of the Lord is truly a God-given gift, Papa," Rebecca said.

He turned to look her in the eye from beneath the brim of his hat. "Thee has plenty of God-given gifts, as well, my daughter."

The prickly sensation of a blush crept up her neck and reached her cheeks. Papa seldom complimented his children, no doubt in order to keep them humble and meek. And so, his every affirmation of Rebecca went straight to her heart for safekeeping. "If I have any particular gifts, I don't know what they are. I am plainer than a pikestaff."

Papa tossed back his head and chortled. "A pikestaff is plain, I'll give thee that. But thee is not at all ordinary. On the contrary, thee has much to offer this world—a spirit of grace and love, a welcoming soul, a determined mind, a diligent work ethic, and a friendly manner. On top of that, thee is prettier than a posy."

"Papa! I've never...."

"Heard me speak in such complimentary terms?"

"I suppose not."

"Thy qualities are exactly what any man would desire in a wife."

She froze in her seat, for she knew what was coming next. "Papa...."

"Gerald Tuke is the man thy mother and I believe to be thy best option for a husband," he said, stopping her mid-sentence. "He will be calling on thee tomorrow night, as thee knows, and you two can discuss the arrangements."

Rebecca prayed for composure. "Papa, I don't want to think of him as my best option. I don't even love him."

"Sometimes, it takes years to fully appreciate another individual."

Years? She couldn't imagine waiting that long to have romantic feelings for her own spouse. Frustration stirred in her chest. "Did thee love Mother when thee married her?"

Papa looked out over the rolling hills on either side of the road, then lifted a hand and ran it through his short, silvery beard. "I did, yes, but I love her far more today than I did then. And thee will surely feel the same about Gerald Tuke."

"But your marriage started with love. Mine wouldn't."

"Gerald Tuke is a good man. He runs a fruitful farm and does well for himself. He is most honored that we have given him our blessing to marry thee."

"Papa, how could thee bless something when I had no part in the decision? I would much rather remain single than wed someone to whom I feel not even the slightest attraction. Thee knows of my strong desire to participate in the Underground Railroad. I have always been led to believe that women in the Society are encouraged just as much as men to make their own choices, to live according to God's will and direction, and to involve themselves in important missional causes. We are to walk in the Light of Truth, which, of course, is the Holy Spirit, and to allow that Light to guide us down life's paths. It would seem to me God would speak to me specifically if He wanted me to marry Gerald Tuke."

"Has thee kept an open mind and a willing heart?" Papa asked. "Perhaps He has told thee, but thy heart is too closed off to hear His still, small voice."

Rebecca gave her father a sidelong glance. Hadn't Mother said almost the same thing? *O Lord, am I missing something vital?* Rebecca prayed. *I don't wish to block Thy voice from getting through to me.*

She dropped her chin to her chest and looked at her folded hands. "I shall try harder."

"That is good." Papa gave the team of horses a sharp tap of the reins and a firm "Getup!" and that marked the end of their conversation.

When they reached the city, the wagon's jostling, combined with the dreadful odors of horse manure, fried fish, smoke from the nearby factory district, and strong ale, and then the memory of Papa's talk of her inevitable marriage to Gerald Tuke, gave Rebecca a queasy stomach. Papa had to veer and swerve several times to avoid colliding with oncoming buggies, not to mention dogs, chickens, pigs, and pedestrians darting out in front of the wagon.

Rebecca didn't relish the commotion, and yet city life still held a certain appeal. The farm was far from quiet, with the nickers of horses, squeals of pigs, squawks of chickens, and moos of cows. Oh, and the occasional thunderstorm. Then, there was the commotion of a houseful of lively children. But that was quiet compared to the constant clamor of thuds, crashes, jingles, and jangles in the City of Brotherly Love.

Papa parked the wagon and hitched the horses along Chestnut Street, just past the United States Hotel and directly in front of Bulkley's Hat Store. Then, after donning his hat and adjusting his jacket lapel and tie, he left Rebecca at R. H. Hobson's General Store and Food Market, next to Bulkley's, to fulfill the requirements of Mother's list while he went to conduct some business at Philadelphia Bank and Trust.

Rebecca climbed down from the wagon, gathered her skirts, and stepped onto the concrete sidewalk. She paused in front of Bulkley's to admire the many beautiful hats in the display window. When a lavishly attired couple breezed past her and entered the store, she felt a stab of envy at the sight of the woman's full-skirted violet gown, ornate floral hat, and dainty purple parasol. With a quick prayer for forgiveness, Rebecca tugged at her untied bonnet strings and hurried her plain self next door to Hobson's.

Papa's business gave her plenty of time to fulfill Mother's list of wants and needs for the homestead. Rebecca strolled from one aisle to the next, her large basket filling fast and growing heavy. The grocer had already set a tall bag of flour, a sack of sugar, and a bushel of potatoes by the door. The Albrights grew potatoes in their garden, but last year's harvest had been nearly exhausted.

Rebecca scanned the list as she started for the front of the store, where Robert Hobson would complete her order from his inventory behind the counter. On the way to the register, she paused to read a sign posted on the inside of the door.

100 DOLLARS REWARD!

Runaway from the subscriber on the 25th day of April, my Black Woman, named ANNA, sixteen years of age, well grown, black color; has small, whimpering voice. She took with her one dark calico and one blue and white dress, a red gingham bonnet, and a brown and white striped shawl and slippers. I will pay the above reward if found and returned to

Hovington Plantation in Amelia County, Virginia

—Thomas H. Waldron

Anger rose in Rebecca's chest. It wasn't the first such sign she'd seen, but the age and gender of the slave being sought made her bubble up with indignation. Her sisters Frannie and Lydia were around that age, and the thought of one of them running for her life made Rebecca shudder.

"Was there anything else you needed, Miss Albright?"

"What?" Startled out of her reverie, Rebecca turned to the proprietor. "No, I— Yes. I mean, I was just reading this poster."

"Oh, that." Mr. Hobson nodded glumly. "The Fugitive Slave Law obliges me to allow folks to post these signs."

"And who posted this one?"

"Who? I can't rightly say. Somebody just came along and put it there. I don't always notice."

"And they can just do that? What if thee was to protest?"

He lifted his gray eyebrows and widened his beady eyes. "Not sure why I'd do that. I don't wish to stir up any trouble."

"But this is a free state. We should be assisting slaves to reach freedom, not helping slave catchers to haul them back into captivity. This particular poster refers to a girl of only sixteen. She will likely be brutally beaten if returned to her master."

"Shh." Mr. Hobson held a forefinger to his mustached lip.

A woman peered around from behind a shelf and glared at Rebecca. Near the door, a man eyed her with suspicion, and the woman with him held her young child closer to her chest.

"No need to get all riled," Mr. Hobson stated, quietly yet sternly.

"But I am riled," Rebecca maintained. She refused to back down. "It is not right for human beings to be treated as personal property just because of their skin color."

Mr. Hobson dropped his chin until it almost touched the top button of his shirt. "And it is not right that you should come in here and make a disturbance. Now, if you'll kindly hand me your list, I will complete your order."

Rebecca let out a loud breath and handed him the wrinkled paper. He retrieved a pair of wire spectacles from his pocket and placed them on the tip of his wide nose, then briefly studied the list. "I believe I have all these items." He turned hastily, no doubt wanting to be rid of her as soon as possible. He was reaching for a jar of olives when the bell above the door jingled. Mr. Hobson turned and smiled broadly. "Mr. Albright, how nice to see you. Your order is almost filled." He took in a deep, close-mouthed breath that made his chest expand. Then his eyes roamed from Papa to Rebecca.

To Rebecca's relief, the proprietor did not bring up the matter of the poster she'd objected to. She felt compelled to tell her father what had happened, but she wanted to wait until they were on their way home. She supposed Mr. Hobson was right—it wasn't her place to cause a public disturbance.

After leaving Hobson's, they stopped at a lumber mill to purchase materials for Papa's furniture business, then at a chandler's shop, and, last, at a blacksmith's to buy a new pot for Mother. She'd been complaining that her old kettle wasn't cooking food evenly, and Papa said she would be thrilled with his unexpected purchase.

"Thee said *what?*" Papa boomed when Rebecca broached the subject of the wanted poster. They had just reached the main road leading back to Sunset Ridge.

"I simply told him I wasn't happy about the sign advertising a hundred-dollar reward for the return of a young slave girl named Anna. She is only sixteen, Papa, and her master calls her 'his woman.' I was quite appalled, and I let Robert Hobson know it."

Her father stared straight ahead, his hands firmly holding the reins, as he maneuvered the horses down the dusty road toward home. "Thee should not be so reckless with thy tongue, Daughter. One never knows who may be listening. We may live in a free state, but that does not make it lawful to assist runaway slaves in escaping to freedom."

"I'm only glad I didn't say as much as I wanted to." Rebecca sighed. "Where do the runaway slaves go after they've received rations and assistance from the Railroad? Do they all move on to Canada?"

"No, many of them remain in the States. But they are not treated well, so they must find remote areas in which to settle. Some fear that the freed slaves will take away jobs from white folks. But I never speak freely about such things to anyone, lest I arouse suspicion."

"But the Friends support abolition."

"Yes, but we must all look out for each other. We may support it, but that doesn't mean we ought to speak of it in public."

They drove the next several miles in sober silence, as Rebecca deliberated her father's words and silently prayed that her frank speech at Hobson's would not rain down trouble on Papa. Finally, she broke the stillness between them. "I wish to accompany thee on thy next mission, Papa. I can help pack supplies and offer encouragement to the women."

"No."

She blinked. "Thee didn't take even a moment to consider thy answer."

"I have considered my answer over a period of time, Rebecca, and I won't have thee involved in something so dangerous. Has thee not noticed that not even thy mother participates in my efforts, other than to help me load necessary items into the wagon bed? For her own protection, I never inform her of my destination; that way, if perchance the authorities should stop by and inquire as to my whereabouts, she won't have to lie."

Rebecca slumped back in her seat, a feeling of defeat sweeping over her. Was that to be her lot in life, then—to be trapped in a loveless marriage, her passion for assisting runaway slaves forever squelched? Her anxiety diminished at the remembrance of a Scripture from the Psalms: *"Cast thy burden upon the* Lord, *and he shall sustain thee; he shall never suffer the righteous to be moved."* Rebecca meditated on the truth of that verse and chose to keep quiet for the remainder of the trip.

5

*B*eneath an inky sky lit by a full moon and billions of twinkling stars, Clay sat before his dwindling fire and sipped his hot coffee. He considered chopping another branch to rekindle the dying flame, but after two days of riding, he was too tuckered out to worry about it. He figured Horace Spencer and his younger brother had likely hunkered down somewhere during the day, so if Clay set out again after catching a few hours of slumber, he wouldn't fall too far behind them.

In the last settlement he'd passed through, he'd struck up a conversation with a peddler, then casually inquired as to whether he'd happened upon two dark-skinned men on his journeys. Interestingly, the peddler reported having sold, that very afternoon, a pair of boots to two Negro men. The older of the two, who'd paid for the boots, had said the purchase was for his master's son who wore the same size as the younger man. But the younger man's feet had been blistered to the point of bleeding, the peddler added. He told Clay that he'd found the story suspect, and wondered if they might be runaways, but had been too distracted by a headache to report the men to the local authorities. He did, however, recall seeing them continue north on the same road by which he'd driven his wagonload of wares into town. "Headin' toward

Philly, I'd say. Suspect they made camp somewhere in the woods along the way, since runaway slaves tend not to travel by day," the scrawny hawker said. "I'd say you're likely to find them if you continue north. Unless, o' course, they disappear on that Underground Railroad folks talk about." The peddler looked him up and down. "You one o' them slave catchers, huh?"

"Not exactly."

"What are y', then?"

Clay thought for a moment. "Just an interested party."

"Uh-huh." The fellow gave him a dubious nod.

Now, hours later, Clay wondered if Spencer and his brother weren't holed up just a few miles ahead of him.

He would find out soon enough. After a couple of hours' sleep, he'd be ready to head out again. He might even be lucky enough to seize them before the end of the day tomorrow.

Rebecca took care not to allow her arm to brush against Gerald Tuke's as they sat side by side on the porch swing. It had been a bore of an evening, but she'd managed to keep her manners intact. Earlier, Gerald had taken her for a ride in his carriage, and they'd stopped in a wooded area and spread out a blanket to eat the picnic supper Mother had packed with meticulous care.

Gerald Tuke had said little, whether from shyness or a naturally reserved nature, and so Rebecca had found herself leading their conversation, asking him questions—mostly about his farm—to which he provided concise answers. Nothing he said made her anxious to spend more time with him. And not once did he inquire after her interests.

"Is thee chilled?" Gerald's somewhat high-pitched voice shattered the quiet.

"I'm quite fine, thank thee," Rebecca assured him.

"But I noticed thee shivering. Here, thee may borrow my summer jacket." He began to remove the garment.

"The air is comfortable enough, but I do thank thee. It's a thoughtful gesture."

"Well, all right, then."

Their conversation halted once more, Gerald began to twiddle his thumbs while gently propelling the swing back and forth with his foot.

Rebecca gazed up at the starlit sky and tried to figure out a polite way to excuse herself. She produced a yawn and covered her mouth with her palm. "My, it's getting late."

"Yes, I suppose it is," Gerald conceded. "But before we say good night, I think we should discuss…um…our future. Doesn't thee?"

Rebecca bristled at the thought, but then she recalled Mother and Papa's encouragement that she keep an open mind and heart. "Go on," she said, trying to remain calm.

"Thy father has given me his blessing to marry thee."

A suffocating sensation made her throat clench. "So he has told me."

"I've known for some time that I wished to marry thee. I've watched thee in meeting every First Day and also at quarterlies, and I've somehow always known thee was the one for me. I hope the feeling is mutual."

Rebecca gulped and found she had nothing in her dry throat to swallow. How was she to tell him that her feelings were far from romantic without breaking his heart? "I…I think thee is a fine man."

He smiled and took her hand without warning. Although he'd been calling on her for weeks now, it was the first time he'd actually reached out to touch her. The bold gesture shocked her, considering she'd believed him to be shy.

"That's a good start, then, right?"

She hadn't meant for her comment to encourage him. She tried to remove her hand from his, but he kept a firm grip on it.

"Gerald, I—"

"We'll make a fine couple, and before thee knows it, we'll have a houseful of little ones."

The remark caught her so completely off-guard that it produced a coughing spasm, and Gerald released her hand in order to give her a couple of swift thumps on the back.

Rebecca finally stopped coughing and quickly clasped her hands in her lap.

"Is thee all right?" Gerald asked.

"Yes, I thank thee." She turned and studied his concerned countenance.

He was a nice enough man, for certain—thoughtful, too—but she couldn't get past his lanky frame, crooked teeth, bulbous nose, and stringy brown hair. On top of all that, there were those wire spectacles that made his grayish eyes look twice their actual size.

Just then, she felt a stab of conviction for her lack of Christian benevolence. Gerald had been nothing but kind and caring toward her. Why couldn't she extend the same spirit to him?

"I'm well aware these things take time, Rebecca," Gerald ventured as the porch swing squeaked back and forth. "Thee shouldn't fret if thee doesn't love me yet. Thy father and I have set the date for Eighth Month. That should allow plenty of time for thy feelings of love to grow."

Feelings of love? Rebecca's stomach took a sickening tumble. Surely, God wouldn't have her marry a man she didn't love, even if that was what her parents desired.

Beginning tonight, she would start asking the Lord to plant a seed of love in her heart for Gerald Tuke. Anything was possible, as Jesus promised in Matthew 19:26:"*With men this is impossible; but with God all things are possible.*"

"I'm sure thee is right," she finally said.

"Good," Gerald said with a nod. "Then that's settled."

He visibly relaxed, but Rebecca did just the opposite. In his mind, they were as good as betrothed. Before she knew it, Papa would be making an announcement about their intentions at First Day. The "clearness committee" would convene and begin the process of addressing potential difficulties. After that, they would meet with Rebecca and Gerald for a time of questions and answers, and to discuss the spiritual nature of marriage. If the members of the committee approved, they would then recommend to the meeting that Rebecca and Gerald be married. Her heart pounded exceedingly hard as she pondered the matter.

"Does thee have anything else thee wishes to know about me?" Gerald asked, stretching his arm around behind Rebecca and resting it on the back of the swing.

Rebecca cleared her throat. "I do, actually. What is thy stance on slavery?"

His shoulders arched in a half shrug. "I suppose I have not given it much thought."

"Thee doesn't have an opinion on the matter?"

"I haven't given it enough thought to form an educated opinion."

Rebecca couldn't help her agitation. "Well, my 'educated opinion' is that, simply put, one human being has no business 'owning' another. Friends are strongly opposed to the practice, as thee surely must know."

"Yes, of course." He bit his lower lip as the smallest of frowns furrowed his brow. "My parents live in the South but don't own slaves. My mother's parents, on the other hand, have always owned slaves, as do some of my aunts, uncles, and married cousins on my mother's side. That said, I suppose I have mixed feelings."

It suddenly occurred to Rebecca that she barely knew the Tuke family. She was aware that Gerald had moved to Pennsylvania from Georgia five years ago to take over his grandfather's farm, and that his grandparents on the Tuke side were staunch Quakers, but she had never met his parents, and the knowledge that there were lifelong slaveholders in his family made her queasy.

"Well," Rebecca said, "thee shan't be happy to know that I should very much like to aid slaves in finding places of refuge." She sat straighter to emphasize the strength of her conviction. "If you'll remember, I attended the Philadelphia Female Anti-Slavery Society's convention last June. That is where my heart of compassion for slaves grew tenfold."

Gerald grimaced. "Yes, I recall that. But we were not yet courting, so my knowledge about your experience is quite limited. However, since the passing of the Fugitive Slave Law, it's been illegal to assist runaways. And, as thee well knows, good Quakers are law-abiding citizens."

"Any good Quaker knows that injustice is the true atrocity, Gerald. Has thee not been listening during the quarterly meetings? The legality of aiding slaves in finding safe haven is a moot point."

Gerald took three deep breaths of night air. In the distance, a hoot owl sang a woeful tune, while a chorus of crickets chirped in one accord. He lowered his hand to her shoulder, and his touch sent prickles up her spine. "Are we having our first argument, Rebecca? It seems silly that it should center on the topic of slavery, of all things."

Rebecca glanced up and caught the glimmer of a smile on his pasty face. Refusing to return a smile, she looked down at her hands, which were clasped in her lap. Whatever would he say if he learned about Papa's involvement in the Railroad? Best not to mention it—for Papa's sake. Papa had made it clear that volunteering for the Railroad was extremely risky.

Rebecca rose to her feet before Gerald could stop her. "I thank thee for the nice evening, but I believe the time has come for me to say good night."

Gerald stood almost simultaneously, and the porch swing slapped against Rebecca's leg. "I hope I haven't upset thee."

"No, not at all. It's just getting late."

He lowered his head, as if he intended to kiss her, so she dodged him and moved toward the door. He reached over and put his hand on the knob. She didn't look up.

"Well, good night, then, Rebecca. I will call on thee again next week. In the meantime, I will see thee at meeting."

"Yes."

She had but three short months to come to love Gerald Tuke. How could she possibly endure it?

Only by God's grace.

6

When Clay awoke, glittering stars still lit the sky, but he felt rested enough to resume his slog up the trail in pursuit of Horace Spencer. Clay threaded his fingers together, inverted his hands, and stretched his arms over his head, then rolled his shoulders backward to relieve the stiffness from sleeping on the hard ground. He inhaled a deep breath of fresh air, then slowly let it out as he combed his fingers through his grimy hair. What he wouldn't do for a hot bath right now. At least Julia wouldn't see him in such an unkempt state.

He'd thought a lot about Julia during his travels yesterday. The couple had not resolved the issues that had precipitated their argument—there hadn't been time enough to do so. But Clay figured there would be plenty of opportunity to smooth matters over upon his return.

He wondered how Julia had held up at the funeral service and burial of her father. Clay was sorry not to have been there for her, but she'd insisted she didn't need him at her side. She had her brothers to lean on, after all. What she really needed, she'd said, was for him to bring Horace Spencer back to Magnolia Hill Plantation and give her a front-row seat at the gallows where Spencer would take his final breath. The hateful, bitter statement had shaken Clay, but how could he fault her for desiring the death of the man she believed had murdered her father—and a slave, at that?

Clay's family never had occasion to own slaves; he and his sisters had grown up simply yet comfortably in downtown Durham, North Carolina, where their father had operated a pharmacy. His mother still lived in his childhood home, and his sisters, now married with families of their own, resided not far from there. Clay's father had died when Clay was only fifteen, the victim of a murderous thief who'd come into the pharmacy at closing time. The thug had been caught almost immediately, thanks to quick acting by several witnesses, but he'd hanged himself in his jail cell one week prior to his scheduled trial.

It was the violent loss of his beloved, highly respected father that had catalyzed Clay's decision to pursue law enforcement. He'd worked his way up the ranks, starting out at nineteen as an assistant deputy. By twenty-one, he'd achieved sergeant status and at twenty-two, deputy. The following year, an opportunity had opened up in Ellicott City, Maryland, and so, to the chagrin of his mother and sisters, Clay had packed his belongings and moved north to assume the position of captain. So impressed were his superiors by his efficiency, his work ethic, and his moral standards that they named him chief trooper when he was twenty-five. His climb at such an early age was almost unheard of, but his passion for justice, his upright character, and his reputation for fairness and integrity made him an excellent candidate for sheriff. Thus, at the young age of twenty-six, Clay was elected to the position by Delaware County, and he'd fulfilled that role for two years so far.

In those two years, Clay had never worked a case that came so close to home. With the toe of his boot, he kicked dirt over the remains of his fire to make sure he'd extinguished all the embers. He folded his blanket and tossed it over his arm, then picked up the gear he'd put by the fire—a coffeepot, a tin cup, a plate, a fork, and the pan on which he'd soaked some white navy beans for breakfast—and stuffed it inside the saddlebag of his horse, Star, named as much for the white shapes on his dappled body as for the badge Clay usually wore but today carried in another pouch. Then he mounted up, grasped the reins of the extra horse, and urged both animals out of the secluded brush and onto the road leading north toward Philly.

⟨⟩

Rebecca held a squirming Chrystal in her lap and did her best to keep the girl entertained by playing church steeple with her own fingers. It was First Day Meeting, and Friends from all around had gathered at Arch Street Meeting House in downtown Philadelphia to experience the appointed hour of silence. Everyone was to become inwardly and outwardly still, quieting the mind and body, to create an opportunity to experience the presence of the Holy Spirit.

Such was not always easily achievable when holding a wiggly two-year-old. For the most part, though, Chrystal was coming to understand that something different occurred at First Day Meeting, and Papa and Mother expected her to do her best to quiet her tongue and still her fidgety body.

Due to their belief that each person was guided by the inner light of the Holy Spirit, the Religious Society of Friends did not count either church or clergy necessary for bringing them closer to God. Thus, their "ministers" consisted of elders and appointed Friends who usually arrived early at the meeting house on cold winter mornings to fire up the basement furnace, then closed up the building once the worship had concluded. It was one of these individuals who sat down first to initiate the act of expectant waiting during the appointed hour of silence. Rebecca loved the simplicity of the meetings, even if the format wasn't always practical for those with youngsters in tow. She often left Meeting feeling more frazzled than filled. So, at home, on the rare occasion she could afford to escape, she climbed to a high spot on Sunset Ridge—as close to the heavens as she could scale—and listened for God's voice.

Over Chrystal's head, Rebecca glanced about the meeting house. Like many Quaker homes, it was built with little ornamentation and had been left unpainted. The seats and balconies on either side were rather sparsely populated today, and Rebecca wondered if the unseasonable heat had discouraged certain people from coming. Papa would never allow weather to interfere with the family's attendance. Last winter, in the middle of a snowstorm, he'd insisted the family of ten pile into the covered wagon and make the two-and-a-half-mile trek to Arch Street Meeting House.

In one of the elevated pews at the front, elder Florence White sat as straight as a razor's edge, her hands folded in her lap, her prayer cap perfectly situated on her head of white hair, her lips pursed in obvious disapproval of the slightest disturbance. Florence and her husband, Harold, had no children, so she probably did not understand the restless nature of youngsters.

Scanning the room once more, Rebecca's eye caught that of Gerald Tuke, seated two rows ahead of her on the men's side. He leaned back slightly and winked gawkily at her through his thick-lensed spectacles.

Rebecca immediately lowered her gaze to Chrystal. Good gracious, would Gerald think she was purposely seeking him out? She thought about their visit that week, and how he'd told her that she would come to love him in time. She found the idea doubtful, even after bringing the matter before the Lord last night and also reading the Scriptures by lantern light for a full forty-five minutes prior to retiring.

Someone cleared his throat, and Rebecca looked over to see Elias Fox rising to his feet, apparently feeling led to speak. Elias faced the front, as if addressing the four elders seated in the elevated benches, but he intended his message for everyone. He began by sharing Psalm 37:23: *"The steps of a good man are ordered by the Lord: and he delighteth in his way."* "Without divine guidance, none of us knows the path we should take," he explained. "For that reason, we must consciously remain in a state of continual prayer and reliance upon the Holy Spirit that lives within us. If we fail to communicate daily with Him, we lose our connection to Him. One must make a deliberate decision to pick up the Sword, which is the Holy Word of God"—he held high the thick, black book with its tattered cover for all to see—"in order that we might learn to be His faithful followers. It is a delight to follow God's precepts, and when we remain united with Him, we experience the joy that only He can give."

After a few additional minutes of exhortation, Elias Fox sat once again, and the congregants resumed their silent worship. As Chrystal wriggled with obvious impatience, Rebecca tried her best to ignore the distraction and to contemplate Elias Fox's message. She was especially struck by the admonition to remain united with God by abiding in prayer. She had quite a journey ahead of her if she wanted a full experience of the presence of God in her life.

Finally, Florence White shook hands with one of her fellow elders, indicating that she felt led by the Spirit to break meeting. As was customary after morning meeting, a brief business meeting followed. When the room was dismissed, Rebecca made a point not to look at Gerald Tuke. Instead, she focused on helping her mother corral the children toward the exit. Her plan was to go straight to the wagon and wait there for her family, in hopes of avoiding Gerald altogether. It wasn't very Christian of her, she knew, but she simply couldn't drum up any excitement over seeing him.

At the back of the meeting house, the female Albrights met up with Samuel, Milton, and Levi, who'd been sitting in the youth gallery in the balcony. Across the aisle, Rebecca saw Papa speaking to Elias Fox, his hand on the man's shoulder. He was probably thanking him for his oration.

Outside, people were gathered in clusters to socialize, their laughter a stark contrast to the silence observed inside the sacred space of the meeting house. Frances crossed the yard to greet her friends, and Milton darted across the lot with one of his peers. Mother chatted with several other women, while their husbands formed a circle of their own.

Rebecca looked around for her best friend, Charity Duncan. Charity had married last year, before the first snowfall, and Rebecca had hardly seen her since then. Charity was nowhere in sight, however. Nor were her parents, leading Rebecca to presume they'd gone somewhere together for the day.

A tug on Rebecca's sleeve drew her attention downward to Henry, standing beside her. "I have t' go to the outhouse," he informed her.

"Thee does?" Rebecca glanced around and saw Milton nearby. She summoned him and asked him to take his little brother to the privy.

Milton winced. "Do I have to?"

"Yes, and thee has to hurry." Rebecca grinned as she gave him a gentle push. "When thy brother has to go, there is no waiting around."

Milton acquiesced with a groan, and the pair scuttled off, leaving Rebecca with baby Chrystal still squirming in her arms, clearly wanting to be put down. When Rebecca set her on the ground, the girl toddled off with a happy giggle, having no idea where she was headed but enjoying the freedom of deciding for herself.

"Ah, there thee is."

The voice of Gerald Tuke caused an involuntary shiver to work its way down Rebecca's spine. Forcing a smile, she turned to acknowledge him. "Good morning, Gerald." She checked Chrystal's whereabouts and watched as the youngster wandered up to a circle of children. A young girl of about ten scooped up the newcomer and carried her over to Mother, as Chrystal's protests carried across the yard.

"It is a good morning, indeed. Going to be another scorcher, I'm afraid." Gerald squinted through his thick spectacles at the glowing sun and cloudless sky. "At least it is my day of rest. I wanted thee to know that Bernard and Elizabeth Balch have invited us to sup with them, and I took the liberty of accepting." He dipped his head a little closer and whispered, "I think this is as good a time as any to let the Friends know we are courting. We'll be receiving more dinner invitations, I'm sure, which will give us opportunities to socialize as a couple."

"Gerald, thee should not have made that decision for me. I'm afraid I...I...." Unfortunately, Rebecca could not come up with a reasonable excuse.

Gerald gave an artful grin and cleared his throat. "If the clearness committee is to approve our upcoming marriage, then they must first observe us as a couple, Rebecca."

"Thee must remember I haven't yet agreed to marry thee."

Gerald raised his scraggy eyebrows so that they were level with the top rim of his glasses. "But thy father has ordained it."

"I am considering what Elias Fox said in his message this morning—that God will direct our path when we fully surrender to Him and remain in a state of prayer. Has thee done that in regard to the future?"

"Of course. And it is clear to me that thee would make the perfect wife."

Rebecca sighed. "That's good—for thee. But now I also must seek God's direction for my future. I shall thank thee to respect my wishes in this matter."

Gerald's head snapped back as his eyes showed alarm. "Thee would defy thy father?"

Rebecca drew a deep breath to compose herself. "I would not willfully disobey my father, Gerald, but I must seek the Lord's guidance."

"I suppose I can understand that," he finally acquiesced. "In the meantime, while thee ponders God's direction, we should continue courting so that we can become better acquainted."

Rebecca guessed it couldn't hurt to have a meal at the Balches.' If she became bored with Gerald, she could always converse with Elizabeth Balch and her two delightful children.

"All right," she told Gerald. "I shall inform Papa of our plans, and let him know I'll be home later."

Papa didn't see her approaching, so she hung back, not wanting to interrupt his conversation with Daniel Hallstead and Terrence Furman. "I shall bring supplies tonight," Papa was saying. "Thee said it is mostly canned goods, blankets, and soap they need?"

"Yes," Daniel Hallstead affirmed. "And some bread, if either of you can spare a few loaves."

"I'll speak to my wife," Terrence put in. "I'm certain we have more than enough."

"Same place, I presume?" Papa asked.

Daniel nodded. "Same place."

"Dusk will be upon us, so I'll bring a lantern for my return trip," Papa said.

Rebecca was determined to figure out where her father was going tonight, even if it meant having to follow him at a distance. She could get herself into serious trouble with Papa, she knew, but her fascination with the Underground Railroad far surpassed her fears.

Suddenly, she was no longer dreading an afternoon with Gerald Tuke. While he droned on during the meal, she could politely pretend to listen while mentally concocting a workable plan for trailing her father to his nighttime destination.

7

Clay crouched down to study two pairs of similarly sized footprints. Ever since Amos had donned boots with a deep tread, Clay hadn't had any trouble keeping track of the Spencer brothers' journey over the dusty dirt paths. At least he hoped his hunch was right about the tracks belonging to Horace and the boy. If they'd gone off the trail and traveled through a wooded stretch or waded along a stream, Clay inevitably found the place where the tracks rejoined the road.

Judging by the look of these prints, which were slightly faded and partially effaced by the tracks of wagon wheels, they had to be a few hours old. Clay checked to make sure the halter of the trailing horse was secure, then mounted Star and pressed on, hoping to catch up to the brothers before they reached Philadelphia. If they made it to the Canadian border, his chances of locating them would most certainly shrink to nothing.

Around two in the afternoon, he came upon a tiny no-name hamlet with a livery. He climbed down and handed off his animals to an old scruffy-looking fellow he asked to feed, water, and brush them. Clay removed his money pouch from his saddlebag and handed the toothless man a couple of coins. "You must see all kinds come through this town, eh?"

The man chuckled, baring his toothless gums, as he greedily palmed the money. "First off, this ain't no town t' speak of. But, sure, we see all kinds. Ruffians an' crooks an' the like. We keep t' ourselves, though, and most of 'em don't cause us no trouble." He gave Clay a hasty up-and-down glance, and Clay wished he had time to wash up somewhere, and reclaim at least a semblance of the tidy appearance he typically maintained.

"You ever see any Negroes pass through here?"

The man removed his tattered hat from his head and scraped a hand through his thin white hair. "Sure 'nough, but we don't pay them no attention. We mind our own business 'round here. It's fer our own good."

"Then I don't suppose you'd tell me whether you'd seen any recently…as recent as this morning, even?"

"Sure, I'd tell y'." The man picked up a currycomb and started brushing Star in a lackadaisical manner. "In fact, y' just missed some. There was two male Negroes came through here a few hours ago. Asked if I could spare some water. Looked to be in a great hurry. I took 'em out back to my pump, an' they filled their water jars."

"Two of them, you say? How old would you put them?"

"Oh, I'd say late twenties, for the one. Other couldn't've been more than fifteen."

They had to have been Horace Spencer and his brother, Amos. "Did you happen to find out where they were headed, or gather any other details about them?" Clay inquired.

The liveryman paused in his brushing and frowned. "They didn't say much, but I overheard the younger one ask the older how much longer till they reached the station. Guess they was plannin' on catchin' a train in Philly."

"Is that right?" Clay hoped the fellow would hurry up and get some food and water for the horses. He needed to get back on the trail. "You happen to hear what the older one said in reply?"

"Sure did." The man eyed him askance. "But what's in it fer me if I tell y'?"

Clay rolled his eyes as he opened his money pouch a second time and handed over a couple of coins.

The old codger snatched the coins and stuffed them in his pocket. "All right, then. He said somethin' like, 'We'll be there by sunset.' Mentioned somethin' about Hallstead somethin' or other. When I glanced back, I saw 'im lookin' at a map. They were on foot, so my guess is, if they 'spect t' get there by nightfall, they're headin' toward Philly. Don't know how many Hallstead farms there is, but y' might start doin' some askin' around the closer y' come to the county line." He paused and stared with bloodshot eyes at Clay. "That's all I know, mister."

Clay thanked the man as he shoved the coin pouch back in his saddlebags.

"What're y' up to, anyway?" the fellow asked him.

Clay eyed the man incredulously. "I thought you said folks around here tend not to ask questions of strangers."

The guy slapped his hat on his head again and gave a sly grin. "Well, now, I guess I did say that. Didn't hurt t' ask, though, did it?"

Clay smiled back. "No, sir."

The man turned on his heel. "Guess you'll want these horses fed an' watered sooner than later, huh?"

⤐

Rebecca lifted a corner of the curtain covering her bedroom window and peeked at the barnyard below. In the light of the new moon, she could see her father loading the wagon with boxes. As soon as he left Sunset Ridge, she would sneak out the back door and follow at a safe distance on her horse, Stoney. Her heart pounded with a mixture of guilt over lying to her parents in saying she was retiring early, and excitement at the prospect of finding out what it was, exactly, that her father did to assist runaway slaves. Then maybe she could convince him that she was capable of helping the cause. She felt almost as if God were calling her to this work. Of course, He probably wouldn't approve of the conniving scheme now under way. She would seek His forgiveness later.

Of course, Father wouldn't approve. Nor would Gerald. Good gracious, after their brief discussion the other night about her interest in helping slaves to reach places of refuge, Gerald would scold her mightily if he learned of her intentions to follow her father on his nighttime journey. Briefly, she recalled the time they'd spent as a couple at the Balches' farm after meeting. It had been pleasant enough, but only because she'd had the children to dote on and Elizabeth to keep her company. All told, she'd barely spoken to Gerald during the meal. Afterward, she'd insisted on helping Elizabeth with the dishes, to give herself a break from his presence. She and Gerald hadn't actually made conversation until the ride back to Sunset Ridge, when she'd asked him all manner of questions about his farm to avoid any discussion as to their relationship.

The bedroom door opened, startling Rebecca. She dropped the curtain and whirled around to see Lydia entering.

"Coming to bed so early?" Rebecca asked, forcing a cheery tone. "I thought thee was supposed to be in Frannie's room, helping crochet some squares for the birthday quilt for Mother." Frances was privileged to have a room to herself, but only because it was a tiny space barely big enough to fit her narrow bed and small dresser. Rebecca and Lydia got along well enough that neither complained about having to share a bedroom. Lydia could be a bit of a whiner at times, but Rebecca had learned to ignore her sister's complaints.

"I grew bored. I told Frannie I would work on the quilt again tomorrow after my morning chores." Lydia closed the door behind her and approached the window. "What was thee watching outside?"

Lydia reached for the curtain, but Rebecca stopped her. "I was… only inspecting the seams of the drapes, to see if they need mending." Guilt over her outright fib immediately pricked her conscience. "All right. If thee must know, I was watching Papa load the wagon, and wondering where he might be taking the supplies."

"Ah. I figured as much. Thee is truly fascinated by the Underground Railroad. Ever since attending that anti-slavery convention last summer, thee has been trying to lap up all thee can about abolition. I saw thee reading that poetry book—*The North Star*, was it?"

"Yes, it's a wonderful collection of the poetic works of John Greenleaf Whittier, a fine Quaker. Thee should read it, as well, and be enlightened."

"Humph. I'm sure he is, but I shall leave the enlightening to thee. At any rate, thee should follow Papa tonight."

Rebecca gave a jolt. "What?"

"Don't act so astonished, Becca. Thee was already planning such a scheme, was thee not?"

Rebecca gasped. So much for keeping her plan a secret.

"Just go. I shan't tell."

"I…I truly didn't have a plan, or much of one. Just to follow Papa. I had hoped thee would stay in Frannie's room until I'd returned."

"Did thee expect us to crochet all night long?"

Rebecca bit the corner of her lip. "I suppose not."

"Becca, Becca." Lydia clicked her tongue. "Thee must learn to be shrewd if thee intends to work for this secret railroad. I have seen thy look of longing. I knew it wouldn't be long before thee tried such a scheme." She turned and tramped across the room to the corner wardrobe, threw wide the door, then quickly opened a drawer and yanked out several blankets and a straw-tick pillow.

Rebecca folded her arms across her chest. "What exactly is thee doing?"

"Just watch, Sister, dear." Walking over to the big bed they shared, Lydia pulled back the light wool blanket and the linen bedsheet. She piled everything on Rebecca's side of the mattress, plumping and shaping it into a long, rounded form, which she then draped with the top cover. Finally, she turned to face Rebecca, sweeping an arm over the bed. "There, now. Thee is sleeping as sound as a duckling snuggled beneath its mother's feathers."

Rebecca stared in amazement. "Lydia Albright, thee is a conniver if there ever was one!"

Lydia giggled, and Rebecca laughed along, even though her heart still hammered against her ribs. "Oh, my. I'm nervous as a rabbit in a snake hole."

"Don't be. It shall all go fine, as long as thee stays far enough behind Papa."

Out in the yard, there was the jingle of harnesses and the thump of hoofbeats. Lydia hastened to the window. "Papa is bringing the horses around. Thee had better go now."

Suddenly, a queasy stomach had Rebecca reconsidering her notion. "I…I don't know, Lydia. I'm afraid something will go awry."

Lydia's brown eyes rolled upward. "Rebecca Albright, if thee desires to involve thyself in this illegal venture, thee had better be ready for some rebellious behavior. And besides, if Papa and Mother consider thee old enough to marry Gerald Tuke, I should hope they think thee entitled to leave the house whenever thee chooses."

Rebecca heard a loud snap of reins and the crunch of gravel beneath wagon wheels.

"Go now, or thee will miss thy chance," Lydia urged her.

The sisters embraced, and then Rebecca slipped out of the bedroom, ran down the back stairs, scooted out the door, and raced behind the house and across the yard toward the barn. She glanced over her shoulder and saw Papa's wagon cresting Sunset Ridge. She would have to make haste if she expected to track him.

She followed him at a distance, maneuvering over the hill and then down into a ravine and around several bends before climbing yet another steep incline. Stoney cooperated perfectly, to her great relief. There were several times when Rebecca feared that Papa's wagon would tip over, the way it pitched about with the weight of its load. When they rounded a large cluster of trees, Rebecca recognized the driveway to Daniel Hallstead's farm. She reined in Stoney and stroked his neck to quiet his snorting as she peered through some nearby bushes. The night sky glittered with stars, and the moon peeked out from behind a floating cloud, providing just enough light for her to make out the figures of Papa and some other Friends. She decided to search for a better vantage point from which to observe the unfolding events. After dismounting, she wrapped Stoney's reins around a thick tree branch, then crouched down and slinked quietly forward until she reached a fallen tree with a thick trunk. Then she lowered herself to the ground and lay on her stomach behind the trunk, raising her head for an occasional peek before quickly retreating.

She found that if she kept utterly still and held her breath, she could even make out some of the men's conversation. "Four crates and two trunks…" she heard. "…Canada station in a couple of days…."

Rebecca's gaze darted from one man to another but always returned to Papa, who hefted box after box from the back of his wagon and carried it over to another wagon hitched to a team of four horses. The back of the wagon was already laden with thick hay, and the driver was perched on the buckboard, reins in hand; his back was to Rebecca, making it impossible for her to identify him. Were there runaway slaves hidden beneath the hay, ready to depart for their next stop on the road to freedom? Her heart pounded with excitement.

Something snapped behind her—a fallen branch, perhaps, or a raccoon. She whipped her head around but saw nothing out of the ordinary, only her own thick curls of hair blocking her peripheral vision. Satisfied that she had nothing to worry about, she faced the wagon again, adjusting her prone body in hopes of finding a more comfortable position. In the next instant, something cold and hard jabbed into the back of her neck, making her whole body jolt in terror. "What—"

"Shush, little missy," growled a low, gravelly voice. "Don't utter so much as a whisper, and don't move a single muscle, until I tell you to. Hear? In case you weren't aware, that's a gun poked in your neck."

Rebecca crimped her lips together, squeezed her eyes so tightly shut that it pained her, and gave her head a couple of violent shakes. *Lord, help me.* A large hand came down and encircled her arm just above the elbow, then yanked her up from the ground. She couldn't contain the little yelp that escaped her throat.

"Quiet!" the man hissed. "Slow and easy, now. Step out into that clearing." His breath was hot and damp on her cheek. With his left arm, he drew her against his solid side, and with his right hand, he raised his rifle and pressed its barrel into her temple.

Since Friends were pacifists, Papa didn't own a gun. Rebecca had seen men wearing or carrying firearms in the city, but never up close—and certainly never pointed directly at her. Something deep inside her wanted to kick her captor hard in the shin and escape his firm hold, but then she remembered his warning.

They moved closer to the wagons, where Papa and the other men were finishing the loading and checking the horses by the light of the moon and stars above.

The man brought Rebecca to a halt. Then, with his gun still pressed against her head, he shouted, "I demand that you hand over Horace Spencer. It's his life for this little lady's, here."

Rebecca's chest vibrated with her every heartbeat. Was this how she would meet her end? *Oh, Papa, I'm sorry to have disobeyed thee. Please tell Mother and the children I love them.*

⁓

Thanks to several witnesses along the way, Clay had tracked the Spencer brothers to this very spot, and he was almost certain to find the two hidden beneath the load of straw in the wagon. He hadn't planned on taking a hostage, but it seemed he would need a negotiating tool, now that Horace Spencer was surrounded by a group of men who were clearly committed to helping him flee to freedom, and probably had no regard for the Fugitive Slave Law. It still fried him plenty to have discovered his money pouch missing when he reached into his saddlebag for a drink from his canteen a couple of miles back. That lousy liveryman. If he'd had time, he would have ridden back to Ellicott City and demanded the return of his pouch—and his badge, for crying out loud. Fool had no wits about him, stealing from a sheriff.

For now, Clay put the whole thing behind him and concentrated on the girl he now held captive. He had no idea who she was, but he'd figured she had some connection to the group of men loading the wagon of runaway slaves; if he shoved her out in front of everybody and made his threats sound convincing enough, someone would surely force Spencer out into the open. Clay waited, his left hand encircling the slender girl's upper arm.

A man stepped forward. "What do you want with this Spencer fellow?"

"Papa!" the girl screamed. "Stay back. He has a gun."

Great stars in heaven, he was holding the man's daughter captive? Clay's bargaining tool was proving even more useful than he could have imagined.

"Rebecca?" The man craned his neck and lowered his eyes. "What are you—"

"Not your concern, sir. Just hand the man over, and no one will be hurt." Clay readied his rifle. Not that he intended to shoot the girl, but he wanted to show that he meant business.

"Are you a slave catcher?"

"Who I am isn't important. But if you want to save your daughter's life, you'll surrender Horace Spencer. I care nothing about any other slaves you might be harboring. The only one I want is Spencer."

"Papa," the girl wailed.

Still nothing. Clay began to worry. Did the man not take him seriously? Would he truly sacrifice his own daughter for the sake of a runaway slave?

There was a rustling of hay in the wagon, and then a shaky voice said, "Y' ain't takin' m' brother, He didn't do nothin' wrong 'cept defend 'imself." From the shadows emerged the figure of a young black man— and he held a rifle. Clay's chest constricted. He didn't want to shoot the kid or his captive. He needed to do some quick thinking.

"Look here, boy. This isn't your battle. We can do this peacefully. You drop that weapon so nobody gets hurt, hear? There's already been one shooting. We don't need another one."

The boy cocked the rifle and raised it. "Horace ain't comin'. Y' turn yo'self on around and get outta here."

"Amos, put dat gun down," said another male voice. "I's comin'."

Just then, a boom shook the ground, and the girl shrieked as a bullet whizzed past. Clay raised his gun, but the obscure lighting made it impossible for him to get a clear shot at the kid. Another boom, and Clay screamed as searing pain ripped through the side of his neck. The girl slipped from his clutches as he released her to press a hand to the wound, warm blood spurting between his fingers. Through blurry eyes, he watched chaos break loose. With his right arm, he struggled to raise his rifle, wanting to defend himself against any further shots. But the boy had vanished, and there was no sign of Horace, either. A sharp yell split the air, followed by the sound of rumbling horses' hooves. Clay reached out to steady himself but found nothing to grab. Reeling with pain and disbelief, he took one, two, three, steps backward, then lost the battle for balance and landed on the rock-hard earth, his head striking something sharp. He gasped for breath as the world closed in on him, fast.

"What is thy name, young man?" The voice sounded a thousand miles away.

Clay opened his mouth to speak, but he had neither the wherewithal nor the wits to answer. The very life seemed to be draining from him. He felt himself falling, falling, as if into a dark, deep pit, despite his desperate efforts to claw his way out.

8

Rebecca watched, speechless, as Papa crouched beside her captor and applied pressure to his bleeding neck with a cloth he'd taken from the man's saddlebag. She was still trying to process what had occurred in the past several minutes—a period of time that had felt like hours.

Terrence Furman peered over Papa's shoulder at the man. "What does thee think, Edward? Should we notify the sheriff?"

Papa stroked his heavily whiskered chin. "I'm thinking on that. He would want to know what we were doing, and we'd be hard-pressed to disguise the fact that we were blatantly defying the Fugitive Slave Law. This would no longer be considered a safe haven for runaways, and we would likely be fined or even imprisoned."

"Then what are we going to do about…?" Terrence nodded at the man lying motionless on the ground.

Papa blew out a breath. "For now, I'll take him home with me to convalesce. Once he has recovered, the man is free to do as he pleases: either report the shooting himself or continue his search. But I'd appreciate it if one of you would ride out to summon Dr. Fleming. Not only does this man have a bullet wound in his neck, but he has an awful gash where his head struck that sharp rock when he went down."

Rebecca couldn't believe her ears.

"I'll go," Elias Fox volunteered. "But, Edward, I don't think it's wise for thee to house him. He nearly killed thy own daughter. And what will Laura say when thee brings him through the door? Thee has enough bodies under thy roof already."

"Does *thee* wish to take him, then?" Papa asked.

With a jerk of his head, Elias quietly answered, "My wife would have me skinned."

"Well, we can't leave him here to die. God would not have us abandon him, slave catcher or not."

"I suspect that young fellow and his brother knew this man was tracking them," said Daniel Hallstead. "Wonder how the younger one got his hands on a rifle. A few inches over, and the bullet intended for this man would've leveled Rebecca, instead."

"Let us not go there with our thoughts." Papa brushed a hand through his hair and glanced up, in the direction of the wagon clattering up the road.

Rebecca's own thoughts kept getting stuck on Papa's intention to take her captor home to convalesce at Sunset Ridge. "Papa, does thee truly intend to nurse the man who would have killed me?"

"No, Daughter. That shall be thy job."

She nearly choked. "W-what?"

"Thy disobedience has caused us all much strife. As penance, thee shall tend this man's wounds, under the auspices of Dr. Fleming."

"But...but Elias Fox is right in expecting Mother to be most upset. Thee knows that Mother relies on me for doing much of the housework and for looking after Chrystal. I don't see how I will have time to see to the well-being of this—this slave catcher."

"We shan't speak of it further until we get home, at which point we shall draw up a workable plan with thy mother's assistance. In the meantime, thee needs to search thy soul and uproot the seeds of rebellion that caused thee to sneak out and follow me."

"Forgive me, Papa, but I only desired to know more about thy work in order that I might make a case for my helping. I yearn to become involved in assisting slaves to reach freedom."

Papa did not reply but accepted the help of several other men in loading the wounded man in the wagon, laid on his back with a couple of old horse blankets propped on either side to keep him from rolling around. A moan escaped the brute's lips, and Rebecca entertained the fleeting notion that he might die before they reached Sunset Ridge. The thought provoked a stab of guilt, for had she not gone after Papa, the man would not have come upon her, and his method of attempting to apprehend Horace Spencer might not have caused him such injury.

As predicted, Mother was not particularly thrilled with Papa when he walked through the door and announced the incoming boarder— a perchance dying one, at that. Nor was she pleased with her oldest daughter. "And what is *thee* doing, Rebecca Albright? I thought thee had gone to bed hours ago."

"We can discuss that later," Papa said brusquely.

Rebecca wanted to remind them both that, at twenty-one years old, she ought to be able to do as she pleased. But then she realized that the act of sneaking out to follow Papa did not exactly become a mature adult, so she kept quiet.

Mother jumped into action with no further questions. She instructed Papa and the men who had accompanied him back to the farm to set up a cot in the room off the front parlor and lay the unconscious man there. Then she ordered Rebecca to prepare a kettle of hot water and to gather some clean rags and towels, a bar of soap, a jar of healing salve, and a pair of scissors.

Rebecca went to the kitchen and begrudgingly began to gather the items Mother had requested. After delivering a load of supplies to the sickroom, she went back to fetch the steaming kettle, wrapping the handles with towels to keep from getting burned. She set the pot on a small wooden table beside the cot.

"We should see what we can do to clean up his neck and head wounds before Dr. Fleming arrives," Mother was saying.

"Thy hands are plenty full with household chores," Papa said to her. "I've already assigned Rebecca the duty of nursing him back to health. It's the least she can do as penance for following me without my permission."

"But he would have killed me, Mother," Rebecca protested.

"Thy father has told me. Thee should have stayed home. Just look at the trouble thy willful behavior has caused." Rebecca had wondered when the chastisement would come. "Now then, let us clean his wounds. First, we shall cut off his shirt. 'Tis a bloody mess."

Rebecca turned her face away for a moment. But then, remembering her charge to oversee his recovery, she forced herself to watch. It was then that she got her first good look at his features—which were not altogether unattractive, in spite of his injuries: square jaw with a dusting of whiskers; sandy-colored, sun-streaked hair; and muscular shoulders as broad as a bear's.

Mother first examined the wound on his neck. "It looks to be more of a bad scrape where the bullet skimmed through his neck. If that is the case, then the Lord had His eye out for him. But, gracious me, he has quite a bump on his skull. See, here?" She gently turned the man's head to the side and indicated the place, and everyone else leaned in closer to see the horrendous bump and horrid-looking gash.

"He landed on a rocky mound," Papa said. "I heard the crack when he went down."

Mother pressed her palm to the patient's broad chest. He gave a groan but kept his eyes closed. "His breathing is somewhat labored, but I can't see how he could be at risk of dying, unless from internal blood loss. We shall await Dr. Fleming's evaluation."

Dr. Fleming arrived within the hour, along with his wife, Norma, who often assisted him. The woman's presence seemed to put everyone at ease. The couple worked as a team, and it was obvious they'd done so for many years, the way Norma handed her husband exactly what he needed before he even asked for it.

After a careful examination, Dr. Fleming deemed the neck wound superficial. The bullet had passed through several layers of skin and then exited, amazingly missing several critical arteries and veins. After applying some medicine to the wound, he covered it with a large bandage. He warned of the possibility of infection setting in but said he was more concerned about the gaping gash that would require suturing, as well as about the man's unconscious state. He examined the pupils of his blue eyes, conducted a few other tests, and finally concluded that he'd probably suffered a concussion. His wife took out the necessary items for suturing the gash, at which time Rebecca turned her head away. She'd never seen such a wound, much less one that required stitching, and the sight made her a bit weak-kneed.

"I'll remove these in about seven days," the doctor mumbled as he finished. With Mother's assistance, the doctor's wife stepped forward and proceeded to wrap a cloth bandage over the wound and around the fellow's large neck. "Only time will tell how severe the injury is," Dr. Fleming said. "I'll leave some laudanum here in case he complains of pain when he finally does awaken. But, due to the nature of his injury, I want to wait until he awakens on his own. Hopefully, by morning, he'll have regained consciousness, at which point I'll assess him further."

Once the Flemings and the other men had taken their leave, Frances, Lydia, and Levi came downstairs to see what was happening. Mother gave them a brief explanation, and when she told them that Rebecca would be seeing to the care of the wounded man, Lydia glanced at Rebecca and raised her eyebrows. Rebecca gave a subtle shake of her head. She wished to awaken and discover this whole thing to have been nothing more than a ghastly dream.

All through the night, Rebecca and Mother took turns tending the injured man, mostly applying a damp cloth to his forehead as a soothing measure—not that it seemed to be making much of a difference, considering how he thrashed. The use of shifts was only a temporary option, Rebecca knew, for Mother had a household to run. Rebecca had her own chores to do, too, but she had a feeling most of them would be reassigned to Lydia and Frances for as long as Rebecca was minding her "patient."

Now, hours later, the first ray of morning sun slanted through the window and glanced off the wood floor that Mother had mopped the day before. In the straight-backed chair where she'd spent much of the night, Rebecca yawned deeply, then glanced at the man sleeping fitfully in the nearby cot. She rinsed the washcloth in the basin beside her chair, wrung it out, and applied it again to the man's forehead. The dampness caused the light brown hair at his temples to curl, and she couldn't help but notice its soft-looking texture, although she fought with all her might not to test her theory. What a ninny she'd become due to sleep deprivation! The sooner she had this man restored to health, the sooner she could send him on his way. Hopefully, he would forget about Horace Spencer and just return to wherever it was he'd come from.

"Got to find him," he mumbled.

As fast as a lightning streak, Rebecca tossed the cloth into the basin and slid forward in her chair.

"Julia…" he mumbled. "Julia…my wife…to…."

Julia. So, he was a married man. The knowledge somehow brought Rebecca a measure of relief. Now she need not blush so much at the sight of him.

"Shh," she urged him. "Thee must rest."

At the sound of her voice, his eyelids fluttered open. "What…?" He waved one of his arms erratically.

Rebecca leaned over and pressed a hand to his burly forearm, pushing it down upon the mattress. What line of work had made him so brawny? Had he fought in many barroom brawls? She considered fetching Mother but decided against it. "Lie still, or thee will do thyself more harm."

Calming, he lifted his head and focused blinking eyes on her face. "Who…? What…?"

"The doctor says thee is to lie still. How does thee feel?"

"The doctor?" He furrowed his brow. "Where am I? Who are you?"

Rebecca blew out a sigh. "I'm here to help thee recover from thy wounds. Thee has been grazed by a bullet, and thee likely suffered a concussion."

"What...?" He tried to reposition himself, wincing as he did so. "I...I don't understand."

"Thee will understand in time. Thee has been unconscious for some time. What is thy name?"

He gave her a glazed-over look. "Clay...something. I can't think of my last name right now."

She tried to reassure him with a gentle pat on his shoulder. "Don't worry thyself. That will only make things worse."

He closed his eyes again, and for a moment, it seemed he'd drifted back to sleep.

"Why do you keep saying 'thee' and 'thy'?" he mumbled.

"We Quakers have a plain way of speaking. But I will try to remember to address thee in a more conventional manner, if it would make thee more comfortable." She paused. "Where do you live? We should contact your family, particularly Julia."

His eyes popped open. "Julia?"

"Thy wife."

He squinted with a look of confusion. "My wife?"

"You don't remember her?"

He shook his head. "How did you say I got here?"

"I didn't. You were in pursuit of a man named Horace Spencer. Someone shot at you, and my father insisted on bringing you to our home to rest and recover."

"Horace Spencer?" He shook his head. "The name means nothing to me. I was pursuing him, you say? Why ever for?"

His ignorance stumped her. "You really don't know?"

He shook his head slowly back and forth, which caused his bandages to make a crinkling sound. As he lifted his hand to the sites of the wounds, a panicked expression washed over his face. "I have to get out of here." He struggled to sit up and throw the blanket off.

Rebecca held him down with one hand to his shoulder. "No, you need to rest and recover. Besides, without your memory intact, you have no place to go. Just lie down for now. Please. The doctor said that rest is the very best thing for you right now. Try to get some sleep, and we'll talk more later."

He stared at her with a look of annoyance. "I don't understand."

"Shh," she uttered as soothingly as she could. "Just rest."

In mere minutes, he had drifted back to sleep.

9

Clay yanked the bedsheets higher under his chin and stared at the ceiling. He couldn't seem to find a comfortable position. His neck throbbed, and his head pounded like rapid rounds of thunder, pulsing with every beat of his heart. His body kept alternating temperatures from chilled to hot. One minute, he couldn't get warm enough; the next minute, he was tossing off all his covers, save for a single thin sheet.

Two young boys stopped outside the doorway and peered in at him. They stared for a few moments, and finally the shorter one spoke. "Hi. I'm Henry."

"Hello, Henry." That was about all he could muster, being that he had the energy of a stick.

"And I'm Milton," the older one said.

"Hello, Milton. I'm Clay...I guess."

"Thee isn't sure?" Milton asked with a stunned expression.

Clay gave a slight groan. "Nope." He rolled painfully onto his side to get a better look at the boys.

"Why?" asked the one named Henry.

"I'm...not sure." Clay's voice sounded odd, his tone shaky. He shivered as a cool breeze drifted in the window. "How many people live in this house, anyway?" All day, he'd seen people of all sizes walk past his door, and he kept wondering when the pretty girl who'd tended him last night planned to reappear. If she'd told him her name, he couldn't recall it. And no wonder, considering he couldn't remember his own name. His memory had been nothing but a jumble of mysterious images and strange thoughts.

"There're eleven of us," said Milton.

"Yes," said Henry. "There's Mother an' Papa, an' Rebecca an' Levi an' Frannie an' Lydia an' Samuel an' Milton an' me." He held up a finger for each name. "Oh, an' baby Chrystal. Everybody calls her that, 'cause, well, she's the baby!"

Clay's head pounded the more, and he broke into a sweat. "That's…a lot of kids."

"Mother says there were twins once, but they died," said the older one, whose name Clay had already forgotten.

"They's in heaven," said Henry. He dipped his chin and tilted his face at Clay. "Is thee goin' t' heaven, Mister Clay?"

"Not soon, I hope." Truth was, Clay had no clue where he was headed after he breathed his last. Did anybody?

"Thee has got t' be a Friend if thee wants t' go t' heaven," Henry told him matter-of-factly.

"I see." Clay managed a nod. "I guess I'm a pretty good friend." He dug around in his head but couldn't come up with the name of a single acquaintance, let alone a friend, which agitated him. Maybe he didn't have any.

"No, he means a Quaker," the older boy said. "Thee has got to be a Quaker Friend."

"Oh." Clay frowned. "Well then, I guess I'm outta luck."

"What are you two doing in here?" The matriarch of the household marched into the room, her heels clicking on the floor. "Scoot!" She pointed her forefinger at the door.

The boys obeyed her order, but not without waving good-bye to Clay.

Clay managed to lift a couple of fingers and flutter them in return. Then he smiled wryly at the boys' mother. "They were just educating me on my eternal destiny."

She walked around the bed, tucking in the blankets. "And what did they tell thee?"

"That I had to be a Quaker to get to heaven."

The woman gave a partial grin as she mopped his forehead with a soft cloth. "Thee is quite feverish."

"Hot one minute, cold the next," he muttered.

"Here, have some water." She took the glass from the table beside the cot and held it to his lips while he drank.

Clay felt as helpless as a newborn. After two whole swallows, he fell back against the pillows, exhausted.

The woman planted her hands on her plump waist and assessed him with sharp eyes. "I'll be interested to see what the doctor has to say. He was to have come this morning, but something must've held him up. He's a busy man. Is there anything I can get for thee?"

"No, but I thank you for your kindness."

"How about a bit of vegetable broth? It would do thee well to take in some nourishment."

He couldn't determine whether he had an appetite or not. Something told him he didn't, and that putting anything on his stomach could backfire in a big, bad way. He squeezed his eyes shut and tried to block out the pain shooting through his head. "I'd better not."

"Thee needs sustenance, even if it's just a few sips. I'll have Rebecca bring thee some."

"Rebecca?"

"My eldest daughter. She's the one who's been tending to thee. She sat with thee all night, and I sent her for a good long nap following breakfast."

"I see." Curse his impaired memory. Those two youngsters had listed off the names of all their siblings, but now he couldn't remember even one. What was wrong with his brain? "Thank you, Mrs...."

"Thee may call me Laura," the woman said.

"Thank you, Laura. I appreciate all—"

"Never mind. No more talking now. Just rest."

He didn't have the strength to argue with her.

Laura turned and walked to the door, then made an abrupt turn. "By the way, thee doesn't have to be a Quaker to secure a spot in the glorious hereafter. The Quakers are Christians who live simply and follow certain practices that have no bearing on one's eternal destiny. Thee has only to confess thy sins to God's Son, Jesus, and ask His forgiveness. Then thee must turn from thy wicked ways, read the holy Scriptures, and pray daily."

Clay nodded. "Thanks." Another list he would likely forget within the next few minutes.

When Rebecca arrived with a crock of steaming soup, Clay obliged her by forcing himself to swallow several spoonfuls. He kept his eyes trained on her, but she clearly avoided his gaze. She pursed her pretty lips in concentration as she fed him, and he felt like an invalid. But when he tried to feed himself, he dropped the spoon, splattering his blanket with broth. He uttered a curse under his breath, then quickly apologized when he saw Rebecca grimace.

All he wanted to do was go home. Then again, where was that, exactly? *Home*. It seemed a foreign word right now.

"Dr. Fleming will be coming out sometime today, though I can't say when."

"Dr. Fleming?"

"You don't remember him?"

He shook his head. "Should I?"

"He was here yesterday. But then, you were mostly unconscious, so it is quite understandable if you can't recall him. Do you remember Julia yet?"

"Julia?"

"Your wife."

"I'm fairly certain I'm not married."

The tiniest smile turned up the corners of her mouth. "You'd best remember her soon, because you'll be going home to her when you recover."

Panic knotted his insides. He heaved an enormous breath and laid his arm across his forehead. "Something's wrong with my brain. I can't remember anything."

"Don't fret. The doctor will be able to help you, I'm sure. And I have been praying for thee."

The mention of prayer somehow took the edge off his fear. "Thank you." He allowed her to feed him a few more sips of broth before he shook his head and turned away. "I can't eat any more. I might…you know."

"Retch?"

The soup he'd consumed sloshed around in his stomach. "Maybe."

"I'll bring a basin just in case."

He closed his eyes with a groan. "Sorry for being such an inconvenience."

But she had already left the room.

Rebecca went to the kitchen and began rummaging around in the lower kitchen cupboards, searching for a large kettle.

Mother looked up from the counter where she was making dinner preparations. "What might thee be looking for, Daughter?"

Rebecca sat back and wiped her sweaty forehead with the back of her hand. "He's feeling sick to his stomach. I need…something, in case he…."

"Take that bucket under the sink."

She hauled out the vessel with a groan. "As much as I dislike pulling weeds, I'd rather be doing that than taking care of this man. Has it occurred to thee that we don't know anything about him? What if he is a murderer? When his memory returns, he may kill us all."

Mother chuckled. "I see that the sleep thee lost during hours seated at his bedside has awakened thy imagination. Now, get in there with that bucket before he loses his soup."

Dr. Fleming arrived just as Frances and Lydia began setting the table for the evening meal. Rebecca ushered the doctor through the parlor and gave a light knock on the frame of the open door to the sickroom. "Clay? The doctor is here to see you."

Clay opened his eyes and managed a weak smile.

Rebecca quickly pushed a chair closer to the bed and invited Dr. Fleming to sit. He did so while opening his black leather bag and removing from it a couple of instruments. "My apologies for taking so long to get here," he said to Clay. "I had three babies to deliver, all by different mothers, mind you. Never had such a day. Now then, how are you feeling, young man?"

Clay shrugged. "I've been better."

The doctor touched a hand to Clay's forehead. "You're running quite a fever. I worried this might happen." He stood and slowly peeled away the bandage from Clay's bullet wound. "Have you changed the dressing, Rebecca?"

"Yes, Doctor. I changed it in the night while he slept, and cleansed the sutured wound with soap and water."

"Good, that's good. Even so, he seems to have developed an infection. It's not unusual, but I had hoped to avoid it. I'm going to apply this ointment in hopes of fighting off the infection. I'll leave it with you and ask you to apply it after each cleansing and before you reapply his bandage. He should drink plenty of fluids, as well—water, tea, and apple juice, if you have any." The doctor then put his stethoscope to Clay's chest and moved it from place to place, each time asking him to take a deep breath. Then he sat back and let the stethoscope dangle from his neck. "Are you experiencing much pain?"

"My head is pounding."

Dr. Fleming nodded. "That would be the concussion. I can give you some laudanum to ease the pain and perhaps help you sleep better. Anything else?"

"I still can't remember a blasted thing."

Mother appeared in the doorway and leaned against the frame, arms crossed over her chest, as she listened intently.

"Amnesia," Dr. Fleming said. "It sometimes results from a concussion, depending on which area of the brain is most affected."

"Amnesia?" Clay muttered.

"Loss of memory. The condition isn't common, but it can result from serious head trauma. Tell me how far back you can remember."

Clay's mouth twisted with exasperation. "Yesterday."

"You really don't remember anything prior to that? Your childhood, your parents, whether you have siblings, the house where you grew up…?"

Clay shook his head in a show of despair.

"He doesn't even remember his wife," Rebecca put in.

The doctor looked at her. "Is that so? How do you know he's married?"

"He mumbled something like, 'Julia, my wife.'"

"Ah." Dr. Fleming turned and angled his head at his patient. "You have a wife awaiting your return. That fact should compel you to try with all your might to remember your past. Do you know your occupation? The name of your birthplace? The town where you now reside?"

"Not a clue," Clay muttered, his face grim.

Mother unfolded her arms and stepped into the room. "Edward made a thorough search of his saddlebags for some type of identification. He seems to think someone robbed him, because no wallet was present. There were no initials engraved on his rifle."

The doctor scratched his temple, then turned to Clay. "I'm quite confident your memory will return, it's just a question of when. Unfortunately, you're not in familiar territory, or the process would probably occur more quickly. Sometimes, seeing the faces of friends and family members, hearing songs and stories, and even smelling certain odors will spark a recollection that precipitates the restoration of one's memory. The brain is a complex thing, and a fall such as the one you took can cause quite a commotion in there." He rolled up his sleeves and leaned closer to Clay. "Let's have a look at that bump while we're at it." Using his fingers, he parted Clay's sandy-brown hair and examined the wound to his scalp. "There's still a great deal of swelling, but that will go down in time. For now, I want you to remain in bed. You're still too weak to move about, and concussions can cause dizzy spells. We sure don't want you falling again. So, no walking around—not even to the necessary."

Rebecca's gaze drifted to the white pail Papa had shoved under the cot, and a blush crept up her neck all the way to her cheeks. "My father and Levi have been assisting him in that area," she explained quietly.

"Good, good." The doctor sat back in his chair and looked at Clay. "Right now, I'm more concerned about the fever. As I said, you can have some laudanum. Some of the other symptoms of concussions include headaches, difficulty sleeping, and even periods of crankiness." With a wink, he added, "You best not get cranky with Rebecca, though, or she might throw you out."

Clay managed a slight smile and lifted his gaze until his droopy eyes made contact with Rebecca's. "I'll try my best. She's been taking mighty good care of me, as has Mrs."—he looked at Mother—"I'm sorry, I've forgotten your last name."

"It's Albright, but I told thee to call me Laura."

"Oh, yes, that's right. Laura."

"As for that fever," Dr. Fleming continued, "keep up with those cold compresses on his face, chest, and arms. And give him some laudanum powder mixed with water. You'll find the dosage directions on the bottle."

"We thank thee, Dr. Fleming." Mother turned to leave the room, then paused. "Would thee like to stay for supper? It's all ready."

The doctor gathered his instruments and returned them to his bag. "Thank you, but I have several more calls to make. I'll return tomorrow to check on things."

"I feel like a big nuisance," Clay grumbled when the doctor had gone.

"You aren't a nuisance," Rebecca said. *You only took me hostage, and might've killed me if someone hadn't shot you first.* She lifted a fresh cloth from the nearby basin, wrung out the excess water, folded it, and laid it across Clay's forehead. "Would you like some water?"

The only response she got was a snuffling sound. In the span of a minute, he'd closed his eyes and drifted to sleep.

10

*C*lay couldn't get his teeth to quit rattling. He was cold as December one minute, hotter than coals the next. People had been fussing over him for who knows how long, even though he kept pushing them away. He wanted to escape—*needed* to escape. But he felt trapped, as if locked in a tiny prison cell. Groans kept coming out of him, despite his efforts to control them. At one point, he screamed in terror when he saw a cobra, warm and vicious, slither across his body, its mouth wide open, as if about to devour him. His chest expanded as he heaved for breath.

"He's delirious," said a female voice. "Should we fetch the doctor again?"

Slowly, slowly, he started crawling out of what felt like a cavernous hole, dark and desolate.

"He was just here yesterday evening, Becca, and then again this morning," said a woman. Was it the matron of the house? "And we're doing everything he said to do—cold, damp compresses when he's burning up; extra blankets when he's chilled."

"Is it time for another dose of laudanum?" This voice came out deep and rumbly. "That should at least help to calm him."

"Soon, Edward, but let's first try to give him a sip of water," came the matronly voice.

A hand came around the back of Clay's neck and lifted him slightly. He opened his eyes to mere slits and saw a dark-haired beauty, the one who'd cared for him from the start. Sadly, her name escaped him, and he didn't have the strength to study her for long. Water slid down his throat, and the tickling sensation caused an eruption of coughs. He tried to catch his breath but only choked. He flailed his arms as his body thrashed.

"Here, let's sit him up," said a man. "Levi, lend me a hand."

Two strong arms came around him from both sides and lifted, and then someone else gave his back a good thump.

Finally, Clay caught a strangled breath, and the spasm subsided. He managed to open his eyes again and saw several people standing around his bed. In the dimly lit room, they looked like dark statues. Was he dying? It sure felt that way.

"What...?" The effort of uttering even that simple word caused his head to throb from front to back. He feebly raised his hand and touched it to his face, knocking the damp cloth off his brow.

"He's awake, Mother, he's awake." The utterance came from a young boy, but Clay couldn't make out his face through his own blurred vision.

"Is thee sure, Samuel?"

The round face of a boy with snappy brown eyes came so close, Clay felt his breath on his face. "Yes, I'm sure. He's looking right at me."

Next, the dark-haired beauty bent over him. Rachel, was it? "Well, I'll be a cooked hen. He's finally waking after two long days."

Two long days? What did she mean by that?

"Are you in pain?" she asked him.

An older woman moved closer. Laura? For some reason, that name stuck with him. "How does thee feel?" she asked.

"Sick," was all he could manage.

"Indeed, thee has been mighty sick," spoke the man standing just behind Laura.

Slowly, it came back to Clay: Someone had shot him, for a reason he didn't remember, and a Quaker family had taken him in. His brain was nothing but a dense fog, and the harder he tried to think, the foggier it got.

"When did I get here?" he croaked out.

"It is Third Day—Tuesday, to thee—just after ten," said the woman he believed to be Laura.

Tuesday meant nothing to him.

"Thee came here on Sunday night," Laura added.

Sunday to Tuesday. How many days did that make? Clay didn't have the energy to calculate it.

In the shadows, he made out the woman's rounded frame. She stepped forward and placed a cool palm on his head. He shivered at her touch. "Thy fever has gone down some. Thee has been quite delirious, but seeing thee awake and hearing thee speak a few sensible words makes me think thee may have turned a corner. I'm Laura Albright, in case thee doesn't recall, and this is my husband, Edward." She then gestured to the others standing at the foot of the cot. "These are some of our children: Samuel, Levi, Frances, Lydia, and Rebecca, the one who has spent the most time at thy bedside, tending thy fever."

It took some effort, but Clay moved his gaze from one person to the next, until his eyes came to rest on Rebecca. Ah, now he remembered her. "Yes, it's slowly coming back to me. How long have I…?"

"Two days," Rebecca answered before he could finish his query.

"Huh?" He could barely grasp the news. His head spun with questions. "Have you figured out who I am? Where I'm from? How I got here?"

The Albrights all looked at one another. For a moment, no one said anything.

"We've been too busy working to get thy fever down," Laura finally said.

"You mentioned Julia several times," Rebecca told him. "She must miss you terribly."

"Julia?" he asked, his mind as blank as an artist's fresh canvas.

"Thy wife," said Laura.

"My *wife?* No, I…I don't think I'm married."

"Well, whether thee *thinks* so or not, thee has a wife," said Edward. "Dr. Fleming believes thy memory will return in time, probably in small increments. We must get thee well so that thee can return home—wherever that may be. For all we know, thee may have a child or two."

"A *child?*" Clay's head pounded. "No, I'm sure I…." But he wasn't sure of anything. This was too much to take in.

"Don't worry thyself now," said Laura, patting his arm. "Everything will work out in God's perfect time."

God's perfect time? He wondered at that, until his head began to throb.

"I'll get the laudanum," said Rebecca to her family. "I think you can all go back to bed now. I'll sit with him a bit longer and then get some rest myself."

Clay couldn't come up with the proper words for thanking these kind folks. He hoped they could read the gratitude in his tired eyes.

⌐

Rebecca sat by Clay's bedside as he slept off and on with a rattling wheeze for the next hour or so. His fever spiked yet again, but she brought it down with wet, cold cloths. He repeatedly thanked her in his lucid times and mumbled gibberish in the moments of incoherence. She couldn't help but study his face while watching him struggle, or to wonder about Julia. Was she worried about her husband? Or was she accustomed to his long absences while he went in search of runaway slaves?

The past few days had certainly been suspenseful for the entire Albright family, as everyone had been pitching in to ensure Clay's survival. Dr. Fleming had somberly admitted that he couldn't be sure Clay had the strength to fight off the infection to his wound, and said he could do nothing more for him than to leave him in the hands of the Almighty. Nonetheless, Rebecca felt an inexplicable certainty that he had survived the worst of his ordeal and would improve from this day forward. As little as she relished the thought of tending him for days and nights on end, she did recognize the fellow as one of God's beloved. The words of Jesus from Matthew 25:40 reminded her of her Christian duty to help this man, slave catcher or not: *"Inasmuch as ye have done it unto one of the least of these my brethren, ye have done it onto me."* If she could envision herself as caring for Jesus, instead, it made tending him a bit more bearable. And so, she prayed for his full recovery, as well as for a heart of willingness to help him as best she could.

When Clay's breathing had settled and he'd returned to a slumbering state, Rebecca stood and stretched. It was well past her usual bedtime. The old clock in the dining room had struck two gongs about ten minutes ago. She went to the window, pulled back the curtain, and gazed up at a sky glittering with millions of brilliant stars. In the pasture below, Rebecca could see the family's two cows, Henrietta and Coral Belle. Most nights, the bovines made their bed in the barn, but Papa had been so busy helping with Clay that he'd decided just to leave them outside overnight. An owl hooted from its perch on the barn roof, and Gracie the dog responded with a bark.

"W-what time is it? And where am I?"

Rebecca turned at the sound of Clay's voice. It was stronger than before, which encouraged her, but his confusion hadn't cleared.

"It's shortly after two a.m. Wednesday morning," Rebecca said gently. "Thee—you're in my family's home, recovering from a wound."

"Wednesday?" He frowned. "I thought it was Saturday. I was... looking for someone."

"Yes." She nodded. "You were looking for a man named Horace Spencer. But that was almost three days ago."

"Three days ago?" He adjusted his position on the cot, then winced. "Oh, that's right. And someone shot me." He touched the bandage on his neck, then moved his hand upward to his scalp. "My head's all bandaged. Why?"

Rebecca sighed. How many times would she have to retell the story? "You fell and struck a sharp rock. The gash is...quite infected, I'm afraid."

"Oh, yes. I think I remember now."

"Do you?" She doubted it. "Can you tell me your name?"

He blinked. "Clay…something. The last name escapes me."

"And how about your wife's name?"

He frowned again. "I'm not married."

"How do you know that for certain if you can't remember your last name?"

Now a sigh whistled out of him. "I can't think straight. Why can't I remember anything?"

"Because you suffered a concussion, according to Dr. Fleming."

He didn't respond but only lay there, staring at the ceiling, no doubt trying to process all that he'd just learned, even if it was for the third time. He moved his head from side to side, his wrinkled brow denoting confusion.

A wave of sympathy washed over Rebecca. She left the window and approached his cot, leaning over to touch his forehead. She found it cool yet sweaty. "Your temperature feels normal. That's good."

"I probably stink like an old dog, though," he muttered.

"Worse." She grinned.

Without moving his head, he rolled his eyes in her direction. "A skunk, then?"

For the first time since she'd assumed the care of him, she laughed. "Maybe not quite that bad."

"I know I could use a bath. My horse probably smells better. He was washed down and combed a few days ago."

"Is that so? Can you remember where?"

"A livery in some little town." Surprise flashed across his face. "I remember!"

Exhilaration over his improvement awakened Rebecca's senses. There was the matter of the second horse he'd had with him, which he apparently didn't recall right now. But perhaps he'd acquired that animal somewhere along the way, after visiting the livery. "Try to think of the name of that little town."

He glanced about the room as if he expected to find the answer written on the walls.

"Try hard," she urged him.

"I'm trying, but I can't…can't think. My head pains me. All I know is, I got off my horse and…and handed him over to someone."

"Can you picture the person who took your horse? Maybe, if we had some more details—"

"I don't know. I told you, I can't remember." An agitated growl came out of him, which triggered a coughing spell.

Rebecca immediately regretted pushing him too far. "It helps if you sit up when you have one of these attacks." She put her hand behind his back and, summoning every ounce of her strength, helped him to a seated position. Once he was upright, his coughing slowed to a series of small gasps and sputters. Rebecca propped two tick pillows behind him for support, and he settled back against them and relaxed, his breathing still raspy but improved overall. When she offered him the glass of water from the table beside his bed, he shakily accepted it and started slurping.

"Don't drink too fast, or your spasms will start all over again," she cautioned him.

He handed her the glass and issued a dour expression. "Yes, Nurse. Thank you, Nurse."

In the lamplight, she caught the tiniest twinkle in his blue eyes. She quickly averted her gaze as she returned the glass to the stand.

"You're the prettiest nurse I ever had, you know that?"

She whirled around. "What?" No man besides Papa had ever complimented her beauty, not even Gerald. "Don't say such things. It isn't proper."

"What makes it improper?"

"Thee is a married man, and don't try to convince me thee is not. Thee has mentioned this Julia woman enough times to make me believe it's true."

"Is it against your religion for men to pay compliments to women?"

The warmth of a blush crept over her cheeks. It relieved her to know that in the dim lamplight, he wouldn't be able to see it. "It isn't against 'my religion,' no, but men simply don't say such things."

"They're probably just too shy."

"Oh, gracious me, let's talk of something else. How is thy head feeling? Has the pain subsided?"

He groaned. "I'm tired of talking about me. Tell me about yourself."

"What? No, I've nothing to tell thee. If all thee wishes to do is talk, then I shall go off to bed. Thee may have gotten plenty of rest these past days, but I have not."

"And a lack of sleep makes you a cranky Quaker?"

She was in no mood for his sense of humor at two in the morning. "Thee should not make light of my faith."

He quickly sobered. "I didn't intend to do that. I respect you for it."

No one had ever told her that, either. What a strange man she was discovering him to be.

"Does your faith prohibit you from talking to men who aren't Quakers?"

She scowled. "Well, of course not. I've been talking to thee all along, haven't I?"

"I have no idea. I've been asleep." His full lips formed a teasing half grin.

Again, she looked away. "I'll see to it that Levi brings the tub to thy room and assists thee with a bath before he goes out to the fields today."

Clay nodded. "That should take care of the skunk smell."

"It wasn't I who suggested thee smelled like a skunk."

"Oh, that's right. Just a sweaty old horse."

She couldn't keep herself from smiling. "That's probably a closer comparison." She yawned then, quickly covering her mouth with four fingers. "I should really get some sleep, or I will have bags under my eyes when Gerald Tuke comes calling this evening."

One of his sandy eyebrows rose. "Gerald Tuke?"

"My...fiancé." She wished with all her might that she could cancel her evening plans with Gerald, but Mother had invited him to supper, and Rebecca supposed it wouldn't be proper to *un*-invite him.

"Ah, so you're engaged. There, you see? Someone else appreciates your fine looks. When are you marrying this fellow?"

She ignored his forward remarks. "In Eighth Month. August, to thee."

An expression of unidentifiable emotion etched his face. "August. How far away is that?"

"We're nearing the end of May."

He shrugged. "I guess time means little to a guy who can't remember how many fingers he's got." He held up his two hands and counted each digit. "Ten," he said at last. "Did I do that right?"

He was toying with her. She smiled. "I'm proud that thee can count as high as thy fingers will allow. Now, good night."

"Are you ready for marriage?"

That question brought her up short. "I think thee is due for another dose of laudanum."

"Well, are you?"

She didn't appreciate his persistence. She put her hands on her hips and slanted him a stern look. "I do not wish to discuss Gerald Tuke with thee. But, if thee must know, of course I'm ready." Of course, she wasn't, but he need not know that. "Here is thy medicine." She spooned the previously stirred liquid hastily into his mouth.

He swallowed with a wince. "That stuff is awful."

"So I've heard." She feigned a second yawn. "I'm going upstairs now. Is there anything else thee needs?"

He leaned over the edge of the mattress and peeked down in the direction of the white metal pail.

Rebecca's cheeks heated with the warmth of a blush. "Well, I can't help thee with that."

"If you could just pull it out for me, I'm sure I'll manage fine."

She didn't like the thought of him toppling out of the cot. "Perhaps I should go awaken Papa."

"No need for that." He lifted off his bedsheet, swung his powerful-looking legs over the side of the bed, and sat there momentarily, as if to gain his bearings. Rebecca tried not to dwell on his muscular frame and silently thanked the Lord that her father had dressed him fully, albeit in a pair of loose-fitting cotton pants that Mother had made for Papa years ago but he'd never worn because they were too large, and one of Papa's oversized button-down shirts, wrinkled beyond help from Clays' having lain in a pool of sweat. The top buttons had come undone, and Rebecca purposely averted her eyes so as not to see the light brown chest hairs protruding through the opening.

She squatted down beside the bed, grasped the pail by one of its handles, and dragged it out, then quickly stood. "Are you sure I shouldn't get Papa?"

Clay nodded, and Rebecca hated that she noted how handsome he was, despite his tangled head of hair, with tufts shooting out in all directions. She stuffed her hands in her apron pockets. "I'll leave thee, then."

"Have I thanked you for taking such good care of me?"

"Several times."

"Well, several times isn't enough. Thank you again."

He could be quite nice when he chose to be.

Rebecca walked to the door, then turned around. "You are welcome. Again. And you'll get that bath later this morning."

"I shall look forward to it."

"Good. Perhaps while I'm sleeping, you can think about Julia."

He chuckled. "I would if I could picture her."

"She's your wife. I'm certain her likeness will come back to you in time."

"So you say." He rolled his eyes. "You'd think I'd remember an important person such as that."

"Yes, wouldn't you? Well, wrack your brain."

He granted her a smile that disappeared in seconds. "Now, there's a novel idea—wracking my brain. Why haven't I tried that yet?"

"Good night."

"Don't you mean 'Good morning'?"
She ignored his question and left him without a backward glance.

11

Rebecca stepped onto the front porch and breathed deeply of the sweet, fragrant air, which seemed to revive her energy, in spite of the little sleep she'd gotten. Sunset Ridge was never more beautiful than at this hour of the early morning, when the sun began its ascent, gilding the distant hills with yellow light. She started toward the barn, looking forward to the prospect of tackling a task other than nursing her patient. For this morning, at least, that was Levi's job.

As she made her way across the yard, she was struck by the parched appearance of the fields beyond the barn. This spring had been unusually dry, with only a few scattered sprinkles of rain, and she knew Levi was worried about the crops.

Giving her bonnet strings a mindless tug, Rebecca glanced heavenward. "Father, Thee knows our needs, and I trust Thee to supply them as Thee sees fit. A good, soaking rain would be most helpful." Then, for no reason other than that she'd just checked on a sleeping Clay, she prayed for him, as well. "And if it be Thy will, grant Clay a full recovery of body and mind. May we, as a family, show forth Thy love and goodness so that he might be compelled to surrender his life to Thee and turn from his evil profession of hunting down runaways. In Thy name I pray, amen."

By now, she'd reached the barn. The big door squeaked and squawked as she pulled it open, prompting a lively response from the barn residents. Henrietta and Coral Belle mooed in their stalls, Morris the mule began braying, and the goats, Mary and Hilda, uttered shrieks that sounded eerily human. "Good gracious," Rebecca muttered. "Thy cries are enough to wake the dead."

The rest of the animals—several horses and a mean old rooster who'd chased some stray hens into the barn behind Rebecca—started kicking up a fuss. A couple of barn cats came running in search of attention, their whiskers still wet with fresh milk from their metal dishes. They mewed loudly as Rebecca bent to pet them.

"Good morning, Becca." Her father emerged from his adjoining workshop. "What brings thee out here at this hour?"

Rebecca stood up straight again. "I wanted to assist with the morning chores, since I've asked Levi to prepare a bath for Clay and help him wash."

"How is Clay?"

"His fever seems to have gone, at least for now."

"That's good. It's been a long stretch for all of us, but especially for thee. I hope thy mother was right in saying he seems to have turned the corner."

"I hope so, too. The simple act of eliminating his stench ought to make a significant difference. Once Levi has gotten him bathed, he's going to help him out to the living room so that Frances may change his bedding."

Papa chuckled. "Nothing like ridding oneself and one's surroundings of the pungent odors of sickness."

"My aim is to get him well so he can return to his wife as soon as possible. Of course, he first must remember where he lives."

Papa nodded. "Dr. Fleming is still confident his memory will return. Patience is the key."

Patience. A virtue Rebecca did not have in reserve. Thank goodness Papa was patient with her. She studied the scuffmarks on the toes of her boots as she considered what she needed to say by way of an apology. "Papa, I want to ask thy forgiveness for sneaking out and following thee that night. It was irresponsible of me, and perhaps none of this would have happened had I not been there."

Papa released a long-suffering sigh. "I've thought much about that night, Daughter. Thee was very determined to learn the ways of the Railroad, or thee wouldn't have put thyself at risk. Do not blame thyself for what happened to Clay. Perhaps it happened for a reason—Clay's coming here, that is. Perhaps he needed to learn from us about God's saving grace."

A gray cat—the one Lydia had named Oscar—rubbed against Rebecca's leg. Rebecca crouched down and scooped him up. "I have wondered the same, Papa. And I have been praying for him."

"I consider thee a responsible young woman, Becca," Papa said. "Thee is kind and compassionate, and the Railroad needs compassionate folks. Perhaps thee can come with me tomorrow night."

Rebecca dropped the cat as her head shot up, knocking off her loosely tied bonnet and leaving it to dangle at her throat. "Really, Papa? Thee would permit me to come along?"

"I consulted with the other men, and they agreed that it would be acceptable. I haven't told thy mother yet, though. I don't suspect she will be very happy."

"I'm grateful for the chance to help, Papa. I appreciate thy confidence in me."

"And I appreciate thy enthusiasm for a worthy cause. Only promise me thee will be careful. Thee knows this is dangerous work."

"Yes, but it doesn't dampen my desire to help. I shall make thee proud, Papa," she assured him.

"It is not I that thee should seek to make proud, but only thy heavenly Father."

"Of course." Rebecca nodded. "Well, would thee care to assign me a less dangerous job for now?"

Papa smiled. "There's the pitchfork. Stalls need mucking."

It wasn't her favorite barn chore, but it wasn't her least favorite, either. She smiled back at him. "It shall be my pleasure."

⁓

Clay sat on the edge of the cot and gazed about the room as he gathered his strength. Long fringed curtains hung over the window, and a woolen rug with a subtle pattern covered the oak floor. A small pine bureau stood across the room, and atop it was a simple washbasin, a pale blue pitcher, and a lantern. The room wasn't much bigger than a large closet. Clay had gathered that it was Edward's study, and that they had moved his desk out to make space for the cot and small chest. Just feet away was a chair—the one in which Rebecca had spent long hours watching him. Across the back of the chair was draped a knitted shawl, and he envisioned Rebecca wrapping herself in its warmth as she dozed, sitting upright, during his own fits of comfortless sleep. The image incited strong feelings of appreciation for her, along with another emotion he couldn't quite identify.

Clay felt better and a good deal stronger after his bath that morning. When Levi had carried the big copper tub into the room and then made several trips back and forth from the kitchen with pails of water to fill it, Clay had experienced a vivid recollection of a childhood memory. A woman—his mother, most likely—said in a teasing tone, "If you don't wash off all that dirt, somebody's bound to mistake you for a black bear." Behind her, two girls, all vim and vigor, rushed into the room, their young faces framed by long blonde braids. Did Clay have sisters? His heart had leaped at the thought of family, of someone awaiting his return.

Now and again, something specific elicited a memory—an aroma from the kitchen, a flavor, perhaps a color or a specific word or sound, and even the sound of the Albright children's laughter. He never knew quite when one of these moments would occur, as they came without warning.

He pushed himself up from the bed, preparing to walk to the window for a glimpse at the outside world. But his weak legs gave way, and he collapsed onto the mattress again.

Rebecca entered then, and his heart took an unexpected flip. The woman had an undeniable effect on him. For now, he chose not to address it, specifically since it seemed there was a woman named Julia in his life. "Hello, Clay. What are you up to?"

He cast her a half grin, then nodded at the window. "Just planning to take a peek outside at the weather."

"Not without help, you're not," she said sternly. "You may be showing signs of improvement, but you are not to walk anywhere unassisted, at the risk of hurting yourself. Here, put your hand on my shoulder."

"You're an ornery one."

"Only when the situation calls for it."

Doing as told, he rested a hand on her shoulder and stood, using her as a crutch. Right away, he noticed her flowery scent, and his heart pumped a little faster than it ought to have. Holy cats, he barely knew her, despite the hours they'd spent together in close proximity. He'd been asleep for most of that time, and their conversations had mostly centered on his convalescence—her asking him about his basic needs or drilling him on his identity, as if her persistent interrogations would hasten the return of his memory. He could understand her desire to have him out of her hair as soon as possible, and he wanted his memory back, too, so he could cease being a burden on the Albright family. But he couldn't help his wish to get to know Rebecca a little better before he left. Then again, what right had he to think such things? Hadn't she told him that she was betrothed? She'd mentioned an August wedding. He couldn't figure out why a twinge of jealousy pinched him at the center of his chest. Land of liberty, not only had he lost his memory, he'd lost his capacity for rational thought.

They took one step, and then another, and another still, until at last they reached the open window. It felt good to get on his feet. Clay surveyed the side yard, where a couple of hens pecked at the ground, and two cats darted up a tree in pursuit of a squirrel. He chuckled at the sight, then sneezed when the warm breeze tickled his nostrils.

Rebecca glanced at him with concern in her eyes. "Are you chilled?"

"Chilled?" Clay chuckled again. "It's hotter than blazes outside. I mean, fire—hotter than fire. Is 'blazes' improper vernacular for your Quaker ears? I'm afraid I keep forgetting about your religion."

She giggled. "My 'religion,' as you say, does not define me. It is the Lord living inside me that makes me who I am. Quakerism is more about personal faith in Christ. Yes, we Friends lead simple lives, but we do so as a recognition of who we are in comparison to our Savior. It isn't something we *must* do but something we *choose* to do. You do not need to change your way of speaking or even your way of living in my presence. That is between you and God. True change begins in the heart, not with the outward appearance or with one's manner of speech."

"I see," said Clay. "Well, that makes sense, I suppose. Never did like having people try to push religion down my throat."

Her eyes gleamed with apparent curiosity. "And who used to do that?"

"My grandmother."

They stared at each other for almost a full minute. Clay's mouth hung open, but he couldn't summon the sense to shut it, so overwhelmed was he at having recalled someone specific from his life.

"You remember your grandmother!" Rebecca finally exclaimed. "What else do you recall about her?"

Clay realized that he had yet to remove his hand from Rebecca's shoulder. Even so, she did not step aside. He stared out past the barn. "I remember spending time with her and Grandpap. They had a big farm somewhere in South Carolina, I think, and I helped my grandpap plow the fields." Emboldened by his own excitement, he gave her shoulder a squeeze. "I'm starting to remember, in bits and pieces."

Her smile was broader than he'd ever seen it. "Dr. Fleming said that your memory would return, he just didn't know when." Then she sobered as she studied him a moment. "Do you remember whether you accepted your grandmother's religious instruction? Did you have any sort of relationship with God?"

The questions gave him a strange sense of uneasiness. "I don't recall that I did, only that my grandmother used to harp on me about my sins. Have you always 'had a relationship with God,' as you put it?"

Her smile widened. My, was she ever a beauty. "Oh, yes! Not as well as I do today, mind you. Everyone must ultimately choose either to follow after God or to turn in a different direction."

"I see." But he didn't, really. He just knew that, right now, he wanted to drink up as much of Rebecca Albright's presence as possible. And if that meant standing here talking about God, then so be it. "You smell so good. What is it that you put in your hair?"

As if suddenly awaking, she moved a good foot away from him. "Thee must not ask such questions. It isn't proper."

"Why not? It was a simple question, wasn't it?"

"Simple, yes, but thee is married. Thee shouldn't be noticing the— the scent of my hair."

Even as she spoke the words, she fingered a few wayward strands that had come loose from the braid down her back, and tucked them behind her ear. She wasn't wearing her Quaker cap, and he would've liked to take a tiny lock in his fist. He'd get a real scolding for that, though.

He cleared his throat. "This Julia person that you say I mentioned while sleeping...maybe she's a friend, or a cousin. Or even a sister. I do believe I have a sister or two."

Rebecca kept her eyes trained on something across the yard. "I distinctly remember thee saying the word 'wife' in relation to Julia." She shrugged. "It does not matter. The fact is, Julia exists, so thee must consider thyself married—*happily* married," she added. "Besides, as thee will recall, I am betrothed. Gerald Tuke is the only one with the right to compliment me in such a manner."

He raised his eyebrows at her, but she kept her gaze averted.

"Rebecca Tuke," he mused aloud. "Good Quaker name, I suppose. And are *thy* desires for him strong and keenly passionate?"

Now her head jerked up, and she pierced him with a not-so-friendly glare. "If thee will excuse me, I shall go help my mother in the kitchen. Gerald Tuke is coming for dinner, and we are preparing a hearty feast."

"I didn't mean to chase you away," Clay insisted. "It was just another simple question."

She walked to the door, her spine stubbornly straight. Ah, so he'd struck a nerve.

"Aren't you going to help me back to my bed?"

She stopped in the doorway and turned around. "I believe thee can manage perfectly without me. If thee should fall, I shall send Frances or Lydia. In fact, perhaps it is time I relinquish thy care to someone else. Thee is quite improved and shouldn't require my services much longer."

A grin came forth, despite his efforts to remain somber. "Who knows? Perhaps I'll be out of your way in the next day or two."

She paused only a few seconds before replying, "Yes, and I look forward to that day." Then she disappeared from view, leaving him to his private thoughts.

In time, Clay tired of standing and shuffled slowly back to the cot and slumped upon it, sweating from even so low a degree of exertion. Out of her way in a few days? Strangely, he wasn't in any hurry to leave, not since laying eyes on Rebecca. Every one of the Albright sisters was a beauty, perhaps Frances most of all, but Rebecca was the one who'd caught his eye from the start. She was the one he wished to get to know on a deeper level.

If only he could figure out this Julia person's identity and rid Rebecca of the notion that he was married to her.

12

At the sight of Gerald Tuke riding his horse up the dirt driveway, Rebecca stepped outside to greet him. She wasn't the least bit happy to see him, but she had to feign enthusiasm if she were to marry him in less than three months. The very notion still made her queasy, and it didn't help that Clay had chosen to plant himself on a wicker porch chair, from where he, too, watched Gerald's approach.

Oh, how it had irked her to discover him sitting there after he'd made a trip to the privy—his first since coming to stay with her family. He claimed not to have the strength or even the desire to return to his room just yet, but Rebecca was certain he just wanted to get a good look at Gerald. She had hoped that her betrothed would at least come dressed in his First-Day-Meeting clothes.

Gerald's gap-toothed grin revealed his pleasure at seeing her. He reined in his horse, jumped down, and tied the animal to the hitching post before swiftly taking Rebecca in his arms.

"Gerald, please," she muttered softly as she pushed him away. "We aren't exactly alone."

"Yes, I see the man on the porch. Thy patient, I presume." He put his hands on her shoulders and gently squeezed. "Remind me again why he must stay in thy house?"

"He shouldn't be with us much longer," she assured him. "He's making excellent strides toward recovery."

"Humph." Gerald lifted his shoulders with a deep inhalation, then released his breath on a loud sigh. "I haven't even kissed thee hello." He leaned toward her with lips puckered, but she turned her face so that his mouth merely brushed her cheek.

He laughed. "All right, my dear. But I shall wish to kiss thee before I leave tonight."

Her cheeks burned with embarrassment, for she had no doubt that Clay watched, most likely with amusement. At least Gerald's appearance was unusually neat, with his dark suit, tie, and hat—no matter that he was sweating profusely in the sultry evening air.

She forced herself to loop her arm through Gerald's and allowed him to escort her up the porch steps. She was still trying to figure out what to say by way of introduction when Clay beat her to the punch, gingerly rising to his feet and extending a hand to Gerald. "You must be Mr. Tuke," he boomed affably. "I'm Clay. I'd tell you my last name, but I can't recall it just yet. I'm well on the way to recovering it, though, thanks to your lovely bride-to-be, here."

Gerald shook his hand unenthusiastically. "Gerald Tuke, but then, I guess thee already knows that." There wasn't even a glimmer of warmth in his voice.

Rebecca dropped her eyes to her shoes peeking out beneath the hem of her long skirt. She'd sewn it last week and was quite happy with the way it'd turned out, although Gerald seemed not to have noticed it. Mother had purchased an entire bolt of the coral fabric with the intention of making it into curtains, but she'd not had a chance to start them yet and had offered Rebecca a section of material to sew herself a nice skirt for special occasions—not that she considered a visit from Gerald Tuke to be special.

How she wished her parents would not push him on her. But with no other suitable gentleman on hand, what was she to do? *Gerald will make a fine provider, Rebecca.* Her mother's words from that very afternoon echoed again in her ear. *Thee must lay aside the fact that thee does not fully love him yet. The feelings will come in time.* But would they? Rebecca feared she would never feel anything beyond common civility for the man. *Are thy desires for him strong and keenly passionate?* Even now, Clay's question rocked her; first, that he'd asked so intimate a question of her, and, second, that she hadn't been able to answer in a truthful manner. It annoyed her that Clay seemed to see right through her.

"How is it thee can remember my name, yet thee cannot recall the most important details of thy life?" Gerald asked.

Clay smiled, though she wasn't sure how much of it was forced. "It is odd, isn't it? The doctor said my memory should return in full, but until then, it'll come in bits and pieces. You have to admit, the name Tuke is rather unforgettable."

Gerald cleared his throat. "Well, let us hope thy most essential memories return quickly, such as where thee lives, so that thee may make for home. I'm certain thee must be anxious for that day—so thee doesn't wear out thy welcome."

"Yes, let us hope so. You won't mind if I sit, will you?" Without waiting for an answer, Clay dropped into the rocker once more, and Rebecca observed beads of perspiration on his forehead.

"Does thee need assistance getting back to thy room?" Rebecca asked him. "I'm sure Gerald would be happy to help thee."

Clay chuckled. "Yes, I'm sure he would. Thanks, but I believe I'll sit out here for a spell."

"Lydia or Frances will bring thee a tray of food shortly. Would thee like to take it out here?"

"That'd be real nice, Rebecca."

The men stared at each other until the front door swung open and Lydia poked her head out. "Ah, thee is here." She ducked back inside. "Mother! Gerald has arrived."

From the kitchen, Mother replied, "All right, Lydia. No need to announce it to the barn animals, too. Invite him in."

Lydia smiled at Clay. Her expression faded to neutral acknowledgment when her eyes alit on Gerald. "Please come in. Supper awaits." She gave a little curtsy, then grinned again at Clay before disappearing inside.

At the table, Gerald was unusually chatty with everyone but Rebecca. Papa asked about Gerald's farming endeavors, and beamed when Gerald boasted of a good haul at market with the sale of over a hundred chickens. He made a decent income from the sale of eggs and from his impressive inventory of livestock, including beef cattle, milk cows, and fattened hogs. None of it much interested Rebecca.

When Frances rose to refill the water pitcher, Lydia jumped up, too, and carried the bowl of potatoes to the kitchen, saying she would add more. The two returned several minutes later, their eyes glittering with amusement, and Rebecca wondered if they had been discussing what an awkward match she and Gerald made.

After dessert, Rebecca rose to help clear the table, but Mother insisted she entertain their guest instead. "Perchance you could go for a moonlight stroll," she suggested.

"Excellent idea," Gerald said.

"I'm rather tired," Rebecca said simultaneously.

"Nonsense," Papa said. "You two go along, now."

Rebecca hid her sigh by affecting a yawn. She did not wish to be alone with Gerald, but how could she avoid it? At least there would be no Clay to contend with. As far as she knew, he'd retreated to his room after eating his supper. She resisted the urge, surely born out of habit, to go check on him. On the way to the front door, she looked past the parlor to his room. The door was ajar, and there was a dim light emanating from within. Did he need a fresh glass of water? Did he have a headache? Was his wound causing him discomfort, such that he might need some laudanum to ease the pain? She decided she would check on him after bidding Gerald good night.

Gerald opened the door and waved a hand for her to go ahead of him. On the porch, Rebecca leaned forward against the railing and gripped it tightly, lest Gerald attempt to clasp hold of her hand and draw it to his lips. He'd expressed his intention of giving her a kiss good night, but she wasn't in the mood for one of his smooches—not on the hand, not on the cheek, and certainly not on the mouth. What could she say or do to deter him?

"I am very much looking forward to the next meeting of the Philadelphia Female Anti-Slavery Society," she announced.

Standing shoulder to shoulder with him, she detected his head turning sharply toward her. "Thee is still wrapped up in that folly? I don't think it's a good idea, and I'm surprised thy father is allowing it."

"The Society is a perfectly civil organization, and theirs is a noble cause. I wish not for thee to challenge me on my involvement."

"I don't wish for it either, my dear; but, since thee is to be my wife, I believe it is within my rights to question thy activities."

Oh, but he rattled her brain. She would not marry a man who insisted on telling her what she could and could not do, especially in matters of morality—and slavery was a moral issue. Perhaps she should talk to Papa herself, and let him know that Gerald did not approve of her involvement in the Society. Would he not then see the error of their union? Surely, a husband and wife should agree on the most important of subjects.

What would Gerald say if he knew of her participation in Papa's latest mission with the Railroad? It seemed she would need to keep her involvement a secret once she and Gerald were married—*if* they were married.

He lifted his eyebrows until several wrinkles creased his forehead. "I can see thee is going to be a hard one to break in after we marry." Then he chuckled.

Rebecca failed to see the humor. "I shan't need any 'breaking in,' Gerald. And if thee thinks I do, perhaps thee should look elsewhere for a wife."

"I have no desire to look elsewhere, my dear. In fact, I would much rather marry a feisty woman than one who is meek and mundane. I believe I'm up for the challenge."

How maddening. She did not wish to be his "challenge."

He put a finger under her chin and lifted it. She allowed it, but only because she felt guilty for being so ornery. She knew that she was to honor and respect others, even if they didn't necessarily agree with her personal convictions.

Gerald lowered his face and planted a firm kiss on her lips. She waited to feel something, but no yearnings flickered in her chest.

She stepped aside to end the intimate encounter.

Gerald searched her face, his expression confused. "Is something wrong, love?"

"I don't know how to say this, but...but I must. I don't have any feelings of love for thee. Thee is a kind man, and thee deserves a wife who will love thee in return."

Gerald shook his head and merely straightened his shoulders with resolve. "I am not the least bit worried about that, Rebecca. As I said before, the feelings will come with time, and with a little effort on thy part. Be patient, and try not to be discouraged. And remember, thy father has put his stamp of approval on our union. He has but only to announce our betrothal in Meeting on the day of his choice, and then we shall go before the clearness committee. Do not worry; thee will grow more attracted as the day draws nearer."

It was useless to argue with him. Papa and he had practically already carved the marriage in stone. Good gracious, what was she to do?

"Come," Gerald said, extending his hand. "Let us take a walk around the yard."

She didn't wish to walk, but she allowed him to take her hand and guide her down the porch steps. "I am quite weary, but I suppose a brief walk will be fine."

They strolled around the house, past the forsythia and rose bushes and then the magnolia tree. Rebecca glanced at Clay's window and, of all things, discovered him standing there, gazing out. Had he spotted them walking hand in hand?

Gerald said nothing until they reached the big oak tree. Several years ago, Papa had built an octagonal wooden bench around the massive trunk. It had held up well, considering how many people had sat on it—or skipped along it, in the case of the younger Albright children.

Gerald exhaled a noisy sigh as he lowered himself onto the bench. "When does thee expect that Clay fellow to take his leave?"

Rebecca sat next to him. "I don't know, Gerald. It will depend upon when he regains his memory and his strength. Right now, he is not well enough to travel."

"Unless he is faking his condition."

"I don't know how thee could suggest such a thing. He had a raging fever. No one can fake that."

"I don't like his being under thy roof."

"I am not the one who invited him to stay with us, Gerald. My papa insisted upon it."

"But it has been thy responsibility to see to his care. That, in itself, is improper."

"Papa would never assign me a task he considered 'improper.'"

"I don't like the idea of my fiancée looking after another man."

"Oh, Gerald, don't be silly. There is nothing unseemly about my doing that. It isn't as if the two of us are ever alone in the house. And Mother looks in on Clay about as much as I do."

"Humph. I felt he looked at thee in a particular way tonight."

Rebecca could not believe her ears. "And what 'way' might that be?"

Gerald scratched the side of his head and frowned. "I don't know, exactly. But it seemed as if he were jealous."

What a foolish notion. "Is thee sure it is not thee who is the jealous one?"

Gerald hung his head and kicked the dirt around with his boot.

"Besides," she went on, "we have reason to believe Clay is married, to a woman named Julia. He uttered her name the other night during one of his feverish fits."

"Julia could be his dog, for all we know," Gerald muttered.

"Gerald!"

"Or his horse. We ought to go to the barn and see if the animal will respond to the name."

"He has two horses, both of them geldings, not mares. And since when is Julia a male name?"

He took her hand in his and, before she could stop him, drew it to his mouth, kissing her knuckles. "Thee is so lovely, Rebecca, and I shan't put up with another man looking upon thee with desire. Is that clear? Thy heart belongs to me." Then he squeezed her hand so tightly that she winced.

When he released her, she quickly tucked both hands inside the folds of her skirt and pretended to shiver. "I must go inside now, Gerald."

She stood, and he leaped up beside her. "But we've barely been alone tonight. Won't thy parents think it odd if thee goes in so soon?"

She covered a contrived yawn with her palm. "I shall just tell them the truth: I am quite fatigued."

"It's because thee has spent so much time nursing that moocher back to health."

"Gerald! As Christians, are we not to show Christ's love to all?"

"I suppose."

Rebecca took Gerald's arm once more, and they started the trek back to the house. A rabbit scampered across their path, and Gracie set off after the furry creature, failing to catch it and succeeding only in compelling it to scurry into a hole under the barn.

They climbed the porch steps, and when they reached the door, Gerald turned Rebecca toward him. "May I claim that good-night kiss?"

Her heart filled with dread. "Gerald...."

"This is what betrothed couples do, Rebecca."

She sighed. "Oh, all right. But just a little one."

He didn't have to lean down very far, for he was only a few hairs taller than she. Rebecca closed her eyes as his lips met hers, again waiting to see if she would experience an extraordinary rush in her veins. Nothing. She stepped back and looked at him. His spectacles made his eyes appear larger than Mother's teacup saucers. "Well…good night, then."

"Good night, my love."

She forced a smile, wishing she could make it more sincere. He opened the door for her, and she slipped past him into the foyer, then closed the door without a sound and leaned against it. She could hear her sisters and mother conversing in the kitchen, and Chrystal squealing with delight. Overhead, there came a pitter-patter and a clunk of footsteps from one end of the hall to the other, and she imagined her brothers wrestling, perhaps tossing pillows at one another. In the parlor, Papa napped on the sofa, his lips parted slightly. She glanced past the parlor to Clay's room. Seeing the light still on, she decided to go check on him. After all, it was her job. At least, that is what she told herself.

13

Clay was sitting in the chair beside the open window, enjoying the evening breeze and reading by lantern light from the Bible he'd found on the chest of drawers near his bed, when he heard footsteps outside his room. He glanced up, and his pulse skipped when Rebecca peeked her head in the doorway.

Why she had such a powerful impact on his heart, he couldn't say; but there it was, as clear as the evening sky. She was a beauty, no question, even though she dressed as plainly as a pauper. She had a distinct elegance about her that set her apart from her sisters. No wonder that Tuke character had snatched her up so quickly. Women like Rebecca Albright weren't easy to come by.

Clay closed the worn cover of the Bible and smiled. "Sent your betrothed home already, have you? It's not even fully nightfall."

"I told him I was weary." She stood in the doorway and fiddled with her bonnet strings.

"I see. And are you weary?"

"Yes, very, but I thought I would check on you before I retired for the night. How are you feeling?"

He couldn't help grinning. "I'm gaining strength by the hour, all thanks to you."

"Let us not forget that I have prayed for you, as has my family. The glory goes to God our Father for preserving your life. He has a purpose in all things."

Clay glanced down at the Book in his lap. "I find it hard to believe that God cares more than an owl's hoot about my life, or that He has some sort of purpose for me."

"Oh, but He does." Rebecca stepped into the room and gazed steadily at him. "God has a special love and purpose for each member of His creation."

"If you say so."

"You would do well to continue studying His holy Word." She nodded to the Bible in his lap. "You will gain insight with each reading."

Clay had picked up the Good Book out of simple curiosity, not to seek out some deep truth. He wanted to change the subject. "So, did that Tuke fellow take you in his arms and speak sweet words to you?" Even in the shadows, he could see the crimson hue of her face, and he immediately regretted his outright nosiness. "Sorry. I don't know what comes over me sometimes. May I blame it on the concussion?"

She raised her eyebrows. "That would be a far stretch of the truth."

"Well then, if we're being truthful, I found your fiancé rather rude, quite frankly. I could tell right off he didn't like me when you introduced us."

She sniffed and then, with one little tug, removed her Quaker cap. Several strands of hair came loose from her bun and fell in curls that clung to her cheeks. "Thee should not trouble thyself about what Gerald thinks. It is true he is not happy with thy presence here, but I assured him that nothing unseemly has happened between us. Nor will it, ever."

"Tell me why you're marrying him."

She raised her chin. "My parents fear I am passing the marriageable age."

That gave him a little jolt. "You're agreeing to an arranged marriage to a guy you don't even love?"

She set the cap on the back of the chair. "I didn't say I don't love him." Her cheeks flushed pink, then turned a chalky white.

"So, you do love him?"

She glanced at the glowing lantern on the bedside table, the light of which set off a flickering in her dark eyes. "It is not for thee to know."

"Why would you marry someone you didn't love?"

"My parents are very wise. They know what is best for me."

"And you don't? Is this one of those Quaker things?"

She crimped her brow and allowed her eyes to meet his. "No, it is not a 'Quaker thing.' It is merely my parents making a strong suggestion that my chances for finding a man of like faith are growing slimmer as I get older."

"And just how old are you?"

"Twenty-one, not that it's any of thy business."

"Twenty-one? That *is* old."

She glared at him.

He laughed. "I'm teasing." He set the Bible on the bed. "I'm twenty-eight, myself."

"Really?" Her tone grew excited. "You're remembering more, then."

"Yes. I'm feeling optimistic, Rebecca. I mean, I still haven't fully regained my strength, but my appetite's coming back little by little, and the headaches seem to be subsiding. Hopefully, more and more important memories will begin to resurface."

"Yes, let us hope so."

He stood then and started toward her.

"What are you doing?" she asked, folding her arms defensively across her chest.

"I thought I'd take a stroll outside. I've been cooped up in this room for days, and I'd like to do a little exploring. Want to show me around?"

She dropped her hands to her sides. "Oh, I...I couldn't."

"Not even to provide some assistance? You are my nurse, after all."

"I am not thy nurse. I've merely looked after thee. But then, so has my family. Besides, I already told Gerald I was tired."

"Which was really just an excuse to send him on his way."

She gave an indignant gasp. "It most certainly was not."

"Of course, it was. Come on, now. Show me around the farm. I'm curious."

She peered over her shoulder, as if to check for eavesdroppers. She chewed her lower lip, and he could almost see the war going on inside her head. "Well, I suppose a short walk couldn't hurt."

They passed the living room, where Edward napped on a sofa. Back in the kitchen, Laura and her elder daughters chatted while they worked. Not that it mattered, but he was just as glad that no one saw the two of them walk out together. As they descended the porch steps, Clay automatically took Rebecca's elbow, then dropped his hand to his side when their feet hit the ground. Stars had just begun to dot the sky above, where a half moon shone brightly. The treetops swayed gently in the mild breeze, putting him in mind of a dance. A faint memory of attending a ballet performance with a woman at his side flashed in his mind, and the recollection made him halt his steps.

"What is it?" Rebecca asked, her eyes on him.

He didn't look at her, just gave his head a little shake and resumed shuffling toward the barn. "Nothing. Just a hazy memory."

"A memory of what?"

"Going to the ballet."

"The ballet?"

"Strange, isn't it? I don't exactly seem like the type." He grinned at her as they walked side by side, their arms gently brushing against each other, and it pleased him to see her smile in return.

"It's interesting, the remembrances that are conjured by the littlest of things."

"It sure is. I've had fleeting visions of my mother, and I'm almost certain I have a sister, maybe two."

"Have you remembered anything yet relating to Julia?"

"I haven't, sorry. I'm sure you'd like me to recall more recent details, so I can be on my way as soon as possible. I'm trying my best."

"Perhaps you're trying too hard. Dr. Fleming urged you not to fret, as worrying will only tire your brain and lead to frustration. And, as

Papa has said, you needn't worry about leaving until you are certain of where you live."

"Your father is extraordinarily kind...as are you."

She waved him off. "I don't think of myself as extraordinary in any way."

"Ah, but you are."

She didn't respond but slowed her steps to keep pace with him, for which he was grateful. He still had a headache and wasn't extremely sure on his feet. However, it felt good to be taking a different path from the one that led to the necessary. He surveyed the big two-story, L-shaped barn with its two gabled roofs and the banked construction on one end. Off to the side of that was a chicken coop surrounded by a wire fence with so many gaping holes that its presence seemed extraneous. Case in point, the chickens roamed the yard quite freely, pecking at the ground in search of who knows what, instinctively moving out of the way for Clay and Rebecca. Behind the chicken coop was a pigpen with a lean-to, inside of which were a number of fattened pigs. Down in the valley, tucked between two rolling hills, was a stone springhouse along the creek bed.

As they reached the barn, Clay stepped ahead and pulled the door open for Rebecca. The entry area was illuminated by a perpetually burning lantern that hung from a hook on a wooden post.

Rebecca pointed at a bench off to the side. "Come and sit," she said, pointing to a nearby bench. "You would do well to rest after that long trek."

"Thanks. Don't mind if I do." He lowered himself onto the bench and released a long sigh. "Impressive farm your family has. I don't think my grandparents raised quite as many varieties of animals."

"There were once a lot more cows, when my grandfather ran the farm primarily as a dairy. But with Papa's bum leg, he can't hold down the farm as Grandfather Albright did. Thank goodness he has his carpentry business."

"What happened to your father's leg?"

"He broke it several years ago, in a fall from a hayloft."

"Does it pain him?"

"Probably some, but he never complains. Perhaps he reserves his grumbling for Mother's ears alone."

"Are you close to your mother?"

Rebecca considered his question for a moment. "I've never felt overly close to her, but I'm not sure any of my siblings does. It isn't that there is strain or strife between us, only that Mother comes off as staunch and stern. Even so, she is a very caring person."

"I can see that." With his legs stretched out before him, he examined his worn boots. "One of your brothers—I believe it was Milton— mentioned you had twin brothers who died long ago."

"He did? That surprises me. It's something we almost never talk of, as Mother is very touchy about the subject. Truth be told, I didn't even know Milton had any knowledge of the twins. At any rate, yes, my brothers Clarence and Howard died two days apart of a deadly fever shortly before their second birthday. I have only a faint recollection of them. I was four at the time, and Mother was so terrified of my falling ill that she shipped me off to live with another family of Friends. I recall staying with them for several weeks…and feeling lonely. Looking back, I imagine Mother wanted to clean the house of every possible germ after my brothers died, but I also think she was too exhausted to see to my care. When I finally returned home, I recall Papa's eyes being sad for months afterward, and Mother's looking…well, vacant. She took to her bed, so unlike the woman she is today, and didn't get up for weeks. Friends and neighbor women came by every day or so to clean and make meals. Some even gave me a few toys; the dolls are the ones I remember. I would cling tightly to them in my bed at night, drawing some sort of comfort from them." She stared off. "I sometimes wonder how the twins would have turned out, had they lived."

"I'm sure the loss of them is something you think about often."

"Not as frequently as you might expect. Like I said, I don't remember too much about the twins. My memories of living with that family and then coming home to a dark, quiet house are more vivid than my memory of my brothers." She turned to look at him, blinking. "Goodness, I've been doing all the talking. I wish you could tell me about yourself."

"Believe me, I wish I could, as well. But I enjoy listening to you."

"Oh. Well, I could go on and on until I've bored you to tears."

He chuckled. "I doubt that."

"Are you ready for a tour of the barn?"

He nodded, then summoned his strength and stood.

"Over here are Henrietta and Coral Belle, our milk cows," she began. "Papa usually keeps them out by day and brings them in at night, although some nights he lets them roam the hillsides. He'll be out later to check on everything. The cows we saw out in the field belong to our neighbor up the road. We share pastures."

"I see."

A black-and-white dog entered the barn and rushed to Rebecca's side. She bent and kissed the dog's nose, a simple gesture that, for reasons beyond his understanding, moved Clay profoundly. He had a soft spot in his heart for Rebecca, and he had no idea what to do with it.

"And this is Gracie. You've probably heard her more than seen her. She's a herder, and when the sheep get out, which happens about once a week, she is adamant about putting them all back where they belong." She gave a little giggle as she patted the dog's head.

Clay stepped forward to pet the dog, and as he did, his hand brushed against Rebecca's. The connection gave him a jolt, and he withdrew his hand almost instantly. He had no idea whether she'd felt it or not; but, for him, there was no denying it.

Just then, a field mouse skittered past, followed by a cat in hot pursuit. Gracie joined in the chase, and the moment between him and Rebecca quickly faded.

From around the corner, a horse neighed. "Is that Star?"

Rebecca stared at him. "What did you say?"

"I said, 'Is that—'" Then it dawned on him. "My horse! I remember him, and his name." Excitement swelled within him, and he hastened in the direction of the familiar-sounding nicker, anxious to lay eyes on his horse in hopes that seeing the animal might spark yet another reminiscence. Rebecca's footfalls sounded behind him as he moved from one stall to the next.

The horse neighed again as Clay finally laid eyes on the tall dappled creature.

"Star! So good to see you." He reached his hand over the stall door, and Star leaned forward to nuzzle it with his nose.

It was a happy event, this reunion, and it gave Clay reason to hope that the remaining details of his life would soon return. His life since the shooting and the resulting concussion had become a puzzle of sorts, with pieces scattered everywhere.

Rebecca climbed up next to Clay and reached over the rail to caress the horse's neck. Her lovely scent reached Clay's nostrils, but he kept quiet about it, recalling how the last time he'd mentioned how lovely she smelled she'd taken offense, saying it wasn't proper of him to notice.

"So, this is Star, is it? We'd been wondering what to call him. Does the other horse have a name?"

"What other horse?"

"You rode in on Star and brought this one"—she nodded to the gray horse in the adjoining stall—"with you on a lead."

"I don't recognize him. I wish I did. He looks like a good ol' boy."

Star nickered again, then extended his giant head over the stall door and snuffled in Clay's face. Clay laughed, overwhelmed by the affection he felt for this animal that was the closest thing to an old friend he had right now. He patted the horse tenderly, then glanced over at Rebecca—and spontaneously kissed her cheek.

It was a quick peck, nothing more, but it was enough to whet his appetite for another taste of her. He drew back and searched her face. Her large brown eyes showed disbelief as they locked with his blue ones, and she stared, her body unmoving, her voice mute. His mouth was already moist and ready for meeting hers, and without another thought, he leaned close again, tilting his head first one way and then the other as he tried to figure out how best to position his lips. To his surprise, Rebecca didn't try to flee. In fact, she stayed fastened upon the stall door, her hands clinging to its top board, her feet making no move to hit the ground and run.

Their mouths met and melded, and for one brief instant, Clay thought he might collapse out of pure joy. He managed to keep his focus, though, as he grasped Rebecca's waist and, with his lips still on hers, lowered her to the ground with little effort. Then he turned her body toward him and gathered her closer, putting one hand in the small of her back, the other hand clutching the rounded portion of her shoulder. Rebecca's arms slowly encircled his broad back, and he felt her hands lock together, as if she had no intention or desire to escape his embrace.

Clay's pulse whirled and skidded. This kiss utterly transported him to a different place, a higher plane. But the familiarity of the act of kissing, and the troubling guilt that ensued, made him slowly pull away.

"Oh!" Rebecca leaped back, putting several inches between them, and covered her mouth with her hand. In the pinch of moonlight coming through the barn window, Clay could see the rush of pink that had stained her cheeks. "That..." she sputtered. "I didn't—"

"I'm sorry, Rebecca," he said past the knot in his throat. "I didn't intend for that to happen. Not at all, I promise. It took me quite by surprise."

"I—I'm at a loss for words."

"As am I. Don't worry, it won't happen again."

"I'm so ashamed. No one must know."

"Of course not, but you needn't be ashamed. We've done nothing wrong."

"How can thee say such a thing? I am betrothed to be married, and furthermore...furthermore...thee *is* married, most likely." She steepled her hands and lifted her gaze heavenward. "O Father, forgive me."

There was a creak of hinges as the door at the front of the barn opened, giving Clay a start. It was followed by the shuffling of footsteps.

Rebecca gasped, her eyes wide, and hoarsely whispered, "It's Papa!" She held a forefinger to her lips, then whirled around with a swoosh of her skirts and ran to a nearby feed barrel, disappearing behind it.

Clay stared after her, gape-mouthed. If the situation hadn't been so grave, he might have laughed. Out the corner of his eye, he saw Edward Albright approaching.

"Clay?"

Clay cleared his throat. "Edward."

"What is thee doing out here?"

"I…I came out to see my horse, sir."

"Thy horse? Thee remembers him, then?"

Clay grinned. "I sure do." He hoped his demeanor wouldn't give away the fact that he'd just kissed the farmer's daughter. "I even remember his name. Star. Not very imaginative, I suppose, but it's what came to mind when I first saw those spots covering his body."

"Well, I'll be. Thee has begun to recall some important memories. What about this other horse?" Edward pointed at the gray gelding.

Ironic that he'd just had this same conversation with Rebecca. Clay scratched his temple. "Afraid my memory is only coming back in spurts."

The older man stepped forward and put a hand on Clay's shoulder. "Don't worry thyself. No point to it. One day soon, it will all come flooding back."

Clay nodded. "I know you're right." He could just see the top of Rebecca's head over the lid of the feed barrel. She seemed to be struggling to keep her balance. When she made a rustling sound, he coughed loudly to cover it up. Edward seemed not to notice. "I'm hopeful I'll regain enough of my memory to be able to head back home—wherever that may be. Goodness knows I've burdened you and your family for long enough."

"No burden, my friend." Edward sniffed, then finger-combed his gray hair. "Well, I came out here to check on the livestock. Thee had better return to the house and get some rest. Thee appears a bit pale in the face. Rebecca will check on you in the morning, I imagine. I haven't seen her since she set off on a walk with Gerald Tuke."

"Is that right?"

Edward nodded. "Strangest thing, though—the fellow's horse is gone."

"Perhaps he took Rebecca for a ride on horseback." Regret flooded Clay's conscience for misleading the man. Edward Albright had been nothing but kind to Clay from the moment he'd taken him in.

"That is exactly what I thought. Nice night for it."

"Yes, it's a fine night."

"That man will win her heart yet."

Clay took a hasty glance at the big feed barrel. "You mean, your daughter isn't in love with her intended?"

Edward sighed. "Not yet, but I keep telling her to be patient. Gerald Tuke is a good man. He's got a fine farm, and he'll do right by her. Love need not precede marriage."

"I suppose not." There was much Clay wanted to interject, but he knew his place, and it wasn't to argue with Edward Albright about the wisdom of giving away his daughter to a man she didn't love and probably never would.

"Perhaps one day soon thee will recall the day thee said thy vows to Julia."

"I hope you're right, sir."

Julia. Had Clay ever spoken vows to her—or to any woman? The memory of the kiss he'd shared with Rebecca released a fresh surge of guilt. What if he really *were* married? How would he ever come to terms with his newfound attraction to Rebecca if he had a wife waiting for him? He vowed right then to avoid being alone with Rebecca again, at least until he figured out who he was and where he belonged. It simply wasn't fair to her, or to himself.

"Well, I will say good night, then," Clay said.

"Good night, Clay," Edward echoed. "I wish thee a restful slumber."

The men's gazes met and held. Clay liked Edward Albright and could almost envision him making a fine father-in-law.

Foolish thought. After stealing a final glance at the feed barrel, he turned and walked out of the barn.

14

When Rebecca turned in for the night, Lydia was still awake, of course, and demanded to know about her "moonlit stroll" with Gerald Tuke. Rebecca hadn't the courage to tell her she'd ended it quite quickly and instead spent time with Clay. Lydia would have a terrible time keeping that a secret, and the interrogation she was sure to administer made Rebecca feel the beginnings of a headache.

Merciful stars, what had come over her, allowing Clay to kiss her— and with such passion? Why, they hadn't known each other for more than a week. The worst part was, she couldn't blame the incident entirely on him, because she'd been a willing participant. Never in all her days had she experienced such a moment. Yes, Gerald had kissed her, but his kisses were nothing compared to what she'd experienced with Clay—an explosive current racing through her, making her heart lurch madly and her legs go as weak as wilted flowers.

Thank the Lord above that Papa had not come upon them in the act, or—heaven forbid—found her hidden behind the feed barrel while he tended to his nightly chores. When he and Clay had finished talking, Papa had moved to another part of the barn, giving Rebecca an opportunity to make her escape. She'd scampered silently to the door, then run like the wind across the yard to the house.

As the two sisters prepared for bed, Lydia made it more than clear she didn't consider Gerald a good match for Rebecca. She described him as a "weasel," then went so far as to make up a silly song, which she sang in a deliberately discordant tone: "Gerald is a weasel, a funny-looking goon. His spectacles make his bug eyes look bigger than the moon."

"Stop it," Rebecca scolded her as she sat at the dressing table and began running a brush through her dark, wavy locks. "That's not very kind." She had to choke back a giggle, for, sadly, the little ditty did describe Gerald quite perfectly.

"Thee can't marry him, Rebecca. Thy children will not look normal."

At that, Rebecca turned abruptly to face her sister. "Lydia May Albright! What would possess thee to say such a thing?" She'd never even discussed the topic of children with Gerald, and now that she thought about it, her nerves jumped with dread.

"Well, it's true. They might have little heads and big eyes…and be very puny. Thee doesn't want puny children with big heads running around thy farm. I mean, it's possible they would look like thee—which would be a good thing, I suppose."

"Thee *supposes?*"

"Well, thee does have fairly big eyes, thyself."

"I do?" This was all so very enlightening.

"They're not as big as Gerald's. Thine are quite nice, actually. His are large and green and grossly big, especially behind those spectacles."

"He can't help the spectacles," Rebecca explained, but her giggles had already started.

"He'd look better without them, even if it'd mean he'd be groping around blindly. Can thee imagine it? Arms stretched out, trying to feel his way around, and suddenly he smacks into a chair, stumbles over it, and falls on his face, breaking his nose. His nose is already too big for his head."

"Lydia!"

By now, the sisters were being noisier than two screeching cats; and the more Lydia talked, the sillier she became. Their laughter escalated—until Mother opened the door.

"What on earth has gotten into you girls?"

"Nothing, Mother," they said in unison, going solemn in an instant. Mother could probably sober a hyena if ever she came face-to-face with one.

Mother pursed her lips and raised one eyebrow. "Well, if you carry on much longer, you'll wake up baby Chrystal, and then we shall see who is laughing."

"Yes, Mother." Lydia climbed into bed and yanked the hem of her lightweight sheet to her chin. "We shall be quiet now." Her voice quivered with repressed laughter, and Rebecca well knew the effort it took for her sister to restrain herself.

"Well then...." Mother started to turn but stopped when she met Rebecca's eyes in the mirror. "Did thee have a nice walk with Gerald Tuke?"

"Yes, lovely," Rebecca fibbed. Nothing involving Gerald Tuke was ever lovely.

"I am glad to hear it. Wedding bells will soon be ringing. Thy papa has said it won't be long before he announces your betrothal at Meeting."

Betrothal. Rebecca swallowed hard. She didn't wish for the news to go public quite yet. Somehow, she had to convince Papa that marrying Gerald Tuke wasn't God's will. But then, what did she really know of God's will? It wasn't as if He had spoken audibly to her. How did anyone know for sure if he was following the path God set for him? If only the Lord would wave a flag under her nose that said, "This is the way. Walk ye in it."

After Mother had closed the door, Rebecca rose from her stool and extinguished the lamp. Mother's mood had changed the tenor of things. In the dark, Rebecca and Lydia exchanged a few more comments, but the giggles had gone out of them. Before long, Lydia drifted to sleep, leaving Rebecca alone with her thoughts—and the memory of Clay's kiss forever imprinted on her heart.

The next day, Rebecca did her best to avoid Clay. She simply couldn't allow herself to look him in the eye. She prepared his breakfast, as usual, but asked Levi to deliver it. At lunchtime, she did the same, having Lydia take the meal to him. When Lydia raised her eyebrows in question, Rebecca pretended not to notice and began scouring the butcher block. She managed to avoid Clay all the way till mid-afternoon, when she was returning from delivering a bucket of slop to the hogs and found herself traveling toward him on the narrow path leading to the outdoor privy. She'd had her head down, so didn't see him until they were just a few feet from each other.

"Well!" she sputtered when she noticed him.

"Yes, well."

Both of them gawked at each other for all of thirty seconds before Rebecca stepped to the side, intending to go around Clay. He moved simultaneously in the same direction. There was an eruption of nervous laughter before they tried again, this time clearing a path for each other. Even so, and in spite of the awkward, uncomfortable nature of the encounter, they stayed firmly planted in place.

"Is thee having—" she began.

"I hope you—" he said simultaneously.

"Oh," she said, giving way to another uneasy giggle. "Thee was saying?"

"I was going to ask if you were having a nice day."

"Yes, I thank thee. It's been lovely thus far. And how is thee feeling?"

"I'm feeling quite well, thank you. Getting stronger."

"Oh, good. I'm happy to hear that. Have any new memories surfaced?" Their conversation sounded so proper and stiff, Rebecca almost curtsied.

"Not today."

More gawking.

"Well..." he said.

"Yes, well."

"I'll be on my way, then." He gave a slight nod of his head, then slipped past her and continued to the outhouse.

Rebecca watched him for a few moments. Would either of them ever feel normal in the other's presence again?

That evening after supper, Rebecca helped Papa load the wagon with a variety of supplies—some food staples, a couple of donated blankets Rebecca had collected from the AFASS, and several new pairs of hand-knit socks. As she did, Rebecca thought about how she took all the conveniences of home for granted: cold water from the well whenever she wanted it, hot meals prepared on the cookstove, garments aplenty, and eating utensils, to name a few. She ran her hand over one of the wool blankets and pictured the precious young child of a fugitive slave snuggling under its warmth.

Papa dropped a sturdy piece of canvas cloth over the assembled wares, secured the load with some twine, and then walked around front to the horses and untied their reins. "Ready, Daughter?"

"I am, Papa."

The four-mile drive did not take as long as Rebecca anticipated, and she found her pulse rate increasing as they drew closer and closer to their destination. What would they find when they reached the pickup point? How many fugitive slaves would there be? Would they be malnourished and exhausted? She tried to prepare herself mentally, and Papa seemed to be doing the same, if his silence was any indication.

"The fishery is just ahead," Papa murmured as the road skirted the riverbank. "I don't see any signs of activity yet."

Rebecca sat as tall as she could, holding tight to her cap, since the wind had picked up. "Nor do I—but there's a skunk!"

Papa pulled back abruptly on the reins, and Rebecca prayed that neither horse would spook. The last thing she wanted was to be covered in smelly spray. Once the black-and-white critter had crossed the road and disappeared into the underbrush, she let out her breath, and Papa clicked his tongue at the horses, prompting them to resume their unhurried gait.

When they arrived at the fishery, Papa steered the team to a grassy patch, then sat back and wrapped the reins loosely around the brake lever. A few fishermen were just coming off the docks with poles and buckets in hand. They nodded at Papa and Rebecca as they walked past.

After a moment, Rebecca whispered, "It's so quiet. Is thee certain this is the right spot?"

"It is, Rebecca. One often must wait."

"Perhaps the boat didn't make it across the Delaware. Oh, Papa, I hope no one drowned."

"Hush. Thee mustn't think such things."

The chill in the air, combined with her sense of suspense, sent a flurry of shivers through Rebecca's body. She gathered her shawl to her neck, thankful that Mother had handed it to her on her way out the door, and determined to muster her courage. She didn't want Papa worrying that her fear might compromise the entire operation.

"I had a good case of the jitters my first time or two," Papa confessed, evidently seeing right through her façade.

She'd never thought of Papa as being anything but cool and collected. "What first compelled thee to participate in this endeavor, Papa?" she asked quietly.

"I suppose it was the same thing that has compelled thee, my dear: a desire for justice and freedom for all." He cleared his throat and surveyed their surroundings.

A rustling nearby made the hairs on Rebecca's arms stand up. She scooted closer to Papa.

"Who dat?" said a voice from the bushes.

"The horses are in the barn," Papa said, using the code he had explained to Rebecca.

From the edge of the woods, one, two, three, four, and then five men emerged, their skin as dark as the night, their clothes nothing more than mere rags. Papa climbed down from the wagon just as a sixth Negro—a woman carrying a small child—joined the men. As Papa held aside the canvas flap so that the runaways could climb in, Rebecca couldn't help herself; she grabbed a fistful of her skirts, jumped down to the ground, and went to the young woman. "Here, let me help thee."

The woman's eyes went as white as a full moon as she gathered her child closer to her bosom. "You cain't take 'im."

The woman's obvious terror unleashed a flood of pity within Rebecca. "It's all right," she assured her. "Thy child is safe. Is thee hungry? We have ample provisions aboard the wagon, including fresh drinking water, loaves of bread, and apples."

"Mama, I hungry an' thirsty," the weeping child said between sobs.

"Shush yo' mouth," she ordered him, pressing his face into her chest. Still she hung back, eyeing Rebecca with a look of desperation. "I's scared, miss. I hear bad stories o' betrayal."

"My papa will not betray you, and neither will our heavenly Father," Rebecca assured her.

The woman's large brown eyes welled with wetness. Rebecca noticed that the hairs on her arms stood on edge. She quickly removed her own shawl and wrapped it around the woman's sturdy shoulders. "Think of God when you wear this. Picture Him wrapping His warm arms around thee and keeping thee safe wherever thee goes."

"I shall," the woman whispered. "And I shall think o' you, too."

Once she had joined the others in the back of the wagon, Papa closed the canvas door. The last thing Rebecca saw was the little boy eagerly devouring his wedge of soft bread.

When they reached the intersection of Lewis Street and Delaware, another wagon was waiting, just as had been planned. Papa had explained to Rebecca that runaway slaves were not as apt to be tracked when several parties aided their escape. At Papa's request, Rebecca remained seated as the small group of fugitives hurried out of the Albrights' wagon. The woman, whose child now lay limp and slumbering in her arms, paused and glanced back at Rebecca. She didn't speak, just nodded solemnly.

"I will pray for thee," Rebecca whispered after her.

"Thank y', and thank y' fo' the shawl."

Rebecca smiled back. "Thee is most welcome."

"Hurry, Gemma," one of the men urged her.

Gemma. How lovely. Rebecca decided that if ever she had a daughter, that would be her name.

The ride home was anything but quiet and reflective, for, as hard as she tried, Rebecca could not stop the flow of her words. Papa was surely weary, but she didn't care; there was so much to talk about. "Did thee see Gemma's face when I put that shawl around her? Thee doesn't think Mother will mind that I gave it away, does thee? I could hardly just stand by and let her shiver. And, oh, her little boy, so sweet and helpless. He must certainly wonder where they're going—and yet, he is so trusting at the same time. Oh, to be that trusting. I often wonder where I'm headed, myself—and then I realize I must trust my heavenly Father to lead the way. I thank thee for allowing me to participate tonight. Will I get to go again? When is thy next mission?"

She went on and on, hardly pausing long enough for Papa to respond to her questions. As it was, he provided only one- and two-word answers. Finally, she paused for a breath.

"Has thee run out of words, Daughter?"

Rebecca's cheeks went hot from embarrassment. "Quite."

Papa chuckled. "Thy enthusiasm cheers me."

"But thee shouldn't need cheering. Not after what we accomplished tonight."

"Ah, but we didn't accomplish even a particle of what needs doing."

His simple statement gave rise to the bitterness of reality. "Thee is right. And I feel now more than ever before that I must continue to assist on the Railroad. Do I have thy blessing, Papa?"

She studied his profile in the moonlight: his whiskery chin, firm mouth, straight nose, and thick brows under his tall black hat. He nodded. "Yes, Daughter."

His approval thrilled her, but it was quickly dampened by the memory of what was to take place three months hence. "And what of Gerald Tuke? I cannot keep my involvement a secret from him if we are to wed. What if he does not approve?"

Papa held the reins loosely as the horses trotted along at an easy pace, their hooves kicking up dust. "Thee must abide by thy husband's wishes."

"Even if his wishes conflict with a core conviction of mine? That hardly seems fair, Papa. Shouldn't a husband and wife be like-minded, especially regarding important matters such as this? Mama supports thy efforts. And yet Gerald Tuke is not in favor of the Railroad."

"I don't believe Gerald Tuke opposes the Railroad. If anything, he would forbid thy involvement out of a fear that any harm might befall thee."

"But if we are to help the oppressed and beaten down, we must be willing to sacrifice our own well-being, are we not?"

"Thee can continue thy meetings with the AFASS. There, thee will have opportunities for assisting with the Railroad efforts without endangering thyself. I'm sure Gerald would not disapprove of thy attending the meetings and staying informed."

"But I much prefer to be in the thick of the action, Papa."

He said nothing for the next little while, just gazed straight ahead. Had she overstepped her bounds? Spoken out of turn?

When they rounded the bend that brought Sunset Ridge into view, Papa slowed the wagon to a stop. The horses pawed at the earth and snorted loudly in protest. "We shall talk further about thy involvement in the Railroad, Daughter. If thee feels a tugging at thy heart, it may well be the Lord's calling. Speak not about this to Mother. As for her support of my involvement, it is not wholehearted. She worries about my safety, so I know she worries doubly for thine. She is anxious for thee to marry, in hopes that thee will settle down and set aside thy determination to participate directly in the Railroad."

She started to protest, but Papa held up a hand. "Thy mother has already lost two children, Becca. Granted, it happened many years ago, but a mother never forgets."

His words stunned her into silence. Of course, a mother never forgot the loss of a child. Was that the reason for the sometimes seemingly hard, protective shell Mother kept around herself? The reason she often came across as stiff and unyielding, especially when it came to Rebecca's dreams?

They rode the rest of the way home in silence.

15

At the sound of the rooster crowing, Clay opened his eyes and stared up at the barn ceiling, where the swallows were stirring in their nests. A week ago, he'd made the hayloft his home. Laura Albright had objected, insisting he remain in the house, but he'd told her he'd more than outworn his welcome, and that bunking up in the barn would suit him just fine.

Since making his move, Clay had grown stronger, and now, for all practical purposes, he was completely healed—on the outside, that is. His sutures had been removed, and his wounds were turning to scars. Most days, he worked in the fields with Levi and did various other jobs around the farm. It felt good to rebuild his muscles and make himself useful. He enjoyed watching Edward build furniture and was glad to offer assistance when asked.

His mind still had a ways to go, though, for he still had no idea where he lived or what he did for a living. It frustrated him no end that he might never recall all the details of what had landed him in Philadelphia, and how far he'd traveled to get there.

On his latest visit to the farm, Dr. Fleming had declared him well, save for his lost memory. He told him not to let discouragement settle in, assuring him that it was still early, and that, from what he'd read, memory retrieval could sometimes take months or even years. *Years?* Clay couldn't imagine waiting years. The doctor had claimed that his memory would return in segments, like the chapters of a book, but not necessarily in the correct order. Clay thought about the possibility of never recovering his true identity. If he ended up staying on at Sunset Ridge, he would convince Rebecca not to marry Gerald. The Lord knew he didn't relish the thought of leaving her, not after those tasty kisses, and he certainly couldn't picture her married to Tuke.

He pushed the borrowed bedsheet off himself, sat up, stretched his arms over his head, and rolled his shoulders to relieve the tension. He couldn't say a mound of hay made the most comfortable bed, but it beat sleeping on the ground beneath the stars, which is what he would be doing if he left the Albrights' farm—wandering the countryside, wondering where to go.

Lately, he'd been remembering more and more pieces of his childhood. He could picture his mother and his two sisters with clarity, and he even recollected climbing trees and hunting and fishing as a boy, when he wasn't helping out at his father's pharmacy. He was almost certain he'd grown up in North Carolina, but he couldn't recall in which town. He even pictured the two-story house where he'd lived. Sadly, he couldn't recollect his sisters' names, but he seemed to remember his mother's being Irene. He also recalled that his father had died, and that it hadn't been by accident. Somebody had killed him in a robbery, but the details were hazy, at best. As for Clay's supposed relationship with someone named Julia, no matter how much he wracked his brain to remember her, he simply couldn't. In fact, he'd begun to wonder if she even existed. Perhaps in his fevered state, he'd mumbled something that Rebecca had misconstrued.

In the meantime, he was enjoying getting to know the Albright family. He'd taken to riding his horse in the evenings, and Samuel and Milton often joined him on their ponies, showing him around the property and pointing out their favorite spots. The boys were good riders, and one day Clay had remarked to Samuel that he would make a fine cowboy. To that, Samuel had said, "Naw, I want to be a judge when I grow up. I'd rather be a sheriff, but Quakers really can't be sheriffs."

"Is that right?" Hearing the word "sheriff" had given Clay pause, and he'd wondered what the significance might be. He'd studied his surroundings, as if to find his answer there, but nothing of importance came to him. As he'd gazed out over the rolling Pennsylvania hills, he'd asked, "Why can't Quakers be sheriffs?"

"Because we are peacekeepers," Samuel had explained. "We aren't supposed to carry weapons."

Clay had been aware of this, of course; he'd merely wanted to draw out the subject a bit, to see if any pertinent memories might surface. Dr. Fleming had said that sometimes a single word could lead to a string of remembrances. Could it be possible that Clay himself was an enforcer of the law?

"Does thee gots a weapon?" Milton had asked, sitting higher in his saddle.

"I think I do, somewhere," Clay had replied. "I think your father must have put it out of reach. Funny that I hadn't even thought of it till now."

"Thee should ask to see it," Samuel had suggested. "Maybe it'd help thee to remember something about thyself."

Smart kid. "I think I'll do just that."

"The day after thee arrived here, Papa looked in thy saddlebags for some clue about thy identity, but he didn't find any—not even a purse. He said somebody prob'ly robbed thee."

Clay had nodded. "He told me that."

"Maybe thee lost everything," Milton had mused. "I lost my lunch pail on our walk to school one time, and Samuel had to share his sandwich with me. He wasn't very happy. Good thing Mother gave him two apples that day. We found my pail on the way home, and Samuel made me give him most everything that was in there. Well, everything 'cept the bread. It had ants on it."

"Don't talk so much," Samuel had chided his brother. "Thee will make Clay regret inviting us on his evening rides."

Clay had chuckled then. "Not at all," he'd assured Samuel. "I enjoy your company. You're very mature young men."

"He called us 'men'!" Milton had exclaimed.

"*Young* men," Samuel had reminded him.

⌒

Now Clay gave his head a quick toss to shake out his meandering thoughts as he slipped into a cotton shirt, then snatched up the smelly overalls he'd shucked the night before, and pulled them on. They'd gotten so stiff with caked mud that if he didn't wash them soon, they were apt to up and walk away. Before leaving the loft, he gathered a bar of soap, a towel, and an outfit that seemed presentable enough for a Sunday service. He'd decided to accompany the Albrights on their weekly trip to Arch Street Meeting House. It was the least he could do as a show of honor and respect. And so, after tending the animals, he planned to give himself a good scrubbing down at the creek.

Edward had insisted it wasn't necessary for Clay to help with the livestock, but Clay found the mundane tasks of feeding and watering the animals and, milking the cows and goats to be oddly rewarding. It gave him a sense of satisfaction to feel he was earning his room and board. He disliked living the beggar's life, being obliged to accept secondhand clothes. Last Sunday, when the family returned home from Meeting, he'd looked up from brushing one of the horses and had seen Rebecca standing just inside the barn, a wooden crate overflowing with clothes. The way she'd stood there with the sun's rays casting a halo-like glow around her silhouette had made him think of an ethereal being—until she spoke. "Clara Fortman's husband died," she'd stated flatly as she plunked the crate on the ground, making the dust fly. "She wanted thee to have his clothes."

"Oh." He'd set the horse brush on a nearby box, brushed his hands on his pant legs, and approached Rebecca. "Well, that's nice of her. I'm sorry about her husband."

"Yes. He fell from a ladder and broke his neck. Died instantly."

Clay's body had jolted involuntarily. "Oh, no. that's awful."

"It happened two years ago."

"Oh."

"And since she's getting ready to remarry, she figured it was time to clean out her bureau."

"I see." He'd grinned, until he remembered that he hadn't shaved, at which point he'd felt self-conscious. Yet that hadn't kept him from stepping closer to her. "You think they'll fit me?"

She'd given him a quick scan from head to toe, as if she needed to assess him. "He was a towering fellow," she'd answered. "I expect they'll fit thee just fine."

"Towering, eh?"

"Mother says thee is to join us for dinner. It will be ready in thirty minutes."

"That's nice. Thank you."

"Of course." She'd given him a tiny glance. "All right, then." As she'd turned away, her long skirt had flared enough to reveal a tiny portion of one slender ankle.

"Rebecca."

She'd halted in her tracks and looked over her shoulder at him. "Yes?"

"You don't have to be so formal with me."

She'd lowered her eyes and toed the barn floor, grinding a little well into the dirt with the tip of her boot. "I'm not being formal."

"Yes, you are." He'd moved closer, stopping within arm's length of her, and she had turned fully to face him. He'd known what she was thinking. It was all he'd thought about for days. He'd taken a deep breath. "It was just a simple kiss." A lie, of course. Nothing about it had been simple.

Her head had jerked up, and her bonnet had come loose, the thick curls of hair beneath it pushing outward. He'd wanted to take a fistful of them, just to remember their texture, but he'd suppressed the urge. Her cheeks had turned a soft pink. "We promised not to speak of that day."

"We did? I don't recall promising any such thing."

"Well, maybe we didn't exactly promise out loud, but…oh, never mind. We mustn't discuss it. In fact, we must pretend it never happened."

He'd chuckled. "A little easier said than done."

"Not for me." This she'd said with her chin jutting out and her shoulders pulled back in a show of stubbornness.

At this point, he'd dared to reach up and sweep away several strands of hair that had fallen across her face. He'd held them between his thumb and forefinger for the briefest moment. "Is that right?"

She had turned again, forcing him to drop his hand, and left the barn. "Don't forget to come in for the noon meal," she'd called without looking back.

"Oh, I won't. My stomach will remind me. Will your betrothed be joining us, as well?"

She hadn't answered him but had merely marched forward, her steps determined and swift.

Gerald had not joined them that day, but he had shown up the last two Wednesdays for supper with the family, followed by a stroll around the property with Rebecca. The routine irked Clay, although he knew he had no right to let it. Why didn't Rebecca just call the whole thing off? She no more loved Gerald Tuke than a rabbit loved a rattlesnake. Clay suspected that her loyalty to her parents, and to Quaker traditions, ran deeper than even she realized. And if she ever found a man she loved who *wasn't* a Quaker, she wouldn't consider marrying him unless he joined the Society.

Perhaps that was part of the reason Clay wanted to accompany the Albrights to Meeting this morning. That, and he wanted to thank Clara Fortman, or whatever her new married name was, for the generous donation of her deceased husband's clothes.

The old rooster crowed again, reminding Clay to get moving. In the back of the barn, Henrietta and Coral Belle started mooing, and Morris the donkey brayed. Clay cringed at the whining sound. It was another day on the farm—another day of not knowing who he was. Plenty of people had said they were praying for him. Maybe it was time to try a prayer of his own. "Lord, if You're listening, I'd appreciate just one little clue…something…anything."

⌒

Ever since their apparent betrothal, Gerald had been acting more and more familiar with Rebecca when they saw each other at First Day Meetings. Rebecca didn't like it, but he ignored her pleas to act with more discretion. Papa and Mother were no help; so set were they on her marrying Gerald that they fairly glowed whenever he was around. Meanwhile, Rebecca recoiled whenever Gerald grasped her by the shoulders, took her hand in his, or, heaven forbid, kissed her cheek. And she could almost feel his eyes on her throughout the meeting, which interfered even more than Chrystal's squirming with her ability to focus and quiet her inner self.

She was quite surprised the day Clay decided to join the family for Meeting. He sat in between Samuel and Milton, who seemed to idolize him, much to Rebecca's chagrin. Following the service, everybody headed outside for the annual picnic. In the yard, wooden tables had been set up with benches surrounding them; serving dishes and baskets anchored the tablecloths, lest the rare breeze lift one of them off. At this time of year, the weather was often hot—sometimes unbearably so. Rebecca wouldn't complain, though, because at least there was a breeze. The air could have been as still as a corpse.

The Albright family dispersed in all different directions—Mother chatting with some friends while they set out silverware and arranged the serving dishes, Papa going to speak with some of his fellow elders, and the older children gathering with their peers to natter, while the younger ones raced to join in a game of tag. Even Clay had found some fellows to talk to, and Rebecca found herself left alone with Gerald. When he moved away, giving her a reprieve, she took a deep breath, relishing the solitude.

Minutes later, she noticed her best friend, Charity Glasgow Duncan, hurrying toward her with a wide smile on her face. "I see thy boarder has joined the family for Meeting today," said Charity with a glance in Clay's direction. "My, but he is a fine-looking specimen."

"Charity!" Rebecca admonished her. "Whatever would Albert say if he overheard thy comment?"

Charity flicked her pretty wrist. "He wouldn't worry. He knows he has my heart. Besides, what woman, married or not, couldn't help but notice him?" She grinned. "I wonder what Gerald Tuke thinks of him."

Rebecca sighed. "Let us just say Gerald will not grieve long when Clay moves on."

Charity gave a bubbly little giggle. "He's jealous, then. I wonder if thee has given him reason to be."

Charity had always been skilled at prying information out of people, especially when they had no intention of spilling it. Rebecca made up her mind that her friend would not succeed at doing that with her today. "Of course not. He's not a Quaker, anyway."

"So, thee would be interested in him if he were?"

"I didn't say that."

"Perhaps he is a Quaker and simply doesn't remember. Now, wouldn't that be something?"

"Yes, wouldn't it?" Rebecca's gaze wandered across the yard to Clay, still engaged in conversation with several other men. She couldn't help but wonder what they were discussing. Across the yard, she noticed that Gerald had taken her father aside to speak with him in private. A strange ball of anxiety rolled around inside her. What could they be talking about? Not her, she hoped, or the matter of their betrothal.

"He still can't remember much about himself, then?" Charity asked.

Rebecca looked back at her friend. "Not really. He recalls tidbits here and there. The doctor says it's a rare malady, and I think he is fascinated by Clay's condition. He often comes to the farm to check on his progress, and he remains optimistic that his memory will return in full. And Papa has insisted he remain with us until that happens."

Charity scrunched her nose. "That must be so strange, not knowing from whence one came—or even what one did for a living." She lowered her voice. "Albert says there is reason to believe he is a slave catcher. Does thee think that's true?"

"I don't know," Rebecca said quietly. "It's difficult to tell. He seems to have a good heart and a belief in human equality, but it could be that he simply forgets his true opinion on the matter."

"Humph. Well, at any rate, I can scarcely imagine how strange it would be to suddenly forget everything about oneself. Then again, there are times when I remember too much, especially the things I'd sooner forget."

Rebecca laughed. "Like the time thee put an oversized toad in the schoolmarm's desk, and she screamed till kingdom come when she opened her drawer to fish for a pencil. Thee was a character, Charity Glasgow."

"Thee means Charity *Duncan*. And, yes, it's times like those...but let us talk of something else. Last Meeting, thee mentioned thy involvement in thy father's...project. How many times has thee accompanied him on one of his deliveries?"

"Shh," Rebecca cautioned her. "We are not supposed to speak of that in public settings."

Charity flicked her wrist once more. "No one can hear us."

Rebecca glanced around. There didn't appear to be anyone nearby.

"Well?" Charity prodded her.

Rebecca sighed. "I've gone along three times," she said quietly, "and, I must confess, I feel it's something I've been called to do. I have met all kinds of people, Charity. They are oppressed and frightened, but also determined and brave. I cannot imagine myself in their shoes."

"Albert has an appetite for joining," Charity said in a hushed tone.

"Really?" Rebecca had known of Albert's involvement in the American Anti-Slavery Society, but she hadn't realized he was interested in becoming more directly involved in freeing slaves.

"A certain opportunity has come up, Becca." Charity leaned in closer. "We are in the process of moving to Chester."

"Chester?" Rebecca's heart sank. "That's so far away."

"Only fifteen miles or so. Just too far to continue attending Arch Street Meeting House. Albert secured a job at a law firm in Chester, and he also plans to establish a station in the house we're buying." She snuck a glance around. "I've divulged more than I should, so we'll talk more about this later. Anyway, I have something else to tell thee, and I'm nearly dying from excitement."

Rebecca felt too numb to guess. "What is it? I can't imagine."

"Thee must keep mum about it—at least for the time being."

"Thee has my word," she stated dryly.

Charity glanced one way and then the other before leaning forward and whispering in Rebecca's ear, "I am with child."

Rebecca gasped. "Thee is?" She embraced her friend, then placed her hands on her shoulders and set her back. "That's wonderful news. You must be beside yourselves with joy."

Charity giggled. "Me more than he, I'm afraid. He wanted to wait at least another year. Of course, he's thrilled now that he's had some time to digest the idea."

Rebecca scoffed at her own naiveté. Would she ever understand the workings of her own body? Mother never had been one to discuss such things as procreation with her children, and she certainly wasn't about to ask now—not at twenty-one years of age. "When does thee expect the baby to arrive?"

"Around Christmastime. Can thee imagine a more perfect gift?"

"I certainly cannot." And she couldn't—unless it was to marry a man she truly loved. Lately, about all Mother talked about was "Gerald this" and "Gerald that." *You two shall marry at Arch Street Meeting House, of course, and then we'll invite the guests to Sunset Ridge after the ceremony for a lawn party,* she'd said only that morning. *Oh, what a grand day it will be.*

Seeing her friend's excitement, Rebecca was again struck with her inability to imagine a life with Gerald Tuke. How unfair that would be, to her and to him. On the other hand, Papa and Mother were determined to see the two of them wed, and Rebecca did respect them wholeheartedly. She scanned the yard and saw that Papa had resumed speaking to the elders, while Gerald had found a place to sit in the shade. She tried to envision herself falling in love with him. Anything was possible, she supposed, but love?

16

During the Meeting and at the picnic afterward, the Friends lived up to their name, all friendly and warmhearted toward Clay. The sole exception was Gerald Tuke, who seemed to view Clay as the enemy. It was as if he feared Clay would steal Rebecca out from under him. When Clay had just finished filling his plate and was making his way toward the tables, Gerald stepped out of line to confront him. "Thee had better not plan on sitting at the Albrights' table."

The words brought Clay's steps to a halt, and several carrots rolled off his plate. "My presence makes you uncomfortable, does it?"

A cold smile formed on the man's mouth, but he made no reply.

Clay couldn't help but laugh. "Have I given you some reason to fear me?"

"Fear thee?" Gerald chuckled. "No, but I do despise thee."

Clay gave an exaggerated gasp. "You're not a very good Quaker, are you?"

The hard smile stayed in place. "Quaker or not, I advise thee to sit somewhere else. I'm sure it would make Rebecca more comfortable, as well, if thee complied with my wish."

"Oh? Should we ask her?" Clay asked impishly.

"We should do nothing of the sort. Kindly do not make a scene and seat thyself at a different table. Today is to be a special day."

"Oh? In what way?"

"Thee will find out soon enough."

"I can hardly wait." Clay brushed past the exasperating man and walked straight to the Albrights' table, his plate brimming with delectable-smelling foods. Considering these kindly folks avoided meat in their diet, they certainly knew how to create tasty meals out of breads, eggs, cheeses, vegetables, and greens. Strangely, not once had he found himself longing for beef, chicken, or hog.

"Clay!" Samuel exclaimed. "Sit by me!"

"No, sit by me!" chirped Milton.

"Sit here, Clay!" Henry whined, patting the place next to him.

Clay's eyes fell to Rebecca. "Maybe I should sit next to your sister, here."

She said nothing, just sent him a threatening glare, which made him laugh out loud.

"Lydia and I can make room," Frances said, scooting away from her sister Lydia.

Clay grinned at the three brothers. "Sorry, boys. I believe two lovely roses have beckoned a thorn to share their bench."

As the boys gazed at him with obvious confusion, Clay happily settled in between two of the Albright beauties. As soon as he was situated, baby Chrystal toddled over and tapped on his arm, so he lifted her up and set her on his lap. He could hardly wait for Gerald to arrive. With a little luck, the poor sap would lose his appetite.

Clay couldn't think of a time when he'd enjoyed himself more. Granted, his memories were sparse, so of course this meeting-house picnic would stand out as one of the best days of his life. Conversation topics around the table ran the gamut, and now and then various Friends approached the family to chat and to extend a greeting to Clay. He wondered what it was about these people that prompted them to be so warm and welcoming. Was that what living a life with Jesus as the focal point did for a person? During the Meeting, a few men and one woman had stood and addressed those gathered, sharing heartfelt messages about Christ's abiding love, with accompanying Scripture passages that had given Clay much to ponder.

To his surprise, Gerald said nothing further to him during the course of the meal. Even Rebecca remained silent, and seemed somewhat sullen, picking at her food and pushing it around on her plate with her fork. Had he made a mistake by imposing himself on her? It seemed unlikely, considering how eager the rest of her family seemed to be to include him at their table.

Rebecca's sisters, on the other hand, didn't lack for things to say. Frances talked almost incessantly about the dearth of good-looking boys her age at Arch Street Meeting House, and Lydia gabbed about how much she missed her school friends now that it was summer vacation. Chrystal babbled happily as she roamed from table to table like a friendly pup, looking for nibbles of food.

As folks were finishing their meals and eyeing up the display of desserts, Edward Albright stood and asked to have everyone's attention. Silence fell over the yard, save for the clatter of utensils being set on empty plates, as all eyes turned to Edward. "I wish to make an important announcement." His gaze trailed a path to Gerald and Rebecca. "First, I will ask that my eldest daughter, Rebecca, and her beau, Gerald Tuke, would please stand."

Now there were murmurs and whispers circulating among the tables. Clay had the unexpected experience of his stomach knotting into a tight ball as he turned to watch the pair get to their feet. Gerald straightened his shoulders and puffed out his chest with obvious pride, while Rebecca's face showed surprise—and not the pleasant type. Clay wanted to rescue her but could only sit and watch in silence, like everyone else.

He redirected his gaze to Edward, who smiled broadly. "I wish to publicize the upcoming marriage of Gerald Tuke and our eldest daughter, Rebecca. Provided that the clearness committee sees no reason to delay the ceremony, it will take place on Eighth Month, sixteenth day."

The crowd broke into loud shouts of congratulations and thunderous clapping.

On either side of Clay, Lydia and Frances gasped.

"She didn't know Papa was going to announce that," Lydia murmured. "Poor Becca."

Frances leaned over the table to say around Clay, "But she knew it was coming, eventually."

"He still should have told her," Lydia maintained.

"She'll be fine," Frances whispered. "Don't worry so. That means I'm next in line. I only hope I find someone more appealing than Gerald Tuke. Anyone but a farmer." Then she joined in the applause.

Clay didn't feel like clapping, but he applauded halfheartedly out of politeness, and so that no one would suspect him of being envious of Gerald. No point in giving anyone reason to suspect he had feelings for Rebecca.

"No one should have to marry unless it's for love," Lydia murmured for his ears alone. In that exact moment, the image of a woman flashed across his mind, and the name *Julia* sounded like a whisper in his head. Was he himself engaged—and to someone he didn't love? The picture blurred, and as hard as he tried to call it back, it would not return.

He gave Lydia his full attention. "You're right about that."

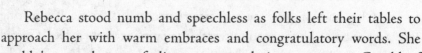

Rebecca stood numb and speechless as folks left their tables to approach her with warm embraces and congratulatory words. She couldn't remember ever feeling a stronger desire to run away. Gerald, of course, beamed with pride, and why wouldn't he? The whole announcement had been his idea, designed to catch her off guard. Why had Papa agreed to participate, when he knew how she felt about Gerald? She took a moment to glimpse at Mother and found her smiling as broadly as Gerald. She must have colluded with him to convince Papa. When would Rebecca become old enough to make her own decisions? Anger surged within her, but she held it at bay and put on a smile for her well-wishers.

"Congratulations, Gerald." Clay extended his hand.

"Why, thank you, Clay." Gerald sniffed proudly, his upper lip curled in a sneer. "I'm sure thee can imagine how happy I am."

"Yes, I'm certain you are," Clay said, as his gaze roamed to Rebecca.

When their eyes connected, she quickly lowered her head. What an awkward exchange. Clay somehow knew she didn't love Gerald. Had his congratulatory words been intended to embarrass her? If so, they'd done a fine job.

"So, August sixteenth, is it?" Clay said. "That's coming up right quick."

"It can't come soon enough." Gerald put his arm around Rebecca's shoulders and drew her against his side. Rather than try to escape his hold and thereby make a scene, Rebecca put on a brave front. Her throat had gone as dry as sand, and she swallowed hard.

"Becca!" Charity pushed her way through the crowd and stopped to catch her breath once she'd reached Rebecca. "Becca, I didn't know! My goodness. I suppose it's my turn to congratulate thee."

"Yes…I suppose so."

Charity tilted her head to one side and assessed Rebecca with narrowed eyes. "Thee and I will have to talk soon. Perhaps I will drive out to Sunset Ridge this week."

"That would be lovely." Rebecca put a hand to her parched throat, then turned to Gerald. "I need to refill my water glass."

"Shall I do it for thee, darling?"

Even though he'd used endearments before, the sound still made her squeamish. "I'll do it myself, thank thee."

"All right, but hurry back. Folks are clamoring to see thee," he said, completely oblivious to her emotions. Had Clay noticed anything amiss?

She picked up her empty cup and promptly left the table, her eyes stinging with tears.

"Becca!" Charity called after her. "Slow down."

She ignored her friend, swinging her arms with each purposeful stride, her heart racing with the exertion.

At the pump, she caught her breath, then started driving the handle up and down—fast, hard, and furious—until water started surging from the spigot onto the ground. It soon formed a small lake, with only a few droplets actually making it into the cup that trembled in her shaking hand.

"What is going on, Becca?" Charity caught hold of her wrist, stopping her pumping in mid-motion. "Why didn't thee tell me earlier of thy betrothal to Gerald Tuke? I knew you two were courting, but I had no idea it was *that* serious."

"Papa did not tell me he planned to make the announcement today. Oh, I knew it would come eventually, but I would have liked a forewarning."

"Of course, thee would have. Did Gerald know?"

"I'm certain he did. I witnessed him and Papa having a discussion before the meal. I don't even love him, Charity. But my parents say I will *grow* to love him." She searched her friend's face through blurry eyes. "Will I?" Desperation circled in her stomach until she thought she might retch.

"Here, sit down." Charity led her to a grassy mound behind the meeting house and helped her to the ground. She took her cup from her, hastened back to the pump to fill it, and quickly returned. "Take a few sips. Slowly. Breathe deep. Thee is looking quite pale."

Rebecca did as she was told, and in a few moments, she felt a sense of calm come over her. "I'm feeling better, thank thee."

Charity plunked herself down next to her, worry in her expression. "Thee should not marry a man thee cannot vow to love, honor, and obey."

Rebecca took another sip of water and swallowed, then expelled a loud sigh. "Tell that to Mother and Papa. It is not so simple, Charity. Mother is set in her ways, old-fashioned. She wants me to marry a good Quaker, which Gerald certainly is; someone who will provide for me, which Gerald can; and someone who loves me, which Gerald does."

"And what of thy feelings? Do they not matter?"

She closed her eyes and inclined her head skyward, welcoming the warmth of the sun on her wet eyelids. "Apparently not. I'm twenty-one... well past the age of marriageability. Mother is terribly worried."

"And thee?"

"I'm not worried. Spinsterhood may very well be my lot.

After a moment of pensive silence, Charity said, "I would not have married Albert if I hadn't been desperately in love with him. If thee is to marry, thee must desire to be married."

"I agree, in principle. But I don't want to disappoint my parents."

"Well then, when you go before the clearness committee, thee must be truthful. They will not approve the marriage if thee doesn't love thy intended."

"I suppose that's true, but I'd rather not go before them at all. It's plain humiliating."

"Then tell Gerald thee will not marry him."

She made it sound so uncomplicated. "Thee doesn't know Mother as I do."

"'Tis true, thy mother is set in her ways."

Rebecca took another sip of water, then set the cup down. "I just keep praying, and telling myself that the Lord will help me to sort it all out so I may do the right thing."

If only He would hurry to answer.

17

Two days later marked a rare occasion when the entire Albright family gathered together around the large farm table for a weekday breakfast. Levi and Clay were prevented from going out to the fields due to the torrential downpour that had been soaking the dry earth since the night before.

After the prayer, Papa broke the silence by saying, "I have a delivery to make at the Hallstead farm several days hence, Becca. Does thee wish to accompany me?"

Rebecca met Papa's gaze. "Not this time, Papa, but I thank thee," she said just before biting into a slice of warm bread.

Since his surprise announcement of her betrothal to Gerald, they had exchanged very few words. He knew she was upset with him, and although she regretted the wall that had come up between them, she did not feel compelled to talk to him just yet. The same applied to Mother. Rebecca completed all her usual household chores, but she didn't initiate any unnecessary conversation. Frankly, she didn't know exactly what she would have said, anyway.

"I'd be happy to go along," Clay announced. "If you'd have me, that is."

Rebecca eyed her father with alarm. What would he say? Surely, he was not prepared to make Clay aware of his activities.

"I would welcome thy company," said Papa.

Rebecca could hardly believe it. She had to mentally tell herself to close her gaping mouth. Papa was really going to allow Clay, presumed to be a slave catcher, to join in his efforts?

⌒

By noon, the rain had let up, so Clay accompanied Levi to the fields. They headed back to the house an hour later when flooding impeded their work. Levi said it would probably take a day or two before they could resume. As they neared the yard, Clay saw Rebecca standing at the clothesline hanging wet laundry, her hair blowing free, the sun drenching her face with a golden glow, and her floral skirt flying up about her pretty knees. Clay couldn't imagine a finer sight. She had rolled up her sleeves to her elbows, looking for all the world like somebody's wife. And that was just what she would be in a number of weeks, unless she came to her senses.

Not for a second could Clay envision her married to Gerald Tuke. Clay would do just about anything to stop their union, but he had to first figure out his own marital status. He'd been praying every morning for God to allow him to remember who he was, where he lived, and how a woman named Julia fit into his life. But he had yet to see a difference. What, exactly, would it take for God to listen? Or maybe He had been listening and simply chose not to answer. Worse, perhaps Clay wasn't good enough to merit an answer from God. He wondered what he might have done in the past to make God unhappy with him. Was there any way for him to seek forgiveness for something he couldn't remember doing? Edward would know. Clay would ask him if the opportunity presented itself.

Once the men dismounted, Clay gratefully accepted Levi's offer to feed, water, and brush down Star. As Levi led the horses to the barn, Clay strolled toward Rebecca. It appeared she had another wicker basket of wet clothes yet to hang, and it had been several days since they'd talked in private. He knew he was about as dirty as a duck in muck after assessing the fields with Levi, but he couldn't resist the opportunity to speak to Rebecca when no one else was about. He wondered how she was doing, now that the news of her betrothal was public.

"Hello there, Becca," he called across the yard. It was the first time he'd used the nickname, and it felt natural to do so.

She peeked out from behind the bedsheet she'd just hung. "Hello, Clay."

"I see you're taking advantage of the sunshine now that the storm has passed."

She put her face toward the sky and smiled, and the sight made his heart dance. "Mother said we were going to do laundry even if it would mean having to drape the damp clothes all around the house. I'm thankful that wasn't the case. I do enjoy hanging laundry, though."

"You do? I don't know many women who would say that."

She grinned. "And how many women do you know?"

He smiled back at her, then drew in a deep breath and raked a hand through his hair. "Every now and then, I think I know several, but then the memory leaves me. Sometimes I get a feeling that a recollection is this far away, you know?" He positioned his thumb and pointer finger about half an inch apart. "And then, whatever it was... it vanishes."

Rebecca glanced over at Gracie, who chased a squirrel up the trunk of a nearby tree. "I'm sure that's very frustrating. Have you remembered anything of significance?"

"I suppose you're referring to Julia."

She looked back at him, her gaze steady. "Not necessarily." Then she bent over and lifted another bedsheet from the basket.

When she reached into her apron pocket for some clothespins, Clay grabbed the bottom corners of the sheet so they wouldn't touch the ground.

"Thank you," Rebecca said. "I meant, have you remembered anything at all that you consider important?"

"I had a recollection last night during the thunderstorm—up in that hayloft, the sounds of the wind and rain are really amplified—but it wasn't of anything you'd call 'important.'"

"Really?" She pinned one corner of the sheet to the clothesline, then took another clothespin and fixed it several inches away from the first. "What was it?"

"Well, when I was just a boy—probably somewhere between the ages of Milton and Samuel—I was walking home from school when a big windstorm blew in. The gales were so strong, I could hardly stay upright. So, I took shelter in an abandoned cabin that was built into a hillside, figuring I would wait out the storm there."

"How long did you have to wait?" She reached into her pocket and took out another clothespin, and then another, moving toward him along the clothesline as she affixed the sheet to it.

Clay chuckled as he held his corner of the sheet to the line to make it easier for her. "A lot longer than I should have. You see, a schoolmate of mine had the same idea. He lived just over the crest from that cabin and followed me inside when the wind picked up. He was a few years older than me, and most kids were afraid of him—including me." The corners of his mouth turned up in a wry grin. "It wasn't long before the weather had calmed, and this guy thought it'd be fun to lock me inside the cabin by barring the door with a big plank of wood he found inside."

"How awful!" She was only a couple of feet away from him now, her flowery scent wafting over the air to his nostrils. "You must have been terribly frightened. And I can only imagine what your mother must have thought when you didn't return home after that storm!"

Clay chuckled again. "I'm not sure how long I hollered for help before I nearly gave up hope that someone would find me. Hours later, my mother showed up. She'd gone searching for me, tracing my route from school. My sisters had made plans to go home with friends, so they didn't know I hadn't made it home. When Ma finally found me trapped in the cabin, I told her what had happened. I'd never seen her so angry. She blustered and fumed all the way up the hill to that prankster's house."

"Your mother sounds like a wonderful woman."

"Indeed she is." Like a flash, the name of his schoolmate popped into his head. "Herb Robinson. That was the name of the prankster."

"You remember?" Her brown eyes lit like two gold stars.

"Isn't it strange, the insignificant details I recall, while the most important things remain a mystery?" He sighed. "I can't tell you how tired I am of this. It's been weeks."

She fastened the final clothespin, then tucked her hands inside her apron pockets and turned to face him. They stood between two hanging sheets. "It's frustrating, I know, but you must view every memory you conjure as a step in the right direction. Dr. Fleming said you would regain thy memory faster if you were in familiar territory, and you are living with a lively bunch of people who probably don't resemble your former surroundings even remotely. Perhaps you and your wife are accustomed to a small, quiet household—unless you have children."

"I don't have any children. Or a wife, I'm fairly certain."

"But how can you be certain?"

Again, he raked a hand through his hair. It was sticky with sweat. He needed another bath. "I don't know how I know, I just do."

She lifted one perfectly sculpted eyebrow. "Is that so? Well, you'll need more than a hunch for something as important as that. Soon you will remember, I'm certain of it. I've been praying the Lord will make things clear."

"As have I, but He doesn't seem to be listening."

"Have you given Him reason to listen? You cannot expect God to answer your prayers if you are not fully His child."

He considered her words. "I'm not sure I'm good enough. Besides, how can God forgive sins I don't even remember committing?"

"He remembers each one. 'Tis not important that you do."

"I'm not a Quaker, either."

"You do not need to be a Quaker to be born again."

"Born again?" Now, there was a term he hadn't heard before. He felt like a dunce.

As if she'd read his mind, she said, "In simple terms, it means saying good-bye to your former life and hello to the new."

"Well, it seems I've done that already."

She smiled. "I'm speaking in spiritual terms, silly. The one prayer God always answers is the prayer a sinner prays when seeking forgiveness, as long as it is prayed in earnest. The ears of our heavenly Father are most keen to the prayer of a repentant soul."

"I see." But he didn't, really. What he saw was her hair, and he dared to snag a tiny lock between his thumb and forefinger. "Tell me, do you actually plan to go through with this marriage to Tuke?"

Their eyes met and held. "I haven't found the proper way to address my shock at Papa's unexpected announcement at First Day Meeting. Gerald knew it was coming, but my parents conveniently kept me in the dark about it."

"That wasn't fair." He rolled the lock of her hair between his thumb and forefinger. "You're not going to marry him, are you?"

Her lips opened, then closed with a faint gust of breath. She lowered her chin. "I'm considering it."

"You are?"

She gave a little shrug of her shoulders. "I cannot deny that Gerald would be a steady provider and a devoted mate."

"You would marry just because he'd make a decent mate? Rebecca, no one should marry unless it's for love."

She raised her chin resolutely. "Oh, but plenty of people do that, Clay. In many cases, it's perfectly proper, practical, and workable."

He tossed back his head and laughed for a moment. "And you want me to believe you'd be happy?"

She turned away, forcing him to drop her wisp of hair, and walked back to the laundry basket. She retrieved a pair of socks and secured each one to the line with a single clothespin. Then she picked up another pair, her movements halfhearted. He watched and waited for her to respond. "It doesn't matter what thee thinks, now, does it?" she finally said.

He stepped nearer to her. "I would hope it mattered to you."

"Well, it doesn't."

He took another step closer and encircled her wrist with his hand. "It does, and you know it."

She twisted out of his grip and turned to face him. "Stop right there, Clay. Thee is married, and I cannot have another kiss from thee on my conscience."

He smiled. "Is that what you thought I was going to do—kiss you? Right here, between the sheets?" Then he winked. "Thee is a discerning woman indeed."

She let out a huff of indignation. "Go on, now. Thee must have something better to do with thy time."

"I can't think of one thing."

She pursed her lips and resumed the task of hanging one piece of laundry after another, nudging him out of the way as she moved down the clothesline. He took a kind of enjoyment in watching her struggle with her emotions. She clearly felt something for him, and just knowing that was enough for now. It had to be.

"Clay?"

He whirled around at the sound of the male voice, startled out of his reverie. "Edward."

"Papa," Rebecca choked. She cleared her voice. "Clay was just relating a memory that came to him during the storm last night."

"Is that right?" The man stood at the end of the clothesline, peering down the tunnel formed by the two sets of hanging sheets. "Thee must tell me about it."

"I will." He turned to Rebecca and whispered, "I'll talk to you later."

She did not acknowledge him but only kept pinning wet laundry to the line, her spine as straight as a rod.

He left her there and started toward Edward. "How's your latest project coming along?" he asked. It took great effort to keep his tone steady and nonchalant.

"I'm fashioning a table for a family in Connecticut," Edward said as the two men strolled toward the barn. "The pieces have all been cut and sanded. The table should be assembled and ready for staining tomorrow, and I hope to ship it next week." He wiped his brow with the back of his hand. "Orders keep coming in, so I never manage to get ahead."

"Not a bad thing, right?"

Edward nodded. "Keeps food on our own table."

"Want me to lend a hand with anything?"

Just then Milton and Samuel bounded up to them, blocking their progress. Gracie was at their heels, barking happily. "Clay!" Samuel shouted. "We're going swimming down at the creek, and we want thee to come with us!"

Clay grinned. "What about your papa? Maybe he'd like to go, too."

Milton's eyes widened as he looked at his father. "Would thee, Papa?"

"I would, but I can't. I've too much to do."

"How about if I take over for you while you go swimming with your boys?" Clay offered. "I'm a quick learner."

Edward looked pensive for a moment. "I've noticed that about thee, but I'd better stick to my task. Go with my sons. They enjoy thy company."

He hesitated only a moment. "All right, then." He looked back at the boys. "You two go get ready, and I'll be right with you."

They gave a loud cheer, then raced like two colts toward the house. Edward watched them with a faraway look in his eyes. "I do wish I had more time to spend with my children."

"You're a good father, Edward. You do your best, and your family appreciates it."

A deep furrow marred the older man's brow. "I thank thee for thy words, Clay. Thee, too, is a good man. I can almost envision thee as a family member."

That comment gave Clay a good jolt, but he managed to keep the reaction internal. "I can, as well, sir."

"Thee must tell me later about that memory Rebecca mentioned."

"I will—but, first, while we're on the topic of Rebecca...." He considered how best to present what he wished to say. "Are you entirely sure she should marry Gerald Tuke?" There. He'd voiced the question. Now to await a reaction.

Edward raised both eyebrows. "Does thee happen to know of another good Quaker fellow?"

"Must he be a Quaker? I recall Laura once telling me that a person doesn't necessarily have to belong to the Society of Friends in order to find God."

"And she is correct. But I prefer that my children marry into the faith."

"By 'the faith,' you mean the Society of Friends."

"It would be best, yes."

"Is there a reason for that, sir?"

"Is there a reason why it shouldn't be the case, Clay?"

Clay swallowed hard, and then the lump that had been sitting on his throat came right back. "She doesn't love him."

"Her mother and I are aware. We are also confident she will come to love him in time."

"How can you be sure? What if you are sentencing her to a lifelong, loveless marriage?" His own boldness made him cringe. The last thing he wanted to do was create a barrier to their friendship.

Edward's expression turned formidable. "We believe thee to be a married man, Clay. If thee has any interest whatever in my eldest daughter, thee would do best to shake it off."

"Of course, sir. I understand completely. I'm merely suggesting you...." But what was he suggesting? That Edward call off the betrothal because Clay might want to marry her? It was a losing battle for someone who didn't even know whether he was available. Moreover, Clay didn't have a Quaker bone in his body.

Edward's face was sober. "Thee was saying...?"

"Nothing, sir. Nothing at all."

Clay heard a door slam, and youthful squeals ring out. "Sounds like your boys are ready for some fun. I'd best go find something appropriate to wear for swimming." He started for the barn, then stopped and turned. Edward's eyes were still trained on him. "I look forward to accompanying you when you deliver those supplies, Edward—that is, if I'm still welcome."

"Thee certainly is. Tomorrow night. We'll leave at seven."

"I'll be ready."

18

That evening after supper, the kitchen still buzzed with activity. While Rebecca washed the dinner dishes, Lydia snapped string beans for tomorrow's noon meal, Frances peeled potatoes for a salad, and Mother kneaded bread dough. A big family called for constant work, and Rebecca and her sisters followed Mother's orders to the letter, like soldiers after their sergeant. Baby Chrystal moved from one person to the next, pulling on their skirts and vying for attention. The sisters tossed various items her way in an effort to keep her entertained—mostly pieces of silverware and wooden spoons, which were dropped frequently on the floor with loud clatters. Upon drying the final plate, Rebecca set it on top of the others, then hefted the tall stack into the dining room, where she set it on a shelf in the oak sideboard Papa had built. Just then, her three youngest brothers rumbled down the stairs like a herd of wild stallions, chattering with excitement. "Hey, whoa! What's all the commotion about?" Rebecca asked them.

"Clay's gonna teach us baseball," hollered Samuel on the run.

"Baseball?"

With shouts of glee, the three boys filed out the door from oldest to youngest, the screen slamming shut with a loud clunk behind Henry.

Baseball. Funny how Clay recalled so much general knowledge yet couldn't conjure up a memory of key people from his life—not even his beloved Julia.

Rebecca was familiar with the sport, but she had never seen anyone play it. She untied her apron and tossed it over the back of a chair, then went to the front parlor to look out the window. Clay stood in the shade of the giant oak, waiting for the boys. In one hand, he held what looked like a mop handle; in the other, he tossed a rubber ball in the air and caught it again. Soon the boys gathered around him, and as he talked, he pointed to the stretch of property between the outbuildings and the cornfield, no doubt setting up some boundaries for play. Next, he held the mop handle at an angle against his shoulder, then extended it in front of him with a swift swinging motion. Henry jumped back and laughed, his high-pitched giggle carrying on the breeze. Clay handed the rod to Samuel, who mimicked the motion, giving a couple of good swings before handing the improvised bat to Milton. At last, it was Henry's turn. A smile erupted on Rebecca's face just watching her youngest brother's awkward attempts, his little shoulders pulled taut with determination.

Papa appeared in the doorway of the barn and leaned against the frame, his arms folded across his chest, his straw hat pulled over his brow. What did he think of the boys' interest in a worldly sport? Rebecca was pleased that their father didn't put a stop to the lesson. When it appeared the boys were ready to start playing, Rebecca went outside and plopped herself down on the top porch step.

Clay glanced her way and waved. "Want to join us?"

Good gracious, try to swing a mop handle at a ball? What did he take her for, a tomboy? "No, I'll just watch." She pushed down the urge to pretend she was a kid again.

When they took up the game, Levi came in from the fields to join in. Clay assumed the position of pitcher, and the three younger boys trying their hand at striking the rubber ball with the makeshift bat. None of them managed the feat, so then Clay took several steps closer to them and gave each of them another chance. Neither Samuel nor

Milton struck the ball, but little Henry swung and actually made contact. Without any forethought, Rebecca leaped to her feet, clapping and cheering, as Clay urged him to run to first base—one of three barrels he'd brought out from the barn and positioned in the shape of a diamond. He ran as fast as his short legs would allow, while Levi scooped up the ball and chased after him, feigning the inability to tag him. By this time, Mother and Rebecca's sisters had come out to see what was going on, and they added their applause. Papa crossed the yard to join them, wearing a wider-than-usual grin.

"Edward, thee should play, too," Mother said.

Papa grunted. "With this leg?"

"Oh, go on," she said. "If thee happens to hit the ball, thee can walk the bases."

"If I 'happen' to hit the ball?" he said with mock indignation. "What does thee mean by challenging my skills?"

"I'm sure Levi will grant thee a handicap, as he did for Henry."

"How kind of thee to group me with a four-year-old."

Mother laughed. "Prove thy skills, Edward Albright." She gave his shoulder a playful shove.

Seldom did Papa and Mother spar for the pure fun of it, and Rebecca rather enjoyed watching.

"I want to play," said Lydia. "Come on, Papa." She tugged on his shirtsleeve. "And thee, Becca."

"I'd rather watch."

"I'll go," said Frances, skipping down the steps and looping her hand around Papa's other arm.

"Frannie?" was the unison response from Mother and Rebecca, who exchanged glances of disbelief.

Then Rebecca added, "Isn't that the girl who shrieks when a single spot of dust soils her pretty skirts?"

The two sisters succeeded in dragging Papa to the crude playing field, and soon it was just Rebecca, Mother, and a wiggly Chrystal on the porch. Mother set the baby down, then nudged Rebecca in the side. "Thee should play, as well."

Rebecca laughed. "I could not hit that ball with a stick if it were sitting on a stump."

"Thee doesn't know if thee doesn't try."

She considered Mother's words but kept her feet firmly planted, as much as she wanted to move them.

"I suppose we don't reserve enough time for carefree frolic, do we?" Mother mused. "There is always so much to do to simply survive, I fear I employ my children to work more than I permit them to play."

"Thy children do not mind, Mother, although recreation is good and necessary," Rebecca replied. "Look at Papa. How often does he take time to enjoy himself? He holes up in his workshop day in and day out. Of course, he loves what he does, but everyone needs to find time for fun and amusement, or else life will pass them by."

Mother watched the game in silence for a moment. "Thee is right, of course. Even with that limp, thy father is enjoying himself. He is quite a man."

"He certainly is. Thy marriage has been a good one, has it not?"

"Indeed. Our love has grown stronger with each passing year…just as I'm sure thy love for Gerald Tuke will grow, even if it is not yet the size of even a tiny seed. I'm certain—"

"Mother, I don't wish to discuss Gerald right now." Rebecca immediately regretted the sharp tone she'd used. She'd purposely put off discussing the ambush announcement of the betrothal, wanting to wait until God gave her the proper words.

"But…thy wedding day is drawing near, and there are more than a few decisions to be made in regard to the event. I thought this would be the perfect time to discuss thy nuptials, since there is no one to interrupt us."

"Gerald and I haven't even gone before the clearness committee."

"Well then, Gerald should make an appointment."

"I'd rather he not," Rebecca murmured to herself, and she tuned out her mother's next string of sentences.

"…and then perhaps we could have our guests come to Sunset Ridge for a picnic. Wouldn't that be nice?" Mother was saying.

Rebecca closed her eyes and gave her head a quick shake. Then, taking a deep breath for resolve, she opened her eyes again and straightened her shoulders. "I believe I'll join in the game, after all."

"What?" Mother sputtered. "But…."

Rebecca gathered her skirts, scrambled off the porch without a backward glance, and jogged over to the field. Her cap strings came loose, and her hat flew off her head, the wind blowing her hair in every direction. Clay looked over, and she smiled at him. "Does the invitation to play still stand?"

With a wide grin, he nodded his approval.

The game proved more fun than Rebecca had expected, with loud spurts of laughter coming from every corner of the field, lots of overlooked errors to accommodate the novice players, and a newfound closeness that came from tossing aside the concerns of the day and spending time together as a family. Rebecca was even able to dismiss, at least temporarily, the notion of her betrothal to Gerald, never mind that he was coming to see her the following night. In retrospect, she should have told Papa that she would go along on his Railroad mission, after all, because that would have given her a reason to cancel Gerald's visit. But it was too late now, with Clay going in her place. She still wondered how Papa was planning on explaining what they were doing. What if the mission conjured memories of Clay's former occupation?

"Get the ball, Becca!" Milton shouted.

Startled out of her reverie, Rebecca blinked as the ball hit on the ground in front of her, then bounced over her head. She ran after it, scooped it up, and threw it to first base, but Levi managed to make it all the way to third. She was not cut out for baseball, but that didn't put a damper on her spirits. Mother had left the porch and was sitting in the grass with Chrystal, an expression of pure pleasure on her face, as if she hadn't a care in the world. It was probably the only time in memory that Rebecca had seen her mother with nothing in her hands to keep her busy, like a knife for peeling potatoes or needles and yarn for knitting. Rebecca glanced at Clay, who patiently pitched the ball to Milton, and she realized it was he who'd brought the family together like this.

Just then, a sentiment she cared not to explore burst through her heart's door. What would she do when all his memories came flooding back, and he had to leave? Heedless now of his probable outrage over her family's efforts to free fugitive slaves, she swiped at a tear with the cuff of her sleeve. Then she scolded herself for allowing these inappropriate emotions to wend their way into her soul. *Lord, he is married. Please guard my heart from loving him.*

After they'd played for almost an hour, Mother invited everyone to come inside and cool off with a glass of sugared tea on ice. No one objected. The younger ones, still full of squeals and giggles, raced for the house. Mother and the others followed on their heels, while Rebecca purposely lagged behind, relishing the chance to ponder in solitude. She also didn't want to give Clay even one second of her attention, lest he notice something different in her eyes.

When everyone had gathered in the kitchen, Mother poured drinks for all and set out a tray of oatmeal cookies.

"Can we do that again tomorrow?" asked Samuel, helping himself to a second cookie.

"Oh, can we?" Milton chimed in.

"I don't know about tomorrow, but sometime soon," said Papa, to Rebecca's surprise. Here, she'd wondered if he would put a halt to the game because of its worldly nature, and he'd seemed to enjoy himself as much as the children. For a brief instant, Clay's gaze connected with Rebecca's. She immediately averted her eyes and gathered Chrystal in her arms. "I believe I'll take the baby upstairs for her bath."

"Thank thee, dear," said Mother. "I'll ready Henry." She assessed the others. "Looks like all of you could use a bath."

"Let's go down to the creek for a swim," Levi suggested.

"Good thinking," said Papa. "Take some soap with you for scrubbing."

"I'm up for that," said Clay.

"Me, too," Lydia and Frances said in unison.

"Does thee wish to come along, Rebecca?" Frances asked.

Rebecca started for the stairs. "No, I'll be busy putting Chrystal to bed," she said over her shoulder. Strange, but as she climbed the steps, she could almost feel Clay's eyes boring into her back. At the top of the stairs, she paused and glanced down. Sure enough, her theory proved true.

⌣

Clay reclined on his straw mattress with his hands behind his head and stared at the barn ceiling. Memories had been flooding his mind— almost too many to keep up with—and they came to him in jumbled pictures, just as Dr. Fleming had said they might, like pieces of a puzzle that he couldn't quite put together. It had started during the baseball game. For some reason, he was able to recall all the rules of play; and after he'd explained the rules to the boys, he'd remembered pitching baseballs in an open field to some of his adult friends. He could put faces to some of them, and had even dredged up a few names: Harmon Clark and Walter...something. But now he wondered if Harmon Clark might actually be two men, Harmon and Clark. The name Piper popped into his head, too, but its significance was lost on him. He also envisioned a pleasant town with a few busy streets trafficked by horse and buggies.

Again, as much as he concentrated on calling up the memories and trying to see actual images and names, he failed. In fact, if he thought too hard about it, his headache returned with an ornery vengeance. Very slowly, with an effect like looking through a foggy mist, a beautiful woman emerged, and he wondered if he weren't looking at Julia. He uttered her name a few times, to see if the image would sharpen, but the only result was the image of Rebecca Albright flashing before his mind's eye.

"Oh, God...if You are here, if You are listening...would You help me make sense of my thoughts?"

He waited for something mystical to happen. And he was still waiting when he drifted off to sleep, thunder rumbling in the distance.

19

It was another rainy morning. Fortunately, Rebecca and Lydia had retrieved all the dry laundry from the clothesline before the skies opened up. All night long, the rain had fallen in torrents, and now Levi fidgeted and paced the house, moving from room to room and looking out every window, as if a different perspective might show a more promising weather forecast.

Of all the Albright children, Levi cared about the farm the most. Papa always said he'd inherited his passion for farm work from his grandfather. Papa much preferred his woodworking business and was happy to delegate the bulk of the responsibility for running the farm to his eldest son. Levi had an inbred sense about farming, a keen awareness of the environment, a strong work ethic, and a pure love of nature. He spoke often about his plans to one day buy the acreage surrounding Sunset Ridge. He certainly had lofty goals.

Rebecca watched him now and marveled at his unusual maturity. Most young men his age were intent on spending their weekends in Philadelphia, looking for pretty girls. But not Levi. More often than not, one could find him holed up in some quiet corner, away from the family ruckus, working numbers on paper and doing what he called "strategizing." Rebecca had no idea what that entailed, but Papa would grin as he pulled up a chair beside Levi and sat down to reason with him about the best way to manage the farm's profits. College didn't seem to be in Levi's future. No, he would spend his life in the fields, steering workhorses down straight rows of soil while sowing seeds, then tending those seeds until they blossomed into mature plants. He would reap the harvest of his hard work during summer and fall, take some time off in the dead of winter, and then happily jump back into his routine come springtime. Rebecca hoped always to live close enough to Sunset Ridge to watch it grow and flourish for years to come.

"That's an angry sky," Levi muttered now, holding one of the window curtains aside. "We go weeks without rain, and worry that the crops will shrivel…and then it pours so hard, we worry they'll all drown. Either way, the harvest will be compromised. And by the blackness of that sky, it's not going to let up anytime soon."

"The Lord will provide," Rebecca assured him. "He has never failed us."

On rainy days, the younger children naturally grew restless and hauled out every toy they owned—or had improvised. They made puppets out of old socks, played checkers or hide-and-seek, and sometimes even rolled a ball back and forth if Mother wasn't watching. She did not prefer indoor play, and so, as soon as the rain stopped and the sun peeked out from behind a gray cloud, she always shooed everyone outdoors—except for the older girls, for whom she always had one chore or another to assign.

While Levi paced, baby Chrystal walked around, toting a homemade rag doll in one hand and a wooden block in the other. Samuel and Milton were playing dominoes on the floor, and Henry was putting together one of the many wooden puzzles Papa had made. Lydia and Frances sat at the table playing cat's cradle and giggling softly, taking a break from their long list of tasks. Having dusted all the furniture in the kitchen and dining room, Rebecca moved to a window with a view of the barn and swiped her cloth over the sill. In truth, she wanted to catch a glimpse of Clay. She'd seen him at breakfast, of course, but then he and Papa had gone back to the barn to work in the woodshop. As she watched, a lightning bolt came out of nowhere, accompanied by a blast of thunder that nearly knocked the stone house off its foundation. Rebecca jolted backward. Chrystal screamed, and everyone else sat like statues, wide-eyed and gape-mouthed, their play having ceased abruptly. Soon Henry joined in Chrystal's concert of tears. "My gracious, that was loud," Mother exclaimed, comforting her two youngest by caressing their heads. "Levi, can thee tell whether the lightning struck anything?"

He was already putting on his hat. "I'll go check."

"Thee can't go out in this storm," Rebecca protested.

He opened the door and stood there for only a second before making a mad dash outside and around to the side of the house. Through the window, Rebecca observed Clay exiting the barn. He sprinted across the yard to meet up with Levi, while Papa watched from the barn doorway. When the two disappeared from view, Rebecca moved to the side window and gasped. One of their ancient oaks lay sprawled across the yard, split down the middle of the trunk, the outhouse having been crushed beneath it.

"Oh, no," Milton whined, coming to stand beside Rebecca. "The outhouse. And I have to go. Bad."

"Thee can use the emergency crock in the upstairs washroom," Mother told him. "It doesn't look like any of us will be using the necessary until Papa builds a new one. You boys will have to go outside behind one of the sheds."

"I won't mind that," said Milton, grinning.

Samuel laughed. "Me, neither."

"I'll dig the new hole," Milton announced. "I'm strong."

"Me, too," Henry piped up.

"Thee isn't big enough, nor one bit strong," said Samuel.

"Am, too," Henry insisted, puffing out his tiny chest.

"Huh-uh."

"Stop it, boys," Mother scolded them. "This is no time for bickering."

Milton left the gathering and ran upstairs. Everyone knew his intentions.

When the rain let up, around noon, everyone headed outside. The menfolk started sawing apart the tree that had demolished the outhouse, so that the pieces could be hauled away. Rebecca and her sisters, with the exception of Chrystal, chipped in by collecting small branches and carrying them to the side of the woodshed to be used as kindling. Every so often, Henry ran over with a twig or two, but his attention span lasted all of three minutes before he was on to something else.

That evening after dinner, Papa and Clay set off on their excursion, while everyone else—including Gerald Tuke—sat on the porch, sipping lemonade and watching the brilliant sunset. Rebecca found herself thinking far more about Clay than her would-be husband seated next to her. Every so often, he pressed his leg against hers, prompting her to readjust her position. She could hardly wait to hear how the mission went, and what Clay thought about it. But she would have to ask Papa instead of Clay. She could not afford to initiate conversation with Clay, lest he kiss her again—a temptation she feared would be difficult to fend off next time. How she had been praying the Lord would take away her increasing feelings for him! But, alas, his helping the family today had only made that warm spot in her heart for him grow even larger.

"Let us discuss the wedding arrangements, shall we?" Mother said, her eyes roving from Rebecca to Gerald.

A knot formed in Rebecca's throat so that she couldn't swallow. She quickly seized her glass and took a couple of swigs of lemonade. Lydia and Frances said nothing, just looked at their hands, and Levi gazed off, as if oblivious. The younger boys were too busy kicking each other under the table and having a regular heyday in Papa's absence that they apparently hadn't even heard Mother's statement.

"Yes, let us," said Gerald. "I've made arrangements for us to meet with the clearness committee next week, fourth day."

Rebecca gave a jerk of her head and looked at him. "That soon?"

"Yes. I assumed it would work well for thee."

"Oh, that's wonderful," Mother assured him. "Let's discuss a few other details while we're all together. Lydia and Frances, I thought you two could bake the pies. We'll need several dozen. Levi, Samuel, and

Milton, you will see to it that the yard is in proper order. I thought I would make several tea cakes, and—"

"Mother, I don't wish to talk of this right now," Rebecca blurted out.

"Thee said that yesterday, when it would have been the perfect time. We must not dawdle any longer. Thy papa will soon be leaving for Dover, Delaware, for his next preaching trip, and I wish to have most of the planning out of the way before he leaves. If thee wouldn't have hopped off the porch to play baseball with the rest of them, we could have started discussing matters."

Gerald dropped his jaw. "Thee played baseball?" he nearly screeched.

Rebecca ignored him. "I didn't wish to make plans yesterday, Mother...nor do I today."

"Thee played baseball?" Gerald repeated.

"Yes, and she has quite a knack for it," Lydia answered with a sly grin.

"Indeed," said Frances, daintily picking up her lemonade glass and looking over the rim of it at Gerald. "We all played, and it was quite grand."

Gerald frowned at Rebecca, but she didn't grace him with a glance.

"I should think thee would know better, Rebecca, than to participate in a worldly sport such as baseball."

"I couldn't agree more," Mother said, shaking her head at Rebecca. "I was quite appalled that thy father encouraged it."

"Edward permitted this game?" Gerald asked.

"It was a family event," said Levi, quietly yet firmly. "Our father had a fine time, as did the rest of us." Then he sent Mother a piercing gaze. "And I saw thee laughing throughout the game, with no indication that thee was in any way scandalized. As a matter of fact, Lydia tells me thee urged Papa to join in."

Silence fell upon the group, from sheer amazement at Levi's bravery. Mother's mouth sagged, but she said nothing.

Gerald cleared his throat. "Well, I suppose we needn't fret too much over the matter. It was just thy family, after all."

"And Clay, of course," Lydia put in.

Gerald rubbed the back of his neck and frowned. "Just when will that fellow be on his way?"

"I hope he never leaves," said Levi. "He's been a great help around the farm."

"If he is well enough for farm work, I should think he is well enough to go out on his own and make a living."

"He's got no place else to go," Milton put in. "This is his home now."

"Well, I wouldn't go so far as to say that," said Mother, reclaiming her voice, although the strength in it had dwindled some. "He shouldn't be here much longer."

"Papa says he's to stay until his memory returns," Levi said as he stood to his feet, bringing the conversation to a welcome close. Rebecca could only imagine the tongue-lashing he would get later for embarrassing Mother in front of company. But, if she knew Levi, he would shake it off quickly.

If only she could do the same with Gerald Tuke. As he took her hand, ready to commence their routine stroll, she recoiled, per routine. It was becoming increasingly evident that she needed to devise a suitable plan for living apart from Mother and Papa—and from Gerald Tuke.

20

"We've reached our destination." Edward directed the horses up a narrow wooded path to a secluded spot. Clay had refrained from asking too many questions of Edward during the journey, but it seemed his suspicions were correct. This was no routine delivery but an undercover mission to assist runaway slaves on the path to freedom.

Night had fallen, making it difficult to see, but as the wagon slowed, Clay made out a good dozen or so Negroes standing huddled together. A baby started wailing, and the woman who held it desperately tried to shush it by alternately swaying back and forth and bouncing up and down. Poor thing was probably hungry, tired, and perhaps in need of a clean diaper cloth.

"Whoa!" Edward drew back on the reins, bringing the horses to a stop.

The Negroes looked up with fear in their eyes, no one saying a word.

"The horses are in the barn," Edward quickly added.

At that, the tallest man stepped forward. He wore a bedraggled-looking sweater with holes in the sleeves, and trousers too short for his legs. Clay immediately shucked his own lightweight jacket and handed it down to the man. The fellow's eyes grew to twice their size. "Oh, no, suh. I couldn't take dat."

"You need it more than I. Please."

The fellow ran a work-worn hand over the woolen fabric of the hand-me-down from Clara Fortman, then looked up with eyes full of gratitude. "I thank y', suh."

"You're welcome." A deep sense of satisfaction settled in Clay's chest, and he reflected that if he'd been a slave catcher by trade, he must have been a hardhearted oaf in his former life. He scrambled down from the wagon, and when he did, the group of Negroes stepped back in apparent fright. "Don't worry," he assured them. "We're here to help you."

At his own words, an image flashed before his eyes of several other frightened Negroes from another time and place. It had been broad daylight, and there'd been a tragedy of some sort, on a plantation. Someone had been injured, or even killed. And Clay felt a sense of responsibility associated with the act. Had a slave been to blame? A slave named Horace Spencer, perhaps? And had someone hired Clay to find and bring him back, dead or alive? He pushed aside the troubling notion and wondered what sort of torment these folks had endured to get to this point. "You're looking mighty tired, all of you."

"We is, suh, but we sho' do 'preciate all da hep folks been givin' us on ar' journey," the tallest fellow put in. "We be fine, suh, jes fine."

The baby continued crying while the young woman tried to calm it. She bounced the babe, then shifted it to her other arm, but to no avail.

Edward had climbed down from the wagon and now stepped up beside Clay. "Where is the driver who dropped you here?"

"He done left, suh, but he give me these here papers to give y'," the tallest man said. "Ain't a one of us can read, suh. He ses you'd understand."

Edward took the paper and read it, then handed it over to Clay.

Drop cargo at corner of Trent Road and Barber. Follow path to Trent, drive five miles north until you reach Barber. Station house there. I must pick up another shipment.

There was no signature.

Clay passed the paper back to Edward, who folded it and stuffed it in the pocket of his pants. Then he addressed the group again. "We'll be taking you to a station house approximately seven miles from here. There you will rest for the remainder of the night and all day tomorrow before setting off again tomorrow evening. You are welcome to settle in Pennsylvania, but, as you know, staying leaves you vulnerable to capture."

"Das why most of us is goin' t' Canada," the tallest man spoke up. "'Cept fo' this mama and her littl'un. She goin' t' Union Village, New York, t' be with 'er sister. With the Lord's help, we'll take 'er dat far, den continue into Canada."

"Is the baby sick?" Clay asked.

"We don't believe so, suh. She be awful tired and cranky, tho'."

Edward and Clay exchanged a glance. "May I have a look at the baby?" Edward asked.

The man stepped aside, and Edward slowly approached the woman. She held the wailing baby close to her breast, her eyes round with terror. "I just want to have a look." His tone was soft and reassuring. "I won't hurt thy baby, I promise."

With obvious trepidation, she peeled back the blanket surrounding the baby. Clay noted that it was nothing more than a filthy rag.

"We all comes from different plantations in de Carolinas. Dis woman, here, though—she go by de name Rose—she come from Monroe County, West Virginia. She started out with some others, but she couldn't keep up, so she done make it on her own most o' the way. She be plumb tired out. We met up with her jes' after we cross over from New Jersey. She don't say much. Don't trust no one, neither."

"Thank thee, Mr...."

"Shepard. Jeb Shepard."

"Thank thee, Mr. Shepard." Edward turned to Rose. "Will thee follow me? I have some provisions for thy baby." He led the woman by the arm to the back of the wagon, then gestured for her to lay the baby in the bed of the wagon. After he gently unwrapped the rag that served as a diaper, he remarked, "She's drenched clear through. Clay, there are some diaper cloths in that crate at the front. Would you mind…?"

Without hesitation, Clay leaped aboard, located the crate, fished out a clean cloth, and handed it over.

Edward nodded his gratitude. "She's got a bad rash, too." He turned to Rose, who looked on with obvious worry. "Try to keep her as dry as possible. When thee comes upon a stream, rinse out the wet cloths as best you can, and don't reuse them till they're dry. Best way to cure a red bottom is to keep it aired." He then proceeded to diaper the infant, and Clay was struck by the man's skill. As a father of eight, he'd probably watched Laura change enough wet diaper cloths to know the procedure. "In the back of the wagon, thee will find a box of baby clothes," Edward told Rose. "Be sure to sort through those and take whatever thee can find to fit thy daughter." He handed the quieted baby back to her mother. "Has thee enough milk for nursing?"

Rose gave a timid nod. "I been givin' 'er all da nourishment I can, suh."

"Thee has done well, Rose." Edward put a hand on her shoulder. "There are also clean blankets in the back. Please select a new one for thy baby, and we'll throw this one away."

"Thank y', suh." She produced a shy smile. "The Lord's been with me. He be my provider an' protector, and He use people jes like y'rselves all along da way. Jes yes'erday, I be prayin' fer a new blanket for my Jewel, and jes' look what happen."

"The Lord promises never to leave or forsake thee. Thee must always remember that." Edward then cast a long look at the weary travelers. "God be with all of you. May He continue to guide and protect you."

"Amen," several chimed in unison.

"Now then, climb aboard, and we'll set out for your next stop."

Within minutes, everyone had boarded the wagon. Edward issued each traveler a blanket, some food, and a canteen of water, then offered a prayer for protection before lowering the large piece of canvas that covered the back door. Then he climbed up to the buckboard beside Clay and nudged the horses forward, up the narrow wooded path toward Trent Road.

After an hour of travel, Edward's bad knee had grown stiff and sore, so Clay took the reins. The baby had quieted, and Clay hoped the travelers were getting some much-needed rest. Now and then, a small animal would scurry across their path, or an owl would hoot in the distance. A full moon lit their way, and the clear night sky glittered with stars—a welcome sight after the heavy rains of late. Edward maintained a pensive silence, leaving Clay to his thoughts. A few more memories had emerged, albeit shifting and mysterious in nature. The names Joseph and Corinne had materialized, and seemed to hold significance in regard to Julia. Were they her parents? Possibly so. Clay also pictured a three-story house with a long driveway and acres of property, including sprawling fields of fruitful crops tended by dozens of slaves. If Clay were indeed married, did he live in the big house with Julia? And did he help oversee the slaves? He couldn't envision himself in the role of overseer or slave owner, not when he felt such compassion for the people in the back of the wagon. He certainly couldn't imagine himself working as a slave catcher.

"For now we see through a glass, darkly, but then face to face: now I know in part; but then shall I know even as also I am known." The passage from 1 Corinthians he'd read just last night revisited him, and he pondered its meaning. Was it possible that God was speaking to him, even though Clay hadn't fully surrendered his life to Him yet? Observing Edward's lifestyle of faith made Clay hungry for the same, but there seemed to be a big step between the faith he felt now and the ability to say, "God, I give my life entirely to Thee; please forgive me of my sins." When he made that decision, he wanted it to come from the deepest part of his soul. He knew so little about the workings of God and the ways He moved that he worried he might not distinguish the difference between God's voice and his own imagination.

Shortly after ten o'clock, they reached the station—a two-story farmhouse about the same size of the Albrights', which belonged to Burt and Blanche Wilson. The horses were in need of rest and nourishment, so Edward accepted Burt's offer to put them up in the barn for a few hours. Burt then insisted Edward and Clay come inside to visit, partake of the meal his wife had prepared, and enjoy some respite themselves. Neither man refused the generous offer.

After the runaways used the necessary in the backyard, Burt quickly ushered them into the house and showed them down to a secret hideaway in the basement. Out of curiosity, Clay followed the group down a ladder through the trap door in the floor. Multiple lanterns lit the expansive room, and there was a table laden with food, supplies, tableware, and pitchers of drinking water. Nearby were several crates overflowing with blankets, clothes, and wooden toys. There were two rocking chairs, and several cots lined the stone walls. Rose settled wearily into one of the chairs and began rocking her daughter, who, Clay noticed, was wrapped in a fresh blanket.

Burt spoke to the group, explaining that they were free to come and go to the outdoor privy as needed, but that they should not linger long in the open, lest someone see them and report their presence to the authorities. He prayed a prayer of protection over them, then told them he intended to close the trap door behind him, but they could easily push it open if they needed to use the necessary.

Clay returned to the kitchen with Burt. After a hearty meal, he sat at the table with the Wilsons and Edward, sipping coffee, as Burt shared one story after another about the rewards and pitfalls of operating a station for runaway slaves. "It's a dangerous undertaking," Burt said in summary. "While we are doing the Lord's business, we are also violating the law. But, as Christians, we must do our part to bring justice to the oppressed and downhearted. The Almighty has protected us thus far, and we have received a good many reports from individuals who have passed through our station and gone on to reach freedom. That gives us much joy and compels us to continue." The gray-haired man looked at his wife. "Blanche and I are in God's hands, and we lean on Him for guidance as we move forward with our mission." He nodded at Edward and Clay in turn. "I applaud both of you for your own involvement."

Edward caught Clay's eye and smiled. No sense in telling Burt that Clay was just along for the ride, or that he had a probable past as a slave catcher.

They left the Wilson place at two o'clock in the morning, the stars and moon even brighter than when they'd first arrived. It would be a long journey back to Sunset Ridge, but Clay wouldn't have traded the experience for anything. Something had happened to him on the journey. He'd birthed a passion for assisting slaves to freedom. When he told Edward, the older man chuckled. "Is that so? Well, I wonder what thy old self would say to that."

"My old self, whoever that was, will have no say in the matter." He joined Edward in mild laughter. "The whole thing is odd, Edward, but I'm beginning to believe it's true that all things *do* work together for good. I just finished reading the book of Romans, and I especially like what it has to say on this topic. If we trust the Lord, He will turn the bad things that come our way into good. I feel like that has happened to me in many regards."

Edward turned his head, and Clay caught a glimmer in the older man's eyes. "Has thee determined to follow Jesus, then?"

"Yes, I believe I have." At his quiet declaration, an impalpable peace washed over him. It was not followed by some grandiose emotional experience but only an indescribable sense of calm.

"That's good, son. That's mighty good. I wonder what thy wife will have to say when thee returns to her."

Clay stared straight ahead, his elbows resting on his spread knees, his hands clasped together. "I don't know, Edward. But if it turns out that I'm married, I will do everything in my power to convince my wife to make the same decision. For now, all I can do is wait—and pray for more memories to surface."

"Amen to that."

They jostled along the road in silence for half an hour or so, each absorbed in his own thoughts, until a man on horseback abruptly blocked their path. "Hold up right there!" the man said, pointing a rifle at them. Edward yanked on the reins, drawing his team to a stop.

The "chk-chk" sound of the dark stranger's cocked rifle sliced the air. Back at Sunset Ridge, Clay had asked Edward if he might bring his gun along, and Edward would have none of it. "The Lord is all the protection we need," he'd said. And Clay agreed; however, sitting here defenseless against an armed man didn't make a lot of sense to him right now—no matter that, just moments ago, he'd stated his intentions to trust the Lord from this day forward. Man, was he fickle.

"What is it thee wants?" Edward asked, as calmly as the air before a storm.

"One o' them Quakers, eh? What's y' got in the back of that wagon, Mr. Quaker?"

Clay swallowed his anger. "We've got nothing of interest to you, sir," he answered for Edward. "Have a look, if you want."

"I might do just that." The man clicked his tongue to urge his horse forward, and soon he was close enough for Clay to see the whites of his eyes. "How 'bout the two o' you climb on down from there?" the man said, raising his rifle a notch. "And bring that lantern with you."

"Now, why would you want us to do that?" Clay asked with a shrug.

Edward nudged him in the side. "Just do as he says." He then retrieved the lantern from where it hung by a metal hook over their heads, and proceeded to climb down. As Clay followed suit, the man pulled his horse alongside them and followed them to the back of the wagon. "Pull back that drape, there," he ordered. "And stick y'r lantern inside so's I can see."

Edward reached to lift the canvas, then poked the lantern inside the back of the wagon.

The fellow peered in. "What's in those barrels way up at the front?"

"They're empty," said Clay.

"Uh-huh. Y' sure y' don't gots a slave in there by the name o' Jeb Shepard? I been trailin' him, but I lost his scent yesterday."

"Feel free to climb up there, yourself, and take a look," Clay said, ignoring the man's comment about Shepard.

The man gave a coldhearted chortle, coughed, and then spat on the ground, lowering his rifle in the act.

Careless oaf. If Clay could somehow wrangle the gun from his grasp, he would easily overtake him.

"Put y'r hands behind your heads," the man ordered them. "And take a few steps back so's I can dismount."

Edward immediately obeyed. "Do as he says," he muttered to Clay.

Clay began backing up, slowly. He decided to play along with the worthless fool. "You a slave catcher?" he asked.

The man shrugged. "Might be. That ain't none o' y'r business, is it?"

"We want no trouble," Edward said. He remained calm on the exterior, but Clay could sense his inner anxiety.

For reasons he couldn't quite define, Clay felt equipped to handle the guy, gun or no gun. *Don't let me get too cocky, Lord. I'm asking You for guidance and protection.*

The man never took his eyes off Clay and Edward as he swung one leg in front of him over the saddle horn, then slid down the side of the horse, landing on the ground with both feet, his rifle still trained on them.

Determined to distract him, Clay pointed at the wagon. "Help yourself."

"Put that hand back where it belongs," the man ordered him.

"Don't be so jumpy," Clay told him. "Do we look armed?"

"And don't *you* be a dumb ox."

"I'll try my best."

"Clay…." Edward murmured out of the side of his mouth. "Mind thyself."

"All right, now, Mr. Religious Quaker. You go on in there and tip them barrels over for me so I can see inside."

"Go ahead, Edward," Clay urged him. "Prove it to the fool."

Without hesitation, Edward approached the rear of the wagon.

"You." Glaring, the fellow waved the end of his rifle at Clay. "Get on up here in front o' me, where I can keep my eye on y'."

Clay stepped forward, watching and waiting for the prime moment to seize the man's weapon and turn the tables on him. He moved in front of him and immediately felt the icy metal of the rifle's muzzle poking him in the back.

"I got my gun on y'r friend, Quaker," the man snarled. "Y' best do as I tell y'. Now, tip one o' them barrels over and roll it toward the back of the wagon so's I can see inside."

The fingers of Clay's right hand closed into a tight ball, his mind and body readying for a skirmish. He just had to find the right moment. *Help me, God, and don't let me get ahead of You. I don't want to do anything reckless and cause Edward injury.*

Edward set the lantern on the floor, then tipped the barrel over and rolled it to the door of the wagon. "As thee can see, 'tis empty."

"That one is, but what about the other?" the man growled. "Do the same with that one."

The rifle tip moved a bit as the guy adjusted his stance. Clay's fist clenched tighter, the muscles in his arms and legs going so rigid, they almost hurt.

Edward tilted the second barrel on its side, but instead of rolling it, he stood beside it, looking back at Clay.

"What are y' doin', fool? Roll that barrel this way," the guy barked. The gun barrel shifted again, and Clay prepared to make a sudden turn, his feet in position for swiveling.

Edward threw Clay a hasty glance, as if trying to relay a silent message, but Clay couldn't quite read it.

"Roll the blasted thing!" the guy yelled.

Edward gave the barrel a strong push, so that it went rushing off the wagon. The gun-wielding man gave a jolt of surprise, presenting Clay with the perfect opportunity to propel himself into action.

Quick as a whip, he swung around and thrust his leg in the air, his boot coming up hard to kick the underside of the guy's wrist, thereby weakening his hold on the rifle. The weapon soared through the air and landed with a thump on the ground a few feet away. The fellow's eyes registered confusion first, then rage. He came at Clay, but Clay blocked him with his left arm, then used his right fist to punch him hard in the chin, the connection swift and solid. The guy's head snapped back, and he started to lose his footing, but he quickly recovered and came at Clay like a caged bear breaking free. The force of his head plowing into Clay landed them both on the ground, where they rolled around in the dirt, each attempting to strike the other with hard blows. In the tussle, Clay somehow ended up pinned on his back. The guy started pummeling Clay's face, but Clay wrangled a hand free, grabbed a fistful of his attacker's hair from behind, and pulled with all his strength. The guy yelped in pain, and Clay managed to free his other arm, then lifted himself enough to throw a solid punch to the guy's jaw and knock him backward. The man lay there for a moment, giving Clay just enough time to scramble to his feet and spring for the rifle. "Clay, watch out!" Edward yelled. Out of the corner of his eye, Clay saw the brute come at him. Just in time, he rolled to his side, and the fellow's fist missed its target, hammering hard into the earth instead. He bellowed in pain, and in one swift move, Clay straddled him and pulled his arms behind him. "Edward! Get me a piece of rope!"

Edward moved quickly to the front of the wagon and returned moments later with a long section of twine. "Is thee all right?"

"I'm fine," Clay said, breathing fast and hard. He took the rope and began wrapping it around the man's wrists, ignoring his wails. "Shut up!" he growled. "You'll live."

"My hand," the man wailed. "It's broken."

"Looks to be."

"What are we going to do with him?" Edward asked.

"Leave him here for the wolves."

"What?" the guy mumbled into the dirt. "You can't do that."

"I can't? Watch me."

After securing the knot to his satisfaction, Clay tossed the ball of remaining twine to Edward. "Here. Tie his ankles together."

Edward hesitated.

"It's got to be done, Edward."

The fellow on the ground started kicking, so Clay grabbed his legs and held them still while Edward bound his feet, the man groaning and spitting in the dirt. Once done, Edward tossed the ball of rope on the ground beside him.

"Good job," Clay told him, checking that the knot was secure. "Now, would you mind checking his saddlebags to see what sort of ammunition this galoot is carrying? We'll toss his rifle in the woods a mile or so up the road—after we've emptied it, of course." While Edward moved to follow Clay's instructions, Clay stood, then rolled the guy over on his side and, grinning, gave him a pat on the shoulder. "There you go. Comfortable?"

The fellow kicked and writhed, to no avail. Clay stepped over him and bent down to pick up his own hat, then slapped it against his leg to shake off the dust before placing it back on his head and adjusting the brim. The guy continued to flail. "Better not use up all your energy," Clay told him. "You're going to want to save it for wriggling your hands free of that rope, which ought to take you ten minutes or so, if you're diligent. Then you'll want to get yourself to a doctor as soon as possible, to get that hand set in a splint."

"What?" the man spat. "You're just gonna leave me here?"

Clay ignored him and walked toward the man's horse.

"I've emptied the saddlebags," Edward told him.

"Good." Clay took the man's horse by the reins, led him to the back of the wagon, and tied him to the hitch.

"Y' can't take my horse," the guy growled, lifting his head a fraction of an inch.

"I'll turn him loose a few miles up the road. With a little luck, he might come looking for you." Clay shrugged his shoulders. "Then again, he might not."

Edward walked to the front of the wagon and prepared to climb up. He propped his foot on the board, then paused. "Is thee really going to leave him?"

"Do you think Laura would welcome another scoundrel at your house?"

In the shadows, Clay detected a pinched frown on Edward's face.

"Just as I thought. Climb on up."

"I'll take the reins," Edward said.

"You'll get no argument from me." Then Clay gave the fellow one last glance. "You'd do well to change professions, mister. Slave catching is dangerous business."

As the guy continued to squirm in the dirt, Clay climbed up and situated himself on the seat next to Edward. "We'd better get going. He'll work his way free in no time."

Edward snapped the reins and set the team into motion. A mile or so up the road, Clay tossed the man's rifle off the wagon. Another couple of miles, and they stopped so that Clay could set the trailing horse free. At last, they were well on their way back to Sunset Ridge.

After a good half hour of reflective silence, Edward spoke. "I wish to thank thee for what thee did back there, Clay. While I hold tightly to the conviction that violence never settles anything, it seems that we might well have been the ones lying in the dirt instead of that lout if thee hadn't taken action."

"Well, you helped by pushing that barrel off the wagon. Smart move on your part."

"I do have a bit of fight in me, don't I?"

Clay's lips turned up in a smile, but not a very big one, since the blows he'd taken to his face made grinning painful. "Probably more than you think. You'd defend your family if you had to, Edward. You really should keep a gun for your own protection."

"Friends don't—"

"I know. You're pacifists."

Edward angled his head at Clay. "Fighting came quite naturally to thee. Thee had all the moves." He paused. "Just as thee did the night we first met. Thee may not remember right now, but the first time I saw thee, thee was holding a gun. To my daughter's head."

"What? Edward, no."

The older man nodded somberly. "Thee was determined to catch Horace Spencer, a runaway slave, and thee thought I would give him up in exchange for Rebecca's life. She had followed me without my knowledge and was spying nearby when thee came upon her."

Clay was completely bewildered by the news, yet the details struck a chord of horrifying remembrance with him. "I was a different person, Edward. You must know I never intended to harm Rebecca. I would never do anything to hurt her."

"I know this, Clay. I just thought thee ought to know the truth."

Clay stared straight ahead. "I'm not a slave catcher, Edward. Never was."

"No? What is thee, then?"

He sucked in a deep breath of air, then blew it out through puffed cheeks. He fixed his eyes on the crest of a hill up ahead. "I'm a sheriff, Edward."

"A sheriff? Is thee certain?"

Clay nodded. "Pretty certain I was searching for Horace Spencer so I could bring him back for a jury trial."

"A jury trial—is that right? I wonder on what charges."

"Murder, I think."

"Oh, my. That's something."

"My mind's still a foggy mess, but the pieces are beginning to come together."

"And Julia?"

Clay shook his head. "I'm still thinking on that."

"The Lord will reveal everything in due time, I'm sure of it."

21

It was just before dawn when Rebecca heard Papa's wagon come rolling up the drive. She threw off her blankets and ran to the window. In the fleeting moonlight, she made out Papa's figure by his limp, Clay's by his size. Both moved somewhat slowly while tending the horses, no doubt spent from their long trip. She wished now she had agreed to accompany Papa. At the same time, she was glad Clay had gone in her place. What had he gained, if anything, from the experience? She went back to bed but only stared into the darkness, too excited to sleep. When she heard Papa's irregular footfall on the stairs, she jumped out of bed again and opened her creaky door to peek out. "Welcome home, Papa."

He paused in front of her room. "What is thee doing up so early?"

"Waiting for thy return. Was thy trip a success?"

"Indeed."

"Were there many runaways?"

"A dozen."

"And everyone made it safely?"

"Yes."

"So, thy trip was mostly uneventful?"

He scratched his temple. "I wouldn't say that, exactly."

"No? What happened, Papa?" Her heart thumped with excitement.

He sighed. "I'm too exhausted to explain. Perhaps later."

"Oh. Of course. Sleep well."

"I intend to." He proceeded down the hall toward his room but stopped midway and turned around. "How was the rest of thy visit with Gerald?"

She let her shoulders slump, no more in the mood for talking about her supposed fiancé than Papa was for telling her about his trip. "I see." He gave a weak smile, then went to his room.

At the breakfast table, Rebecca was not the only one who gasped at the sight of Clay's red and swollen face. "What happened to thee?" Lydia asked as soon as she walked through the door.

He gave a crooked grin because his lip was swollen to twice its size and wasn't able to curve up properly. "Had a little tussle with a bear."

"A bear?" Milton asked, his eyes wide. "How big?"

"He's joking," said Samuel. "C'mon, who hit thee?"

Clay exchanged glances with Papa. "I'll let your father tell you about it…if he wishes to."

All eyes fell to Papa, except for those of the three younger boys, who had gathered around Clay to stare at his battered face. Rebecca's gaze roved from Clay to Papa and back again. What in the world had happened last night? To avoid showing too much concern, she refrained from saying anything.

"Let's sit down for breakfast, shall we?" Papa said.

Rebecca looked at Mother. She hadn't said a thing to her or her sisters while they'd prepared the meal. Apparently, she had determined to leave that to Papa to divulge.

Rebecca ended up seated directly across the table from Clay. Once they had situated themselves, their eyes met, and she found it hard not to stare. No matter that his face was battered, he was still the most handsome man she'd ever seen.

As usual, Papa gave the morning blessing, and everyone began eating in silence. After a few minutes, Papa set down his fork. Everyone, with the exception of Henry and Chrystal, stopped eating and looked at him, clearly hungry for details. "Last night, a stranger came upon Clay and me. He threatened us with a gun and demanded we show him what we had in the back of our wagon. There was a struggle, but Clay managed to wrangle the gun from the man, and in turn, overtake him with his strength but not without a battle, as you can well see by his face. In essence, he saved our lives, and for that I am grateful."

"Good gracious!" said Frances.

"Thee got in a real fight with someone?" asked Samuel. "And he had a gun?"

"Thee is brave!" Milton exclaimed.

Clay raised a hand. "Now, hold it right there. I don't want any of you thinking I wasn't scared out of my britches, but I did what I had to do to keep your father safe. Fighting is usually wrong, but sometimes you have to do it to defend a just cause. Yes, the man had a gun, but God provided protection, or your father and I might not be sitting here this morning."

"That's why I want to be a sheriff," said Samuel.

"Samuel, that's enough," said Mother. "Thee is not going to be an officer of the law."

"Actually…." Papa cleared his throat and traded glances with Clay, then shot Mama a nervous look. "Clay had a significant recollection last night along those lines."

"What was it?" asked Lydia.

"He believes he is a sheriff himself," answered Papa.

Samuel slapped the table. "I knew you weren't a slave catcher!"

Clay turned to Samuel. "No, I'm not a slave catcher. I have vivid memories of being a sheriff somewhere, can even picture my office and the faces of my deputies. Beyond that, I'm at a loss. Your father has said that the Lord will reveal it in His own time, though, and I believe him." He winked at Samuel, then met Rebecca's gaze. She quickly looked down at her plate and resumed eating. Imagine that—Clay, a sheriff! Well, he'd said he couldn't envision himself as a slave catcher. He'd also said he couldn't picture himself married. She kept her head down to avoid his eyes for the remainder of the conversation.

In a moment of silence, Mother cleared her throat loud enough to gain everyone's attention. She set her napkin next to her plate and raised her chin a fraction. "Now that thy memories are returning, I should think it won't be long before thee remembers thy wife. She must be worried sick about thee."

Clay took a quick sip of water. "I'm still not sure I'm married, Laura." He set the glass back down and met Mother's eyes. "But if I am, then I will be happy to reunite with my wife. Either way, I will do my best to leave here as soon as possible. I realize I've more than outstayed my welcome."

"Well, I...."

"Nonsense," said Papa. "Thee will stay right here until it's clear just where thee belongs." The wrinkled, stern-faced frown Papa sent Mother was enough to chill everyone's breakfast. Lydia inclined her head at Rebecca and arched her eyebrows, her chocolate-hued eyes going as round as glass marbles. If the air in the room hadn't been so tense, Rebecca might have giggled.

"Well, I appreciate that more than you know, sir. Just the same, I look forward to recalling all the facts so I can be on my way."

Did he really wish to be on his way? It could well mean he would never see her again. The memory of his kisses burned like searing flames into Rebecca's brain, creating a sudden headache. She wished to excuse herself but fought the compulsion.

She kept staring at her plate, her appetite having long since slipped away. Levi turned the discussion toward matters of the farm as everyone hurried to finish the meal. Even baby Chrystal seemed to sense the tension, for she started crying loud enough to raise the roof and would not be comforted, until Rebecca stood from her chair and went around the table to retrieve her. It provided her a good excuse for leaving the room.

Later that morning, after Rebecca had situated Henry and Chrystal in their beds for a nap, Lydia came to her and thrust a basket into her hands. "Here. Mother asked me to deliver the noon meal to Levi and

Clay, but I think thee should do it. Thee might get a chance to talk to Clay in private."

"Whatever do you mean?" Rebecca held the basket at arm's length. "I don't wish to speak to him in private."

Lydia pushed the basket closer to her. "Of course, thee does. Thee wants to hear all about his debut on the Underground Railroad, for thee knows Papa's version was severely abridged."

She had her there. "What if Mother asks where I've gone?"

"I'll tell her the truth—that I asked thee to go in my place. I'll add that I'm not feeling well."

Rebecca frowned. "But that would be a lie."

Lydia shrugged. "Not entirely. I do have a slight pain in the stomach. Go on, now. I've saddled Stoney. He's tied out front."

"Oh, all right."

Truth told, Rebecca did want to hear the whole story. Forgoing her cap, she hastened to the cornfield, where the stalks had already grown waist high. They would be ready for harvesting around the time of her presumed wedding. What had Gerald and her parents been thinking in scheduling the event when they had? The entire family would be working day and night to gather the harvest, and Papa often hired several of Levi's friends to help. Afterward would be the preserving for the family's own cellar, as well as a series of trips to the city to sell the corn at market. Rebecca had always enjoyed harvest time, and the thought of being married in the midst of it did not bide well with her.

She reined in Stoney, dismounted, and tied his reins to the work wagon that was parked at the edge of the field. The two horses hitched to the vehicle shook their heads at her arrival, then resumed grazing on grass. Several rows over, Levi looked up and waved at Rebecca, prompting Clay to glance over his shoulder. At the sight of him, a familiar shiver of excitement rippled through her, but she suppressed it. Gracious, she needed to quell her nerves before drawing any closer.

"I brought your lunches," she called out, lifting her basket over her head as she picked her way through straight rows of corn toward the pair. Feeling suddenly bashful, she could only pray Levi would not detect her attraction to Clay. Oh, why had she agreed to deliver their lunches?

22

What a sight Rebecca was with her dark hair falling out of its single braid, her cheeks a rose-colored hue, and her timid, but bright, smile warming his insides. "Well, here you go," she said, handing the basket over to Levi. "I hope you enjoy your lunch."

"Wouldn't thee like to join us?" Levi asked.

"Oh, I've already eaten."

"Well then, thee can still sit with us in the wagon while we eat, and enjoy the sunshine."

"It is a lovely day…I suppose I could sit a spell." She fumbled with her skirts, feeling like a schoolgirl. "Perhaps you could tell us more about your adventures last evening, Clay."

"And about the important decision thee made," Levi put in, as the three started toward the wagon.

"Ah, yes. I've decided to give my life over to God."

Rebecca turned her head toward him. "Really? That's wonderful news!"

Clay grinned down at her. "I feel a bit like a fish flopping around on shore, not exactly certain what I'm supposed to do next. I aim to read my Bible every day and pray—and leave the rest to God, I guess."

Levi chuckled. "That's a mighty good start, Clay."

"I can't explain it, but today, I have this deep, settled peace I didn't have before."

"God had a purpose for thy wounds," Levi said. "He knew thee had to be put on thy back before thee would truly look up." Not for the first time, Clay thought how mature Levi was for his eighteen years, already running a farm and having a faith so strong, he made Clay look like a brainless kid.

When they reached the wagon, Levi opened the picnic basket. "Chicken sandwiches. Looks mighty good, Becca."

While the men partook of their meal, the three of them conversed, Levi and Clay sitting at the back of the wagon, their legs dangling over the edge, and Rebecca sitting more toward the middle with her back against a hay bale, her legs stretched out in front of her, crossed at the ankles. While eating, Clay relayed his experiences from the night before—everything from transporting the slaves to the basement hideout and then dinner with the station master and his wife and finally to their encounter with the slave catcher. He also divulged his memory of his being a sheriff. "I still can't recall which town I come from, but I can picture everything about my office and my two deputies. I get different names in my head, but I can't quite associate them with the corresponding faces just yet. Dr. Fleming still says he's confident I'll recapture everything in time."

"I'm confident, as well," Rebecca said.

They sat in silence for a time, breathing in the warm breeze.

"Don't know as I could join the Society wearing a sheriff's badge," Clay said after a moment.

"Oh, I'm sure there are a few sheriffs affiliated with the Society," Levi mused, "though most of the brethren would eschew the occupation because of the violence involved. Frankly, thee would get no argument from me. We believe that government is divinely instituted, and that virtuous men and women are to help it operate as God intended. William Penn is a good example of one who enlisted his comrades into public service. Quakers encourage peace, justice, charity, spiritual awareness, and liberty for the benefit of all. What better way to encourage and protect these principles than to position thyself in a place of public authority?"

"Levi!" Rebecca exclaimed, her hands clasped in her lap. "When did thee come to be so smart?"

A wide smile appeared on his mouth. "I'm not particularly smart, Becca. I just enjoy reading. And, by the way, there were Quakers who fought in the Revolutionary War."

"Yes," Rebecca conceded, "but not without discipline from the elders, I'm sure."

"From what I've read, it depended upon the region. Some Quakers felt compelled by a sense of civic duty to take up arms against the British." Levi shrugged. "At any rate, most meetings leave the matter up to the individual to decide."

"I find this fascinating," Clay said after swallowing his last bite of sandwich. "I'd like to learn as much as I can about the Friends Society. Don't know as I'd ever accustom myself to speaking plain, though."

"I speak plain at home and at First Day Meetings and such, but I don't use it when doing business in the city," Levi explained. "Otherwise, people look at me odd, as if I've lost my front teeth. Again, it's a personal matter. Mother is from the old school, and she about faints if we don't use plain pronouns." Levi took another drink from his jar, then set it down and brushed the crumbs from his lap. "Well"—he jumped down from the wagon—"I want to go check on the potato crop on my way over to the west field. Could thee drive the rig over there when thee is finished?"

"I'd be happy to," Clay replied. "I can come with you now, if you'd like."

"I should be getting back to the house, anyway," Rebecca hurried to say. She lifted her skirts in preparation to stand.

Levi raised a hand. "No hurry, really. Go ahead and tell Rebecca more about your adventures last night, if thee chooses. I'll catch thee later in the west field."

"Okay, then," said Clay. "If you're sure."

Rebecca folded her legs at the knee and hugged them against her chest, anchoring her skirts against the breeze. Clay scooted back in the wagon bed and settled in next to her, resting his back against the hay bale but keeping enough of a distance that his shoulders did not brush hers.

"You proved to be quite the baseball player the other night," he said with a grin.

"Oh, and didn't I?" Rebecca giggled. "I didn't catch the ball once, nor could I throw it worth a nickel." She rested her chin on top of her knees. "I'll admit it was fun, though. I hope we have a chance to play again. The boys thoroughly enjoyed themselves."

"As did your sisters—and let's not forget your father."

"Hm, yes, it was good to hear him laugh. Papa rarely takes time for pleasure."

"That's a shame. He's a good man, your father. I appreciated the chance to spend time with him last night. He told me exactly what happened the night I was wounded...how I threatened your life. I can't believe I did something so base, and I hope you will forgive me."

"Well, after last night, and the incident with that scalawag, I suppose now you know how it feels to have someone point a gun at your head."

He gaped at her, and then, when he realized she was jesting, gave her a playful nudge in the side. "I wouldn't have hurt you, of that I'm sure. I was probably just using you as a pawn, nothing more."

"A pawn!" Rebecca angled him a coy glance. "*You* were a scalawag, then."

He chuckled, then sobered and assessed her with narrowed eyes. "And now? What am I now?"

She lowered her chin to her knees again and centered her eyes on the toes of her boots peeking out from her skirt. "I don't know. Have you sincerely surrendered your life to the Lord? Or are you just pretending, in hopes of impressing our family?"

It was a fair question, but it hurt like a gut punch just the same. She challenged him with her silence, awaiting his reply.

"I sincerely asked Jesus to forgive my sins and take charge of my life. It wasn't an especially earth-shattering moment, but more a deep-down resolve that everything I've observed about your family is authentic, and that I wanted what you had. Then, last night, listening to Burt and Blanche Wilson share their passion for helping the runaways and testify of how they've seen the power of God at work in their mission...well, it struck me yet again that I'd been missing something in my life, and that thing was a relationship with God. So, I made the decision to turn my heart toward Him. I didn't make this choice lightly. I've been reading from that Bible most every day, and it's made an impact on me. I believe Levi was right when he said God had a purpose for landing me flat on my back. It forced me to look up."

Rebecca nodded with a tender smile. "Thank you for sharing all that with me. I'm happy for you." As she studied him further, she frowned. "Your face looks awful."

"Well, thank you very much."

She laughed. "Sorry—that isn't how I meant it. You must have taken some terrible blows last night."

He lifted one eyebrow—the one that wasn't as swollen. "You should see the other guy."

They shared another chortle, and then Rebecca picked up a long piece of straw and rolled it between her fingers. "I wonder what Julia will say about your conversion. Perhaps she has been praying for you all this time while she awaits your return, hoping you will turn to Jesus."

He scratched the back of his head and gave her a sidelong glance. "I rather doubt it. Something tells me that she isn't much for prayer."

"Why do you say that?"

"It's a hunch. I don't get an easy feeling in my gut when I think of Julia. Something must've happened between us before I left. We had some kind of disagreement."

"A *marital* disagreement."

"You are determined to prove me married, aren't you?" Again, he gently poked her in the side, then gave a quiet laugh. "Is that so you can keep yourself from falling in love with me?"

She gave a jolt, and the heavy lashes that shadowed her eyes flew up. She looked him straight on. "Don't say such things."

"Why? Because you can't face the truth? I'll admit it, Rebecca—I've fallen in love with you." There. He'd not only admitted it to himself but to her, as well. He had needed to say it.

She stiffened. "Clay...."

He reached up and snagged a lock of her hair. "You are so lovely."

She didn't move, just sat there rigid and still, staring at him. Tears started forming in the corners of her coppery eyes. Without forethought, he pulled her to him, cupping the back of her head with his hand. She cried quiet sobs into his shoulder, her tears making a damp spot on his shirt. "Don't cry, honey. It's going to be all right. You'll see." He kissed the top of her head. He longed to do the same to her lips, as before, but he knew he must refrain. She was as pure as fresh-fallen snow. To kiss her would be to heap unnecessary guilt upon her. "Will you promise me you won't marry Gerald Tuke?"

She pulled back from him, her tears still falling, but more slowly now. Then she cleared her throat and straightened her shoulders. "I cannot promise thee anything because it is not thy right to ask."

Interesting how she'd chosen to switch to the plain pronouns. He supposed it was her way of detaching herself, keeping things between them more formal—now that he'd opened his heart wide for her to peer inside. "Then make a promise to yourself, Becca. You know it can't be God's will that you marry him."

"I know nothing of the kind. Perhaps marriage to Gerald is to be my lot in life. God is bound to keep me humble, and this is His way of doing it."

"Would you listen to yourself? You think God would have you settle for someone who doesn't bring you joy?"

"Perhaps someday...."

Enough of this silliness. Urgency drove him to kiss her with abandon. Perhaps it was wrong, perhaps not. He'd reached a point of such confusion, he didn't know how to act around her. He loved her, and that was all he knew right now.

At first, she resisted; but then, suddenly, as if awaking from a long winter dream, she gave in and wrapped her trembling arms around his neck, instigating a warm shiver that shimmied up his spine. As the kiss lengthened, he swept her up in his arms, kissing and tasting until it became clear he could never get his fill. "Becca," he muttered between kisses.

"Clay," she whispered back.

The kiss resumed with fervor, until Rebecca slid away from him by a good foot, then gaped at him with obvious shock. "What—? That…that wasn't supposed to happen."

"It's all right." He reached for her.

She slapped his arm away. "No, it's not all right, Clay. It will never be all right." She leaped to her feet.

He jumped up, as well. "And how do you know?"

"Because…because the timing is all off. Thee is likely married, and even if thee is not, there's still a Julia out there, somewhere, waiting for you. We shouldn't have kissed, Clay—not before, and not now. It was wrong, and we were not going to let it happen again. Remember?"

"Settle down."

"Don't tell me to settle down. We never had the right to fall in love."

"Ah, so you admit that you love me."

"No! I admit nothing."

"You just did."

He reached out again, but she evaded him and jumped down from the wagon. As soon as her feet hit the ground, she marched over to Stoney and snatched up the reins as if she were mad at the poor critter. She paused before mounting him. "Do not do that again, Clay. I mean it."

"Do what?"

"Kiss me, you crazy duck!"

He gave his head a little shake. "You participated."

She rubbed the underside of her nose, made a low growl in her throat, and then shoved her foot into the stirrup and climbed into the saddle. To his advantage, she accidentally showed a fair amount of leg in the process. She fixed her skirts before casting him a final glance. "I would prefer it if thee took thy supper in the barn tonight. I will have Lydia deliver it."

He lifted one eyebrow. "Won't your family be suspicious?"

"No, because thee will come up with an explanation."

"I will?"

"Start thinking." She clicked at her horse and soon left Clay in a dark cloud of dust and dirt.

He watched her ride away, her braid fully undone, her hair flying behind her, her skirts flying as wide as an eagle's wingspan. *Lord God, help me…I've fallen hopelessly in love.*

23

*R*ebecca's tears started up again as soon as she left Clay. What a predicament, falling in love with a man who could never be hers—for more reasons than one. How had it come to this? And how was she to stop loving him? Shame constricted her heart. As Stoney veered up the long drive to the house, Rebecca used her sleeve to dab at her wet cheeks. She somehow needed to get Stoney watered, into his stall, and brushed down before she saw anyone, lest she be questioned as to the reason for her bloodshot eyes. She needed time to recover from Clay's kisses—kisses she should never have allowed. *He's probably married, Lord, and I've let him kiss me. Again. Please forgive me for my carelessness.*

Across the yard, Papa was bent over his workbench, sawing lumber for a new outhouse, while Samuel and Milton lugged small branches and twigs to the woodpile. There was still much debris from the fallen tree that would require several more days of work to clear. Henry and Chrystal were presumably napping, and no doubt Lydia and Frances were completing indoor chores Mother had assigned them. Rebecca knew she ought to go help her sisters, but right now, she had to regain her composure.

No sooner had she started brushing down Stoney than she heard the sound of squeaky wagon wheels in the driveway, followed by Gracie's friendly but vigilant bark, which prompted a chorus of noise from the chickens. Rebecca set down the bristle brush, checked to make sure Stoney's lead was securely knotted to the post outside his stall, and then went to the barn door to peer outside. Her heart expanded with joy at the sight of Charity Duncan's wagon. As Charity reined her horse to a stop and then climbed down, Rebecca ran over to meet her,

"Charity!" Rebecca called, running out to meet her. "What is thee doing here?"

Her friend gave her a full smile and a warm embrace. "Didn't I tell thee I was going to try to come visit?"

"Yes, but I didn't think thee would make it, considering thy move to Chester."

"Well, it so happens I'm visiting my parents for the day, and since they live only a couple of miles from here, I figured I'd drive over. Besides, I want to talk to thee about something." She held Rebecca at arm's length to look at her, and then her smile dissipated. "What's wrong? Thy eyes are red and teary."

"I—oh, I don't know as I can say. It's a very long story."

"Thee can tell me."

"I know. It's just that…well…thee will think I've fallen from grace."

"Never. None of us can fall from God's grace, my dear. Whatever thee may have done, it is forgivable. Thee need only to ask the Lord for forgiveness."

"I know, and I have, but I'm ashamed of myself. And I'm sure the Lord is disappointed in me."

Charity dipped her head and furrowed her brow. "It cannot be that bad, Becca. As thy best friend, I demand that thee tell me what it is that has thee all in a tangle."

Determined not to let the tears begin again, Rebecca breathed deeply, looped her arm through her friend's, and pulled her own shoulders straight. "All right, but promise not to despise me."

"I promise." Together, they walked to the barn, Gracie at their heels.

As Rebecca continued brushing Stoney, she told Charity everything. She began with how she'd sat at Clay's bedside for hours in those early days, watching him breathe, studying his profile, and praying for his healing. Then she shared about their lively conversations and laughter, that first forbidden kiss, their subsequent attempts—albeit unsuccessful ones—at avoiding each other, and then the latest kiss. She told of his newfound faith, his recent epiphany about being a sheriff, and everything else she could think to divulge—including that she loved him.

By that time, Stoney had long since been put in his stall, and the two friends now sat side by side on a wooden bench at the back of the barn, beneath the very hayloft where Clay had been sleeping. Rebecca let go a loud, long sigh that told of her emotional exhaustion, and Charity slipped an arm around Rebecca's shoulders, giving a gentle squeeze. They'd stretched their legs out straight, and now both studied their shoes in a moment of silent reflection. Gracie had planted herself in front of them and fallen asleep in a sprawled position, the picture of utter contentment. As usual, Charity had demonstrated her beautiful gift of listening, but now Rebecca anxiously awaited what she had to say about her quandary.

"Well." Charity sniffed and shifted in her seat, retracting her arm and clasping her hands in her lap. "Thee has found thyself in quite a pickle. It seems to me that thee needs to make a list."

Rebecca felt her brow tighten. She angled her friend a quick glance. "What does thee mean, a list?"

"A list of all the things thee needs to do to get thy life in order."

"My life in order? Thee makes it sound as if I'm about to pass on into glory."

Charity giggled. "We'll not go that far, but thee does need to make some drastic changes."

"Such as?"

"For starters, thee needs to pray. God will give thee clear direction. So, if we were making an actual list, thee would write after the numeral one, in all capital letters, 'PRAY.' Second, thee needs to pay Gerald

Tuke a visit and end this silly halfhearted romance. It is only fair to him that thee does that."

"But—"

Charity silenced her with an upheld hand and a stern glance. "Third, thee must tell thy parents, in as nice a way as possible, that thee will decide for thyself whom to marry, and whether to marry at all."

Rebecca leaned back against the plank wall and listened. Charity made it all sound so simple.

"Fourth, thee cannot tell Clay that thee have called off the wedding, lest he think it is solely because of thy feelings for him that thee has done so. It is not for him that thee rescinds thy commitment to Gerald; it is for Gerald and thyself alone. There is no point in divulging any of this to Clay, for he cannot be a part of thy life—at least, not yet." She cast Rebecca a serious face. "Perhaps never. Thee must not allow thy hopes to mount, Becca, because he could well be married; and, even if not, there is still a lady named Julia that he will someday have to face.

"Fifth—"

"Wait, wait." Rebecca giggled as she put a hand on Charity's arm. "Perhaps we really should write this down. Can thee pause long enough for me to fetch pen and paper?"

But Charity remained focused and stern-faced. "As I was saying, fifth, thee must leave Sunset Ridge. The sooner, the better."

"What?" All the humor had drained out of Rebecca. "But—"

"Shh. This is quite perfect, really. Albert and I have talked and prayed about this, and we wish to present thee with a plan."

"And what plan is that?"

"Thee must move in with us. The house is large, so there is plenty of space, and it is already stocked with furniture, albeit somewhat worn, but it will serve us well for now."

Rebecca gawked at her friend. "Would thee listen to thyself, Charity? I can't move in with thee and Albert. The very thought is preposterous."

"Preposterous? Why, it makes perfect sense to me. Albert will be busy with his new job, and I shall be cleaning…and cleaning…and cleaning. Wouldn't thee love to come and help me?"

"I would love to come and help thee, yes, but move in with thee? Even with a baby coming?"

"Especially with a baby coming!" Charity laughed. "I can only imagine how much help I'll need, so I'll admit my motives are somewhat selfish. The idea was Albert's, in fact. With his starting a new job, his hours will be long, his days trying. He said that having thee come live with us for a time would take a heavy weight off his shoulders. He's concerned that the move will create stress and loneliness for me, especially since we know no one in Chester."

Rebecca took a moment to digest her friend's plan. Was the idea all that outrageous? For some reason, she felt a surpassing peace when she considered the prospect. "I would need to find work, of course, to afford the rent."

"Rent?" Charity frowned. "Having thee so close would be compensation enough. But perhaps thee could find a job, and save up enough money to one day rent a place of thy own. Goodness knows thee shan't want to stay under the same roof as a newborn for very long."

Rebecca grinned. "Well, I'll need to pray about it some more, but… but I suppose, as long as thee is sure it's all right with Albert—"

"Oh, Becca, of course it's all right with Albert. I know we will get along just grand! What does thee think? Is tomorrow too soon?"

"Tomorrow?" Rebecca couldn't help the gasp that escaped her lips.

"Why not? Thee need not bring anything but thy personal items. Thee might wish to bring thy pillow and blankets—or perhaps not. Also, bring whatever items thee would wish to use to decorate thy room."

"My room?" The notion of having a room to herself was blissful, indeed—although she would miss Lydia. *Oh, Lydia…and Frances…and Levi…and Henry and Chrystal….* Her heart filled up and spilled out her eyes in the form of more tears.

"Now, don't start crying again. Thee must think in practical terms." Charity wrapped her in a quick embrace, then set her back with two firm hands on her shoulders. "Thy bedroom already awaits, Becca. And after everything thee has told me, it is best thee leaves Sunset Ridge. I think thee knows I speak the truth."

Sniffling, Rebecca nodded, slowly regaining her composure. It wasn't as if she were considering moving across the country or even the state. No, it was a mere fifteen miles away. And Charity was right. It was time. Past time, actually.

They made plans for Charity to return the next morning with her father, Peter Glasgow, to pick up Rebecca. Mr. Glasgow would drive the women to Chester and spend the next several days at the new house, helping Albert with various projects and repairs. In the meantime, Charity and Rebecca would scour the place from top to bottom. The whole notion of moving in with the Duncans began to take form in Rebecca's head and heart, and the more she thought about it, the more it seemed the right thing to do.

After waving good-bye to Charity, Rebecca looked up at the sky, clear blue and dotted with a few puffy clouds, and prayed a silent prayer for wisdom as she prepared to break the news to her parents. "Dear Father, please lend me strength and wisdom regarding this decision. I feel in my heart that this is right, but I desire to do Thy will in all things. Please erect a barrier if I am not to move forward with this plan." A particular calm settled over her, and then Proverbs 3:5–6 came to mind, lending her further assurance. *"Trust in the Lord with all thine heart; and lean not unto thine own understanding. In all thy ways acknowledge him, and he shall direct thy paths."*

"I shall take that as a sign that Thee is leading me, most gracious God," she whispered. She glanced around the yard while dabbing at one last tear. Papa had abandoned his job, and the boys were nowhere to be seen. Papa must have released them from their duties to go play on the big tree swing out back.

She swallowed hard, straightened her spine, and walked to the house. She was about to open the screen door when she overheard her parents conversing and decided to wait outside. She knew she ought not to eavesdrop, but she couldn't help it.

"This whole thing must be resolved, Edward. The date of the wedding is drawing nearer, and I cannot get her to discuss the plans with me."

"She does not wish to marry him, Laura."

"Well, he is her best—nay her only—candidate at the moment. Seeing as there aren't any other available bachelors in the Society, we must act before Gerald slips out of her hands."

"He won't slip out of her hands, Laura. Thee worries too much when thee should be trusting."

"Do not preach at me, Edward. Thee can preach at the rest, but not at thy wife."

Papa let out a long, wheezy breath. "I am not preaching at thee, Laura, merely suggesting. At any rate, Rebecca is a twenty-one-year-old woman. It is difficult to force her into something about which she is not fully enthused. I'm leaving for my preaching trip to Dover tomorrow, so I must devote the rest of my day to preparing through prayer and study. Perhaps thee can speak with her at the supper hour tonight. I understand that matters have to be settled, but I must leave it up to thee."

"When, again, will thee return from Dover?"

"Second day next week."

"I see. Well, if all goes well, our plans will be well under way upon thy return."

"That would be nice. If thee can convince her, that is."

Rebecca gathered her courage, opened the screen door, and stepped inside. "Convince me of what, Papa?"

Her parents turned at her entry, then stood blank-faced with mouths agape. For one wicked moment, Rebecca exalted in their surprised expressions and obvious discomfort. However, this was not about watching them squirm; this was about moving forward and doing what she should have done long ago.

"Thy father and I were just...discussing thy upcoming marriage," said Mother. "Will thee not join us? Come, let us sit down." She gestured toward the living room.

"There is nothing to discuss," Rebecca said quietly. "I am not going to marry Gerald Tuke."

"W-what?" Mother sputtered. "But—"

"You both have known from the start that I don't love him. Oh, I know that you said I would grow to love him. At first, I believed that to be a possibility. I wished only to honor and respect your wishes. I even considered that a union with Gerald Tuke might be sensible, seeing as I am moving past the age of marriageability. However, it is not fair to Gerald that I take things even one step further with him. I shall go see him this afternoon." She paused to catch her breath, feeling unexpected exhilaration at standing up for herself like this. "I'm sorry to cause you disappointment, and probable embarrassment, since the engagement was already announced at Meeting. However, I did not know that thee was going to make the news public when thee did, Papa. Had I known thy intentions, I would have stopped thee beforehand. I realize now that I let things drag on too long, and for that, I am sorry." She chewed her lip, gathering her resolve, then blurted out, "I'm in love with Clay."

Mother gasped, then clamped her hand over her mouth and promptly plunked herself down in the nearest chair, her face instantly drained of all color.

Papa's eyes drilled into Rebecca. "I figured as much. I have seen the way you two look at each other at mealtime. Thee must know it is wrong, Rebecca, especially given our belief that Clay is a married man."

"I know this, Papa. That is precisely why I am leaving Sunset Ridge."

"Leaving?" Mother had found her voice, but it sounded as if she were struggling to breathe.

"Yes. I'm going to Chester to live with Charity and Albert."

"Charity and Albert?" Papa blinked. "Since when do they live in Chester?"

"They just moved there. Albert has taken a new job with a law firm, and he also plans to establish a station on the Underground Railroad. I plan to assist him."

"We won't see you at First Day?" Mother asked, brushing right over her remark about the station.

"No." A surge of confidence bubbled up within Rebecca. The more she spilled her plans, the stronger she felt, and the surer she became of her decision. "I don't wish for Clay to know where I've gone, so you must promise me you won't tell him."

"Well, thee certainly has our promise on that," Mother said.

"I also prefer that you not tell him of my decision not to marry Gerald—at least for now. He and I must put some distance between us."

"Rebecca!" Mother's eyes went wide, her expression aghast. "Has thee committed some—some awful act with him?"

Rebecca raised her chin and looked Mother square in the face. "Of course not. It is merely best that we sever contact."

"It is my fault," Papa said, shaking his head. "I should not have put thee in charge of his care."

"It's no one's fault, Papa. Thee did what thee thought was right. Truly, it was good and proper to bring him under our roof so that we could show him God's grace and mercy. All is not in vain, either, for he has come to know our heavenly Father in a personal way."

"That is reason to rejoice," Papa conceded.

Mother merely sat in the chair with drooped shoulders and a defeated expression. Rebecca felt sorry for her, but she also rejoiced in having finally stood up for herself and done the proper thing. "Now, if you'll both excuse me, I intend to start packing. After that, I'll go see Gerald. I shall convey the news to my brothers and sisters, as well— when the opportunity presents itself."

"Of course," said Papa.

Mother merely nodded.

Rebecca left them and went to her room. Upstairs, with the door closed behind her, she collapsed in an ocean of tears.

24

*J*ust before the supper hour, Clay was reading from *The Liberator* in the barn when Lydia entered the barn carrying a plate of food. "Papa said thee requested to take thy supper out here tonight. Is thee feeling ill?"

"No, I'm…just a little tired, is all," Clay said, setting down the anti-slavery newspaper Edward had loaned him. He'd found the articles compelling, for the most part, but his preoccupied mind was making it difficult for him to concentrate.

"Well, it's no wonder, the way thee works in those fields all day with Levi and then assists Papa in his workshop. Thee earns thy keep, that's for sure."

"I plan to go finish that outhouse after I finish this meal. Now, that'll really be earning my keep."

"I thought thee said thee was weary."

So much for his excuse. "I am," he assured her. "But that outhouse isn't going to build itself, and with your father leaving tomorrow for that preaching trip, somebody's got to finish it. Might as well be me."

"Good." Lydia grinned. "I'm getting mighty sick of having to go down by the creek. Girls don't have it as easy as boys do."

He laughed aloud at her frankness. Lydia had no compunctions about expressing herself, and he liked that trait.

She clasped her hands behind her and glanced at the hayloft. "Is thee comfortable sleeping up there?"

"It isn't so bad." Truth was, he missed the comfort of a real bed. Just that day, he'd had a brief memory of his own bed, in his small yet comfortable, home—and, according to the pictures that had flashed across his mind, he didn't share his bed or his home with anyone, especially a woman named Julia. He wanted to discuss these latest memories with Rebecca, but she'd been adamant about his keeping distant from her, and he had to respect her wishes—for now.

Clay heard a wagon rumbling up the drive. He peeked outside. "Rebecca's coming back, I see. I was beginning to think she was going to miss supper."

He watched as Rebecca parked the wagon in front of the house and then walked with purpose up the porch steps, then disappeared inside. Not once did she glance back at the barn.

"Where did she go, anyway?" Clay asked.

"Mother said she went to visit Gerald."

It felt like a hand had closed around his throat.

"Rather strange, if you ask me," Lydia mused. "Perhaps she agreed to appear with him before the clearness committee, after all. I don't know. Mother wouldn't give me any details." Then she shrugged. "Well, I'd better go back to the house. Did thee need anything else?"

Clay stared at the door into which Rebecca had disappeared. "No, but thank you for asking."

"Of course. Enjoy thy supper." Lydia left him with his thoughts and skipped across the yard to the house.

Clay looked down at his plate full of food and realized he had no appetite.

⌢

That evening, Frances and Lydia sat and watched Rebecca pack her bags.

"It won't be the same around here without thee," Lydia lamented, her face wet with tears. "What are Chrystal and Henry going to do without you? Thee is like their second mother."

"It'll be downright lonely," Frances added. "Not to mention tedious, with all the housework being divided between two of us instead of three."

Rebecca laughed. "Is that all I am to you? Work relief?"

Frances stood up from the bed and enfolded Rebecca in her arms. "Thee knows I love thee, Sister dear."

Soon Lydia joined the huddle, and the three of them sobbed like a little girl who had just lost her favorite doll. After a time, the sniffling sisters removed themselves from the embrace, then wiped their eyes and gathered their wits.

Rebecca cleared her throat. "It's not as if I'm moving a thousand miles away," she pointed out. "And, had I gone ahead and married Gerald, it would have been the same story." Turning to her wardrobe, she picked up a blouse and held it out, assessing its condition.

"How did Gerald react when thee broke the engagement?" Frances asked.

Rebecca tossed the blouse back into the drawer. It was too tattered to take along. "He was displeased, but he didn't appear overly surprised or even brokenhearted. He knew I didn't love him, and I'm certain he didn't love me—not down deep, anyway. He'll find someone else." She looked at Frances. "Perhaps thee can marry him, Frannie."

Frances picked up a pillow and plunked it in Rebecca's face. "Not in a thousand years. I am completely opposed to having Mother and Papa choose a husband for me. I can't believe thee humored them as long as thee did."

Rebecca chortled. "Well, I think perhaps they've learned their lesson about arranging their daughters' marriages."

"There'll be no husband for me unless he sweeps me off my feet," Lydia declared.

"And that is as it should be," said Rebecca. Then she knelt and closed the lid of her trunk. "There. I believe that is that."

Lydia narrowed her eyes to slits. She'd moved to the center of the bed next to Frances and drawn her knees up to her chin. "Remind us again why thee is rushing off. Now that the engagement is no more, thee could just as easily stay at Sunset Ridge."

Rebecca braced herself on the trunk as she stood, then climbed onto the mattress between her sisters. "I didn't disclose my full reasons at the supper table tonight. I wanted to talk to you two privately, and to Levi, as well. Mother and Papa know, but that is all."

"What do they know?" Frances asked, her chest rising with deep inhalations.

"Thee is in love with Clay!" Lydia blurted out.

Had it been that obvious? Rebecca did her best to feign nonchalance. "Whatever would make thee say that?"

"Come now, Becca. I'm not so naive that I don't recognize certain things."

"I had the same suspicions," said Frances. "As did Levi."

"What? But how—? Was it that obvious?"

"Then it's true?" asked Lydia.

"Oh, my darling sisters." Rebecca wrapped them both in another embrace and spilled the same story she'd told Charity.

"It makes perfect sense for thee to move in with Albert and Charity," Frances said when Rebecca had finished. "Especially since they plan to establish an Underground Railroad station for runaways. That is where thy heart of passion lies, Sister. Thy involvement will keep thy mind busy, and help thy heart to heal."

"I happen to agree, but listen, both of you. It is most important that you do not divulge my whereabouts to Clay," Rebecca reiterated. "I do not wish for him to find me, as no good could come of it. Promise me you will not tell him."

"We promise," the girls replied in unison.

"And do not tell him I've broken my engagement to Gerald. I don't wish to give him any false hopes regarding our doomed relationship."

They nodded glumly.

"It's almost like Romeo and Juliet, doomed from the start," Frances said.

Rebecca laughed, albeit minus any humor. "Well, I don't think I'd go so far as to say that, but theirs was an ill-fated love, indeed. In my case, I trust that God has my best interests in mind. He always works things out as He sees fit. Our job is to trust Him in all circumstances, love Him with our whole hearts, and always believe His ways are best."

Lydia's shoulders drooped. "I wish I had thy faith, Becca."

The three drew close once more for another rare moment of true sisterly love, their hearts full with emotion, their eyes damp, and their bond stronger than ever before.

⁓

The next morning, Clay took his breakfast in the house—probably against Rebecca's wishes, but she wasn't present, so he supposed it didn't really matter. He wondered why she hadn't come downstairs for the meal, but he refrained from inquiring, not wanting to arouse suspicion. The family was unusually quiet, but he dared not ask what had made them all tense. Even Chrystal and Henry weren't their normal, jovial selves. Maybe he could question Levi while they worked in the fields later that morning. He couldn't ask Edward, for he had left for Dover at the break of dawn. Perhaps Edward's absence explained it. The children were missing their papa. Laura had left the table five minutes ago and was rattling pots and pans around in the kitchen.

Lydia cleared her throat while assisting baby Chrystal with her cup of milk. "Thank thee for finishing the outhouse, Clay."

"Mm-hmm. We needed it," said Milton.

It was the first real attempt at conversation anyone had made since Clay had sat down.

"You're welcome. Samuel helped. Isn't that right, Samuel?"

"Yep. Made my muscles a lot stronger." He flexed both arms to prove his statement, which produced smiles from Frances and Lydia.

"I'm strong, too!" Henry declared, also flexing.

"Not as strong as me," said Milton, who also flexed.

"No bickering, boys." Frances' no-nonsense tone got the boys' attention and they went back to eating.

"It looks to be a nice day," said Clay after taking a bite of warm bread.

As if on cue, almost everybody glanced out the nearest window. "Yes, doesn't it?" said Frances.

Lydia dipped her spoon into her bowl of oats and stirred rather than ate.

After taking a couple of more futile cracks at initiating conversation, Clay finished his bowl of oats and his two slices of bread, then laid down his spoon. Lydia and Frances began gathering the plates and tableware, marking the end of the meal.

"Everyone sure acted strange at breakfast today," Clay said to Levi after meeting him later at the north field, where they were repairing fences.

"Is that so?" Levi took up his hammer and nailed a fence board in place.

"Everyone was so quiet and distant. Even the youngest two weren't themselves."

"Hmm."

"Couldn't get a conversation going."

"Everyone must've been tired."

Clay shook his head. "It was more than that."

"Well, I can't really say."

"Can't? Or won't?"

Without glancing up, Levi reached in his pocket for another nail, his expression solemn. Clay held up the other end of the board and waited for Levi to secure it in place before they both moved down to the next section of fence in need of repair. He kept his eyes trained on Levi, expecting to see a crack in his demeanor. "Are you going to answer me?"

"Nope."

"Why not?"

"I'm not at liberty to say."

"You're not at liberty? All right, Levi. What's going on?"

"Sorry, Clay, I can't talk about it."

"Does this have something to do with Rebecca? She wasn't at breakfast this morning. Why didn't she come down?"

Levi stopped and looked at Clay, his face as sober as a judge. Then, at the sound of a wagon going by, Levi turned and waved at the driver.

"Who was that?" Clay asked.

"Peter Glasgow. He lives a mile or so up the road." Levi watched the wagon till it disappeared from view, then wiped a hand down his sweaty face. "Let's get this fence done, shall we? We can talk later."

But that never happened. When Samuel rode out to deliver their noon meal, he told Levi that Mother needed him to come fix something at the house. "What is it that needs fixing?" Levi asked.

Samuel shrugged. "She told me, but I can't remember. Something to do with the stove, I think. Or maybe the sink. Anyway, she told me to tell thee when I delivered the food."

Levi sighed. "Does thee want to finish up here?" he asked Clay. "Looks like there's only that one last row there." He pointed eastward.

Clay nodded. "Of course. You go on and tend to matters at the house. I'll see you later." Then he turned to Samuel, "You want to stay here and lend a hand?"

"Sorry, I can't. Mother's got me working in the garden."

"I see." He'd figured he could wrangle some information out of Samuel, given half a chance, but that plan fell flat. Something was fishy. And it appeared he would have to do his own digging to discover it.

Several hours later, when Clay returned the work wagon, Lydia met him in the barnyard with an envelope. "I was asked to deliver this letter," she told him, extending the missive.

"Is that so?" Clay climbed down from the wagon, removed his gloves, and stuffed them in his hip pockets before accepting the envelope. On the front, his first name was spelled out in delicate handwriting.

"It's from Becca."

Clay almost laughed. "Wonder why she'd write me a letter when she could just as easily come out and talk to me."

"She's not here."

"Did she go into the city with Levi?"

"No, she's gone."

"Gone? Where?"

"I can't say, but she left...took her things and moved out."

Now his entire body jolted. "Moved out? Where?"

"I told thee, I can't say. Only that she's moved to another town."

Panic surged through his veins. That explained the family's strange behavior at the breakfast table. "I don't understand."

Her gaze dropped to the envelope. "Maybe thee will find some clarification in that letter." Then she turned on her heel and walked back toward the house.

Clay glanced down at the unopened envelope, then looked up at the horses that were hitched to the wagon. The horses could wait. He could not. He strode to the barn, made for Star's empty stall, and situated himself on a stool before tearing open the envelope and tossing it onto the dirt floor. As the stale scents of straw, old leather, and grain filled his nostrils, he began to read.

Dear Clay,

I have taken advantage of an opportunity to move away from home. It was past time for doing so. I have asked my family to keep my whereabouts a secret, and I would appreciate it if thee would respect this desire and not attempt to ferret out information from them. It is for our mutual benefit that thee and I never see each other again, and I am certain thee knows why. I hope and pray that thy memory will return in full, and that thee will soon be returned to Julia. I wish only God's very best for thee both.

Sincerely,
Rebecca

Clay read the letter three more times before folding it up, then closed his eyes and leaned back against the stall. Was that it, then? She hoped never to see him again, and she expected him to forget her? Yes, there was the matter of Julia and his rediscovering what sort of relationship she had with him. *If* he was married to Julia, he would remain with her, of course. But if he *wasn't*, then he would certainly want to make Rebecca aware of it.

Groaning, he swiped his palm down his face. He was still so green about this matter of prayer, but he struggled to form some words that made sense, and hoped the Lord would read between the lines. "God, what am I supposed to do? Levi said You brought me here for a reason. I didn't mean to fall in love with Rebecca, but I did. What would You have me do with these feelings? Just toss them aside and pretend they don't exist? Please help me recall the details of my past in full. Make it clear to me exactly who I am and where I belong so I can figure out how to move forward. Amen."

He sat there in silence, awaiting some sort of revelation. But after a few minutes of nothing, he dragged himself up and went to tend to the horses.

25

The house in Chester was every bit as big as the Albrights' farmhouse, and it had a stone façade so similar that Rebecca had to fight down a wave of homesickness upon seeing it for the first time. Across the yard were a couple of outbuildings and a fenced-in pasture. The major difference about the Duncans' new estate was, it lacked life. No chickens roamed about, no horses ran to the pasture gate to welcome them, no pigs oinked in the pens, no goats propped their front legs on the fence to peer out at them, and no Gracie barked hello. Of course, this was not a full-sized farm; it was a small plot of land just off Chester's main thoroughfare and within walking distance of the center of town. Given its location and its size, it was the perfect place to establish an outpost of the Underground Railroad. Albert had expressed a desire to have the station in operation by late summer, and Rebecca looked forward to helping make the necessary preparations.

The first morning she awoke at her new residence, she lay in bed, staring across the room and thinking about her family. Mother and her sisters were probably in the kitchen, preparing breakfast and baking the day's supply of bread. She could almost hear the rattle of pans and the back-and-forth banter of Lydia and Frannie. Before long, the boys would come padding into the kitchen, poking around for something to eat, and Mother would shoo them out again, ordering them to be patient.

Mother. Rebecca had spoken little to her before leaving for Chester, but she had detected a sheen of wetness in the older woman's eyes when they'd said good-bye. Mother had never been overly generous with doling out hugs and kisses, nor was she one to show much emotion, so her miniscule tears were noteworthy indeed. Did she regret having urged Rebecca so strongly to marry Gerald? Was she missing Rebecca's help around the house even now? She felt a surge of emotion as images of the youngest children's faces floated across her mind. Were they crying because they missed her morning cuddles? And how had Lydia fared without an evening chat with her longtime confidante? Many had been the nights the two sisters had lain awake talking.

Rebecca hauled in a deep breath, then pushed the covers off and sat up, letting her bare legs dangle over the edge of the mattress. The big four-poster bed had been more than comfortable, and the room itself was relaxing, if not elegant, with its high ceilings and fancy crown molding. All around were exquisite touches, right down to the crystal doorknobs. There were two paintings on the walls: one of some children romping in a garden, and another of a sunset above a hilly landscape of lush trees and wildflowers. Granted, the room needed some sprucing up—as did the rest of the house, having long sat vacant. But Rebecca was confident that she and Charity would have every room shining spotless in under a week. She by no means had the housekeeping skills of her mother, but, having worked under her tutelage all her life, she knew a thing or two about scrubbing down a house until it sparkled. Once they had completed the biggest chores, Rebecca would seek a decent-paying job so she could start saving money for a place of her own when the time came for her to move out.

As soon as she put her feet on the cool wood floor, she made up the big four-poster bed, walking around it to tuck in the sheets and blankets, draping the heavy quilt over the top, and plumping the pillows. Next, she knelt before her wooden chest and lifted the lid, intending to unpack.

In spite of her efforts to ignore it, Clay's image continually came to mind. While she sorted through her clothing and arranged it in the chest, she wondered what his thoughts had been when he'd discovered her absence at the breakfast table. What might he have said to her family? And, more important, what had they said to him regarding her departure? Would Clay drill the children as to her whereabouts, despite the request she had made in the letter she'd left him? She sincerely hoped not. Even though she missed him terribly, it was for the best that she had gone away. It was only a matter of time before his memory returned, and he, too, would leave—would return to Julia. Her heart was so full of emotion that, at times, she found it hard to breathe.

She gathered a set of underthings, along with a skirt, blouse, and apron, and walked to the window to peek outside. This was a far busier place than Sunset Ridge. A train whistle blew in the distance, and the hustle and bustle of city life passed just beneath her window, people scurrying past on their way to work or to market. A newfound energy welled up within her at the thought of exploring the sights and discovering all that her new surroundings had to offer.

She cast her eyes skyward. "Dear Father, Thee has brought me to Chester for a reason. I believe part of that reason is for me to assist with the Underground Railroad, but perhaps Thee has something else in store that I cannot yet see. Please prepare my heart for serving Thee in the best way I can. May I be a blessing rather than a burden to Charity and Albert, and may I view the things of life through Thine eyes and not my own. O Father, Thee knows how empty my heart feels after leaving Sunset Ridge…and Clay. I ask Thee to bind up my wounds, that I may serve Thee with joy in my heart and thanksgiving in my soul. Take away my selfish desires and replace them with a desire only to live for Thee. In Jesus' name I pray, amen."

She inhaled deeply, then slowly exhaled. Feeling suddenly rejuvenated, she dressed for the day's activities and headed downstairs. She found Charity sitting at the kitchen table, looking her usual cheery self. Upon Rebecca's entry, Charity brightened the more. "Good morning! Would thee like some coffee?" She started to rise.

"Stay put, young lady," Rebecca ordered her with a laugh, pressing her friend's shoulders gently so that she would return to the chair. Then Rebecca went to the cookstove and poured herself a mug of black, pungent brew from the hot kettle before padding back to the table.

"How did thee sleep?" Charity asked.

"Like an old dry log. And thee?"

"Albert and I were both exhausted, so we slept soundly, as well. This pregnancy has drained me of much of my energy, but I'll not let it slow me down."

Rebecca placed her hand on her friend's forearm. "Thee *will* let it slow thee down, Charity. I'll see to it, in fact. Leave the heavy work to me. Truth be told, I enjoy it. In fact, I hardly know how to act, sitting down with a steaming cup of coffee first thing in the morning. I ought to be standing at the stove, cooking something."

Charity laughed. "All in due time. We haven't many food supplies yet, so Albert suggested we take the rig to the marketplace this morning before we get too involved in household chores. I shall put thee to work baking bread later today, and then there's this big house to clean."

"I'm happy to help however I can, dear friend. Consider me at thy beck and call."

"Has thee thought much about Clay?" Charity asked with a conspiratorial smile.

Rebecca took a sip of coffee in order to delay her response. Her mind burned with the memory of his most recent kisses. "I have, but I'm trying not to dwell on him. I'm hopeful that, in time, he will be nothing more than a distant memory."

"I have been praying for thee. I know it must be difficult. I'm thankful thee came to live with us. It will do us both good. Is Sunset Ridge continually in thy thoughts, as well?"

"Ah, more than thee knows. But I am eager to explore Chester. I hear the train coming now. How fun to be living so near to the station."

They chatted for several more minutes, then got down to business and began planning out the week ahead, numbering their list of chores according to priority. At times, they giggled like schoolgirls, but eventually they put a plan in place and then divided chores among them, Rebecca taking the more labor-intensive tasks that would require climbing or getting down on her knees. It seemed she would spend the next several days sweeping and mopping the floors, washing the windows, and wiping down the walls in preparation for having them painted or wallpapered—a job Albert had hired out, much to Rebecca's relief.

If nothing else, her new life in Chester would be an adventure, and she meant to make the most of it, doing everything as to the Lord, with joy and thanksgiving in her heart.

Everything at Sunset Ridge was different with Rebecca gone. Mealtimes were beyond odd, with the little ones fussing over nothing and everything, and the big kids being more sober than ever before. Clay realized that his own presence played a part, for Rebecca's siblings— excepting Chrystal and Henry—knew that he was a primary reason behind Rebecca's departure. They simply didn't know how to act around him anymore, and Clay understood that. He wasn't exactly sure how to act around them, either. He would be glad when Edward returned from Dover. Perhaps he'd find an opportunity to talk to him in private and reassure him that nothing unseemly had happened between Rebecca and him—just a few kisses—and that, while it was true he'd fallen in love with her, he accepted that the relationship could never amount to anything, barring a divine twist of some sort.

Time and again, Clay considered packing up his few possessions and fleeing Sunset Ridge. Yet something indiscernible made him stay put, in spite of the strained atmosphere and awkward tension.

The last of the fence lines had been repaired yesterday, so after breakfast, Levi had gone with Frances and Lydia to the city to sell produce. In the meantime, Clay worked in Edward's workshop, sanding down the parts of a table. Gracie was curled up asleep on the cool floor nearby, and he found her presence calming. While he worked, he pondered the Scripture from Isaiah he'd committed to memory earlier that morning: *"Fear thou not; for I am with thee: be not dismayed; for I am thy*

God: *I will strengthen thee; yea, I will help thee; yea, I will uphold thee with the right hand of my righteousness.*" As he meditated on the verse, a peace that surpassed his understanding filled his being, and he knew—he just knew—that, somehow, everything was going to be all right.

Later that day, while Clay was mucking out stalls, Gracie began quite a barking fit. Clay propped his pitchfork against the wall, removed his gloves and laid them on a milking stool, and then walked to the door to see who was coming. Edward was climbing down from his rig when Milton burst out the front door of the house and skipped down the porch steps. "Papa!" he screeched. "Everybody, Papa's home!" At his announcement, the rest of the family filed out into the yard.

Grinning, Clay leaned against the door frame, his arms crossed, his hands tucked in his armpits, and watched the family he had come to love like his own.

Edward hugged each of his children in turn, reserving his final embrace for Laura, who held Chrystal in her arms. When he'd finally doled out the last hug, Henry demanded to know what his father had brought them. Edward reached into his pocket and retrieved what appeared to be an assortment of candy sticks, then handed one to each of his kids. They tore into the treats as if they'd never tasted anything sweeter, even though Laura was forever baking pies and cookies. Clay figured he had put on a few pounds during his stay. Levi walked around to the back of the wagon and hauled down his father's satchel, and then, like a shepherd with his flock, Edward steered his family toward the house.

Clay started to retreat inside the barn, but Edward called out, "Clay, come on inside with us." Clay brushed his hands on his pant legs as he sauntered toward the house, the afternoon sunshine searing his shoulders through his cambric shirt. A knot of curiosity burrowed in his chest as he wondered why Edward had invited him inside.

As everyone got situated in the living room, Laura and the older girls brought out glass tumblers and a pitcher of cold tea. Everyone sat down, save for Chrystal and Henry, who fished around for something to play with in the wooden toy chest.

"How was thy trip, Papa?" Lydia asked.

"Oh, the trip was fine. Elias Fox and I had a fine time meeting with several of the Friends, and I had an opportunity to share in their fellowship. But there is something that I think is important for all of you to hear. As usual, we took our meals in various homes, and yesterday, we had our meal with George and Mary Engstrom. While we were supping, George Engstrom told us about his son who lives in Catonsville, Maryland, which is close to Ellicott City. He mentioned that his son was part of a search party for a missing man—a sheriff from Ellicott City. The whole town had been quite concerned."

Ellicott City. Like an exploding cannonball, Clay's body shot straight off the chair. "Ellicott City?" He pinned Edward with his eyes. "I'm that man, aren't I?"

Edward remained calm. "I believe so, Clay *Dalton*."

Clay sat down again and swept a hand through his hair. "Sheriff Clay Dalton, of Ellicott City," he repeated absently. "Did you say that's in Maryland?"

"Indeed, it is. Delaware County, to be exact—the area of thy jurisdiction."

"Delaware County." Clay heaved a loud breath. "Sheriff Clay Dalton. It's starting to sound familiar. Why wasn't I able to come up with that on my own?" He clutched his head with both hands and grimaced. "I don't understand it."

"Dr. Fleming said himself thy condition was difficult to grasp, that thy memory could return all at once or in segments," Laura reminded him. "I'm sure once thee reacquaints thyself with thy former surroundings, things will begin to take shape again."

"I hope you're right, Laura." Clay turned to Edward. "Did you learn anything else?"

"I did," said Edward. "Namely, that thee is not married but rather engaged, to one Julia Wellesley. It was her father, Joseph Wellesley, whose murder precipitated thy search for Horace Spencer."

"I'm not married?" To Clay, that was the most important detail of Edward's report. He couldn't restrain the grin that exploded across his face. The implications of the news rushed over him like a waterfall, refreshing his senses. He looked around the room, meeting several wide-eyed faces. "I'm not married!"

"Thee still must reunite with thy betrothed," Lydia said in a solemn tone.

That brought his excitement down a notch. "Yes, but…but I'm not married. I knew it all along. I just knew it."

"What's 'married'?" asked Henry as he climbed onto the sofa next to Lydia, a carved wooden horse in one of his pudgy hands.

"It's when a man and a woman get together legally," answered Samuel.

"Legally?"

"They become husband and wife," Lydia said.

"And sleep in the same bedroom?"

"Henry!" Samuel's face went red and blotchy.

Henry's mouth fell. "And then they kiss?" he asked, as nonchalantly as could be.

Samuel groaned and put his head in his hands. "Make him stop."

Everybody laughed, until Levi said, "What is thee going to do, Clay?"

That changed the tone.

"I…I guess I'll be leaving soon. Possibly tomorrow." Clay wished there was a way to reach Rebecca with the news that he wasn't married. Perhaps Edward would give him a hint as to her whereabouts.

"First Rebecca, and now thee?" Milton's lower lip trembled. "It isn't fair!" Tears welled up in his big eyes and spilled down his cheeks. Laura reached over to touch his arm, but he jumped up and ran out before she had the chance.

Clay considered going after him, but Edward must have sensed it, for he said, "Leave him be. He needs time to ponder things. We'll explain to him later in a way he can understand."

Clay nodded, then looked in turn at each beloved face around the room. "I don't even know how to express my thanks to each of you. I mean…this has been quite a journey for me. I…." He could hardly believe it when tears sprang to his own eyes. "It's a lot to take in all at once, I guess." His voice was stiff with emotion.

Sniffles came from some of the girls, but he tried to avoid looking directly at them. They'd say a proper good-bye tomorrow.

Clay cleared his throat. "I need to get this relationship with Julia figured out."

Edward nodded. "Yes, 'tis true."

Clay glanced at Laura and found her expression unreadable. Did he detect a tiny bit of moisture in her eyes, as well? He'd never known her to show emotion, or even much affection.

"Thee never knows," Edward went on. "Once thee meets up with Julia again, thy affections may rekindle. Thee must give it a chance. The Lord will make the proper path clear to thee in due time."

Edward was right, Clay supposed. He would have to give the relationship a chance. Still, something told him it was over—that it had been, even before he'd set off on his search for Horace Spencer. The two had argued, and Clay was beginning to remember why. Julia was a wealthy girl with a sense of entitlement, and she wanted to keep it that way after they married, despite Clay's being a man of humble means. He remembered wondering how he would manage to keep her happy on his meager sheriff's salary.

"Tomorrow morning," Edward said, "we'll put thee on the train. Thy horses will ride on a livestock car, and thee can pick them up at Ellicott City."

26

Rebecca and Charity had accomplished a great deal in recent days, working for hours on end to get the new house spotlessly clean. Rebecca thought often of Sunset Ridge and the family she'd left behind, but staying busy kept her mind occupied and made her body ready for sleep the second she put her head on the pillow each night. Right now, however, she couldn't help but think of Papa, knowing he would have returned yesterday from Dover, and wishing she could hear about his trip. Perhaps later that day, she would sit down at the desk in her room and write him a letter. The house was unusually quiet, with Charity's father having headed back to his own farm and Albert working his first day at the law firm. When the clock struck noon, Charity declared it time to take a break. "We've earned a bit of a rest, doesn't thee think, Becca?" she said. "Wouldn't it be grand to walk into town and take our noon meal at a restaurant?"

"A restaurant?" Rebecca asked. "But we have plenty of food here, after our trip to the market yesterday, and with all the bread I baked."

"Yes, but we need to do some exploring that doesn't include errands, and I'd like some fresh air. Remember that little eatery we saw yesterday? Morningstar Dining Room, I think it was called. Let's go there."

"All right, but on one condition—that thee permits me to treat."

"Oh, I couldn't let—"

"Yes, thee could," Rebecca insisted. "Otherwise we shan't go."

Charity blew out a breath of frustration. "All right, Becca. I'll allow it this one time."

They stuffed their coin purses in their apron pockets and hastened out the door, not even taking the time to don their prayer caps.

"I still can't accustom myself to how different Chester is from Sunset Ridge," Rebecca said as they strolled along the sidewalk, smiling at passersby and relishing the bright sunshine.

"Is thee missing home?"

"A bit, but I'm truly enjoying staying with thee and Albert."

"Well, I, for one, love having thy company," said Charity. "It makes me feel like a schoolgirl again."

Rebecca laughed. "Let's hope that feeling doesn't wear off."

Charity touched her rounded belly. "If it does, it won't be due to thy presence but due to this little person growing inside me."

"Has the baby been very active this morning?"

"Oh my, yes. He really is quite a kicker. Albert says he'll probably kick the first person he sees after he's born."

"So, you believe it's a boy?"

Charity giggled. "Albert hopes so. I have no preference, but I'm expecting a boy so that I'll be pleasantly surprised if it's a girl."

"That's a good way to look at it."

At the corner of Seventh Street and Welsh, they turned left. The restaurant was three doors down. A man entering held the door for them, and Rebecca acknowledged his kind gesture with a nod and a smile. The eatery was crowded, but they found a free table toward the back. Rebecca could not recall the last time she'd eaten at a restaurant. Mother believed dining out was too extravagant—and it was, especially for a family of ten.

They didn't wait long before a middle-aged woman wearing a food-stained apron approached their table with a coffeepot in hand. "Would you ladies like some coffee?"

"Yes, please," they answered in unison.

The woman proceeded to pour the dark brew into their empty tea-cups. "Haven't seen you two in here before."

"It's our first time," Charity affirmed. "I'm Charity Duncan, and this is my dear friend Rebecca Albright. She's staying with me and my husband, who just started work at Wilson and Sons Law Firm. We recently moved to a home on Potter Street."

"Nice to make your acquaintances. I'm Dorothy Waite, the owner of this establishment." She straightened and pushed a few strands of brown hair out of her eyes. "Was it the old Crosby house you moved into? It's been vacant about a year."

"Yes, that's the one," said Charity, "and we just did a year's worth of cleaning in five days."

"Well, it'll be nice to see new life in that old place."

They chatted a few more minutes before placing their order—two bowls of corned beef and cabbage stew, even though neither woman was accustomed to eating meat.

"She's friendly," said Charity when Dorothy had left them.

"Yes, very." Rebecca glanced around the restaurant and noticed a sign nailed to the wall near the kitchen area. It read, "HELP WANTED. Inquire of Dorothy."

Charity followed her gaze. "Is thee going to inquire?" she asked.

"I think I will," said Rebecca, before she had a chance to really think about it. She had never held a job that paid actual wages, and she wondered if she were even qualified for the position being advertised. As if on cue, Psalm 56:3 came to mind: *"What time I am afraid, I will trust in thee."* God always seemed to speak to her at just the opportune time.

Clay peered through the fingerprinted train window as the locomotive's whistle gave a high-pitched squeal and the brakes screeched, bringing the train to a stop. "Chester City Limits," the sign said. Clay pressed his forehead against the glass for a closer look. Chester appeared to be a bustling town, with folks traversing the sidewalks, some toting small children, others carrying bundles of dry goods. He watched an older fellow load several parcels into the back of his wagon, then untie his horse from the hitching post and climb aboard. Another fellow dressed in a dark suit and dapper hat crossed the street with purpose in his step, probably heading back to the office after his noon meal. A large brown dog darted across the road in pursuit of a stray chicken, and on a corner, a young boy was selling newspapers.

As he gazed further up the congested avenue, emotion clogged his throat as he thought about his final morning at Sunset Ridge. The whole family had come out to the driveway to see him off, most of the kids biting on their lips and wearing solemn faces. Edward had climbed up to the driver's seat of the wagon and waited while Laura had given Clay a quick, tight hug. "Take care of thyself, and come back to see us," she'd said. Her demonstration of affection had surprised him, for few were the times he'd seen her embrace her own children. Fleetingly, he'd wondered if she'd even hugged Rebecca before she'd set off to who knows where.

On the ride to the train station, Clay had asked Edward once more to tell him where Rebecca had gone. Edward had refused, saying Clay first needed to find out where things stood with his fiancée. If, after a time, he saw that the relationship was not progressing, he was to notify Edward in writing, at which time Edward would respond appropriately. Otherwise, Edward would assume that he had worked things out with Julia, and he would let the matter rest.

"At least tell me she isn't still planning to marry that Tuke fellow," Clay had said just before boarding the train. But Edward had merely shaken his head in a way that said he declined to comment.

"Lord, don't let her marry him. Please, Lord," Clay quietly prayed now while gazing out the window. He waited for some sort of spiritual insight or a sense of calm to come over him, but in vain. He could not get the woman out of his mind, and somehow he had to find her. Soon.

The train rolled into Ellicott City late that afternoon. Clay's heart pounded against his chest at his first glimpse of the town from the train window. Citizens milled about on the platform, waiting to greet incoming passengers or preparing to board the train themselves. He searched the many faces, but none was familiar.

He picked up the satchel that Edward had given him and proceeded toward the door. Stepping down on the platform, he held his breath and glanced around, half expecting someone to approach him. When several minutes passed with no greetings from anyone, relief surged through him. He would just as soon enter the town with as little fanfare as possible. He headed for the livestock car at the back of the train to retrieve Star. In his final minutes, he'd decided to leave the extra horse with the Albrights, for Milton and Samuel to ride. They were elated and had already started arguing over what name to give it.

Once he'd saddled and mounted Star, he gave a little kick to get him moving. He would rely on his horse to lead the way because, at least for now, Star knew Ellicott City far better than he. Although the place was familiar enough, Clay felt more like a visitor than a longtime resident. What in the world would his deputies say when he walked through the door of the station?

As he rode up the main street toward the busiest section of town, many of the people who spotted him gasped, pointed a finger, waved, or just shouted a greeting. "He's back from the dead," someone said. "Welcome back, Sheriff!" someone else called out. "We've missed you!"

Clay didn't like being on display, but what else could he do? He acknowledged each greeting with a quiet nod and continued on, trusting Star to transport him directly to the sheriff's office. When the horse stopped out front of a wood-frame building that looked vaguely familiar, Clay climbed down and tied his reins to the hitching post. "Good job," he whispered, giving Star a pat on the neck. Then he stepped up to the planked sidewalk, climbed the two wooden steps to the front door, and turned the knob.

Upon entering, he breathed in the familiar smell of his office. There was his desk, still as cluttered and dusty as the day he'd left it. He walked across the concrete floor, the grit grinding beneath his boots, and sat down in his old leather chair. As he pulled open one desk drawer after another, memories flooded his head at the sight of such mundane objects as worn-down pencils, tablets of paper, and keys to the holding cells. He jumped up and went to the adjoining room, but all three cells stood empty. With a sigh of relief, he closed the door behind him, then returned to his desk and spent the next few minutes rustling through a pile of papers. Then he tossed them back where he'd found them and stood to his feet again when a commotion in the street drew him to the window for a look. A large crowd of people had gathered just outside his office. It sure didn't take long for news to travel in this town. He sucked in a deep breath to brace himself.

The door blew open and struck the wall. Standing there were several townsfolk, all gaping at him, and his deputy Harmon Clark. The name came to him from nowhere.

"Sheriff Dalton?" Harmon extended a hand, albeit warily, as if he feared Clay might be a ghost. "We've sent out search parties and had another posse scheduled to leave at dawn. Walter's rounding up his people now and making final arrangements. We feared you might be dead, but we were determined not to give up hope quite yet. Am I ever glad to see you. Been trying to fill your shoes here, sir, and it ain't easy!"

Clay chuckled. "Well, I'm back now, so you can call off any further searches."

Harmon blinked. "But…where have you been?"

"It's a rather long story, I'm afraid."

"Are you all right?" asked Harmon. He put his hands on Clay's shoulders and held him at arm's length. "You seem a little different."

"Oh, I'm different, to be sure." He didn't think now was the time for sharing that he'd lost his memory, found God, or fallen in love with a pretty little Quaker girl.

In the next moment, a man Clay recognized as a local reporter pushed his way through the door, pen and paper in hand. "Sheriff Dalton? Why, it *is* you. My stars, I didn't know if I should believe the rumor or not, but here you are, in the flesh. I'd like to run an article in tomorrow's paper. Where've you been all this time? I know you had set out to find Joseph Wellesley's alleged murderer. What's become of him?"

"Whoa, George." Harmon raised both hands. "Sheriff Dalton just got into town. He's not ready for any interviews. If you want to write a short article confirming his return, then go to it. But you won't get any further details out of him until he's ready to talk. I'm sure he'll answer all your questions later. For now, have a little mercy on the man. He looks plain bushed, if you ask me. Now then, all of you, go on about your business."

"You'll speak to me first, though," George told Clay as Harmon calmly ushered him out. "Can I get your word on that?"

Clay nodded. "You've got my word. How's tomorrow morning?"

"I'll be at your office at eight."

Finally left alone, Clay and Harmon exchanged looks. "Okay, my friend," said Harmon, putting a hand on his shoulder and leading him to a chair. "Let's hear it."

Once they were both seated, Clay started at the beginning and told Harmon everything—except for the parts about the Albrights' work on the Underground Railroad, and his falling in love with Rebecca. Some things were best left untold, at least until he figured out how things stood with Julia.

"So, your memory—it's returned?" Harmon asked.

"Not entirely, I'm afraid."

"Do you think you'll be able to resume your duties as sheriff?"

It was a fair question, and one that Clay had barely taken time to think through. "I don't know, Harmon. Not sure what I'll tell George in that regard, either." He was still committed to upholding the law and enforcing justice, he just wasn't sure if he wanted to keep doing that in Ellicott City.

Just then, the door opened again, and there stood the slender silhouette of a woman.

Clay blinked twice before getting to his feet. "Julia?"

"Clay? Blessed saints, it *is* you! I didn't believe it when I heard it. Oh, Clay!" She ran over, her full skirt skimming the floor, and fell into his arms. He embraced her, waiting for a rush of affection to surge through him. Instead, all he could think about was how much he missed holding Rebecca.

Julia stood on tiptoe and kissed his cheek. "My goodness, it's wonderful to see you. I've been so worried. What on earth detained you? Surely, you found Horace Spencer. Where is he? Have you locked him up?" She started for the room of holding cells, but Harmon stepped in front of her. "Let me in there, Mr. Clark," she instructed him. "I mean to give that man a piece of my mind."

"He's not here," Clay muttered.

"What?" She whirled around and faced him. "Then you hanged him already. Mother will be so happy to hear—"

"I didn't hang him."

She stared at him blankly for a moment. Then her eyes narrowed. "Did you hand him over to a higher court?"

Clay sighed. "I didn't get my hands on him at all. He's undoubtedly in Canada. I'm sorry, Julia."

Her eyes glinted with indignation. "You mean, after all this time…? What on earth were you doing with yourself, Clay Dalton?"

He didn't detect so much as a hint of happiness in her face at seeing him safe.

Harmon cleared his throat. "I think I'll just step out of the office for a few minutes."

"Well, are you at least planning a trip to Canada?" she persisted, ignoring Harmon's declaration of his departure. "Someone has to find that disgusting animal and make him pay for what he did."

Clay shook his head. "Everyone knows that once a runaway crosses the border, it's virtually impossible to find him."

She scoffed, then gave him a quick up-and-down glance. "Well, at least tell me what you've been doing. Did you exhaust all your leads?"

"I was injured, Julia. A bullet wound in my neck, and a head injury that resulted in what's called a concussion of the brain…along with memory loss."

"You lost your memory? Oh, my stars in glory! And you said someone shot you?"

"Yes. Horace's brother, Amos."

"A mere child managed to shoot you? That was a little careless on your part, wouldn't you say?"

Leave it to Julia to blame him and his lack of skill. "I more or less thought of it as a result of my being in the wrong place at the wrong time. I didn't *allow* him to shoot me, Julia. I'd like to take it back and would if I could."

"Well, I should say. My mother and brothers will be extremely disappointed that you failed to apprehend my father's killer. We were so hopeful of bringing justice to that despicable beast."

He could have brought up the fact that several witnesses hadn't painted Horace Spencer as the cruel animal Julia portrayed him to be, or the fact that her father had had a reputation for treating his slaves unjustly. But there was no point in stirring up already troubled waters.

When he didn't reply, she gave her head a quick shake and placed her hands on his shoulders. "Well, never mind that for now. How are you? Have you recovered all your memory? Surely, you haven't forgotten that you and I are to be married this November."

Actually, he hadn't recalled the exact date, only that the wedding was scheduled for sometime this fall. But their nuptials were the last thing he wished to discuss at this moment. "I'm feeling quite fine, thank you."

"What a relief." She gave him an adoring smile and brushed his cheek with her fingertips. "Oh, Clay, I feared you might not come home to me. I know I shouldn't have doubted, but I admit I was starting to worry. Everybody was. Your deputies had started sending out search parties. Where did you say you'd been?"

"I...I don't think I said. I stayed with a kind Quaker family."

She wrinkled her nose if he'd just cussed. "Quakers? How on earth did that come about?"

He hauled in a hefty breath, trying to decide how many details to share. "I had tracked Horace Spencer to a farm settlement that was being used as a station along the Underground Railroad. In an effort to apprehend Spencer, I tried to use a young woman as a bargaining tool.

The plan backfired, and I was shot and injured. Then, to my amazement, the young woman's family took me in in and nursed me back to health. I owe a great deal to them for their care and compassion." He chose to keep the detail about Rebecca's involvement in his recuperation to himself.

Julia brushed something off his shoulder, then dropped both her hands to her sides. Everything about her was so put together, from the intricate floral hat atop her perfectly coiffed head of hair to her gingham bustle dress and right down to her pointy-toed leather ankle boots. It occurred to Clay that he much preferred Rebecca's simple attire.

"Well, I'm sure it was pure drudgery for you to live with such pious folk—and to think they participate in helping runaway slaves escape to freedom! It's against the law, you know. Couldn't you have done something to stop them? Here you were, trying to capture Horace Spencer, and they were undermining your efforts. It's positively shameful."

"First of all, these people were very gracious to me, considering they believed me to be a slave catcher. If they do break the law, it is out of a deep sense of conviction. They believe all men are created equal and that no one individual has the right to own another human being."

Julia snorted. "If I didn't know better, I'd say you sounded like a northerner, Clay Dalton. They didn't get into your head, now, did they?"

He swallowed, preparing himself for the spewing of words that was sure to follow his next statement. "Watching that family—so strong in their faith and loyal to one another—made me realize I was missing something in my life. I…I chose to give my heart over to God, Julia, and it's made a big difference."

She jerked her head back and stared at him with narrowed eyes. "Now I know you haven't fully recovered from that head injury. Do you realize how ridiculous you sound? You were gone just a few weeks, and suddenly you're a religious fanatic?"

Clay sighed. "I'm sorry you view it that way. It's not really about religion but rather about connecting with God in a personal way."

"Oh, pfff." She flicked her wrist. "I don't wish to hear any further religious banter, understood?" She put her hand on his chest. "Now then, I must be getting back to the house. I regret that I can't invite you over tonight. Mother is under the weather—she has been, ever since Father passed—and I should be the one who breaks the news to her of your failed mission. Perhaps tomorrow night you could take me to the traveling minstrel show that's in town this week."

"I—sure, I'll be happy to."

"Good. Come by at five thirty. We'll eat at Harper's Restaurant beforehand."

"That sounds fine."

She reached up and stroked his lapels. "You never did give me a proper reunion kiss." She closed her eyes and puckered up.

Clay hesitated, wondering why the sight of her plump lips put a sour taste in his mouth. He must have loved her at one point, but those feelings had fallen by the wayside. Could he manage to rekindle them? He leaned down and touched his mouth to hers.

27

Three days into her job at Morningstar Dining Room, Rebecca was feeling more at ease in her new role. Dorothy had hired her on the spot. Two of her waitresses had quit the same day, and she was desperate for help. As Rebecca cleared a table recently vacated by a family of five, she smiled at the sight of the plate of barely touched Atlantic cod and hash browns that had belonged to the littlest girl, who couldn't have been more than three—right between the ages of Chrystal and Henry. Oh, how Rebecca longed to wrap her arms around them and kiss their pudgy cheeks. She gave her head a little toss, as if to shake it free of such painful thoughts, and carried the stack of dishes to the sink. She was on her way back to the table to finish clearing it when a male voice said, "Excuse me, miss?"

She turned and locked eyes with the pleasant-looking man she'd waited on twenty minutes ago. He wore a black suit, and on the tabletop in front of him sat a folded newspaper and a fashionable hat. "How may I help you?" she asked as she approached him.

He smiled as he held out his mug. "I know you've already filled it once, but may I bother you for another cup of coffee?"

"Oh, certainly. I'll be right back." Suffering saints! So much for following Dorothy's instructions to anticipate the customers' needs.

Rebecca returned with the steaming pot and proceeded to fill his cup, aware of his eyes capturing her every move.

"You're a new hire, aren't you?" he asked.

"Yes. Do you come in here often?" She was working hard on using informal pronouns when addressing patrons.

"Only on occasion. But now that you're working here, you might see me several times a week." He winked.

She felt her face blush crimson at his flirtatious overture.

"Are you new to Chester, too?"

"Yes." She nodded. "I'm staying with some friends."

"Nice. And where might that be?"

She realized she'd already said too much. "I should be getting back to work."

"Of course. But first, may I be so bold as to ask if I might take you on a stroll through town some evening?"

She clutched at a button on her plain collared blouse. "Um, I'm sorry, sir, but I don't even know you."

"Oh, forgive me. Philip Harrington." He extended a hand. "I own Harrington Furniture and Upholstery, just a few blocks up the street. And you are?"

She hesitated a moment before putting her hand in his. "Rebecca Albright, sir. Pleased to meet you. But I'm afraid the introduction doesn't change the fact that I don't know you well enough to accept your invitation."

He tossed his head back with a chortle. "Fair enough, Miss Albright. Perhaps you will just have to get to know me over the course of my next several meals at the restaurant. Will you wait on me the next time I come in? I have nothing against Dorothy, mind you, but you are far prettier."

She frowned. "Excuse me, sir, but I'm of the Friends persuasion. I don't see why you would—"

"I'm very much taken by you, Rebecca. The second I laid eyes on your lovely face, I knew I had to introduce myself. You don't mind, do you? Must I be Quaker to find you attractive?"

She didn't care for his forward approach. "I'm sorry, but I really must be getting back to work. It was very nice meeting you, Mr. Harrington."

"Likewise, Miss Albright. I'll see you tomorrow, perhaps?"

Did he now plan to visit the restaurant every day? "Perhaps. Good day." She retreated, feeling his eyes following her.

In the kitchen, Dorothy sidled up to Rebecca. "I see you've caught the attention of Mr. Harrington."

"Do you know him?"

Dorothy snorted. "There're few who don't, in these parts. He's richer than buttermilk cake and the most eligible bachelor in town."

"I have no idea why he'd want to give me the time of day."

Dorothy laughed as she picked up two plates of food. "He enjoys a challenge. He probably took one look at your pretty face and knew you were innocent and untouched. He doesn't always play fair, though, so beware."

"Whatever do you mean?"

"Well, he's accustomed to having women fawn over him. Can't get enough of it. He's particular, though, and around the time a woman thinks he's about to propose, he drops her like a hot coal. I wish someone would teach him a lesson."

Rebecca gave a nervous chuckle. "Well, I shan't be the one to teach him any lesson, because I shan't give him a second of my time. He can consider me his 'challenge,' if he wishes, but I do not play games with men." It suddenly struck her that that was exactly what she'd done with poor Gerald Tuke—strung him along until the last second. She should have ended things right from the start and not sacrificed his feelings for the sake of pleasing her parents. Poor Gerald had been so hopeful that she would one day come to love him.

"Well, Philip Harrington is nothing if he's not persistent," Dorothy went on. "He'll do his best to charm you into going out with him, you'll see."

Rebecca turned around and took another peek at the man. He set down his coffee cup, then stood and angled her a cunning smile. She abruptly averted her gaze, mortified that he'd caught her. Would he now think she found him attractive? Nothing could have been further from the truth. If anything, she compared every aspect of him to Clay Dalton and knew with certainty that Philip Harrington didn't stand a hair's chance of ever winning her heart.

After her shift, she returned to a quiet house. She found a note from Charity on the kitchen table.

Becca,

> *Albert and I have gone for a stroll. Be back soon.*
>
> *A letter came for thee today. I set it on thy bed.*

Love,
Charity

The news of a letter filled her with excitement, and she found herself running up the stairs like a young girl. She burst through her bedroom door and picked up the envelope. The return address was her family's farm. Her eyes fell to Mother's handwriting, so elegant, refined, and precise, just like the woman who had penned it. Rebecca sat on the edge of her bed and stared at the letter momentarily, trying to prepare herself for what she might find inside. Then, with care, she unfolded the thin stationery and began to read.

My dear Rebecca,

> *Sunset Ridge is not the same without thy presence. I regret now that I was not forthright in telling thee that I did not wish to see thee go. Thy father and I were wrong in trying to force thee to enter into a loveless marriage, and we offer our sincere apologies. I hope thee will accept them and realize that we only wanted what we thought best for thee.*

Everyone else misses thee, especially Chrystal and Henry, the latter of whom asks every day when thee is coming home. It is difficult to tell him that thee has made a new life elsewhere. I do not wish to cause thee to feel any guilt, though, because I believe what thee did was for the best. Frances has moved into Lydia's room because Lydia did not wish to sleep alone. I think a part of her still wishes to be a little girl, and I cannot fault her for that. At times, I wish I could turn back the clock.

Lately, my thoughts have often turned to the twins. Their passing at only twenty-two months of age left me feeling completely helpless and out of control, and I suspect that is part of the reason why I sense the need to control those around me. The Lord has taught me much about myself in the days since thee left.

I also wanted to tell thee that Clay has left Sunset Ridge and returned home to Ellicott City, Maryland, where he serves as sheriff. Thy father discovered, in the course of a conversation during his preaching trip in Dover, some important details about Clay's life—including that his last name is Dalton. The Lord works in mysterious ways to answer our prayers! Perhaps one day, thee will hear more of the story from Clay himself, although it is not for me to give thee false hope. I fear I cannot say much more on the subject, as it doesn't seem to be my place. Forgive me if I leave thee with more questions than thee had before. Just know this, Rebecca, dear: Thy father and I do wish you nothing but sincere happiness. May God grant that to you in His own sweet time. Further, let me say this one additional thing: we consider Clay to be a fine and virtuous man whose presence at Sunset Ridge was a blessing on us all.

Chrystal has awakened from a nap and is crying, so I must conclude this letter, but I shall write to thee again soon.

Lovingly,
Mother

Rebecca swiped at her tears and refolded the letter, then lay it aside and stared across the room. *Clay Dalton…sheriff…Ellicott City……a fine and virtuous man.* What did it all mean? And how was she to expect to hear another word from Clay? Julia would never permit him to have contact with her, not that Rebecca wished to see him, anyway. What she and Clay had shared would be better left untouched, and she would do well to remind herself of that on a daily basis. "Lord, please help me to wipe Clay Dalton from my mind," she prayed. "I don't want to think improper thoughts about a man who likely has just reunited with his wife—or his fiancée." After uttering the prayer, she could not push aside the nagging feeling that something was amiss. Mother had made no mention of Julia and had even alluded to knowing something she didn't dare pass on, since it wasn't "her place."

Rebecca stood and walked to the bureau, stashing the letter in the top drawer, beneath her underthings. As she closed the drawer, she spied her reflection in the mirror above the bureau. She was a sight after a long day of work, and it didn't help that her eyes were red from crying. She dipped a dry cloth in the basin of wash water from that morning, wrung it out, and used it to dab at her face.

Downstairs, the door opened, and she could hear Albert and Charity chatting happily. Rebecca wished not to bother them with her presence just yet, so she sat in the rocker by the window and resumed reading Nathaniel Hawthorne's *Twice-Told Tales.* She'd found the book in the downstairs library yesterday, one of many titles that had been left there by the previous owners. She didn't know how long she'd been reading when she heard a loud bump and then a tumbling sound, followed by a scream. Rebecca dropped the book and jumped up, ran to the door, flung it open wide, and raced to the top of the staircase. At the bottom of the steps, Charity lay in a heap with one leg turned beneath her. She was moaning and clutching her stomach. "The baby!" she sobbed. "I've hurt the baby."

Seconds later, Albert knelt at her side. "Shh, we don't know that," he soothed her.

Rebecca rushed down the staircase and stopped just above the place where Charity lay. She couldn't speak, so startled and stunned was she by the fall her friend had taken.

"Thy leg—can thee stretch it out?" Albert asked his wife.

Wincing, Charity managed to pull her leg back into its proper position.

"Here, let's check thee for other injuries." Albert carefully lifted her arms and bent them at the elbows.

"I was just about halfway up the stairs when my heel got caught—ouch!" she screamed.

"Is this where it hurts?" Albert asked. "Right here on thy arm, where I'm bending it?"

"No, my arms are fine. It's my—my stomach. Here." She pressed the lower part of her abdomen, and that's when Rebecca spotted the pool of blood forming under Charity's body and spreading over the hardwood floor.

Rebecca jumped up and said calmly, so as not to show her alarm, "I'll go for the doctor. Where is his office?"

"Next street after Welsh," Albert said. "Turn left and go three blocks. It's there on the left. Hurry." His eyes teemed with fear.

Just before Rebecca closed the door behind her, Charity let out a screeching howl like nothing Rebecca had ever heard. She ran faster than ever before, and reached the doctor's office sweaty, exhausted, and breathless. She pounded on the door and then waited for what felt like an eternity until she heard the hurried approach of footsteps. The door opened, and a woman with disheveled brown hair smiled at Rebecca. "How may I help you?"

"My friend…she fell down a flight of stairs. She's expecting a baby, and…and before I left, I saw that she had started bleeding."

"Oh, dear. Where does she live?"

"In the old Crosby house on Potter Street."

"I know it well." The woman stepped back and called over her shoulder, "Herman! Come quick. Your services are needed."

A man hastened down the hall toward them. His white shirt was unbuttoned at the top, and he was dabbing hastily at his mustache with a napkin. "What's the problem?" he asked.

Rebecca quickly repeated what she had already relayed to his wife. Minutes later, Dr. Perkins was following Rebecca on foot to the Duncans' while his wife, Irma, hitched the horses to the wagon. She was to come to the house, in case they would need to transport Charity elsewhere for treatment. All the way back to the house, Rebecca did not cease praying that God would protect Charity and the baby, though her prayers were an unintelligible blur in her mind.

Shortly after ten o'clock that night, Charity lost her baby—a girl, according to the doctor. Charity wailed from pain, physical and emotional, and there didn't seem to be a thing anyone could do to console her. She wept uncontrollably for a full hour after the Perkinses had gone, then finally quieted for the first time, though her face remained a picture of anguish and despair.

Rebecca pulled a chair to the bedside and sat, taking one of Charity's hands in both of hers. "I'm so sorry," she whispered. "That's all I know to say right now."

Charity said nothing but only lay there, staring at the ceiling with bloodshot eyes. Every so often, she emitted a sob that wracked her body. At last, she turned toward Rebecca. "How could I have been so clumsy?" she asked between sniffles. "The heel of my shoe got caught on the step, and I grabbed the railing, but I didn't hold tight enough. I killed my baby, Becca. I killed her." The wailing resumed.

Rebecca bent over her friend and held her close, crying tears of her own that dripped off her cheeks onto Charity's shoulder. Out the corner of her eye, she caught a glimpse of Albert standing in the doorway. He nodded at her with a long face, then turned and left. He had to be just as devastated as Charity. They'd both wanted this baby so badly.

When the tears had slowed, Rebecca sat up, wiped her eyes, and cleared her throat. "I want thee to listen to me, Charity Ann Duncan. What happened tonight was an accident. Thee is not responsible, and I don't want to hear any words to the contrary coming out of thy mouth.

Yes, it will take time for the pain to subside, but there shall come a day when thee smiles again."

Charity shook her head. "I can't imagine smiling again. Not as long as I live."

Albert reentered the room at that moment. As soon as he sat on the edge of the bed, Charity's tears resumed. "I just can't believe what's happened, Albert. Why didn't God protect our baby?"

"There, now." He caressed her arm and cast a hasty, helpless glance at Rebecca. Then he took a deep breath and cleared his throat. "We must not blame God for what happened. Could God have prevented it? Of course, He could have. In fact, I don't think we can begin to count all the times throughout our lives when He has stepped in and saved us from tragedy and harm. He doesn't always divert us from hardship, though, and it is in those times that we must trust Him anyway, holding fast to His promise never to leave us or forsake us. Because He is faithful, we must be faithful in return, my love. Perhaps one day, thee will have an opportunity to minister to another woman reeling from the pain of a similar situation. Think what a comfort thee will be to her." He bent and kissed her cheek.

Rebecca rose. "I'll leave you two for now."

"Thank thee, Becca," Charity said, lifting her gaze. "I'm so glad thee is here."

"God knew she would need thy company," Albert added before returning his attention to Charity. "In a day or so, thy mother will be here, as well. I'll send word with one of my clients who's going to Philadelphia tomorrow. I'll give him money to either deliver the letter himself or hire a courier for me. One way or another, thy parents will receive word. If I know thy mother, she will be on the next train out of town."

That news produced a tiny smile from Charity.

Rebecca tiptoed out of the room. Her heart was broken for her friends, and she felt helpless to do anything but love them and pray that God's tender mercies would fall upon them.

Back in her bedroom, she collapsed across her bed, exhausted. While she lay there, more tears came—tears for Charity and Albert, yes, but tears also for herself, for the things she had lost. She missed Sunset Ridge and her precious family. Even more, she missed someone she could not have, and she wondered how she was ever going to get him off her mind and out of her heart.

28

While Clay's deputies were out tending to various duties, Clay took the opportunity to reread the letter he'd received from Edward Albright that morning. Edward had heard from Daniel Hallstead that, according to an unknown source, Horace Spencer and his brother had arrived, along with several other wayfarers, in an unpopulated area of Canada. Shortly thereafter, Amos Spencer had fallen ill and died. A sadness welled up in Clay for the boy who had shot him. The letter ended on a cheerier note, with Edward sharing that the family was well but the youngsters missed Clay. Edward made no mention of Rebecca's well-being or her whereabouts; but then, he wouldn't—not until such time as Clay inquired. For all Edward knew, Clay and Julia had found happiness once again.

Clay folded the missive and went back to sorting through the piles of papers on his desk. Just as Dr. Fleming had predicted, familiar surroundings had been the key to retrieving his memory, and it hadn't taken long for him to jump back into his duties as sheriff. Over the past several days, Clay had investigated several tavern brawls, resolved a dispute between two neighbors over a fence, arrested three men for the robbery of Frank's General Store, and probed into the explanations for a couple of house fires. He'd also thrown a few drunks in jail to give them time to sober up.

When he bent to pick up a pen that had fallen to the floor, his new sheriff's badge caught his eye, and he took a second to glance at it. Strange how he didn't have the same affinity for the job as before.

George Blackstone had printed an accurate account of Clay's absence in the local paper, but it didn't seem to be enough for the fine folks of Ellicott City. People were continually stopping Clay in the street, at the bank, or in restaurants to welcome him back and, usually, to ask how he'd spent his days with the Quaker family that had taken him in.

The only folks who didn't take an interest in his story were the Wellesley family. With his wedding only a few away, Clay had an important decision to make, and he figured tonight would be the determining factor as to whether his relationship failed or flourished. It was to be his first dinner with the entire Wellesley family present. As usual, Corinne Wellesley would situate herself at one end of the table. The captain's chair at the other end, previously filled by Joseph Wellesley, would sit noticeably empty. Clay dreaded the evening—dreaded greeting the long-faced, judgmental Corinne and her cheerless sons, Joseph Jr. and Richard, who were bound to treat him with anger because he had returned to Ellicott City empty-handed. Neither brother had set foot inside his office even once since his return, either to welcome him back or to question him. It didn't surprise him. He figured he knew their reasons. They needed time to prepare their barrage of questions and accusations, and they wanted everyone in the same place at the same time. Moreover, now that Clay had developed a true aversion to slavery, he dreaded having to dine on sumptuous fare served by house slaves who would never come close to tasting such delicacies.

Since his return to Ellicott City, he'd had very little time alone with Julia. He'd been busy catching up on his duties as sheriff, but, if he were honest, he'd also been deliberately avoiding her. They had gone out to dinner on a few occasions, but Julia had invited other couples he barely knew, and he'd found the conversations stilted and superficial. One night, when he'd driven her home, the hour was late, so he'd turned down her invitation to come in for a cup of tea and instead excused himself with a cursory good-night kiss. She'd pouted, but he'd been too tired to care. His feelings for her had diminished, and he found her company somewhat boring, if not grating. What had drawn him to her in the first place? Had he been so shallow as to appreciate her only for her beauty and wealth? If so, he didn't much care for his former self.

Later that evening, taking a hurried glance at his reflection in the mirror on his bedroom wall, he straightened his collar and pressed down a stray piece of hair that insisted on standing on end. After a few more tries, he gave up on it and went into the living room. His small house was cozy and suited him fine, but over the past several days, he'd come to realize it wasn't truly *home* to him—not in the way it once had been. There was no denying it: He missed Rebecca—missed her smile, missed the sound of her voice, missed her touch, and missed the feel of her in his arms. Without her, he wondered if he would ever truly feel at home again. The few kisses they'd shared had ruined him for Julia's. Saints and souls, even if he never kissed Rebecca again, he would still compare any future kisses to the ones he'd stolen from her.

He checked the clock on the bookcase. It was time to leave for Magnolia Hill Plantation. Before donning his hat, he paused to pray. "Lord, please grant me wisdom, courage, and strength for the evening ahead. May every word I utter be exactly what You would have me say. Give me discernment and insight, and help me to respond with honesty and sincerity to every question asked of me. If Joseph Jr. and Richard treat me with bitterness and disdain, help me to show them mercy and grace in return.

"And regarding my job as sheriff, Lord, I need Your wisdom. I need some kind of sign from You, something to indicate that my feelings for Rebecca aren't pure foolishness. Do You wish for me to remain here in Ellicott City and try to rekindle my love for Julia while also attempting to win her soul for You? Or should I resign from my job and go back to Sunset Ridge in hopes of finding Rebecca before she marries that Tuke character?" With a touch of anger at the mere thought of her marrying

Gerald Tuke, Clay plopped his hat on his head without so much as an amen.

Nothing about his prayer made him feel one hair wiser. If anything, he was more confused than ever. Leave his home and go after a woman he wasn't even sure would give him the time of day? Quit his job when he had no other means of income planned? What kind of fool was he, anyway? He was a fool in *love*, that's what he was! He shook his head, as if that would put a little sense into it, then headed out his front door and mounted Star, who'd been waiting patiently at the hitching post.

He rode through midtown on his way to Magnolia Hill as if he hadn't a care in the world, tipping his hat brim and waving at friendly passersby, all the while pushing down the knot of dread that had tied itself up in his gut. At the corner of Mills and Fredrick streets, he directed Star to the right and urged him into a trot.

"Sheriff!" someone called from behind him. "Sheriff Dalton! Hold up, there."

Clay pulled on the reins to slow Star's gait, then steered him to the side of the road and turned him around. It was his neighbor Earl Hand, a kindly middle-aged fellow with a wife and two grown children, both married and moved away. "Mr, Hand. How are you?"

"I'm fine, Sheriff, just fine. And you?"

"Couldn't be better," Clay replied in as light a tone as he could muster.

"I won't keep you, Sheriff. I know you must be on some errand or 'nother. I hope I didn't interrupt anything too important."

"No, not at all. What can I do for you?"

Earl shifted his weight from one foot to the other and used his palm to shield his eyes from the sun. "I got a question for you. I feel a little foolish, seein' as you just arrived back in town an' all, but…."

"Go ahead," Clay urged him. "I haven't a thing to hide. I assume you want to know how I wound up staying with that Quaker family in Philly."

"No, no, nothin' like that. I read the article in the paper, and Jean and me is just happy everything turned out well for you. My question is a bit unusual, so please don't hesitate to tell me right off if you ain't interested."

"Well, now you've got me curious, sir. Go ahead and ask whatever it is you want to."

"Like I said, I'll not keep you, but, well, Jean's ma, she's been real sick for a couple o' months now."

"I'm sorry to hear that."

"She's doin' much better, mind you, but the doctor says she'll be needin' extra care from now on. Jean's been travelin' by train to see her mother twice a week, and there's a kindly neighbor woman what looks in on her, but Twin Oaks is pretty far, an' Jean wants her to move up here. She refuses to come live with us, but…well, we was thinkin'…if we could find her a house real close to us, she'd still have her independence, and Jean would feel a whole lot better havin' her nearby."

Clay had an inkling of where this was going.

"So, I was wonderin'—that is, Jean and I was wonderin'—if you would ever consider sellin' your house. I already asked the Porters, the neighbors on our other side, and they aren't interested. You probably aren't, either—bein' as you just got back in town—and I know you're gettin' married real quick here. But anyway…."

"Well, Earl, you've posed an interesting question," Clay replied. "I'll have to pray about my decision before I can give you an answer. I hope you understand that."

Earl gawked at him. "Why, Sheriff! Jean an' me pray about every-thing, too. I didn't know you was a prayin' man."

"I wasn't always, but I am now."

"Well, I'll be. That's good news, Sheriff. Not to put any pressure on you, but Jean and me felt the nudge to ask you if you'd consider sellin'—even though it felt a little inappropriate to be askin' at this particular juncture in your life."

"No apology necessary," Clay assured him. "Like I said, I'll pray about it and get back to you as soon as I can."

"I'm much obliged, Sheriff. You have a pleasant evening, now."

"Thanks, Earl. Please tell Jean I wish the best for her mother."

They tipped their hats at each other before Clay urged Star into a trot and headed off again. He couldn't get the grin off his face. When the Lord had a plan in mind, He certainly didn't waste any time in setting it into motion.

The evening at the Wellesleys' did not start out well, with Richard refusing to shake Clay's hand. Clay had quickly retracted his arm, but there was no fixing the awkwardness of the moment. Joseph Jr. did shake his hand, but his face lacked any trace of genuine warmth. Their children—Julia's nieces and nephews—all hung back, which made Clay wonder if their parents hadn't warned them to beware of the man who'd failed to bring their grandfather's killer to justice. Julia's sisters-in-law were only slightly friendlier, yet they maintained a cool demeanor overall. Then, there was Corinne Wellesley, who barely acknowledged his arrival; she merely nodded at him when he came through the door, then suggested that he and Julia go sit in the parlor until Merlene summoned them to the dining room. He followed Julia into the small but stately room, lowered himself onto the sofa near the tall brick fireplace, and studied the pattern of the thick Turkish rug that covered a vast majority of the room's shiny wood floors. He resisted the urge to prop his scuffed boots on the ornate wooden coffee table in front of him. Something told him Julia would never stand for that.

"Well, that went well," he said with sarcasm.

Seated beside him, Julia snuggled up close, and he had a strong urge to go plant himself in one of the two matching chairs facing the sofa. "Don't worry yourself over my brothers and mother," she cooed. "It won't be long before they accept you as one of the family. They are simply still miffed that you didn't find Horace Spencer."

"Oh, I found him, all right. I just wasn't able to apprehend him." No way would he divulge what he'd learned in Edward's letter.

"Yes, you've told me that." She looked at her perfectly manicured fingernails for a few seconds, then quickly lifted her head and gave him a gushing smile. "Our wedding is seventy-one days away. Can you believe it? I counted this morning. Did I tell you I bought my dress long before Father's passing? Mother actually noticed it first and pointed it out to me. It cost her and Father a pretty penny, but that's neither here nor there. I just know you will love it on me. Oh, how I wish Father could've walked me down the aisle. I suppose Joseph Jr. will have to suffice. I could have asked Uncle Arthur—that's Father's brother—but Mother insisted that it would be more appropriate for Joseph to escort me."

All this wedding talk gave Clay a headache, particularly since she wasn't giving him a chance to put in a single word.

"November weather can be unpredictable. I certainly hope we don't get a sudden snowstorm. It's not out of the realm of possibilities, you know. Wouldn't that be awful? But why am I worrying over something I can't control?" At last, she took a breath. "Well"—she straightened a tiny wrinkle in her satin skirt—"aren't you going to say anything?"

He might have laughed at the irony of her question if he'd been in the mood. Instead, he rose and approached the mantel over the fireplace for a closer look at the painting that hung above it—a colorful rendering of the acres and acres that made up Magnolia Hill Plantation, the sun casting its glowing rays through puffy white clouds over the autumn-hued fields of tobacco plants.

"Father commissioned John Redding, a local artist, to do that painting several years ago."

"I see."

She sidled up next to him, her shoulder touching his upper arm. "Are you all right, Clay? You haven't said much."

"I'm afraid I'm a little fatigued, but I'll be fine."

She smiled. "Oh, good." Any concern she'd had for him disappeared, as she looped her hand through his arm again then went up on tiptoe and unexpectedly kissed his cheek.

He felt guilty for failing to return the gesture, but he simply could not muster the necessary feelings.

"You're looking dapper tonight. Did I tell you that?"

"Thank you."

"Do you like my new dress?" She let go of him and did two twirls on the floor, making her full-length purple gown flare from the waist down.

"I do. I meant to tell you how beautiful you look."

She pouted. "Then why didn't you?"

"I—I have no excuse."

"Other than 'fatigue,' I suppose."

He felt like an insensitive brute. He opened his mouth to apologize, but before he could say anything, a Negro woman entered the room and cleared her throat softly. She wore a plain white gown with a crisp-looking apron and a white ruffle-brimmed cap that tied under her chin.

"Excuse me, sir, miss…dinner is served." She gave a quick curtsy, granting Clay the tiniest glance, and it was then that he remembered her from prior visits to Magnolia Hill Plantation. Before, he'd barely taken note of her, but now he observed the bags beneath her chocolate eyes, the slight bend of her spine—perhaps the result of spending countless hours scrubbing floors or lifting objects too heavy for her frame—and the irregularity of her spindly shoulders, with the left side lower than the right, possibly from carrying weighty woven baskets full of supplies.

"Thank you, Merlene," he said. "We'll be along shortly."

The woman's brown eyes rounded with surprise, and she gave another curtsy before turning around and retreating hastily to the kitchen.

Clay looked at Julia, bewildered. "What did I say?"

She issued him a scolding glare. "You are not to thank house slaves for doing what's expected of them. I thought you knew that."

"I was just extending common courtesy."

"Courtesy? With slaves." She scoffed. "They will start taking advantage of us if we treat them with anything more than firmness and authority."

"But slaves are people, too, created by God. Don't you think God loves them?"

Julia's head jerked back, and her brow crimped. "I have no idea. I suppose He does, in His own way."

At last, a good laugh came out of Clay, but it was not the jovial kind. "In His own way? He loves all of us equally, Julia." Then he softened his tone. "He loves Merlene just as much as He loves you."

Now she was scowling. "How dare you compare me to a slave. They are not at all like us, Clay. I hope you haven't forgotten that important tidbit." She shook her head. "You are not the man you once were. I sometimes wonder if you haven't gone a little muzzy in the brain since losing your memory. All this talk about religion, and now your notion that Negroes deserve the same treatment as white folks...why, it's pure foolishness."

His mouth took on a bad taste, and something told him right then that prolonging the evening visit would serve no purpose whatsoever. Julia's brothers detested him, her mother despised him, and Julia herself had no desire to accept the truth about God's unconditional love and forgiveness. She considered herself in a class all her own, and he couldn't imagine why she'd ever wanted to marry the likes of him.

"I think I'd better go, Julia."

"What?" she screeched. "You can't leave. How would that look to Mother and the rest of the family?"

"I'm sure it won't earn me any popularity points. I'm sorry, Julia, but I think you probably realize that things are just not going to work out for us."

"What do you mean? You're jilting me?"

He bit on his lower lip and wrinkled his brow, then shifted his weight from one foot to the other. "I'm truly sorry. I didn't mean for things to end quite this way. I'll go apologize to everyone before I head out."

"No!" She snagged his arm. "You will not humiliate me in front of my family. If you are breaking our betrothal, the least you can do is leave quietly."

"But...shouldn't I at least say good-bye?" He started to walk toward the dining room.

She stopped him with a strong tug on the arm, then turned him in the other direction. "I always knew you weren't meant for me," she said as she ushered him toward the door. "Father always insisted you would continue to rise through the ranks to become mayor, or perhaps a U.S. Marshal...at least, he intended to push you in that direction. He said you had the determination and the skills, and all you needed was the proper guidance."

"Is that right?" Clay took his hat from the coat tree next to the door. "Well, I'm flattered by the confidence he had in me, but I really have no desire to become any of those things. And if that is why you wished to marry me, then our marriage would not have been a happy one, not to mention neither one of us is what you'd call 'hopelessly in love' with the other. Do you realize how very little excitement you showed over my return to Ellicott City?"

She craned her head and looked him in the eye. "Well, I was indeed glad you hadn't died—as the rumors went."

"That's reassuring." He gave her a small grin. "I'm sorry, Julia. We both gave it a good try."

She gave him her usual pout. "I suppose you're going back to that Quaker family. Perhaps you'll even join the religion."

He brushed a hand through his hair. "I don't know. I'm praying about what to do next."

She groaned. "There you go again with your religious nonsense."

A twinge of sadness pinched his heart. He wished he'd been more forthright with her about his newfound faith, but he still considered himself to be a baby Christian and wasn't yet confident in his ability to persuade anyone else to accept salvation.

"What are you going to tell your family when they ask why I left?"

She looked at him sharply. "That you were heartbroken because I broke off our engagement."

He chuckled. "I can't object to that."

She gave a sad smile as they walked to the door, where a Negro man stood at the ready, his hand on the knob. "Good-bye, Clay. Whether you know it or not, I do wish the best for you."

Clay lifted her hand and planted a feather-light kiss on the back of it. "And I for you, Julia."

Then he set his hat on his head, walked outside, and mounted Star. He rode off without looking back.

29

There was little Rebecca could do to lessen Charity's sadness or to relieve the pain of the sprained ankle and swollen knee she had sustained in the fall. But she could at least cook and clean and try to distract her friend with stories about her work at the restaurant, telling of the people she'd met and the little mishaps that were a trifle humorous.

Charity's mother had been a godsend during her several days' visit, preparing meals, baking more cookies and pies than the four of them could consume, and tending to her daughter's needs as only a mother knew how. The morning she left, they missed her immediately. Thankfully, Rebecca didn't have to work that day, and the restaurant was closed the following, so she would be on hand to care for Charity in the next forty-eight hours.

Charity's mother had brought an unfinished quilt for Charity to work on, and Charity was stitching a square right now as she reclined on the parlor chair by an open window, both legs propped on a footstool. A gentle breeze ruffled the curtains.

"That quilt's going to be just beautiful when it's finished," Rebecca said as she took a dust cloth to the bookshelf beside the massive fireplace.

Charity paused to admire her handiwork. "Mama promised to come back when it was time to sew the pieces together." Then Rebecca heard her friend exhale a wistful sigh, and she followed her gaze out the open window to a woman pushing a baby carriage along the sidewalk. "I know in my heart I'll conceive again, Becca," she said as she resumed her stitching. "When the doctor examined me yesterday, he said he saw nothing to indicate I'd have any trouble, although he did suggest we wait a while to ensure I have time to fully heal."

Rebecca tossed the dust cloth aside and sat in the chair next to Charity. "I'm certain thee will have a houseful of little ones. In fact, I can almost hear the hallways ringing now with their squeals of laughter."

"Indeed." Charity smiled. "I'm beyond thankful thee came to stay with us, Becca. I can't say I've been much of an encouragement to thee, though."

"Oh, Charity. Just being with thee has been a balm for my soul."

Charity paused in her stitching. "Our lives are a lot like this quilt."

"How does thee mean?"

"God is designing us, piece by piece, like so many quilts. In the moment, it's difficult to envision what we'll look like in the end, but He sees the finished product, and it is our place to trust Him to put us together as He sees fit. I imagine Him saying something like, 'This piece will fit very nicely right here. It will serve to make My precious creation stronger, and so I shall stitch it in to build her character.' I lost my baby, Becca, yet I am determined not to blame God but rather to trust Him. I still despair over what happened, but I will not lose my faith over it, because I believe what the Bible says in Romans—that God works everything together for our good if we love the Lord and are called according to His purpose."

Tears formed in Rebecca's eyes at her friend's summation of a verse she'd long held dear.

"I know thee has questioned what God has in store for thee," Charity went on. "Thee fell in love with a man thee could not have. Instead of despairing, thee must learn to trust God's seamless plan. Thy own quilt will one day be just as God wants it to be, if thee allows Him to do the designing."

Rebecca swiped at a tear. "How did thee acquire such wisdom?"

Charity released a soft giggle and shook her head. "Clearly, I do not see myself from thy vantage point."

A moment of comfortable silence passed before Charity spoke again. "There's another reason I'm working on this quilt. The pattern is one that runaways are accustomed to seeing along the route. When it's finished, I shall hang it on the front porch as a sign that our home is a safe haven."

Rebecca sat straighter. "Is the plan coming together, then?"

"It certainly is. Albert has made contact with Ernest Walters, the Friend who will be joining us in our efforts, and Ernest introduced Albert to two other Friends from the local Society who are anxious to get our station under way. All of them attended the American Anti-Slavery Society meeting last night and gained much insight as to how to move forward in their efforts."

"When does thee expect the station to start operating?"

"Much sooner than we originally thought. Perhaps as early as a few weeks from now. But there remains much to do. Albert and Ernest plan to wall off half of the root cellar to create a space where we may house runaways overnight."

Rebecca's chest welled with hope at the exciting prospect.

There was a knock on the door, catching them both unawares.

"Who could that be?" Charity asked.

"I'll go find out." Rebecca hurried to the door and opened it. On the other side stood Philip Harrington. The insufferable man! Rebecca sucked in a breath. "Well, hello, Mr. Harrington. What brings thee here?" But she should have known better than to ask. On his daily visits to the restaurant, he had been hounding her to tell him where she lived, and so, before leaving work yesterday, she'd finally told him. Now she could have kicked herself for giving in. She hadn't expected him to come to the door uninvited.

He issued her his signature bright-toothed smile, then quickly removed his hat and bowed slightly. "I have come to inquire as to whether you would like to accompany me on a walk through town. Surely, by now, you can see I'm quite harmless."

She forced a lighthearted laugh. "I can see nothing of the kind."

A train announced its arrival with a piercing whistle. Rebecca poked her head out the door and peered up at the pure blue sky. The setting sun still lent the perfect amount of warmth to the afternoon. She supposed a walk would be nice, but did she dare go with Philip after hearing all the things Dorothy had said about him? She certainly didn't wish to be added to his list of prospective conquests to bait and then cast aside.

Hearing Charity's footsteps behind her, Rebecca turned around. Her friend still walked with a limp, but it had improved from several days ago. Charity smiled at Philip. "Hello, there."

"Charity, meet Mr. Philip Harrington. He's a frequent patron at the restaurant."

"How do you do?" She extended her hand, and he shook it, flashing her an enchanting smile.

"My goodness, two beautiful ladies under one roof," he gushed. "I don't know if I can bear it."

Charity withdrew her hand and gave a nervous giggle. Stars in glory, he'd managed to charm Rebecca's married friend!

"I'm trying to entice your lovely boarder to accompany me on a walk through town."

"Actually, I—believe I'm needed—here." Rebecca silently implored Charity to back her up.

"Nonsense," Charity said. "You two go along."

"But...but I really should stay here." Rebecca raised her eyebrows and shot Charity a piercing stare.

"Whatever for? I'm fine." Then Charity turned to Philip. "I took a fall several days ago, and Becca seems to think I need round-the-clock care."

"I'm sorry to hear about your fall," Philip said. "I trust you're doing better."

"Much better, thank you. A walk would do Becca much good." With both hands, Charity pushed her out the door. "You two have a lovely time. No need to hurry back."

Of all things, Charity was playing the Cupid card. Rebecca would have to set her straight as soon as she returned.

She looked up at Philip with a fleeting smile. "Well, then."

He held out his arm. "Shall we?"

She succumbed, and the two set off toward the center of town.

⌒

"All aboard!" The train had idled at the Chester station for fifteen minutes when the conductor finally called out in singsong to the passengers loitering on the platform, bidding loved ones good-bye as they gathered their luggage and made for the cars. Clay was anxious to reach his destination. Over the past few days, he'd done a lot of soul searching, Scripture reading, and praying—and, consequently, little sleeping. In the end, he'd gone with the choice that seemed the most logical, for it was what he sensed God telling him to do: He would go to Sunset Ridge and try to reason with Edward, explaining his need to find Rebecca. If all went well, and assuming she wasn't still betrothed to Gerald Tuke, he would go after her in hopes of convincing her of his love. He wanted to marry her, but so much hung in the balance. Would she ever agree to marry a man who carried a weapon, considering her Quaker belief system?

"Lord," he whispered against the window, "please help me to place my future, my concerns, and my hope in You. If You have a plan to bring Rebecca and me together, please reveal it to me so that I might follow Your lead. Nevertheless, Lord, not my will but Yours be done."

He couldn't count how many similar prayers he'd uttered since ending his relationship with Julia several days ago. To his great relief, he hadn't heard a word from her or any of her family members. He'd half expected her brothers to show up with the intent of chewing him out. But then, they were probably just as happy to see him gone. Besides, she was to have reported that breaking off the engagement had been her doing.

He'd written a letter to his mother and sisters to tell them he'd ended his relationship with Julia. He knew they wouldn't shed any tears over the news. Upon first meeting Julia, during a visit to Ellicott City last February, Clay's older sister had taken him aside and expressed her concern over Julia's character. At the time, he'd thought her remarks rude, but now he saw the truth behind them, and even admitted as much in his letter. Something told him his sisters would love Rebecca. But there he went again, getting ahead of himself in his dreams about the future.

The giant locomotive huffed to life, hurtling great puffs of smoke into the sky, and its whistle gave another earsplitting blow. Clay didn't flinch but remained lost in reflection, his head still pressed against the window. When someone sat down next to him, Clay turned with a cursory nod to the larger gentleman before returning his gaze to the window. As the train car vibrated with its initial chug-chug-chug movement along the tracks, Clay's eyes locked on a familiar sight. He pushed his nose flat against the glass and squinted with all his might to make sure his eyes weren't tricking him. Could that really be Rebecca, walking arm in arm with a man? Clay peered harder and quirked his brow, his mouth agape. That wasn't Gerald Tuke, or any Quaker man, for that matter. No, this finely attired fellow walked tall and proud with an air of superiority. Had she already met someone else and given him her heart? Desperation drove Clay to his feet. Without so much as a "Pardon me," he dived over the man seated next to him and landed in the aisle, then raced into the next car, and then the next, until he finally intercepted the conductor. The man was making his way down the aisle, collecting tickets from the passengers.

When the conductor spotted Clay, he straightened his frame and put on a stern face. "What do you think you're—"

"Stop the train!"

"What?" The man's chest puffed out in a show of authority, his face going red.

"I need the engineer to stop this train so I can get off."

"And I need to ask you to quit making a disturbance and return to your seat this minute. The train is in motion, and the next stop is Philadelphia."

"No, the next stop is *now*. I demand you tell the engineer to stop."

The conductor scoffed. "By what authority?"

"Go on and sit down, mister," one of the passengers grumbled.

A couple of hefty male passengers even stood to their feet, evidently ready to provide assistance to the conductor.

"By *this* authority," Clay said, reaching inside his jacket for his sheriff's badge and sticking the silver star under the conductor's nose.

Someone gasped. "That's Sheriff Dalton!"

The conductor's eyes went as round as two glistening moons, and the man took a step back. In drawing back the front flap of his jacket, Clay had exposed his holstered gun in all its shining glory. He pivoted to let the would-be vigilantes see it, as well, then watched as they sheepishly sat back down. A hush fell as everyone looked at the conductor.

He cleared his throat. "Follow me, Sheriff. I'll escort you to the engineer's car."

Clay released a heavy breath, his heart pounding as loud and hard in his ears as the locomotive's sputter and cough. He gave the gawking onlookers an apologetic tip of his hat, then nodded at the conductor. "Lead the way."

30

As Rebecca walked with Philip, her companion proved polite, attentive, and even engaging, asking questions that kept her talking. He seemed to take an interest in her Quaker heritage, even saying he would be honored to accompany her to Meeting once she had settled upon where she would attend. Rebecca couldn't imagine wishing to attend anyplace other than where Charity and Albert settled. To date, Albert had visited two meeting houses and wanted to try one more before making a decision, but it sounded as if he were leaning toward the Society to which Ernest Walters belonged.

Philip was, of course, more than eager to offer many details about himself. He had four siblings, all married and living in New York State, and his parents had been deceased for some time. He'd invested a portion of the inheritance he received after his father's passing in a furniture business, in which he partnered with his father's brother. After the death of Philip's uncle, Philip had taken over the business, and, with the help of two additional business partners, the store had thrived enough to open two additional stores, in Baltimore, Maryland, and Alexandria, Virginia. He'd never married, he said, though he'd come close a time or two. That admission came as no surprise to Rebecca, considering what Dorothy had told her, but it did surprise her that he'd admitted it.

The train whistle sounded again, accompanied by the squeal and hiss of brakes.

"I wonder why the train's stopping so suddenly," Philip said, nodding toward the locomotive pulling several passenger cars. "Perhaps there's some problem."

"I should hope not," Rebecca said.

"Shall we turn around?" Philip asked. "It's awfully loud." They had walked south on Potter Street till they came to Fourth, then followed that street east over the bridge at Ridley Creek. Along the way, they had stopped at a tiny bakery where Philip purchased two sugary pastries, which they now nibbled as they walked, still arm in arm.

"Yes, that's a good idea. I should be going back, anyway. Charity may need me."

"She's very dear to you, I see."

"We've been best friends since childhood."

"It must be wonderful having a close friend. Perhaps you could help me with that." She caught the flirtatious tone in his voice, even detected his smile when he leaned closer, his warm breath tickling her cheek.

Not wanting to appear oversensitive, she didn't acknowledge the statement. Neither did she remove her hand from his arm but only directed her gaze straight ahead, wishing she could quicken their pace and reach the Duncans' home in the span of a wink. Somehow, she had to find a polite way to inform this man that she had no intention of falling captive to his charms. She might be the exception to the rule, but nothing about him drew her in, and she would make that clear before he left her at the doorstep.

No man but one had the power to capture her heart. That man was out of her reach, however; and someday, somehow, she would learn to forget him.

Where had Rebecca gone? Clay searched the street where he'd seen Rebecca walking arm in arm with that natty-looking man, but to no avail. In his estimation, a full ten minutes had passed between the time he'd spotted her and when the engineer finally brought the locomotive to a stop. At that point, he had disembarked, then run as fast as his legs would carry him to the very place he'd spied her. Now he stopped and bent over to catch his breath, but only briefly. He did not wish to linger more than a second or two. Nor did he want to go too fast and bypass her on a side street. His guess was that she and her companion were still keeping a casual pace. The thought of her strolling with another man made Clay all the more eager to find her.

He came upon a woman standing in front of a store window, gazing at the goods on display. "Did you happen to see a handsome-looking couple pass by here a few minutes ago?" he asked her.

The woman turned to him with a look of surprise, then gave a slow shake of her head, causing the feathers on her hat to sway back and forth.

"The woman was dressed in plain Quaker garb," Clay added, "and the man wore a dark suit."

She shook her head again. "No, sorry."

"Thanks."

He walked on, peering into window after window, in case the two had entered one of the local businesses. The more time that passed, the more he worried he wouldn't find her. If all else failed, he would return to the train station, buy another ticket for Philadelphia, and continue his original plan to beseech Edward for details regarding her address and situation.

He chided himself for acting on impulse in stopping the train rather than seeking God's direction. All told, there hadn't been much chance to stop and pray about it; and hadn't he already asked God to lead him? Discerning the will of God was no easy matter. With a silent prayer for a calm spirit and for wisdom, he proceeded down the planked side-walk, his eyes on alert. He started questioning everyone he passed, but it seemed no one else had spotted the couple. After he crossed a bridge, he began thinking they must have turned down a side street, and his hopes of finding them began to crumble. Should he return to the train station and purchase a ticket for the next train to Philadelphia? His stomach grumbled with hunger, but he would forgo nourishment until he had exhausted every possible avenue that might lead to Rebecca.

On a whim, he turned down a side street named Caldwell and walked only a block before reaching another intersection that was busy with horse-and-buggy traffic. A sign told him he'd reached Seventh Street, and so, on another hunch, he turned left and continued for several blocks, having no intuitive feeling whatsoever but aimlessly tramping, his eyes roving in every direction, impelled by a deep inner desperation to keep going. After a time, he came upon a bench in front of a store and sat, refusing to acknowledge the sense of defeat that seemed determined to settle in his chest. "God, what am I doing?" he whispered, his hands clasped between his knees, his head hanging as he stared at the wooden walkway beneath his tired feet.

When he lifted his head, his gaze fell upon a brick building across the street. The placard over the front door read "Delaware County Sheriff."

"That's interesting," Clay murmured. Then, with little forethought, he rose from the bench, checked both ways before crossing the street, and proceeded through the door of the building. Inside, he saw that the room was set up much the way his office in Ellicott City was, although this one was smaller and housed only two cells, one of which was occupied by a man curled up on a cot.

"Help you?" a male voice asked.

Clay removed his hat and turned to the fellow in uniform seated behind a desk. "Maybe."

The fellow pointed at the empty chair on the other side of his desk. "Have a seat, if you want. Sheriff's out at the moment. You got some complaint to file?"

"No complaint, no." Clay shook hands with the man before dropping into the seat. "Let me introduce myself. Clay Dalton, from Ellicott City."

The man gawked at him. "Clay Dalton? As in, *Sheriff* Clay Dalton? That was some article in the *Sun*. You can't still be on the hunt for that runaway slave."

Clay cringed. He hadn't intended to draw attention to himself. He wanted to find Rebecca, not discuss his botched attempt to apprehend Horace Spencer. "The hunt's off. Horace Spencer's long gone. Right now, I'm searching for Rebecca Albright. She's a member of the Quaker family that took me in after I was injured, and I saw her out the window of the train as it was pulling into the station. I jumped off, hoping to catch up to her, but she disappeared on me."

The fellow grinned. "Sort of like Horace Spencer, eh?"

His teasing did not sit well with Clay, who stood. "I thank you for your time, sir. I don't think I caught your name."

"Lyle Mercer." The man extended his hand for a shake. "Sorry I couldn't help you more." He creased his brow and tilted his head. "Now it's my turn to ask you a question."

"Sure."

"You wouldn't be lookin' for a job, would you?"

Clay raised his eyebrows. "What sort of a job?"

"Well, I know it's a long shot, with you bein' an established sheriff an' all, but we're real shorthanded right now. One of our best deputies just took another job outta state. It's a known fact you climbed the ranks from a pretty young age, an' as Sheriff Hansen gets ready to retire, he's eager to start groomin' a replacement. You'd start out low on the totem pole, o' course, and have to work your way up. But you're young and could pull it off."

Clay's interest was piqued, but he tried to hold his excitement at bay. "Isn't there anyone else in the force who'd want to step into this particular position? You, for instance?"

Mercer tossed his head back with a chortle. "See all this white hair on my head? Let's just say that when Sheriff Hansen retires, I'll be on his heels. He and I been together for nigh on thirty years. It's time for some new blood in here, and the folks of Chester won't argue that fact none. No one faults you for gettin' shot and failin' to bring back that fugitive. Folks 'round these parts were just glad to hear you made your way home in one piece."

"Well, I appreciate that."

"You come back in here later—if you got time, that is—an' talk to Sheriff Hansen. I can guarantee he'll want to meet you."

"You can, huh?"

"Sure, and you want to know another reason why?"

Clay scratched the back of his neck. "I'd be curious."

"He knew Joseph Wellesley."

Clay blinked twice. "And how's that?"

"Hansen grew up in Ellicott City on a farm real close to Joseph Wellesley's place. Wellesley's old man shot Hansen's pa in a fight over property lines. 'Course, the Wellesleys were rich way back then, and we all know money talks. Wellesley's old man paid off the prosecutin' attorney an' walked free the rest o' his days. Meanwhile, his son— Joseph—inherited his old man's mean streak. Sheriff Hansen's told me all kinds o' stuff he witnessed him doin' as a kid—killin' animals real slow-like, shootin' them in the legs or stranglin' the life outta them. And in the years before Hansen moved here, he heard plenty o' reports about Joseph mistreatin' his slaves, abusin' them like animals. Let's just say Hansen didn't mourn long when he got word that one o' Joseph's slaves had shot him."

Clay's mind reeled at the coincidence. "Interesting story. Sometimes it does seem like the world's a lot smaller than we think." No way would he admit to having been engaged to Joseph Wellesley's daughter. "Well, I'd better head back to the train station, but I'll try to get back here and introduce myself to Sheriff Hansen at some point."

The deputy gave a crooked grin. "Like I said, he'll be pleased to meet you. Because of his connection to Wellesley, he followed your case closely."

Clay set his hat back on his head. "I'll be on my way, then. Thanks for your time, Mr. Mercer. I hope to see you again soon. Real soon."

31

By the time Rebecca and Philip reached the front steps of the Duncans' house, Rebecca was tuckered out. "Thank thee for the walk." She clasped the doorknob and started to turn it.

Philip covered her hand with his. "I thoroughly enjoyed our time together. May I come by again and take you to dinner on, say, Monday night? I realize you work in a restaurant, but the one where I'd like to take you is far more elegant. I will escort you in my brougham."

"Thee is a very nice man, Philip, but—"

"It would just be dinner, nothing more," he inserted.

She swallowed once, then twice. "I appreciate thy effort to make me feel welcome in Chester, but I'm afraid I'm not quite ready to begin courting."

His face dropped. "Not even me?" He wore an expression of utter disbelief. Had no woman ever denied him? "Have I said something you found offensive?"

"No, no, nothing like that. I just—well, I'm frankly...."

"A little shy around me?" he asked, tilting his head at her in a teasing manner.

"No, not that."

"Then you must be a bit awed that I would pay you so much attention." He lifted her chin with his index finger and smiled. "Is it so difficult for you to believe that a man such as myself would be attracted to you, a pure and simple Quaker woman? Perhaps you aren't accustomed to hearing men tell you how beautiful you are."

Awed by his attention? Men such as he? A simple Quaker woman? With each phrase, her ire grew. "I'm sure thee must find it quite impossible to believe a woman *such as myself* would not find thee appealing, Philip, but...."

"I see. It is because you are a Quaker. You cannot allow yourself the temptation." He shrugged. "I suppose I can understand that. Let me assure you that I am a patient pursuer."

"Philip." She laid one hand on his arm. "I am not interested in a courtship with thee. Ever. I have no quarrel with thee, but it is plain we share nothing in common, so I shall not accompany thee on any future outings. Thank thee for thy interest. It has been most flattering to discover that someone 'such as you' would be interested in someone 'such as me.'"

His jaw dropped for a moment. "Well. That does come as a surprise—that you would decline the opportunity to see me again. I could show you a good time."

"I'm sure thee would try, anyway."

He opened his mouth as if to speak, but nothing came out.

She almost felt sorry for him. "Good afternoon, Philip."

He sniffed. "You weren't my type, anyway."

To his obvious dismay, she giggled. "As I've already said, we have nothing in common."

He presented her with a half grin. "Good day, then." He turned and headed down the walk.

"I hope we can at least be friends," she called after him.

He paused and looked over his shoulder, his tiny smile still in place. "I'll see you at the Morningstar. Dorothy's bacon and eggs are too good to pass up."

⌒

Clay headed back up Seventh Street, fascinated by all that had transpired in the Chester sheriff's office. Whether it meant anything, he couldn't be sure, but Sheriff Hansen's deputy had certainly given him plenty of things to chew on. Was it possible that the Lord had directed him straight to the sheriff's office with the express purpose of opening a door for future employment in Chester?

His mind reeled with various thoughts, and then the doubts began to creep in. Perchance the Quaker woman he'd seen on the street wasn't Rebecca at all, but merely someone who closely resembled her. And if that were the case, why had he felt almost duty-bound to enter the sheriff's office? *Lord, how am I supposed to recognize the difference between Your voice and my own mixed-up mind?*

"My sheep hear my voice, and I know them, and they follow me." He'd read the verse a few days ago and committed it to memory, and now he knew why: It had spoken to him for a specific reason. If he were truly God's child, which he surely was, he would recognize God's voice. God, through His Holy Spirit, communed with him daily, even moment by moment, and it was his duty to listen and obey.

With fresh confidence, Clay raised his head, straightened his shoulders, and quickened his steps as he headed back to the train station. If God wanted him on that train to Philly, He would make it happen. If He didn't, He would slam the door shut.

As Clay made his way through town, past various stores and businesses, his stomach growled, reminding him of his long-ignored hunger. He decided to stop at the next restaurant he came across. Hopefully, the place wouldn't be very busy at this time of day, and he'd be served quickly enough to make his connection to Philly.

The first eatery he came upon had a big "CLOSED" sign hanging on the door, so he kept going. It wasn't until he was within a block of the train station that he spotted another eatery, this one a tiny, somewhat run-down establishment. There were delectable aromas drifting out the open windows, so he put his hand on the doorknob. The whinny of a horse made him stop and look, and it was at that moment he saw him— the very man who'd been walking with Rebecca, or the woman who looked just like her. Clay stood frozen to the sidewalk, his hand fixed to the knob, as the man drew nearer. The fellow's gait wasn't nearly as proud and pompous as it had been earlier. Did Clay dare speak to him? What if the man refused to give him the time of day? Or what if it wasn't even the same man he'd seen earlier?

"My sheep hear my voice…."

The man made eye contact with Clay when he was about to pass by, so Clay swallowed his pride and cleared his throat. "Excuse me, sir. Did I perchance see you walking with a Quaker woman a short while ago?" There. He'd asked the foolish question.

"Pardon?" The man halted his steps.

"I'm sorry," Clay said quickly. "I've mistaken you for someone else." He pulled the restaurant door open.

"Why would you ask me such a thing?" the man asked.

Clay paused. "It's nothing. I just thought—"

"I was walking with a Quaker woman, yes, but of what importance is that to you?"

Clay's face felt as hot as a scalding kettle. "She looked like a woman I know named Rebecca Albright."

"Well, Mr.…."

"Dalton," Clay supplied. "Clay Dalton."

"Well, Mr. Dalton, I can tell you that Miss Albright is not interested."

A painful lump formed in Clay's throat, making it hard to swallow. "Is that so?"

"It certainly is."

"Well then, would you be willing to tell me where I might find her?"

"And why would I do that?"

"I'd like to at least say hello to her—if you don't mind, that is."

The fellow frowned. "Mind? Why should I mind? Like I said, she's not interested in courting. If she won't agree to let me court her, I can't imagine she'll give the likes of you as much as a second look."

Clay jolted. Were his ears deceiving him? "She refused your offer of courtship, you say?"

"That's correct. She made it clear she is interested in no one."

"I see." Clay's chest nearly split open wide with relief. "Well, could you tell me where she lives, then?"

"I suppose. But I wouldn't get my hopes up."

Clay ignored his warning, and the man was still rattling off directions when he set off at a run.

⌒

"I can't believe the audacity of that man," Charity exclaimed. "I'm sorry now that I pushed thee out the door. At least thee enjoyed a tasty tartlet for thy trouble."

Rebecca giggled. "Oh, Charity, it's reassuring to see thy bright, sweet smile peeking through the clouds again."

"Thee does have a way of drawing me out, Becca." Charity smiled, then sobered slightly. "Promise me thee will never leave me."

Rebecca laughed again. "How can I make such a promise when Albert may well be the one to eventually shoo me off the premises?"

Charity waved off her remark. "He shan't do that, or he will be forced to move to the desert."

Rebecca quirked an eyebrow at her. "The desert?"

"Has thee forgotten Proverbs twenty-one, verse nineteen? *'It is better to dwell in the wilderness, than with a contentious and an angry woman.'"*

"Oh, Charity. As if thee could ever grow a contentious bone in thy body."

They shared another good laugh, until there came a demanding pound on the front door.

The women stared at each other for a full ten seconds before Rebecca groaned. "He's come back to reason with me. Can thee tell him I am occupied?"

"Occupied? With what?"

"With…with…I don't know. Darning socks. Go! Thee is clever enough to think of something."

"Is thee asking me to lie?"

"Thee shan't be lying. I'll go get the darning needles."

"Then thee must find a pair of socks with some holes."

"I haven't the time. Oh, good gracious! Just tell him I'm—I'm indisposed."

Charity shook her head. "Indisposed? As in, thee has gone outside to the necessary?"

"No! Thee cannot tell him *that*. Oh, for goodness' sake. How dare he return, after I made it clear I am not, nor will I ever be, interested in courting him?"

"Perchance he has developed a whole new plan for approaching thee."

"If so, he can throw his new approach out the window. Why don't we just go to the kitchen and ignore the knocking?"

"Thee may go to the kitchen, Becca, but I cannot possibly ignore that persistent knock."

Rebecca went ahead and sought refuge in the kitchen while her friend went for the door, but she kept one ear open to hear what Philip had to say.

The door opened with its usual squeak. Rebecca listened for Philip's voice but heard only dead silence. She waited. And waited. Finally, there came the sound of hushed voices, followed by uneven footsteps.

Charity entered the kitchen, then stood there and stared at Rebecca, her expression one of utter shock.

"What's wrong?" asked Rebecca.

"Wrong?" Charity blinked. "Why, absolutely nothing is wrong. In fact, everything is so incredibly, painfully, horribly, and wonderfully right."

Rebecca frowned. "That sounds like utter nonsense."

"Why doesn't thee go into the parlor and figure it out for thyself?"

"Certainly not. I've already told Philip—"

"It isn't Philip, Becca."

"Well then, who is it?"

Charity came around behind her and started pushing, in the same way she'd shoved her out the door after Philip. "Go on," Charity urged her.

Rebecca heaved a nervous breath and peeked around the corner. Clay! She nearly lost her footing for the shudder of surprise that raced through her veins. She clapped both hands over her open mouth to keep from screaming. He looked so good—so ruggedly dashing, and so… real. But then, she told herself, she must be dreaming. He smiled, and she forgot to breathe. Questions circled her head like so many fireflies. Was this some sort of cruel joke? Had he merely stopped to show off his fiancée, Julia?

"Hello, Rebecca."

She stood mute, in need of a good shaking to bring her out of her daze.

He stepped a few inches closer. She put out her hand to stop him, and he paused. "Take all the time you need, Becca."

"What are—? I can't— How did—?"

He shifted the weight of his solid frame from one foot to the other. "I've come to tell you something important. Could we sit on the front porch? It's a lovely afternoon." He couldn't seem to get the smile off his face.

Rebecca, on the other hand, was too numb to get her facial muscles working. Clay took her hand and gave a little tug toward the door, and just the touch of his hand awakened her senses. He led her onto the porch, where the warm breeze whipped at the stray strands of her hair. He guided her to a chair and gently helped her into it, then sat down next to her without letting go of her hand.

"I haven't stopped thinking about you since the day you left Sunset Ridge."

Dare she admit that she could tell him the same? Not yet. She had too many questions. "How did thee find me?"

"I was on the train bound for Philly and saw you out the window, walking arm in arm with a man. I managed to get them to stop the train so I could get off, but by then, you'd disappeared."

Rebecca gasped. "We heard the sudden screech of the brakes and thought perhaps there was some trouble aboard the train."

He angled his face at her. "There was trouble, all right. Heart trouble."

"Heart trouble?"

He pressed the palm of his free hand to his chest. "My heart, honey. It's been missing you something terrible."

Honey? Her eyes welled at the simple endearment. "I...I don't know what to say."

He lifted his eyebrows. "Say you've missed me, too."

"But...but Julia...."

"Is someone from my past. Not my future."

Rebecca gave a start. "Thee means...?"

"We were never married, just as I always thought. We were betrothed, but I broke it off several days ago. I made an effort to reconcile with her, but it didn't work out. There was nothing between us any longer. Truthfully, there probably never was. She hardly seemed heartbroken, so I am sure we were never meant to be together."

Rebecca's heart jumped, and she felt the need to clutch her chest. Perspiration beaded on her forehead. Dare she hope? Could this really be happening?

He went on to tell her how he had lost his passion for his job as sheriff of Ellicott City. He described the growth of his faith and told her he'd prayed daily for guidance, wisdom, and direction. He told her that a neighbor had asked whether he would consider selling his house, and that he'd taken it as a possible sign that God meant for him to leave Ellicott City. And he went on to say that his newfound aversion to slavery had him considering helping out with the Underground Railroad.

Then he started firing questions at her: How was she adjusting to life in Chester? Did she regret leaving Sunset Ridge and her family? Was there much opportunity to assist with the Underground Railroad in the local area?

She told him that while she missed her family and the farm, with every passing day, she knew she'd made the right decision to leave. Sunset Ridge would always be home, but, for now, she had to follow the path God had put her on—that of helping Albert and Charity in establishing a station on the Underground Railroad. She also said that she couldn't live with Albert and Charity indefinitely, hence her decision to find a job and begin saving money to one day support herself. She went on to share about Charity's tragic fall and her heartbreaking miscarriage. Clay listened intently, compassion shining in his blue eyes. They talked, and then they talked some more, until it seemed there was little left to say.

He had released her hand some time ago and now clasped his together, holding them between his knees. His gaze dropped to the porch floor. "The thing is, Rebecca...I can't live without you."

She sucked in a cavernous breath and held it in her lungs for a span of several seconds.

He lifted his head and looked at her. "You know I love you."

Her pulse pounded in her brain. "I...I love thee, as well."

He grinned. "I had hoped and prayed *thee* would say that."

She loved that he'd borrowed her manner of speaking, even if he'd done so in jest. She didn't care how he chose to speak, and she didn't even care if he fully embraced the Quaker fellowship, as long as he loved Jesus with all his heart. All she cared about was living the rest of her life by his side.

He took her hand again and gave it a little squeeze. "Come here, you sweet Quaker girl. You are going to sit in my lap."

"I am?" A nervous giggle bubbled forth from her lips as her heartbeat began to throb against her chest. "But...that isn't proper, is it?"

He laughed. "It is when the woman is about to become the man's wife."

"The man's...." Was that a proposal? "*Wife*, thee said?"

"Yes, indeed." He continued tugging at her hand until she stood, moved sideways toward him, and landed gently in his wide lap, his thighs as strong and sturdy as a table. He encircled her with his arms and pulled her against his chest as a contented sigh whistled over the top of her head. She settled in, and he removed her loose-fitting cap, then tossed it aside and kissed her hair. Despite the heat of the day, she broke out in chills. "I love you," he said again. "I'm glad I found you hiding behind that fallen tree all those nights ago."

She sat forward and peered back at him. "Found me and then hauled me up and put a gun to my temple, thee means."

"You had to remind me of that, didn't you?" He pulled her back against his chest. "I wasn't going to hurt you. I knew even then that it was the start of a lasting relationship."

She laughed. "Thee did not."

"Did."

"Did not."

He reached down, lifted her chin, and quickly covered her mouth with his own before she had the chance to continue their silly argument. As they kissed, his hands explored the plane of her back, then moved up her neck, caressing all the way. One of Rebecca's arms was pinned between them, but she wrapped the other one around the bulk of his frame and grasped his shirt with splayed fingers. Oh, how wonderful to claim him as her own, and with no feelings of guilt or self-reproach. He was hers to love. *Hers.*

After endless moments of delicious kissing, Clay swiveled her around in his lap so that she was mostly facing him. He put his hands on her shoulders and gently squeezed, then captured her face with his glittering blue eyes. "I know I'm doing this somewhat backward, because I haven't had a chance to ask your father for your hand, but will you marry me, Becca? I happen to like the sound of 'Rebecca Dalton.'"

"I happen to like it, as well. My answer is yes, of course!"

"Well then, that's settled." The warmth of his smile matched the sweet tone of his voice. "In all our talking, I failed to tell you something else important."

"And what's that?"

"I may already have a job waiting for me right here at the Delaware County sheriff's office. A deputy by the name of Lyle Mercer said he felt quite certain Sheriff Hansen would hire me. It's a long story, but the gist of it is, God led me to that office, Becca. I'm certain of it. I wouldn't take the job if you didn't want me to, though, because, as you can imagine, it would mean I'd have to carry a weapon."

"Of course, thee should take the job," Rebecca answered without hesitation. "Where would our country be without men such as yourself to uphold and enforce the law? Quakers embrace the law as a means of promoting harmony and structure. We only oppose unnecessary violence, and I know thee to be a man of integrity who will pursue peaceful resolutions first and foremost."

He shook his head in a show of awe. "When do you think you'll be free to travel back to Sunset Ridge?"

"Ahem."

Startled, Rebecca and Clay both glanced up. There, at the top of the porch steps, stood Albert, wearing a broad grin. "Sorry to break things up, but I can't greet my wife unless I trudge past thee." He clapped Clay on the shoulder before putting his hand to the doorknob. "I caught the last bit of thy conversation. Just so thee know, I'll be home with Charity all day tomorrow. First Day sounds like the perfect time for taking a trip to Sunset Ridge, don't thee think?"

Charity opened the door and peeked outside. "I couldn't help but overhear, and, yes, tomorrow is perfect."

Albert laughed. "Thee didn't listen in on their entire conversation, I hope…?"

Charity feigned a gasp. "Of course not! But…well, the windows *were* open."

Rebecca giggled. "It doesn't matter, Charity. Thee and I will stay up late tonight talking."

Albert sighed and shook his head. "Best get used to it, Clay. These women share secrets."

The banter continued for a few more minutes until Charity and Albert went inside.

Alone again, Clay and Rebecca shared another tasty kiss…and then another. At last, they sat back and looked each other in the eye.

"Is this real?" Rebecca asked.

"It's as real as the sun and the moon, sweetheart."

And as they exchanged yet another kiss, the birds in the trees overhead rested their wings and whistled a tune of hope and joy.

Epilogue

Though it was Twelfth Month, Twentieth Day, Clay and Rebecca could not have chosen a more perfect date for their wedding. A mild temperature of 55 degrees surprised the multitude gathered at Arch Street Meeting House. Whoever had heard of such pleasant weather so close to Christmas? Why, at this time last year, a snowstorm had buried all of Philadelphia.

The bride wore a long-sleeved gown of chestnut-brown silk with wrist cuffs, simple stitching, and a round neckline. It fit Rebecca perfectly, from the gathered waist right down to the elegant hem of the full skirt. And the best part was that Rebecca felt almost divine wearing it. Frances had woven Rebecca's hair into fancy braids that twisted and twirled like lovely pieces of ribbon gathered atop her head, and they were covered by a headpiece of sheer frothy material, the strings of which Lydia had tied loosely under Rebecca's chin. Around Rebecca's shoulders, her mother had arranged a lovely fringed wool shawl, and the conservative woman had shocked everyone by purchasing some rouge powder at an expensive department store in downtown Philadelphia to lend a bit of color to Rebecca's pale cheeks. Mother delighted in the stares she'd gotten from the clerks who had waited on her, a plain-as-porridge Quaker woman purchasing such an extravagant item.

The groom looked dashing in his form-fitting black coat, matching breeches, neatly tied cravat, and polished boots. One glance at him that morning, and Rebecca knew in her heart no other man on earth compared. She couldn't help the pride that welled up inside at having snagged so fine a man. How the Lord had blessed her!

Gerald Tuke was noticeably absent from the ceremony. The last Rebecca had heard, he'd begun courting a woman who attended a local Mennonite church, and they were quite enamored of each other. The news had cheered her, and she wished them only the best.

Quaker weddings involved very little fanfare, and for that, Rebecca was thankful. During the time of silent worship, she struggled to focus on the things of God as she mutely rehearsed the marriage vows she had memorized. Surely, the Almighty understood her state of mind and would pardon her distractedness. No officiant had been assigned to marry them, per se, for the Quakers considered that job to belong to God alone. Theirs was only to proclaim their individual pledges before God, family, and fellow Friends, after which time they would be married, and the members of the clearness and oversight committees would sign the marriage certificate. It was a simple matter, really, but also a profound one. She could barely believe it, but, tomorrow morning, she would awaken at her husband's side bearing the name Rebecca Dalton.

Rebecca leaned forward and glanced down the bench at Florence White, sitting all straight-laced and stern-faced. Florence gave Rebecca a solemn nod, indicating that the time had come for the couple to stand. Rebecca glanced across the aisle at Clay, seated in the men's section. Moments later, the two stood and met in the middle at the front. Clay took her hand and gently squeezed it before they turned to face each other. Then Clay went first with his vows, speaking with clarity and confidence: "In the presence of God, and before these, our families and friends, I take thee, Rebecca Albright, to be my beloved wife, promising with Divine assistance to be unto thee a loving and faithful husband so long as we both shall live." Then, her eyes brimming with tears of gratitude, Rebecca recited her own vows to Clay. Florence White, Thurston Byer, and Alger Crump signed the marriage certificate, then handed it to Clay, for him and Rebecca to add their signatures. Alger then reclaimed the certificate, which would be signed by several other folks later on, and asked the couple to sit back down before he turned toward the congregation and read the certificate aloud. After a time of various individuals standing at their seats to offer verbal support, heartfelt best wishes, and blessings to the couple, Thurston Byer introduced the new Mr. and Mrs. Clay Dalton. He gave them a few final words of spiritual wisdom and encouragement, then finally freed them to walk down the aisle, an act that not only concluded the ceremony but was thought to make the marriage legal and binding.

Once the two had reached the foyer and were out of sight of the wedding guests, Clay didn't hesitate to enfold Rebecca in his arms and kiss her so thoroughly that she almost melted into a puddle of a million sensations. "That was only a prelude of things to come, my love," he whispered when they separated. "Tonight, you shall be completely mine in every sense of the word."

A tide of passion, not to mention heart-lifting anticipation, ran through Rebecca, followed by a prickling of her nerves. "Oh, Clay, I love thee."

He cupped her face in his hands and touched his nose to hers. "I love thee more."

Before she could protest, he planted another quick kiss on her plump lips, and then a crowd of fellow Friends and family members descended on them. Chuckling, Clay stepped aside to make way for all the hugs, kisses, and well-wishes that followed. When Mother approached them, the masses parted like the Red Sea under the power of Moses' staff. "I am so proud of thee, Becca," Mother whispered, drawing her oldest daughter into a warm embrace. "I am glad thee held thy ground in regard to marriage. Thy father and I are pleased with thy choice and are honored to welcome Clay into our family."

"Thank thee, Mother. That means so much." They hugged again, and over Mother's shoulder, Rebecca saw Papa embracing Clay. What a tender moment.

After Mother stepped away, Rebecca's sisters and brothers approached for hugs and kisses, and baby Chrystal begged to be picked up, so Rebecca obliged. How good it felt to be reunited as a family, if only for today. Tomorrow, she and Clay would board the train for Durham, North Carolina, where she would finally meet Clay's mother and sisters and their families. She could hardly wait. Clay's new boss, Sheriff Hansen, had been gracious enough to grant him five days off so that he could enjoy some time with his new wife.

After resigning as sheriff of Delaware County, Clay had sold his home to Earl Hand. It hadn't taken long for him and Rebecca to find a perfect house within the city limits of Chester, situated a mere three blocks from Charity and Albert. It was a cozy two-story that Rebecca couldn't wait to decorate to her tastes. Best of all, its proximity to the Duncan home made it easy for them to help with the Underground Railroad. Already, they'd assisted with feeding and boarding more than two dozen slaves, whom they had furnished with supplies and sustenance to last them until they reached their next stop.

Clay made his way back to Rebecca as the crowd began thinning out. There would be no formal dinner for the wedding guests, but Mother, Frances, and Lydia had prepared a feast for the family and a few select friends, including Charity and Albert; Charity's parents; Elias Fox and his wife, Agnes; and Dr. Fleming and his wife, Norma. Charity had quietly confided in Rebecca that she probably wouldn't be able to partake of much food, since she'd started experiencing severe bouts of sickness with her latest pregnancy. The news that she was expecting again had cheered Rebecca beyond words.

When it was time to exit the meeting house, Clay tucked Rebecca's hand into the crook of his arm and led her out the door and to the carriage he'd rented for driving her back to the farm. It was an extravagance, he knew, but Rebecca deserved only the best on her wedding day. He couldn't help but compare how very pure and simple this ceremony had been to the lavish one he would've had with Julia. He looked at his wife and knew that no other woman could ever make him happier. He helped her board the carriage, then darted around behind it and climbed up next to her.

"Can we ride with you?" Milton called. Samuel came along behind him, and Henry followed, full of unleashed excitement.

"Boys!" Papa called from his wagon, where the rest of the family was already situated. "Get your little tails back over here and give those newlyweds their privacy."

Milton hung his head and began to turn. Samuel had already started back toward the family wagon, while Henry just stood there, squinting up at them in the bright sun.

Clay and Rebecca exchanged a glance. "We have a lifetime to be alone," Clay said with a grin.

"Exactly," Rebecca replied.

"All aboard!" Clay called to the threesome.

Samuel turned quicker than a rabbit. "Thee means it?"

"Hurry before I change my mind," he answered, laughing.

Samuel and Milton climbed up first, then Samuel helped Henry. Once the boys had gotten situated in the back, Clay waved Papa on, and he followed after them.

Clay held the reins loosely as the carriage jounced along. Rebecca's shoulder and leg kept bumping against his, creating within him boundless waves of excitement that only escalated when she placed her hand on his thigh and squeezed. He wrapped one arm around her shoulders and tugged her close, then kissed the top of her head, loving the way a few wisps of hair fell around her temples and stuck to her pink cheeks. They rode like that for a while, the boys chattering nonstop behind them.

"Someday, we'll have a houseful of our own," Clay said quietly, nodding toward the back of the wagon.

Rebecca glanced at him, her eyes dazzling as they reflected the December sunshine. "How many does thee want?"

"I'm not fussy. A few dozen, maybe."

She laughed. "I think that's a few too many."

He grinned. "Okay, then. I'll settle for as many as you want."

"I expect it will take some time...or not." She dropped her head to his shoulder and gave what he could only term a satisfied sigh, so sweet and soft. "Charity says it can happen when one least expects it," she whispered wistfully.

"She said that, did she?" He chuckled.

In a distant field, a herd of deer played, while overhead an eagle spread its lordly wings and flew across the azure sky. They rounded a bend, and Sunset Ridge came into view, with its rolling hills where wildflowers would once again bloom come spring. The sight took Clay's breath away, imparting to him a true sense of comfort and belonging. He kept the private moment to himself, tucking it into his file of fresh, new memories. He had come to treasure this place called Sunset Ridge—this place where faith prevailed, family mattered, and love made everything right with the world.

A Letter from Shar

Dear Readers,

The Religious Society of Friends has been of great interest to me for as long as I can recall, particularly since my dad spoke often about his Quaker upbringing. Even though he and my mother joined the Wesleyan denomination after they married, and then the Free Methodists, Dad's roots in the Society remained strong, and he adhered to many Quaker tenets throughout his Christian walk. He did so unobtrusively, never pushing those precepts on others. But it was as a young boy in the Society that he first found Jesus.

Founded in England in the 1600s by George Fox, Quakerism was predominantly based on Christianity, and the influence remains as strong today. Members profess the priesthood of all believers, a doctrine derived from 1 Peter 2:9: "*Ye are a chosen generation, a royal priesthood, an holy nation, a peculiar people; that ye should shew forth the praises of him who hath called you out of darkness into his marvelous light.*" In the nineteenth century, a diversification of theological beliefs arose in the Religious Society of Friends; as a result, Quakers today include those with evangelical, holiness, conservative, liberal, non-theist, and universalist ways of thinking. That said, Quaker understandings of Christianity vary widely. Worldwide, approximately 80 percent of Quakers today belong to the "evangelical, programmed" branches of Quakerism—that is, they worship in services with singing and a prepared message from the Bible, coordinated by a pastor. The rest continue to practice "waiting" worship, or "unprogrammed" worship, where the order of service is not planned in advance, is predominantly silent, and may include unprepared vocal ministry from those present. There exists today a small segment of Quakers who still speak with plain pronouns, dress in plain attire, and live a testimony of simplicity.

The following list includes just a small sampling of the countless websites I found helpful, interesting, and informative over the course of my research for this book.

www.QuakerAnne.com

www.QuakerJane.com

http://www.quakersong.org/fgc_and_music/

www.QuakerMaps.com

www.QuakerInfo.org

www.ecwsa.org

http://www.history.com/topics/quakers

http://christianity.about.com/od/quakers/a/quakersbeliefs.htm

http://trilogy.brynmawr.edu/speccoll/quakersandslavery/commentary/organizations/underground_railroad.php

May God's rich blessings rain down on each of you.

Love, Shar

Questions for Personal Reflection or Group Discussion

1. How did you react when you read about Horace Spencer allegedly shooting his master? Do you think there is a place for violence in faith-based fiction?

2. Rebecca Albright was not physically attracted to Gerald Tuke. How important is physical attraction in a relationship? Can a relationship blossom over time, even in the absence of physical attraction?

3. How would you have reacted if your parents had selected a mate for you? Putting yourself in Rebecca's shoes, and also in

the era in which she lived, do you think you would have tried to love Gerald in order to please your parents?

4. Did you connect with the character of Rebecca on any level? If so, how?

5. What was your impression of Clay in the beginning of the story? How does his character evolve over the course of the book?

6. Did Clay's "salvation experience" come across as authentic? What changes did you witness in his life as a result?

7. What was your reaction when Rebecca and Clay first kissed? Did you deem it inappropriate, considering Rebecca's belief that Clay was married?

8. As you read the novel, which aspect engaged you more—the characters or the plot? Which one of the two seemed to be the driving force behind the story?

9. What were some of the main ideas or themes that the author explored (and perhaps inspired you to explore for yourself)?

10. Were there any scenes in the story that struck you as particularly insightful or profound? Identify them, and explain.

11. Did you find the conclusion of the story satisfying? Why or why not?

12. Has this novel altered your beliefs or broadened your perspective in any way? Did you gain anything new from reading it? If so, what?

About the Author

Born and raised in west Michigan, Sharlene attended Spring Arbor University. Upon graduating in 1971 with an education degree, she taught second grade for two years, then accepted an invitation to travel internationally with a singing ensemble for one year. In 1975, she came home, returned to her teaching job, and married her childhood sweetheart. Together, they raised two lovely daughters, both of whom are now happily married and enjoying families of their own. Retired in 2003 after thirty-one years of teaching, "Shar" loves to read, sing, travel, and spend time with her family—in particular, her adorable grandchildren!

A Christian for over forty-five years, and a lover of the English language, Shar always enjoyed dabbling in writing. She remembers well the short stories she wrote in high school, and watching them circulate from girl to girl during government and civics classes. "Psst," someone would whisper from two rows over, always when the teacher's back was turned, "pass me the next page."

In the early 2000s, Shar felt God's call upon her heart to take her writing pleasures a step further, and in 2006, she signed a contract for her first faith-based novel, *Through Every Storm*, thereby launching her writing career. With more than sixteen published novels now gracing store shelves and being sold online, she daily gives God all the glory.

Shar has done numerous countrywide book signings and made several television appearances and radio interviews. She loves speaking for community organizations, libraries, church groups, and women's conferences. In her church, she is active in women's ministries, regularly facilitating Bible studies and other events. She and her husband, Cecil, live in Spring Lake, Michigan, with their beautiful white collie, Peyton, and their ragdoll cat, Blue.

Shar loves hearing from her readers. If you wish to contact her as a potential speaker for a church function or would simply like to chat with her, please feel free to send her an e-mail at sharlenemaclaren@ yahoo.com. She will do her best to answer in a timely manner. You may also find her on Facebook!

Turn the page for a sneak peek into *Their Daring Hearts,*
Book Two of the Forever Freedom Series also
by beloved author Sharlene MacLaren.

Coming Fall 2017

1

*"Since God is in the midst of her; she shall not be moved:
God shall help her, and that right early."*
—Psalm 46:5

The flame of the bedside lamp gave off enough light to cast a long shadow of Allison's small frame across the marred wood floor as she packed the barest of necessities in her tiny valise. Outside the open window, an owl hooted in a haunting way, and Harry, the family's old brown mongrel, gave a single bark. She hugged herself to ward off a chill that crept through her nightgown with its threadbare sleeves.

"Josephine Winters, what do you think you're doing?"

The shrill whisper caught Josie off guard, and she whirled around to face her fifteen-year-old cousin. "Go back t' sleep, Allison. I didn't mean t' wake you."

"What're you doin'?" the girl asked again.

Josie clamped shut the valise. "I'm gonna do it, Allie. I'm joinin' the army."

"Y'are not!" The girl threw off her covers and leaped out of bed.

In the distance, a freight train announced its impending arrival with a long, piercing whistle.

"I am, and y' can't stop me."

"Y' can't join the army. You're a woman, and women aren't allowed."

"Shh, pipe down. I'm not goin' as a woman. I'm goin' as a man."

"A man?" The girl shifted her weight from one bare foot to the other and stared wide-eyed at her. "An' just how d'you propose t' do that?"

"I'm gonna cut my hair and rub some dirt onto my face, and then I'll dress in some of Andrew's old clothes, like his straw hat and work boots. The army'll issue me a man's uniform and a new pair of boots. I'll pass just fine."

Allison crimped her pretty brow and tilted her face. "It's gonna take a lot more than that t' make y' look like a man."

She wouldn't be deterred by her cousin's doubts. "It'll work. You'll see."

The rest of the house was quiet for now, but soon, Aunt Bessie would start shuffling around in the kitchen, and the sounds of rattling pans and clinking dishes would rouse Josie's five other cousins. She needed to get moving if she hoped to escape unnoticed.

"Y' have no idea what you're getting' yourself into, Josie."

Josie shrugged. "Maybe not, but I'll soon find out, won't I? I can't stay here, Allie. I'm an extra mouth to feed. A burden. I see the worry in your mother's eyes when I sit across from her at the table. Sure, I'm an extra pair of hands, but Aunt Bessie needs money more than she needs my help around the house. I'm nineteen. It's past time I started takin' care o' myself." She straightened, stretched her five-foot-three frame to its full height, and stared her cousin in the eyes. "I'll make it just fine. I'm strong and sturdy."

"But…but why the army, of all things?"

"They'll take care o' me. I'll get three square meals a day, and pay, on top o' that."

"But it's war, Josie, vile an' brutal. The news reports are grim. Union soldiers are dyin' every day. Gettysburg was terrible. What if you get caught in a battle such as that? The Union may be winnin', but the Rebs aren't about to surrender. Not yet, anyway. We've already lost Andrew."

Josie's stomach knotted. *Andrew.* Her only brother. She swallowed a stone-like lump. "I'll keep my head down."

"But—"

"I promise I'll write y'. My name'll be Gordon Snipp, so when y' write back t' me, always address your letters to him. The officers're always readin' the soldiers' mail, searchin' out spies an' such." Josie picked up her valise and turned to go.

"Wait." Allison snagged hold of her wrist and gazed at her through teary eyes.

Josie set the suitcase down again and hugged Allison to herself while holding her own tears at bay. After a quick embrace, she straightened, tamping down her sense of regret. "I'll leave it t' you t' tell Aunt Bessie. I can't bear to say good-bye t' her, or anyone else. In fact…." She reached into her pocket, snatched the folded piece of paper inside, and thrust it at her cousin. "I wrote you this letter 'cause I didn't want to have to say good-bye to you, either."

Allie stared at the letter in silence.

"Please, just take it." Josie gave the note a little shake. "I have t' go. Thank your mother for me, but please don't give 'er any details about where I've gone. I don't want her gettin' any hair-brained ideas 'bout sendin' somebody to hunt me down and drag me back here. I need to do this. I've needed to get out on my own for some time, and I believe in the Union's cause, just as Andrew did. I want to pick up where he left off. I feel almost obligated to finish what he started, in honor of 'is efforts. Tell Aunt Bessie I appreciate all that she's done for me over the years. When I start makin' money, I'll send some back for the family."

Allison took the letter and pressed it to her chest, her face long, her eyes misty. "Mother will be put out with you."

"Perhaps, but she'll also be relieved t' have one less mouth t' feed."

Allison didn't argue. She must have recognized the truth of Josie's words. "I don't want you t' die like Andrew did. That would wipe out your whole family."

Her pointed words stung Josie straight to the core. She and her brother had been orphans for eight years, ever since their parents had succumbed to yellow fever. Amazingly, the children had been spared, thanks in large part to the kindly neighbors who had taken them in when their parents were stricken. After Ma and Pa died, the local authorities decided it best to burn their house, thereby rendering Josephine and her brother homeless. Aunt Bessie—Ma's sister—and Uncle Clarence had assumed their care after that. Uncle Clarence's heart had given out last year, and he, too, had passed into glory. Following that, Andrew had joined the army, even though he was too young and lacked any experience. With barely any training, he'd marched into the Battle of Drewry's Bluff in April of '62. A week later, several Union soldiers had visited Aunt Bessie's farm to convey the news that he'd sacrificed his life for the good of his country. The soldiers had given Josie his bloodied knapsack of meager possessions. Because his body had lain for three days before anyone had found him, he'd been buried quickly in the shade of an old tree along with half a dozen other soldiers.

"I won't die," Josie stated, as if she could read the future. "Like I said, I'll keep my head down. I need t' do this. I hope you understand."

"Where will you head first?" Allison asked.

"Well, first, I'll be on the lookout for an out-of-the-way spot where I can transform my appearance. After that, I'll head to the recruitment center on Market Street. It's only a couple o' miles' walk from here. I saw an advertisement about enlistment tacked to a post in front of Fred's Fish Market a month ago. Ever since Gettysburg, the army's numbers have been dwindlin', so they're eager for new enlistments. That's how my plan was hatched."

"The numbers are dwindlin' 'cause soldiers are *dyin'*. I don't want you to be one of them."

"Nor do I." Josie tried to force a grin, but she failed. A period of painful silence passed between the two girls. She'd said everything she needed to say, and time waited for no one. She stepped closer to her cousin and kissed her cheek. "Give everyone a hug from me, and tell them all I'll miss them."

"I will." Allison bit her bottom lip as two tears slid down her cheeks. "I'll pray for you, Josie."

"And I for you."

Without taking even a tiny glance behind her, lest she change her mind, Josie picked up the valise, slipped through the door, tiptoed down the staircase and out the door, and strode across the yard, purpose in her step and quiet resolve in her spirit.

⟝

Levi Albright quickly reread the letter from Mary Foster. Then he carefully folded it again and tucked it inside his sack along with the other dozen or so long missives she'd sent him over the past three months. After closing his reticule, he crossed his outstretched legs at the ankles, lowered his cap to just above his eyebrows, folded his arms over his broad chest, and leaned back against the trunk of an old shade tree—a welcome relief from the suffocating heat—to do a bit of dreaming. He liked Mary Foster—as much as a man could like a woman he'd never met in person. She was a good Quaker, from what he knew of her, and had started attending Arch Street Meeting House shortly after he'd left to join the army. His sisters said she was sweet and pretty, and that he'd be a fool not to come home and marry her. Of course, they would say that; they wanted him to leave the army and return to the farm. *Now.* Quakers were pacifists, and he'd broken the covenant by enlisting. He wasn't the only Friend who'd done so. He'd met more than a few fellow Quakers while serving. One of them had even died in battle. But Levi had spent long hours in thought and prayer before reaching the conclusion that he couldn't just read about the war any longer. He had to join in the cause, and he'd done so in late summer of '61—nearly two years ago to the day. His brothers were old enough to pull their weight at the farm, so it wasn't as if he'd left Papa completely to his own resources. Lord willing, they would muster out his squadron in '64—unless the Union brought the war to a victorious finish before that—and he would go back to the farm. Perchance he'd even wind up with Mary Foster as a wife. He'd already built a fine clapboard house on Sunset Ridge not far from his parents' home, roomy enough for a family.

"Sergeant Albright, ye're bein' summoned," said a voice from behind him.

He jolted to attention and lifted his gaze to his friend and fellow soldier Jim Hodgers. "By whom?"

Jim grinned. "Who do y' think, Sarge? It's Lieutenant Grimms. He's prob'ly gonna throw another one o' his fits. I just saw Captain Bateman and a few of his men leavin' Lt. Grimms' tent. You know how the lieutenant gets after the captain pays him a visit."

Did he ever. For some reason, no doubt due to his calm demeanor and levelheaded thinking, Levi was always the one Grimms wanted to consult after a talk with the captain. He realized Grimms relied on him. But Levi didn't welcome the implication of his expertise. He didn't even relish the promotion he'd received after the Second Battle of Fredericksburg, in which he'd led a small unit of soldiers into battle when a Confederate squad had caught them off guard. He'd acted on impulse, since Lt. Grimms had been further up the line, and Levi hadn't had time to go in search of him. In an instantaneous decision, he'd ordered several men to follow him, and together they'd charged the intruding Rebels, forcing them to retreat to the hills from whence they'd come. Their actions had paid off, precipitating Levi's climb from private to sergeant. He hadn't felt worthy of the commendation, saying he'd done only what any good soldier would have; but Captain Bateman and Lieutenant Grimms had called him overly modest. The captain had added that brave, intelligent, decisive soldiers such as Levi would help lead the Union to ultimate victory.

Levi didn't like this war. He hadn't enlisted in order to receive any accolades. But he did believe in preserving the Union and bringing an end to slavery. If his superiors wished to sew another patch on his uniform, then so be it.

He leaned forward, away from the tree trunk, and stood, brushing the dirt from his army pants and then hefting his knapsack. "Thank you, Private. I'll go see what he wants."

Jim nodded, then walked away. Levi watched him plant himself next to a group of four privates who were playing cards. Then Levi set off for Lt. Grimms' tent.

He found the tent flaps pulled back and the lieutenant sitting in a chair at his makeshift desk, writing something. When Levi knocked quietly on the tent post, the middle-aged officer turned and gave a sweep of his arm. "Come in, come in. Here, have a seat." He gestured toward the large stump in the middle of the tent.

Levi decided to make himself comfortable. He would probably be there awhile. "You summoned me, sir?"

"Indeed, indeed." Lt. Grimms pulled a cigarette from his pocket and lit it, then took a few puffs, blowing a strong-smelling smoke in Levi's direction. It was all Levi could do not to wave the cloud away from his face. "Pity you don't smoke. It's good for the nerves, you know."

"My nerves are quite fine at the moment, sir."

"Yes, well, mine are not." Grimms inhaled again, then exhaled slowly with another blow of smoke. "Captain Bateman just left, and I'm hotter than a cooked hen right now—not because of this awful heat, either." He tossed his pen on his desk, then rotated his body to face Levi. Sure enough, above his graying beard, his cheeks were redder than beets.

Levi maintained his composure. "What did he have to say this time?"

"Doggone it, Levi, we aren't in this war to sit around twiddling our thumbs. These men joined up to fight."

Levi would dare say a high percentage of them were fine with playing cards and checkers, whittling various crafts out of wood, and writing letters home. Any day they didn't have to march into battle was a good day, as far as he was concerned.

"You hear that?" The lieutenant tilted his sun-worn face to one side.

Levi stopped to listen a moment, then nodded. "Yep, sure do. There's fighting going on in the distance. Sounds like some heavy artillery and musket fire."

"And we should be there. But, no, we have 'more important' things to do, according to Bateman. Such as guarding the rear of that lousy supply train for however long he chooses to keep us on that assignment. Can you believe it? What does he take us for, nincompoops?"

"No, sir. I don't believe so, sir."

"Oh, yes, he does." Grimms fired off a slew of cuss words, making the veins in his neck come near to popping. Good Quaker that Levi was, he'd never been one to use bad language, but he had certainly grown accustomed to hearing it while in the throes of war. "When do you suppose he's going to forget about that little mishap at Salem Church?"

Levi bristled but tried not to show it. "I wouldn't exactly call it a mishap, sir. Several Union soldiers died when we mistook them for Rebs. We opened fire on our own men, sir."

"It was unfortunate, for sure, but it was a foggy morning, and visibility was nil. Accidents happen everywhere, even in war. It doesn't make us bad soldiers."

"And you weren't responsible, sir," Levi pointed out. "Those fellows were scared, and they fired out of sheer terror."

"My superiors tell me I'm responsible, Sergeant. I'm always to blame for whatever happens as long as G Company is under my authority. That's just the way of it. And the captain hasn't let me forget it." He blew out a loud breath, and another big cloud of cigarette smoke came with it. "He takes pleasure in reminding me every time he sees me. If he weren't my superior, I'd tell him to go bury himself."

Levi succumbed to the tiniest of smiles. "That's a trifle extreme, isn't it, Lieutenant?" Grimms was a lot of talk and very little bite.

"Might be, but it doesn't change the fact that I'm mad. Shoot! We even had to remain in reserve at Gettysburg."

Levi hadn't minded that one bit. "Give it some time. We'll get a worthy assignment soon."

"Humph. I hope you're right. It's downright embarrassing, if you ask me, guarding the rear of the supply train day in, day out—as if some Reb is going to come sneaking around."

"You never can tell, sir. It's happened before."

He flapped his arm in a show of disgust. "Well, I didn't call you in here purely for the sake of ranting. Captain Bateman announced that we're to welcome seven new soldiers to our company today. Hear they're a bunch of greenhorns."

"We were all greenhorns in the beginning, sir."

"True enough. I'll expect you to add them to the roster and instruct the company to treat them with respect. Private Adams will document each man's specifics. He's been doing a fine job as company recorder."

"Yes, he has. You'll have yourself a nice book of facts by the time this war ends."

"That's the intent. Decades from now, folks will want to know all about Company G from the Twenty-third Pennsylvania Regiment. We'll make history yet."

"Yes, sir."

"There'll be drills first thing in the morning. I'm sure the greenhorns will need some guidance."

"And I'll be sure to offer it, sir."

Grimms put down his cigarette, removed his hat, and gave his head a good scratching before plopping the dusty cap back in place. "How's morale?"

"As good as it can be, I suppose."

"Good, that's good. Army's done a lot of regrouping since Gettysburg. We lost so many soldiers. I suspect the fighting will continue to let up some on both sides till we muster up more soldiers. Hear the government's put out a plea for new recruits, even offered some extra incentives—like higher pay and better meals." Grimms scoffed. "That'll be the day when the meals start improving."

Levi chuckled. "One taste of hardtack, and they'll beg to go back home."

Grimms gave a glum smile, then turned back to his desk. "Well, I've got work to do."

In other words, Levi was dismissed. "Yes, sir. I'll see to those new recruits when they get here, sir."

"You do that."

Out of respect, Levi gave a salute, then grinned to himself and shook his head as he departed the lieutenant's tent with nary a farewell from the man.